C0-DAN-998

THE MORTAL GODS

THE
MORTAL
GODS

First Edition

ISBN 978-0-9998230-0-2
eBook 978-0-9998230-1-9

Artwork by Max Davenport

THE MORTAL GODS

PROLOGUE

It's not human.

Leth repeated the phrase over and over in his mind as he watched the hunched figure dig through the ash. Bodies lay strewn in every direction, each burnt beyond recognition. Countless trees had succumbed to the heat and fallen during the night. The entire forest was a graveyard for men and wood alike. For all Leth knew, he was the only breathing soul for miles. He and the creature now standing before him.

Thousands had come. More than Leth or anyone else could have hoped for. They had gathered, as had been the plan, and were prepared when the signal was given. In the end it hadn't mattered. Even with armor removed, *it* had sat comfortably out of reach and rained fire down from above, destroying everything and everyone in the forest.

Perhaps some made it out alive. Maybe some on the outskirts.

Leth fought a wave of nausea as his nose caught the scent once again. He couldn't give himself away, not after all he'd been through. Over a year of hiding, months of preparation, the long trek, and the night of terror. He knew his chances were slim, but that was enough for him. And if he died, at least he wouldn't feel the guilt any longer.

The creature stiffened. Leth's heart beat faster. The creature slowly stood, fully exposing its bare back to Leth. Sweat mixed with ash on the skin. The creature began to turn, and Leth knew his time was up.

His fingers released the string. The arrow flew through the early morning, weaving between the pair of blackened stumps towards its target. As the creature rotated, it lifted a hand

and Leth felt the end approach. Just as the head swiveled to look, the arrow struck flesh. The creature stumbled, catching itself on a log. The stick and feathers protruded from its shoulder. The creature returned its attention to Leth.

Not enough.

Leth dove behind a tree. The ground where he was standing a moment before burst into flame. A second explosion shook the tree, and Leth felt the heat as the flames wrapped almost entirely around him. Leth ran for better cover, the fire seeming to follow at his heels. He dove behind a boulder and crouched to smother the flames that had caught on his pant leg. He quickly pulled another arrow from his back. One more shot, and then he would die.

A battle cry sounded not far from him. Then another. There were other survivors! Leth heard several pairs of feet pounding towards the Dragon. Pushing aside his fears, Leth was on his feet once again, this time running back the way he had come. The Dragon came into view as it unleashed another spout of flame. Leth watched as a man fell, screaming. Three more men were visible through the scorched trees, racing towards the creature. Leth gave a yell of his own and charged.

The Dragon turned in a slow circle, hand raised, the world burning before it. Leth weaved to dodge another blaze and pressed on. Another man fell, but several more appeared between the trees. The Dragon hesitated for a moment, then dropped its hand. Thick, leathery wings sprouted from its back, and the creature began to flap. It quickly lifted off the ground and began skyward.

"Now!" Leth yelled. "It can't fly and fight at once!"

The men converged on the ground below, and Leth let another arrow loose. A miss. But by his third arrow, he was joined by his companions and the group began to find their mark. An arrow to the leg, then another in the side. The Dragon faltered. Leth drew again, aiming carefully, and sank the projectile into the creature's chest.

The wings stopped beating. The creature began to fall, slowly at first. The wings retracted, and the figure raced downward. Ash puffed into the wind as the half-naked body slammed to the earth, and for what felt like minutes, the group of ash and scar covered assassins watched the figure several dozen yards away lay still in the carnage, not daring to hope.

"It's dead," Leth finally said.

Another arrow sank into the creature. Leth turned to see Jag, tears streaming down his face. The man pulled another arrow and fired again. And again. The rest of the group watched in silence as Jag emptied his quiver, threw his bow at the creature, and finally sank to his knees. His shoulders shook as he knelt face down in the ash. Leth looked back at the body. So much destruction. So much death. Was it really possible that they had succeeded? That it was all … over?

But it's not over. Not yet.

The group gathered around the figure, leaving Jag to his grief. They discussed the creature, and for the first time Leth confessed his involvement. He expected anger in the reaction, but most of his companions just showed resignation. Whatever had brought about the horror of the last several years was a moot point now. It was in the past. Only the future mattered.

And so the discussion began. How to stop this from happening again? Hide the power? But there were six men present, no guarantee that one of them wouldn't seek it again once the others left. And to entrust all of the power to a single being once again was unthinkable. Even dividing, then hiding brought with it certain complications, not the least of which was the fact that each man would have to trust that the rest of the group had done just that. The final conclusion was logical.

"We divide it," Leth said finally. "Each takes a piece with him and gets as far from here as he possibly can. Keep it with you but hidden until you grow old, and entrust it to whomever you choose." He took a deep breath. "And we leave one man behind to warn the future."

The man to his left nodded. "The idea is sensible. All agreed?"

The men nodded. They glanced at Jag as he entered the circle, stooped, and took his share of the responsibility. Leth's heart wrenched.

"Jag ..." Leth said. "You don't have to-"

"I'll see to it that they are never used again." Jag turned and walked away, shoulders hunched.

When Leth turned back, the rest were watching him. He looked back at them. "What are we waiting for?"

The man with the dark beard pointed at the body. "You choose next."

Leth looked around the circle. Five shares remained, but it was obvious what he was to do. Slowly he knelt. The creature was motionless, but touching it still made him shiver. To think he had once known, even loved this thing before him. But much had changed since then. The creature had changed.

When Leth stood, the tension of the group seemed to dissipate. Each took their turn until the last of the Dragon's power had been removed from its corpse. Leth stood as a sentinel, watching as each man began his long journey to an unknown destination. In the distance he heard a whoop of surprise as one of the men tasted his newfound power. As the last of them disappeared from view, Leth turned back to the figure lying in the ash. He knelt by its head.

He laid a hand on the golden locks of hair. As a child he had been jealous of Yorth's good looks. The blue eyes, strong chin. Leth felt a tear slide down his cheek. He would bury the body. The power may have corrupted Yorth, but Leth loved him still the same. After all, they were still brothers. One finally dead, and the other more alive than ever.

CHAPTER 1

To be a god. A *real* god.

The goal was ambitious, to be sure. But ambitious and impossible were two very different things. Particularly given the careful preparations and planning that were behind this goal. King Devvon may have had the same blood as Jag, his forty-third great grandfather, but that was where the similarity ended. He smiled. Particularly

"Here you are, my lord."

Devvon took the proffered object. A glove, its leather worn from years of use but otherwise without blemish. He turned it over, scrutinizing, his eyes coming to rest on the small black stone sewn into the outside of the thumb. He held it close and easily picked out the threads holding the gem in place. But from even a short distance they would be invisible.

"Excellent, Demolick. Your skill lives up to your reputation."

"Thank you, my lord." The young man bowed his head. "It is sufficient then? For my promised payment?"

Devvon nodded, looking up at the man. "It is sufficient. What payment were you promised?"

"My life, sire. I was promised my freedom."

"Ah, yes." Devvon drew his sword. "Your life."

Demolick stumbled backwards. "My lord, you—"

Devvon plunged the sword through the man's chest. After a moment of revelry, he extracted his weapon. Demolick fell to the ground, wheezed twice, and collapsed. His motionless eyes held onto the emotional surge.

Devvon knelt and wiped the blood from his sword on the corpse's leg. "Pity," he said. "Good leatherworkers are hard to find." He sheathed his sword as he crossed the room to the entryway. Carefully sliding the leather glove inside his armor, he rapped on the wooden door.

The door swung open. The soldier that stood on the other side glanced at the body, then at Devvon. "My lord?"

"Get this cleaned up."

"Yes, my lord." The man wouldn't know, nor need the reason for the execution.

Good conditioning, thought Devvon as he strode through the opening and down the stone corridor beyond. A short walk brought him to his second meeting of the morning. He waved as he approached, and another attending soldier pushed the next door open. The three men on the other side jumped from their seats to attention. Devvon waited until the door behind him closed.

"So?"

"Ready, sire."

Devvon looked at the first soldier in the line. The man stood tall, over six feet, and wore a spotless white cape and a gleaming breastplate. *Only three*, he thought, his jaw clenching as he inspected the man. *Well, that's Lexik's problem now, not mine.*

Devvon moved to the second soldier in line and studied his uniform. The browns and yellows were carefully intertwined. The man would be invisible in any forest during the autumn. Devvon looked the man in the eye. "Soldier."

"My lord."

"Who is your king?"

"King Tressle of the northwest, may the Ragdons let him live forever."

Devvon smirked. King Tressle and his people were fond of asking the gods for the impossible. "I could have deduced that from your accent alone."

The soldier nodded. "Thank you, my lord." Once again, an appropriate response from a north-westerner.

Devvon nodded his approval and continued on to the third man, dressed in greens. "And you?"

"My lord, I am bound to King Alder of the south."

Devvon looked closely at the man's face. "How did you get that scar?"

"A raid on Gyon, one of our outlying villages. You should know that, my lord. Your men did the raiding."

Devvon raised his eyebrows. The soldier was surprisingly outspoken. He was about to comment on this, but remembered that King Alder had been making changes of late. Rumor had it he was promoting independence and boasting of the strength of his citizens. *Likely due to his being in Lexik's pocket,* Devvon thought as he smiled at the man before him.

"You are correct. Those were my men that raided that village."

Devvon stepped back to take in the full effect of the three men side by side. "I assume there are no questions."

Two shook their heads. The man in green hesitated. "My lord … you are aware that I have failed."

"I am aware, and I should kill you. However, I haven't the time to replace you. I have made arrangements, and I will correct your mistake."

"Yes, my lord." He threw his chest out further. "Is there anything I can do to redeem myself?"

Devvon took a step forward, bringing them face to face.

"Survive," he hissed.

The man didn't meet Devvon's eyes. "Yes, my king."

"Go, then."

The three turned in different directions and departed through three separate doors. Devvon watched the man in green leave. He flexed his hands.

"Not your king. Not even your emperor," he said to the empty room. A moment later he heard a horse gallop through the courtyard below.

"No. Within the year, I shall be your god."

CHAPTER 2

"For my lady, I shall slay you, beast!"

"Ne'er, for 'tis my lady you speak of and I am the better man!"

Steel hit steel as the two men engaged. The young woman under discussion watched idly from a nearby bench, stifling a yawn in the afternoon sun.

"Ha ha! Today, you have met your match, for I was taught by the royal trainers themselves!"

"Yes," a grunt of exertion, "but that means you were trained by ME!"

The first man's sword clattered to the ground as a final blow twisted it from his hands. "Radgons' fury, take it easy Reon!"

Reon winked. He flipped the discarded sword into the air using his own, his opponent easily catching the handle.

"I was. Care to try again?"

Titan rolled his head from side to side, stretching his neck. "You do realize I have the power to have you beheaded, don't you?"

Reon smirked. "You would have to get my sword away from me first."

"Yes, well, I'm sure if we gather enough men together we could manage it. And I believe you are supposed to refer to me as 'my prince'."

Reon shook his head. "I could never do it with a straight face. I watched you eat dirt as a kid. Not very princely. Besides, we agreed. You beat me at the sword and I start calling you by your title."

Titan lifted his sword. "Again, then. I'll beat some sense into you if it takes all afternoon."

"Not with me watching," Adrianna said, rising from the bench. "You two have been at this for over an hour. I appreciate you both declaring that you are fighting for my honor, but I'm bored to tears."

Titan looked at Reon. "How many times have we gone?"

"Seventeen. I've been counting."

"So, best ..." Titan contorted his face "... eighteen out of thirty seven?"

"Alright then."

Titan rushed him. Four seconds later his sword clanged against the stone wall and dropped to the ground.

"There," Titan said. "Now I feel battered enough to go in."

"Good," Adrianna said as she walked between them. "Take baths. I'll be in the stable."

Titan and Reon agreed and started for the keep proper. The bright blue banners that marked the castle of Titan's father hung from the various windows and balconies. Fluttering in the wind, they looked much like a river surrounding the castle. A moat, suspended in the air.

"You know," Titan said. "My father would be a lot safer during the peace conferences if you went in my stead."

"Nonsense," Reon said. "I've only managed to stay better than you over the last year because I dedicate twice as much time to it as you. And even so, you frequently come close to beating me."

"You call that close?"

"More or less."

"I need to practice more. Close means dead in a real battle."

"You're doing what the kingdom needs. Leave the fighting to us commoners."

"The kingdom doesn't need another diplomat," Titan said. "I've seen enough of those of late to know we already have plenty."

Reon laughed. "Royalty complaining about being around royalty. You must be the first in history to hate having to be around rich, beautiful women." He elbowed Titan in the ribs. "Such as Adrianna?"

Titan responded with a sharper blow. "You have more of a shot at her than I do."

"Being royal and all, can't you change laws like that? What's the point of having power if you only use it to restrict yourself?"

Titan shook his head. "That's a question you'll have to ask my father."

A cool drink, baths, and fresh clothes followed, and the two youth joined Adrianna in the stables. She was brushing the brown coat of her ride, her blonde hair shimmering alongside the rich mane.

"My lady," Reon greeted her, providing an exaggerated bow.

"The horse's hooves need scraping. There's a length of iron over there."

"But my lady, I know how much you enjoy the care of your fine animal. I should be loath to deprive you of such."

Adrianna sighed and turned to Titan. "What's the point of keeping a servant that talks fancy but won't do what you tell him to?"

Titan shrugged. "You just have to realize that Reon is nobody's servant. With the amount of refusing I've seen him do, I'm not sure how he has escaped execution up to now."

Reon shined a stolen apple on his shirt. "I've got friends in high places."

Titan crossed to a worktable and grabbed the metal rod. He turned and lifted a back hoof of the horse. He let it down and examined the other. "These seem fine to me."

"They are. Unfortunately, Reon is right. I like to care for Sienna. I cleaned them off just before you came. I was only asking to make sure our dear, lazy friend hadn't changed over the last year."

"Nary a bit," came the reply between bites.

Titan dropped the piece of metal back on the table and crossed to Reon. The latter offered the apple. Titan took a large bite, wiped a bit of juice from the side of his mouth with his sleeve, and held the apple out to Adrianna. She took the apple and bit in without hesitation.

Reon laughed. "Glad to see you haven't changed either. I hear sharing an apple with men can give a woman disease."

"Lucky for me, you're not a man."

"Titan, I think she just insulted us."

Adrianna shook her head. "I said you. He's a prince. Royalty doesn't carry disease." She handed the apple back and continued brushing. "When do you leave?"

"Tomorrow morning," Titan said. He sighed. "Tomorrow he starts his journey towards the den of asps."

"One of those asps is my father."

"You know what I mean. I don't understand why he leaves his sword out of the conference when none of the other kings do."

"Maybe," interrupted Reon, "it's because he doesn't feel like he needs it. After all, he has the best of the best just outside the door."

Titan smiled. "We've already been through this today."

"Nearly best of the best, then."

Adrianna was watching Titan. "Are you nervous? This isn't your first time."

"Yes, well. Spy reports say some of the other kingdoms are getting restless."

"By 'some of' you mean Devvon," Reon said flatly.

"I don't think this is a good time to go unarmed into a room with a man who obviously has less than honorable intentions."

Adrianna smiled. "Your father isn't a fool. And my father would defend him to the death."

"And if Devvon has convinced the other two to ally?"

Reon sprayed masticated apple. He brushed a piece off of his cheek as he stifled his laughs. "I didn't realize I had hit you so hard."

"Impossible," Adrianna agreed, wrinkling her nose at the scattered bits of fruit.

"Regardless, there is no good reason to give up his sword. He's the only one who does. Year after year, as an outdated symbol of peace, he gives up the only defense he has."

"He'll be fine," Adrianna said. "He's got you. Who could ask for anything more?" She winked.

Reon rolled his eyes and coughed. "Well this isn't awkward. I think I'll check out what's going on at the armory– "

"Forget it, Reon," Titan interrupted. "Everyone in this room knows that nothing is going to happen."

Adrianna cocked her head. "And why not? Don't you think I'm beautiful? Last year while you were away, Reon couldn't stop himself from saying every five minutes that you did."

Titan shot Reon a look.

"Oops?"

Titan looked back to Adrianna. There was a time when he would have been embarrassed to have her know. But the impossibility of the situation made it hard to feel self-conscious. "You know why nothing will happen. It's the law."

"Not my law."

"But it is mine."

"Aren't you the prince? Won't you have the power to change the law? Didn't you just get through saying that your father should change things?"

"Only the laws that don't stand to reason. Our marriage laws have a purpose."

Adrianna folded her arms. "Why can't a royal marry a royal?"

"It would upset the balance of power. Five separate kingdoms that are evenly matched means peace. Uniting two kingdoms would create an unfair balance." Titan looked back and forth between the two. "It must be. I am to marry a western commoner."

"So ... you won't fight for me?" Her voice inflected ever so slightly. The stable grew quiet.

"... Adrianna ..." Titan leaned his head back against the wall.

Reon stood. "Well, Adrianna, I'm still an eligible young man, even if Lord Titey is already betrothed to some unknown peasant."

Adrianna raised an eyebrow. "Unlike Titan, I do have a choice."

Reon winced. "Ouch. Do you have to be so blunt?"

"In most cases, no. But I have found that subtleties don't work as well with you."

The trio halted their conversation as a messenger strode through the stables. "Prince Titan, King Lexik requests your presence."

Titan nodded. "Where is he?"

"In the map room with King Alder."

"Good." Titan turned to the basin beside him and rinsed his hands. Drying them with a hanging towel, he nodded his farewell to Reon and Adrianna and exited the stable. As he left he heard Reon commenting that royals were slaves to their duties.

The castle contained half a dozen spires that rose above a complex of lower hallways and rooms. Situated at the top of one of the lower towers was the map room. In times of war, the king stayed within, guiding the military via messengers, and watching the battle through large windows. The windows and single entry all had heavy wooden doors that, when in place and barricaded, made the room all but impenetrable. Titan climbed the last few stairs and pushed one of the weighty doors open.

Titan stood at attention and waited while the two men across the room finished speaking. King Lexik looked up and gave his son a nod, but didn't beckon him forward.

"Are you still sure about this, Alder?"

"Most sure. You and I both came up with the idea, and it's a good one."

"But wouldn't you feel more comfortable if one of your men—"

"My friend, Titan is *your* son. I trust him implicitly."

Lexik nodded. He abruptly turned and waved Titan over.

"My lords," Titan said as he approached.

"Titan, you remember King Alder."

Titan smiled at the formality of his father's introduction. Alder and Lexik met far more frequently than the annual peace conferences, and Titan was often in attendance. "Of course. How are you, my lord?"

"Very well, thank you. Better sitting in this castle. Every time I do I feel as if I was given the wrong kingdom. It feels like home here."

"Nonsense," Lexik said with a smile. "It only feels like home because of the company you bring to it."

"You know," Alder said, "if we let Adrianna have her way …"

"Alder," Lexik chided. "Let's have none of that."

"As you wish."

Lexik turned back to Titan. "Alder has a favor to ask of you during the peace conferences. He has some possessions he would like to have close at hand. Would you be willing to carry a bag for him?"

Titan cocked his head. "Of course. What possessions?"

Alder shrugged his shoulders. "Assorted valuables. I couldn't leave them home, but I don't want to take them with me. You understand."

Titan nodded. "I do, my lord. I will keep them with me at all times."

"Thank you. I'll repay you in kind by keeping your own kingdom's most prized possession safe." Alder nodded towards Titan's father.

Lexik smiled. "I appreciate the gesture, but just because I won't have my sword doesn't mean I'm defenseless."

Titan cleared his throat. "Father, I've been meaning to talk to you about that."

Lexik turned to him. "You already have. I will not change my mind."

"But why? I don't understand, all four of the other kings keep their weapons. Alder, please tell him."

Lexik set his jaw. "Titan, I said we had already discussed this."

"Why do you insist –"

"Titan!" Lexik's voice echoed through the room. Titan clenched his teeth, physically biting his tongue. Lexik closed his eyes for a moment and exhaled. When he re-opened them, he immediately turned and pulled a map off the table and purposefully rolled the parchment. "Alder, would you excuse us for a moment?"

"Of course." Alder bowed to Lexik and Titan and retreated through the door. Lexik turned his back to Titan and walked away from him.

"Father, I'm sorry. It wasn't my intention to challenge you."

"Yes it was. I raised an independent son, and now I must suffer the consequences." Lexik reached the chest on the opposite wall and opened it.

"So you're not angry with me?"

"Of course I'm angry with you. When I say a matter is closed, you are to respect my wishes. But I understand you as well." He pulled out a long, thin bundle of cloth. "You simply have to accept that there are some things that you just don't understand yet."

Titan closed his eyes and exhaled slowly. "You are right, father. I don't understand why when the other four offer trinkets, year after year you insist on your sword."

"Someday you will," Lexik said as he returned. "I fear sooner than you think. Here. Happy birthday."

Titan hesitated. "It's not my birthday."

"Nor is it any other occasion that merits gift giving, so I simply had to pick one."

Titan gently accepted the bundle and placed it on the table. He cut the twine with his side knife and unwrapped the leather canvas. As the last layer fell away, he looked back up. "Your sword?"

Lexik smiled and tapped the hilt visible over his shoulder. "My sword hangs on my back. This is yours."

Titan looked down again and studied the weapon before him. Black leather with silver threading was bound around the hilt. He looked across the sheath, mesmerized. "It looks like an exact replica."

"My sword has been my faithful companion. I'm asking you to take this instead of mine when you become king. Let mine be buried with me." He looked intently at the weapon on the table. "This sword is a mark of royalty. You are an exemplary son, and you deserve both the sword and the honor it will provide."

Titan gently gripped the sheath and lifted it from the table. He grabbed the hilt and drew the weapon. Though he was expecting it, Titan was still surprised by the tint of the blade. His reflection was clear in the darkened metal. Slowly, he rotated the blade in his hand, noting the black stone on the other side. "Even the gem."

Lexik nodded. "Care for this sword with your life."

Titan nodded as he sheathed the sword. "I will." Attached to the sheath was a leather belt, designed to ride across the chest. Titan lifted the belt over his head, settled the sword across his back, and adjusted the strap.

"Thank you, my lord."

Lexik nodded his approval. "Do you still pray?"

Titan was taken aback by the change of subject. "Not as often as I should, I suppose."

"I would advise against forgetting the gods. The Ragdons are willing to offer their blessings. Let them."

"I will," Titan said. He waited, but Lexik's eyes remained expectant. Titan thought through the various deities and selected Enlightenment. As he raised his arms to begin, Lexik shot out a hand and caught him. "Titan. Never armed."

13

"Of course, my mistake." Titan reached up, pulled the sword from his back and set it on the table. He began again, bringing his hands to his chest. With his palms together, he pushed outwards until they were fully extended in front of him. He spread his arms, opening his chest to Enlightenment, the second of the five Ragdons and his own favorite since childhood. He held the pose for several seconds as a symbol of subjection to the deity's will. After a moment, Titan reversed the order of the hand movements, expressing thanks.

Lexik grunted, handing Titan's sword back to him. "It is vital that we pray without weapons, without armor. Asking the gods for help while armed is hypocrisy. We defend ourselves, but we let *them* protect us."

"I will," Titan repeated.

"Good. Are we ready to leave tomorrow?"

"The regiment will be ready to leave at first light, our horses are being groomed and fed as we speak, and supplies are already packed."

"Very good. Titan, I'll be honest with you. I think you're spot on with Devvon. I imagine he's planning something. The situation at the peace conferences would make him a fool to try anything there, but the road will take us a full week. That's a lot of time and a lot of opportunity for him. Make sure the men are on their guard at all times. Double shifts for the night watch wouldn't be a bad idea."

Titan nodded. "I agree. I'll have it arranged. The men I'm bringing are the best swordsmen in the kingdom. All except Reon."

"He's seventeen. Too young."

"I'm seventeen, and you not only let me come but assign me as your aide."

"You are my son. The closer you are to me, the easier the transition will be for both you and the people when the time comes."

Titan didn't bother to disagree. The changes he wanted to make in how his father governed had been rejected time and time again. Lexik wasn't going to change anytime soon.

14

Arguing over it only increased the king's conviction. "Well, other than Reon, we're as ready as we can be."

"Good. You may go. I'll see you at sunrise."

"Yes, my lord." Titan turned and strode towards the door.

"And Titan?"

"Yes, my lord?"

Lexik smiled. "I'm looking forward to the trip. It's been a while since we spent more than a few minutes at a time together."

Titan smiled. "So am I, father. I'll see you tomorrow."

CHAPTER 3

General Felk rode his white horse towards the looming castle. His army, now no more than forty wounded men, marched behind him at a decent pace, considering their condition. The dark red banners on either side of the gate before them flapped crossly in the wind. *Appropriate.* Felk exhaled through clenched teeth.

The gate opened without petition, the soldiers on either side of the wall saluting in respect. Felk probably knew at least half of the soldiers by name, though he couldn't pick them out while in armor. Those soldiers were used to seeing Felk leave at the head of an army, and more importantly, they were used to seeing Felk return. *Often not at the head of an army*, Felk bitterly thought. There were good men on that wall. Similar to the good men that were left on the battlefield behind him.

The streets surrounding the castle were still as the tiny army marched through. The same scene had been replayed too many times for there to be significant mourning. Those who lost loved ones would cry behind closed doors. Those whose loved ones returned to them would cry for different reasons. The rest would simply watch.

King Devvon's castle stood in the exact center of the city. In the case of an attack, Devvon wanted to make sure that his defenses had as long a time as possible to prepare themselves before an invading army reached them. *Pointless*, Felk reflected. *There hasn't been an invading army in decades.* By placing his people between himself and potential dangers, all Devvon was doing was affirming once again that his life was more important than theirs.

Felk ached for change. He ached for the days when he had served King Hyulit, Devvon's father. Hyulit understood the importance of his people. The days had been peaceful under his rule. He hadn't needlessly thrown away lives for the sole purpose of getting rid of a single general.

Felk's return marked Devvon's sixth failed attempt in the last year to rid himself of the general without outright sentencing him to be executed. Felk knew King Devvon would have no emotional trouble giving the order, but he wasn't stupid. There were too many soldiers within the eastern army who still saw Felk as their ultimate authority. If Felk was beheaded, the city would turn to chaos as the military and populace alike sought revenge.

Devvon hated the amount of influence Felk commanded. The solution Devvon had been employing to resolve the problem was one of conquest. There were many lands outside the rule of the five kingdoms that were unclaimed. The majority of them were infested with armies of bandits and thieves that had formed in the absence of law. Devvon had dedicated his energies to their subjection.

Six times Felk had been sent to conquer what Devvon would call a "small settlement." And six times Felk had arrived to find that the army he had been given was vastly outnumbered by the enemy. Six times he had been bound by oath to conquer or die. And conquer he had.

The small procession reached the castle courtyard, and Felk dismounted. He signaled the dismissal of his men, entered the keep, and walked swiftly down the corridor. As he approached, the doors to the throne room were pushed open by stationed guards and Felk strode through. He crossed the room, sunk to a knee, and dutifully bowed his head.

"I have returned, King Devvon."

"So I gathered," Devvon said dryly. "How went the battle?"

Felk kept his face to the ground. "We achieved victory, but at the cost of many lives. The initial reports we received were inaccurate. The bandits stationed at the river bend were triple the predicted number."

"It would seem my spy network was mistaken. Don't fear, General. I shall find the culprit and he shall be executed for his error."

Felk didn't doubt Devvon would behead the spy who made the count, most likely in the city square in front of the castle. Devvon would give a long and noble speech about the despair he felt at the lost lives. He would even praise Felk for his courage and leadership abilities. And then he would place blame on a single man. A man who had both counted and reported accurately.

"I don't believe an execution is necessary for a simple mistake."

"Isn't it?" Devvon rose from his throne. "I can't let it just pass that an incorrect count, or worse yet, a lie would be the cause of so many deaths." He approached towards Felk, waving him to his feet. "Wouldn't you agree, General?"

Felk rose to meet the king's stare. "I would."

"Then how can you suggest we just stand idly by?" King Devvon's voice dropped to a whisper. "Don't you want revenge, my most honorable general?"

Felk's hand autonomously moved to his axe. Devvon's gaze flickered down, then back. He smirked. "Yes. You want revenge. Why don't you take it?"

Felk lifted his chin. "Revenge will not change wrongs that have already been committed."

"But it will prevent their continuation. By not taking action, you are subjecting your men to future dangers." Devvon's eyes were full of hate and invitation. "You are killing your own men, general. Men who look to you for protection, who trust you with their lives."

Felk clenched his teeth. An angry outburst would only give Devvon a lawful reason to kill him. "Then perhaps it is better that the decision is yours rather than mine."

Devvon smiled graciously, then stepped away. "Indeed." He raised his voice loud enough for all in the room to hear him. "Unfortunately, I am to leave tomorrow morning for the peace conferences. I will be unable to take action for several weeks, during which time the inadequate spy will most likely pass more wrong information." He returned to his throne. "You there, soldier. Find out who made the original count of the bandit force and have him arrested. General, I want you to personally oversee his execution in my absence."

Felk glared. "I believe that it can wait until your return."

"I want you to have the privilege. After all, this man was responsible for the deaths of, what, nearly two thousand men?" Devvon beamed. "For your courage in battle, you've earned the right."

Felk remained silent.

"Good. Have it done before my return." Devvon waved his hand in dismissal. Felk bowed and spun, storming from the room. As he reached the doors, Devvon called from behind. "Thank you for your unwavering obedience, General."

*****

Adrianna grew still as she stared down the arrow's shaft. She raised the bow ever so slightly, exhaled, and released. The arrow's zip was answered with a resounding thud as it buried itself just off center of the target.

"Beginner's luck," Reon said.

Adrianna didn't bother to spare him a glance as she notched another arrow. She took aim. After a long moment, she let the arrow fly. It soared through the air and struck dead center. Adrianna nodded, satisfied. "That's better."

She held the bow out to Reon. "Your turn."

Reon stepped forward and notched his own arrow. "Show off," he muttered. His shot caught the outer rim of the orange circle around the red.

Adrianna gave a low whistle. "You were right. Last time you had trouble hitting the target at all. You *have* improved."

"Ragdons know I have. If it weren't for the cursed crosswind that shot would've split your arrow."

"Ah. A second shot then?"

Reon shrugged. "And make a princess feel bad about all her hard work only earning her second place? That wouldn't be very gentlemanly."

"How considerate of you." She calmly took the bow, notched the last of the four arrows, and fired. Reon's arrow splintered to pieces as the shot passed through the shaft.

Reon eyebrows shot up. "Right."

Adrianna smiled, but not because she had beaten Reon. Both of them knew that the competition was strictly for entertainment. She did, however, take pride in her talent with the bow. Her father always affirmed that she had picked up one of his bows as a toddler and had yet to put it down.

She turned and looked back towards the castle. "What's taking Titan so long?"

Reon was walking back from retrieving the three remaining arrows. "I bet your father just loves how fast you go through these things."

"He's been gone for nearly an hour."

Reon dropped two of them and notched the third. "Titan and his father tend to talk for longer these days. Titan wants to change things, and Lexik doesn't. So Titan can't."

Adrianna sighed. "Not even after Lexik is gone and he's king?"

"Doubtful," Reon said as he let the string snap. The arrow struck several inches closer to the middle than his first had. "Titan may disagree with his father, but he knows Lexik rules well. The people are protected, they have enough food, and they are general happy with management. Lexik's method works, and Titan knows it."

Adrianna crossed her arms. "That may be true for a lot of Lexik's commands, but some of them don't make sense. You for instance. Why aren't you going tomorrow?"

"Somebody's got to stay behind with the pretty girls." Reon winked at Adrianna and shot another arrow. It nicked the outer edge of the target and flipped end over end past it. "You know, make them feel good about their archery skills and all."

"I must admit you're succeeding. I don't know that I've ever beaten someone so badly."

"What do you say we switch to fencing?"

"You dare challenge a lady?"

Reon rubbed his chin. "Yeah, that's no good. Alright, you keep shooting. I'll throw my sword instead."

They turned as the sound of footsteps approached from behind. A young man was just emerging from the trees, headed towards them.

"Hello, there Jaron," Reon greeted the newcomer. "General Jaron, I should say."

"That's not necessary, Reon," the young man said with a smile. He turned to Adrianna. "My lady, I don't believe we've met."

"Nor do I," Adrianna said as she extended a hand. "Adrianna."

The man took her hand and bowed his head in deference. "I suspected as much, your highness. My name is Jaron. I'm very pleased to meet you."

"And you're one of Lexik's generals?"

"Not one of," Reon interjected. "He's *the* general around here."

"There are three of us."

"Yes, but the other two answer to you."

Jaron blushed. "Only as a formality."

"So what brought you to seek our company this fine afternoon, General?" Reon asked.

Jaron spared a glance towards Adrianna. "I was taking a walk and saw you shooting. I thought I might be able to offer myself as a third contestant to lessen the competition."

"Second contestant, you mean," Adrianna said with a smirk. "Only one of us was actually shooting at the target."

"Now is that really necessary, princess?" Reon shook his head. "You really were close to beating me. Don't put yourself down. Just keep practicing."

"May I?" Jaron asked.

"You're the boss," Reon said, offering the bow.

Jaron weighed the bow in his hand before notching an arrow. "This is from the armory?" he asked.

"Yes, sir."

He raised the weapon and took aim, his arms and shoulders relaxed from obvious practice. After a moment, his fingers let go and the arrow whipped through the air. Adrianna gave a gentle clap.

"Very close to center. Better than my first shot. Take another, now that you've seen how the bow shoots."

Jaron shook his head. "I'm afraid it won't make much of a difference. The bow is standard issue, and I've been practicing with them for some time. Eventually I will perfect my shot from this distance, but hitting the bull's-eye by merely making a second attempt would be nothing more than luck."

Adrianna smiled. "Self-awareness is a rare gift."

"Why do you think he's a general?" Reon said. "Only four years older than me, but he's one of the best strategists the kingdom has."

"Is this true?" Adrianna asked.

"Course it is," Reon answered for him. "We haven't had problems with bandits for over a year because of his troop placements and movements. The blokes can't get through."

Jaron shook his head. "We haven't had problems because the men are dedicated to protecting their families." He handed the bow back to Adrianna. "I'm afraid I only had time to stop for a moment and must be on my way again." He paused. "My lady, I assume you are staying here until your father's return?"

"I am."

"... Would you be willing to participate in a rematch tomorrow evening?"

Adrianna cocked her head. "But I thought you said another shot wouldn't improve your chances?"

"It wouldn't," Jaron looked down. "At least not with archery."

Reon raised an eyebrow. "What with –"

"Challenge accepted, General," Adrianna interrupted.

"Thank you, my lady," Jaron said. "I look forward to it." He quickly turned and headed back the direction he came.

Reon watched him go with a scowl. "I don't understand what just happened. What's he improving his chances with?"

Adrianna watched as Jaron disappeared into the trees. "With me."

Reon scratched his chin. "Uh-huh. And ... you accepted."

"What else could I do? He was obviously uncomfortable. Refusing would only have led to embarrassment."

Reon whistled as he looked back towards the forest. "I've never seen Jaron embarrassed before."

CHAPTER 4

Devvon watched as Felk storm through the far doors and turned down the corridor out of sight.

By the Ragdons, why won't he die!?

Felk was infuriating. The real problem was his defiant obedience. The man performed every command with perfection, without hesitation. And so, Devvon had purposefully placed him in situations so dire, so impossible that the only conceivable outcomes were death or dishonor. Either would serve to lose his grip on the people, but neither had happened. Devvon had wasted thousands of lives, lives he needed for the coming months, just to coax Felk's heart into stopping. But on Felk's heart beat, like a pounding headache.

Letting Felk live was unacceptable. The loss of the ten thousand men was better than losing the whole eastern army. The option wasn't perfect, but it was the best available. What infuriated Devvon the most was that he was losing even more men than Felk realized. And Devvon needed these soldiers.

Devvon had known he would need them for the last eighteen years. That was the driving reason behind his population laws. His first act after assuming the throne was to decree that if a woman reached the age of thirty without having three sons to show for it, she was hanged. Women started having children earlier and, as the requirement was three males, many times would produce four or five daughters in the process that could be put to work on farms. More women meant more law-abiding citizens to give Devvon soldiers. Current projections claimed that by the time Devvon died, the army would be four times its current size.

The projections had two flaws: the growth wouldn't take nearly that long, and Devvon wasn't going to die.

Growing an army was less about birth rates and more about signed documents. For instance, within the month Devvon would sign into law a change in the recruitment age. By reducing the age from eighteen to fifteen, his advisors informed him that the army would increase by fifty percent immediately. Of course, that would be insufficient. But, by signing a second document allowing volunteers to reenlist, the army would swell beyond comprehension. Combining an army that size with his careful planning, Devvon would conquer with ease.

So long as Felk didn't get in the way.

With any luck he will refuse to carry out the execution, Devvon thought. *Even the most simple-minded of commoners would see that as blatant disobedience.* And if he did carry it out, Felk would be one step closer to an outburst. It was only a matter of time.

Of course, time was growing short. Devvon waved the guard to his right forward. "Report."

"Your honor guard is ready for your departure. And the men you sent several weeks ago have sent word that they are in position as well."

"Excellent. How many men did they take with them?"

"One hundred and fifty, my lord."

Devvon rubbed his chin, counting. "How fast could twenty riders get to them?"

"Only twenty? No more than three days, if they pushed their mounts."

"Send them."

"Yes, my lord." The soldier strode away.

One hundred and seventy. Given the quality of training the other two kingdoms gave their soldiers, that should be about right. Devvon rose and turned as a servant pushed a side door open for him. The remaining guards in the room stood firm. They had not been ordered to move.

Devvon was met by the captain of the honor guard just outside the door. "We are ready to leave at dawn, my lord." Devvon nodded as the man fell into step beside him. "Are you sure about this plan, my lord?"

"You doubt me, Captain?"

"Of course not," the Captain blurted. "I simply mean that bringing more men with you might prove beneficial."

"They won't be necessary."

"Understood, my lord."

Devvon smiled. The man didn't understand. There wasn't a soul besides Devvon himself that knew the full extent of what was coming.

Devvon dismissed the Captain and continued to the royal chamber. The night was fast approaching, and he knew he would hate the wait. In years past, he would have gone to his wife in search of her beauty. He still thought of it as a pity that she had been barren. He would have liked to have spared her, but the law was the law. And after her execution, no one doubted Devvon's sincerity.

Devvon undressed and sank into his prepared bath. The water was perfect. He let his head rest back and closed his eyes. This coming week would mean the dawn of a new era. No more kingdoms, no more squabbling. One people, under one god. Best get some rest while he still needed it.

*****

Titan swung up into the saddle.

"If I didn't know any better, I'd say you had done that before," Reon commented.

"Only a few times," Titan replied as he adjusted the reins. Reon set himself to securing the saddlebags. Titan looked around at the group of two hundred men and horses. It was comforting to see the blue and green flags mingled together. A treaty between Lexik and Alder was out of the question for the same reasons that a marriage between Titan and Adrianna was impossible. But as far as Titan could tell, the only thing lacking for an alliance was the paper bearing the signatures.

He pulled at the strap on his shoulder. The weight of the sword was unfamiliar, as was the sight of it to passersby. The similarities of the sword to that of his father appeared to be accomplishing King Lexik's intentions. The women and children stared and the men were quicker to salute. For whatever reasons Lexik had, his attempt to have Titan step more fully into the role of heir was working.

"Well, Prince of the Western Kingdom," Reon said as he stepped back, "you ride carefully and ol' Susie here will take good care of you."

"First of all," Adrianna said as she approached, "that horse is male, and second, he is only three years old."

"The gender I can swallow, but how in the Ragdons would you know its age?"

"Lexik gave him that horse last year for his birthday. It was two years old then. Two plus one is three. I'll explain it to you later."

"Math, huh? Very sneaky."

"Very observant," Titan corrected.

"I know my horses," Adrianna said. She smiled sweetly at Reon. "And bows."

"Don't listen to her, Titan. Women always lie about such things."

She turned back to Titan. "Be careful. I overheard my father giving orders. He's nervous."

Titan nodded. "Devvon would be a fool to attack both of us at the same time. That's why we ride together."

"I know. Just be careful."

"We will."

The soldiers were finishing lining up their ranks. "Time to go," Reon said as he watched them. "Can't wait till next year when I'm riding out with you."

"Neither can I," Titan responded. "We need the best we have with us."

"Aw, shucks," Reon said. He kicked the dirt. "Don't make me blush."

"Be safe," Adrianna said. She raised her hands with her fingers together to her forehead, and then extended them outward toward him. "May Vision keep you," she said as she finished the prayer by reversing the motion.

Reon clapped his forearms together. "And Strength bear you up," he said, clapping them again.

Titan felt warmth spread through him. Having another person call upon the deities in his behalf always gave him a good feeling. Having his best friend and his ... Adrianna ... the effect was compounded. He beamed, saluted, and kicked his horse forward toward the front of the gathering.

"Good morning," Lexik greeted him as he approached.

"Good morning," Titan answered. "Are we ready?"

Lexik breathed in deeply, looking at the crisp, blue morning sky. "I do believe we are. Give the order."

Titan turned to the horseman to his left and nodded.

"Forward!"

One hundred men advanced. Lexik and Titan rode at the front, proceeded by their honor guard and followed by lines of horsemen. One hundred men were allowed from each kingdom at the peace conferences. Several hundred feet in front of them King Alder and his men were already moving. During the journey the kings would ride together, but exiting the city instilled hope in both kingdoms. Best to let each king lead his own army.

"You look nervous," Lexik said, eyes ahead.

"I'd be lying if I said I wasn't."

"That's understandable, but your people are watching you. Relax your shoulders."

Titan took a deep breath and obeyed. "He's crazy."

"Crafty, not crazy."

"That doesn't make me feel any better."

Lexik chuckled. "Hopefully it means he'll stay in line."

"And if he doesn't?"

"Well ... than he'll be all that much more dangerous."

Titan shook his head. "He's going to try something."

"He wouldn't be able to move the amount of men needed to conquer the other four without us knowing about it. So, we stay on the road, camp on the high ground, and keep a good watch. Even if he does try something, we'll have warning."

Lexik was right. Devvon knew what he was doing. His confidence led him to action, but his judgment reined him in. Titan took another deep breath and looked around to bid farewell to the city. Banners streamed from second story windows in alternating blue and green, marking the procession's path. The people waved, shouted, cheered. They would be gone for over two weeks, and Titan would miss both the buildings and the people that inhabited them. He loved the road, but he inevitably longed for home.

The gate ahead was like a gaping mouth, the road a winding tongue and the forest innumerable teeth. Titan could see the guards saluting from above. He also picked out two other figures, not in uniform. Since the first time Titan had gone with his father three years prior, Reon and Adrianna had bid him farewell in the courtyard, then raced on horseback by back alleys to beat him to the gate. They both waved energetically, though Adrianna's training gave her the appearance of enthusiasm while Reon's lack of training gave him the appearance of a fool. Titan's position at the head of the small army forbade him from a reply. Titan smiled as his friends waved anyways.

Two hours later, whatever excitement the men had entertained had eroded mostly away, and the two armies began to mingle. Most wouldn't know each other, but in a few instances it was quite possible that cousins or even brothers were being reunited. It wasn't uncommon for westerns and southerns to intermarry.

Alder fell back and rode beside Lexik and Titan. He muttered something about safety and being in the midst of the army rather than at the front. Lexik grinned, nodded, and accepted the excuse without argument. They rode in silence for a time, but Alder was too much of a conversationalist not to seize the opportunity.

"You know, Lexik, we really should just sign a treaty and be done with it. We haven't hidden very well that we are mutually supportive, and all the other kings consider us practically one. So why not?"

"Because," Lexik said, "it doesn't matter what people think. It matters what they say and do. You know as well as I that the alliance tried seventy years back failed miserably."

"Yes, well, one member of the alliance was somewhat hostile towards the rest. The other three had to engage and break it up before the east gained more support."

"Why is it," Titan asked, "that the eastern kingdom is always the one making trouble?"

"Not always." Lexik winked. Titan rolled his eyes. "It's a long story."

Titan raised an eyebrow. "Do you have pressing business to attend to at the moment?"

Alder's saddle shook loudly as he stifled his laughter. Lexik simply shook his head. "Cheeky boy. Well, at the most basic level, the man who became the first king of the east sacrificed much more than the others to conquer the Dragon. The eastern kings at times feel they deserve more by right of heritage."

"What did he sacrifice?"

Lexik glanced at his son. "His wife."

"His wife was killed by the Dragon?"

"Yes, but he lost her long before she was killed."

Titan raised an eyebrow. "That's not very clear, father. Even for a politician."

Lexik chuckled. "No, it's not. But it's all you are getting for now. Order the men to report."

Titan's chaffed at the deflection, but gave the order anyways. The men were divided into groups of ten that were trained to quickly take inventory of their provisions, weapons, and the surrounding forest. The groups' assigned leaders would report to the captain at Titan's left, who would then report to Titan and Lexik. It was extremely efficient, lasting no more than a minute, and didn't require a slowing of the pace.

As the command was carried out, Titan thought about what he know of the formation of the five kingdoms. Roughly a millennium before, the known world was in a state of chaos. An enormous winged creature, now called the Dragon, had appeared and ravaged the landscape. Fire-breathing, impenetrable armor, and inhuman senses. It was said to be invincible. An army gathered to destroy it, but was wiped out in moments. The last five soldiers followed the creature to its home and killed it. Various methods were attributed, though Titan didn't feel like any of the theories sounded plausible. After the deed was done, the five heroes were crowned and their dominions flourished and became the kingdoms of present day.

Beyond the core of the tale, storytellers had spun a thousand different patterns, describing what happened. Some said that the Ragdons endowed the five kings with supernatural abilities. Others said they stole them from the Dragon. The priests themselves were silent on the matter, and as such many stated it was best not to speculate. As Titan thought, he remembered he had heard the offerings at the peace conferences themselves were representative of the sacrifices made to stop the destruction.

Hours stretched into days. Between riding, walking, and staring, the trip dragged on into boredom. Dusk, however, brought enough excitement to keep Titan going. Lexik knew the effect of a royal literally feeding his men and encouraged Titan to join the nightly hunting party. On the fourth night, Titan brought down a doe and was welcomed with cheers from the men.

His stomach full of his trophy, Titan lay down to rest in the tent next to his father's. The Tower was still a three day march ahead of them, but home already dominated his thoughts. *Three more days, a day for talk, and seven to return,*

31

he counted. Of course, both of the kings and their men would be eager for a soft bed. Perhaps with a little persuasion, a seven day trip could be done in five or six. Titan smiled, closed his eyes, and focused on the sound of crackling wood coming from a nearby fire. Ten days until their return. Ten days until ... ten days ... ten ...

Titan snapped his eyes back open as he heard the undeniable flit of an arrow whip through his tent.

CHAPTER 5

Felk smashed his fist against the door for a third time.

"Curse whoever you are, I'm not opening!" came the reply.

Felk growled. "I am your general and I'll have your hands if you don't open before I can axe through the door!"

"A thief that lies!"

Felk turned to his horse, slid his war axe from its scabbard, and with a mighty swing sank the blade deep into the wood. A yelp of fright came, followed by the sound of scraping wood and metal. The door opened an inch and two beady eyes peered through the crack.

"Step forward into the light!"

Felk complied, letting the torch illuminate his scarred face. Another yelp.

"General!" The door was flung open and a short man who was obviously thick of both body and mind ushered Felk in. Felk noted with satisfaction as he stepped through that his axe's blade was protruding through the other side. He grabbed the wooden shaft and yanked his weapon free. The man swallowed.

"My apologies, General. Only thieves trying to spring their criminal friends knock this late at night."

"Open it," Felk commanded as he pointed to the door opposite them.

"Of course." The swollen man ran to the far wall, upending a chair in the process. He yanked a ring of keys from a nail and began fumbling for the correct fit. Felk crossed to the locked gate at the other end of the room and waited as four keys were tried before the telltale click sounded. "Anything else I can do for you, General?"

Felk swiped the keys from the man. "Close your front door, don't allow anyone through it, and don't follow me in."

"Yes sir," the man squeaked. Felk turned towards the black opening. He pulled the nearby torch from its bracket, took a deep breath, and duck in. He began down the stairs into the pit that contained every arrested criminal in the kingdom. The king insisted that lawbreakers rot in darkness. It allowed Devvon time to sort through a collection of citizens that possessed certain skill sets that were harder to find among honest men. The gifted were pardoned. The rest were hanged.

Felk pushed the door at the bottom open with his axe and began down the corridor of cells. Each was a box just too small for a grown man to stand fully upright in. Those inside shielded their eyes from the flame as Felk passed. He stopped halfway down the row and turned to the nearest wretch.

"You there. A man was brought in here within the past several days. Which is he?"

The man didn't bother to raise his head, but pointed down the line of cells. Felk continued for several more strides and repeated the question to another inmate. Further direction came. He finally found his objective lying down, facing the opposite wall.

"Soldier," Felk said.

The man didn't answer.

"I am your general. You are bound to answer me."

"I haven't been no soldier for two days now," the man replied without turning, "meaning I isn't bound to do nothing."

"Are you the man who counted the bandits at the river bend prior to the latest raid?"

The man didn't respond. Felk lowered his voice.

"Do you want out of here?"

Silence. Slowly, the man rolled to his back and let his head fall to the side. He rubbed his eyes and squinted. Felk waited as the man's vision adjusted.

"General Felk?"

"Did you make the count?"

"Yeah, I made it."

Felk stepped closer. "Do you remember?"

"Yeah."

Felk's heart pounded. He knew wrong numbers had been passed before, but had never had a chance to verify that Devvon was changing them. "Tell me."

The man stared at Felk. "And then I get out?"

Felk answered with a nod.

"Then open the door first."

Lucky you're not still a soldier. "I am to be your executioner tomorrow in the city square. I have no qualms finishing the deed here instead. Tell me or even the Ragdons won't be able to stop me."

The man shook his head. "The way I sees it, I got nothing to lose either way. Open the door."

Felk studied the dirt streaked cheeks, the unkempt hair. This man had lost everything. Felk's threat had hinged on the man valuing his own life, on him fearing death. He didn't. He had accepted it.

Felk wedged the torch between two bars, retaining his axe. The man watched from his back, expressionless. His eyes were curious. Felk reached the keys held in his other hand, found the fit, and twisted. Several other prisoners turned at the metallic click. Felk took several steps back and brought his axe forward.

The man hesitated, then rolled to his side. He pushed the door, eyebrow rising as it creaked open. He crawled through and used the opposite bars to pull himself up. He stretched up, rolling his shoulders like a cat after waking. He dropped them to his sides and sighed.

"Now don't that feel just perfect."

"The count."

The man scowled. "I sat in that tree counting for three days. Near broke my back doing it." He laughed. "I didn't think I'd end up breaking it down here."

"The count, man."

The man held up a hand. "I haven't stood for no two days. You just wait." He reached up again, his back offering several cracks of appreciation. "I owe you, General. Alright, I'll tell you. The count's the same as what I passed. One thousand."

Felk started. "One thousand?"

"Yep, just like I said to the runner. One thousand men, couple dozen horses."

Felk stared at the man. The original report he had received had been for one thousand. He had taken twice that amount to ensure victory. All but forty of those two thousand soldiers were now dead at the hands of a grossly underestimated force. The man standing before him had passed one thousand, and Felk had been told one thousand. Devvon hadn't made an alteration. The group of bandits truly did triple during the two week period.

Felk let the blade of his axe smack against the stones at his feet. "Thank you, soldier." Felk stepped to the side.

The man didn't move. "Just like that?"

"I told you I would. There's a man upstairs that I refuse to kill for you, but escape is yours."

"And … what about you? Even if I kills the man, all these men down here seen you and heard you. Devvon isn't going to be happy that I been sprung, and he going to figure out who done it."

"My word is my bond. I'll handle Devvon."

"He'll kill you."

"Almost undoubtedly."

The ensuing silence was broken only by several hushed whispers of neighbor prisoners. The freed soldier glanced around him, then back at Felk. "You know, I heard about you,

General Felk. Men say you the last good leader. You care about you men."

"I do," Felk said. "Please, go quickly."

The man still didn't move. "Where to?"

"To the Ragdons' inferno for all I care. Just GO!"

"See, problem is, I haven't got nowhere *to* go. Devvon will reward anybody who sees me. I'd have to run to another kingdom, and they'll know me by my accent. Be hated no matter where I go."

"I agreed to get you out. You figure out where you'll be able to manage."

The prisoner wiped his nose with a filthy wrist. "I apologize, General. I think I isn't going to make good on our deal."

Felk lifted his axe several inches. The man snickered.

"Now there isn't no need for that." He stretched again, then sighed, shaking his head. Chuckling, he turned and ducked back into his cell. "I suggest you lock the door before leaving."

Felk furrowed his brow. "What are you doing?"

"You blind, General? I'm sitting."

Felk approached and rested a hand on the open door.

"The way I sees it, General, you can save lives if you alive." He held Felk's gaze. "My friends' lives. Me? I'd just be running. That isn't no life." The man leaned forward, grabbed a bar of the door and wrenched it from Felk's gripped. He slowly closed it and crossed his arms expectantly.

Felk shook his head. "I promised I would let you escape."

"And you did. I just chose to come back. Now lock the door."

Felk didn't move. The ring of keys in his hand turned to lead.

"Lock the door."

Felk lifted his wrist and numbly turned the lock. The nearby murmurs died with the echoing click.

The prisoner smiled as he rested his head back against the bars. "You have a good night, General. I'll see you tomorrow."

*****

Adrianna awoke again. She peered out the window to find the night dark and quiet. How many times had she drifted in and out of dreams? Trying to remember made her tired. Just not tired enough to fall asleep again. With a sigh, she pulled the blankets back, crossed the room, and rang for a servant. Less than a minute passed before there was a soft knock at the door.

Adrianna opened it to find a young maid in mid yawn. "I'm sorry," Adrianna said quickly. "I didn't mean to wake you. I assumed there was a servant on duty."

The girl smiled and shook her head. "Don't worry, my lady. I'm the servant on duty. I dozed off." Her cheeks grew pink.

Adrianna felt ashamed at the unimportance of her request. Still, the girl was already here. "I was just wondering the hour. I can't sleep and I'm tired of waiting for sunrise."

"It is just past the second watch. I'm afraid dawn is still at least three hours away."

"Thank you," Adrianna said. The girl curtsied and headed back down the hallway. Three hours. Adrianna looked back at her rumpled sheets, like quicksand dragging her back into them. She rubbed the back of her neck and crossed to the open balcony beyond. Leaning against the railing, she watched the stars above. Thousands of them, always constant, but only offering hints of light. Somewhere out there, her father was out under those same stars. So was Titan.

Titan. Adrianna shook her head as a new sense of weariness set in. He was the most aggravating person she'd ever met. Noble enough to step in to protect commoners, strong enough to not feel the need to compete against other men, and yet ... so ... aggravating. She had always heard that love and grief were faithful companions. If only he would --

Stop it, she told herself. *Reon is right. Titan is bound by his law, and he will never change it. It's pointless to think about him as anything more than a future sovereign.* The law was unbreakable, as Titan was fond of saying.

Adrianna cocked her head. Unbreakable, yes, but ... unbendable?

If he wouldn't break the law, and he wouldn't change it even for love, that left only one option: abiding by the law. Adrianna stood and went to the servant bell once again. The response was significantly faster. Adrianna raised an eyebrow.

"I decided to wait a little nearer, my lady. You're too bright to simply stay up all night. It was only a matter of time before you thought of something to do with these hours."

Adrianna grinned. "I'm hopelessly predictable. Would you bring me a copy of King Lexik's laws?"

"All of them, mistress?"

"Oh ... no, not all. Just those dealing with royal marriage and succession."

The maid cocked her head, then curtsied and turned back the way she had come. Adrianna went to her desk and began moving the books and ornaments to the ground. She pulled out a stack of fresh paper, a bottle of ink, and several quills. A soft knock at the door announced the return of the maid, now bearing two scrolls. She deposited them on the cleared desk.

"Does my lady require assistance writing?"

"No, thank you," Adrianna answered. "You try to get some sleep, even if you are on duty. No sense in both of us being awake." The maid nodded guiltily before retreating once again. Adrianna sat and began unrolling a scroll. She edged the candle closer.

As the Ragdons have not dictated with whom a person should fall in love with, neither is it lawful for a ruler to decree to whom that same person should marry. As such, it is within the right of each man within the kingdom to marry any woman of his choosing, regardless of station, allegiance, or age. No restrictions are in place except those of fidelity imposed by the priest performing the union.

The exception to the law is the king himself. He and his second are required to marry in order to produce heirs, but they shall neither propose nor accept a proposal of marriage to a royal. A marriage to royalty from another kingdom produces a union which will upset the balance of power between the five and as such is forbidden.

Marriage is a binding union. Divorce is outlawed and infidelity is punishable by imprisonment for a month. In the event of a premature death, the widow or widower may marry again, assuming they abide by the aforementioned laws and their second spouse is made aware of the prior marriage.

Adrianna's quill hovered above the empty page beside the scroll. She tapped her nails idly on the desk as she reread the text. Every king's intentions were the same. Draft laws that restrict undesirable actions of subjects while maintaining complete freedom for the sovereign himself. Loopholes were pervasive, but usually subtle. With her own page still blank, she rolled up the first scroll and moved on to the second.

The king is given all rights to rule and reign. His word is law to the extent that it doesn't contradict current law. He is subject only to the unanimous voice of the people, as judged by the priests of the church, who may dethrone him if his conduct becomes distinct from the Ragdons' will. His reign lasts until his death. Stepping down would have the potential of creating divisions among the people, and as such is only permitted when it is in line with the Ragdons' will, as determined by the priests of the church.

Upon the death of the king, his oldest surviving son succeeds his reign. Should he be without male heir, the generals are to assume the throne, in order of rank. If the king has no heir and the generals are for whatever reason dead or incapable of rule, the priests will appoint a ruler from the common class.

Adrianna frowned at the stubbornly empty paper. Titan, in his current station, was required to marry a commoner, and would retain the throne until he was removed by the gods themselves through death or divine decree.

Alright, she thought, pushing herself back to her feet. She crossed the room and, with a twinge of guilt, rang the servants' bell once again.

CHAPTER 6

"Stop." Devvon waited as the approaching silhouette obeyed. "Report."

"Ready, as promised. Just waiting on you."

"Spread them out. All at once would raise suspicions."

The figure leaned against a tree. "Just because I'm not yours doesn't mean I'm stupid."

Devvon clenched his teeth. He had set many things in motion throughout the years as he prepared for his rise to omnipotence, but none that repulsed him to the extent this deal did. Any other option would have been preferable. But supremacy had its price.

"You are mine. You've sworn loyalty."

"You, of all people, talk to me about loyalty?"

Devvon yanked his sword from his hip. "You dare accuse me of betrayal?"

A chuckle wafted through the chill night. "I thought that was what this whole plan was about."

"I'm not betraying them."

The shadow shrugged. "I'll take your word for it. But where I'm from, you're walking the line."

Devvon growled as the shadow was reabsorbed into the night.

*****

Titan flung himself from his bed as the first scream pierced the darkness.

"Attack!"

Titan snagged his bow and sword as he charged through the tent door. The yell had come from the south. He watched as a sea of darkness flowed up the hill towards the encampment. The forward edge reached the line of sentry torches, and steel clashed as the guards engaged the enemy. Lights from behind rose and arced gracefully over the skirmish. Like falling stars they streaked towards the tents below.

"Cover!" Titan dove behind a pile of crates. The arrows cut through the camp. Tents burned and men screamed. Titan shoved himself to his feet, counting the seconds in his head as he ran to his father's tent. Lexik burst through the door, brandishing his sword, and Titan yanked him behind a supply wagon. Another volley hit, but was rewarded with fewer cries.

"Report," Lexik said as he peered around the edge of the cart.

"Attack from the south. Men on foot, archers behind with fire."

"Count?"

Titan shook his head. "Too dark to see."

"Ragdons' fury." Lexik lifted his sword above his head and began yelling orders. "Form up! Firsts, bows, seconds, left flank, thirds, right flank, fourths with me!" And with that, the king charged towards the skirmish.

Titan raced after him. Another arrow zipped over his head as the men from both the southern and western armies scattered to their positions. An army this small left them somewhat vulnerable, but it meant that Lexik could directly command all of the men. No time was lost passing commands through the ranks, so movement was entirely efficient. By the time they reached the conflict, more than forty men were already with them.

Titan parried an attack, spun, and sunk his blade into flesh. The man's cry cut off with a second swing. Two more figures charged Titan. He darted left, causing the men to reach him a second apart. The first swung an axe overhead. Titan sidestepped and sliced into the man's arm with his own weapon. He whirled, parried the second man and swung wide and high. Hitting nothing but air, he swung again, this time finding steel. Over his assailant's shoulder three more figures materialized. Titan gritted his teeth. Four to one would not be good odds.

Between blinks, the shaft of an arrow appeared, jutting from his opponent's throat. Another sliced through the night, fell the lead of the oncoming trio, and prompted his companions to dive for cover. Titan ducked behind a tree and glanced down the line. His father stood over several corpses two dozen feet away. Alder was at the end of the line beyond, sweeping towards them with his honor guard.

Titan whirled back at another scream. The line to the other side was breaking. "Archer's, right!" he yelled. Men in that direction dove for cover before the first volley hit. Titan's own attackers seized the moment's peace to close the distance.

He dodged left. A javelin sunk into the wood, then yanked back out. The short sword swung low and hard. Titan parried, whirled, and swept his own sword out wide. Both men jumped back, then rushed forward. Titan sheared the shaft of the javelin in two, but the tip of the other man's sword caught him across his calf. Pushing through the pain, he drove the swordsman back in a series of blows. He waited patiently, then twisted neatly and impaled the other as he approached from behind with the sharp end of the javelin. Titan snatched it from the air as the man collapsed, turned, and reached up to catch the inevitable attack. With his hands and weapon held above, the javelin easily found its mark in the swordsman's gut. Titan pulled away as the man fell.

Titan looked again to the west to see the enemy soldiers at that end fleeing. To his left, his father and King Alder were having similar success, and a moment later the hillside fell quiet.

Lexik pointed at a soldier. "Follow them. Make sure they don't double back." The man saluted and waved at three companions. They disappeared quietly into the darkness.

Titan knelt to examine his leg. His father approached. "How bad is it?"

"It's superficial. Should heal up in a few days."

Lexik clenched his teeth. "I'll kill Devvon."

"Are you sure it was Devvon?" asked Alder, approaching with two soldiers in tow. "Could have been a group of bandits. They know about our yearly trip."

"It was him," Lexik said. "Bandits don't pray." He pointed to a man half way down the hill. He was still moving. His motions were sluggish, but Titan recognized the hand movements of the plea to Protection. The man's arms went limp as he finished.

A soldier approached. "Report," Lexik commanded.

"Thirty six killed, my lord. Another fifteen wounded. They're being seen to as we speak."

"Sixteen wounded." Lexik motioned to Titan's leg.

"Father, I'm fine."

"See a healer," Lexik said, then turned back to the man. "And from King Alder's?"

"Forty two dead. Twenty two wounded." The man bowed his head. "Captain Toque is among the fallen."

Alder cursed. "Alright, Lexik. We'll kill him together."

"More than half the army wounded or dead," Lexik said. "What of the enemy? Did we get a count?"

"Yes, my lord. Estimates put their numbers at one hundred seventy. Roughly two thirds were killed."

Alder shook his head. "Devvon is an idiot. How could he possible think to take our army with fewer numbers during an uphill battle?"

"Perhaps this attack was preparation for another that is still to come," Lexik replied.

Titan looked around the camp. With the damage already done... "We won't survive to make it to the peace conferences."

"Yes, we will," Lexik replied. "Devvon will be expecting us to move slower because of our wounded." He turned to the soldier who still stood at attention. "Give the order. We move out as soon as the injured are bound. Leave the supplies that would have been needed for the fallen, and use the extra space in the carts to haul those who can't ride." He turned back to Alder and Titan. "The Tower is impossible to enter if even a small force is defending it. We race there as quickly as possible and wait for the other kingdoms to arrive. The defensive position combined with two hundred men from Tressle and Yuoran should be enough."

"Unless Devvon is already there," Titan said. "Then what?"

Lexik watched the dark forest before them. "Let's pray that he's not."

*****

At the top of the steps, Felk's crimson cape flapped in the breeze, an unwilling slave bound to perform its function. At the bottom his battle axe, freshly sharpened, leaned resolutely against the executioner's block.

The crowd spread throughout the square and for blocks down the side streets. As his last command before leaving the city, Devvon had sent out a proclamation that an execution was to be held and that every citizen, regardless of age, was to be present. Disobedience was punishable by death, and roaming patrols had been out all morning.

Felk glanced at the blazing sun above. Too much light. Nothing was hidden. Nothing to obscure the murder to come. It seemed that even the weather bent to Devvon's authority. Felk hated himself for standing as he was. He reminded himself that this blood was on Devvon's hands, it was his decision and his power. Felk was doing only what honor demanded.

Honor. Bile rose in his throat.

The execution was a tool, and an effective one at that. Disobeying Devvon's command would give him leave to sign Felk's own execution order. If Felk died, how many of his men's lives would be lost to further Devvon's purposes? Lives weren't valued as they should have been, either by the king or the other generals. But by obeying Devvon, an innocent man would die. Felk would perform the deed in front of the entire city, losing the trust of thousands. And he would hate Devvon for it. Hate bred betrayal. Betrayal merited death.

A wooden cart was pulled into the square by a pair of mules. Silence smothered all else as the cage was drawn closer and closer to its final destination. The man inside sat, calm, arms crossed. Just like the night before as Felk turned his back on him.

"Ragdons help me," Felk muttered under his breath.

"Sir?" Felk heard the solider shift his weight.

The procession plodded onward. Slow, but determined. "Does this man deserve death?"

"The king has so sentenced him."

"Yes. And we must obey." Felk closed his eyes. "I just ..."

A pause. "I know, General."

Felk looked to his side. The man spared a glance and returned his gaze ahead. He smiled grimly and nodded.

The cart creaked as it came to a halt below. The driver stood, brushed invisible dust from his pants, and climbed down. The prisoner waited patiently for the cage door to be opened, then walked to the block and knelt, letting his eyes drift lazily across the crowd before him.

Felk's pulse pounded in his ears. He cleared his throat.

"This man has been found guilty by his Lordship Devvon of inaccuracies that cost thousands of lives. Because he is unable to be present, his majesty has requested that I stand in his place. You are all gathered to assure that justice be done." Felk waited for a reaction. Any reaction. None came.

"Does the prisoner have any last words?"

The man glanced over his shoulder, smile full of teeth. "That I does." He turned back to the crowd and eyed them. He took a deep breath and scream.

"To the inferno with the king! Long live the General!"

Silence suffocated the echo.

He slowly turned back to Felk. "Thank you, sir."

Felk urged his legs forward and began the descent, step by step. His blood was molten lead, weighing his body and burning his mind. He reached the ground and stopped before the chopping block as the prisoner lowered his forehead to touch the wood. Felk pulled his axe from its scabbard.

Felk watched the back of the man's neck as a bead of sweat slid off of it. Twelve hours ago he had given this man freedom. The man's honor, his desire for the safety of his companions persuaded him to decline the gift.

Honor. The highest virtue in Felk's mind. Yet here he stood, his hand tied to an executioner's axe. His axe. Felk lifted it over his head.

"General?"

"Soldier?"

"Take care of them."

"... you have my word. May the Ragdons' ... take you."

"And may they keep you, sir. For a good while yet."

CHAPTER 7

A loud knock at the door jolted Adrianna upright. She took a deep breath, shook her head, and stood. More thumps sounded as she crossed the room. Irritated both at the interruption and impatience, she swung the door open to reveal Reon with his fist hanging in the air. "Morning, princess," he said with a smile.

"Yes, it is," she retorted. "What may I do for you?"

Reon frowned. "You can catch my sarcasm, for one. It's past lunch, and nobody in the castle has seen you. I came to make sure you were still breathing." He looked down at her robe. "You're not even dressed? That's considerably lazier than how I remembered you."

Adrianna turned to the window. Light cascaded in, the sun obviously well overhead. "Sorry," she said. "I've been reading. I guess I got carried away."

"Must be a good book," Reon said as he followed her into the room. He spotted the small mountain of scrolls on the desk, crossed to them, and read a line or two from several. "Bleh. Law is as dull as a training sword."

Adrianna nodded as she sat. "Yes, it is."

"Then why are you in here? Or is there a story about a scandalous romance buried in that pile somewhere?"

"Just law," Adrianna said. She picked up a scroll and held it out to him. "I need a fresh voice. Read and I'll listen."

Reon stared at the paper. "Seriously?"

She nodded. Reon hesitated before he reached out and took it. "You owe me a kiss for this." He cleared his throat, pushed invisible glasses up his nose, and carefully unrolled the parchment. "'Marriage'", his voice rose with emotion, "'may occur between any man and woman and requires only mutual consent and a witness to take effect. Tradition holds that it is sealed with a kiss. In a marriage involving differing ranks or allegiances, the woman joins the man. A woman commoner marrying a royal man becomes a royal, while the two in reversed roles would then both be commoners.'" He rolled the paper reverently and held it towards her.

"That's it?" Adrianna asked, reopening the scroll.

"The entire tragedy, as performed by your humble servant." Reon bowed low.

Adrianna reread the lines. "That's simple enough."

"That's not our law, though."

"No, it's not. It's *our* law." Adrianna returned the paper to the stack and grabbed another.

"Studying up for our looming ascension to the throne, are we?"

"Not exactly," Adrianna said. She held out another scroll.

"What then? I don't want my theatrical talents to be wasted on lesser endeavors." He took the paper and glanced at it. "Succession to the throne? I would think you would already know this part of your law fairly well." He considered her. "What are you up to?"

Adrianna didn't meet his eyes. "I'm trying to marry Titan."

Reon chuckled. "You've been trying to do that for a couple years, now. What are you really up to?"

Adrianna pushed away from the table. "Titan won't change the law. So I've been looking at the law. Very closely."

"And?"

"... I'm still looking." Reon burst into laughter. Adrianna glared. "It's got to be there. You of all people know that every rule has its loophole. Every law has some caveat that the rulers leave in to let them do whatever they want to."

"I resent that whole 'you of all people' bit. And you forget one thing, princess."

"And what is that?"

Reon looked at the mound of scrolls. "Lexik made our laws."

Adrianna sank back into her chair and sighed. "No, I didn't forget that." She stared at the pile in front of her. "He didn't leave many extra freedoms for himself, did he?"

"Nope," Reon said. He smiled contentedly. "I think that's one of the reasons why the people love him so much."

Adrianna massaged her temples. "I've been comparing our two laws. On most points they are exactly the same. The only differences are those concerning what the king can and can't do. Lexik holds himself to the exact same standards as he does everyone else." She closed her eyes. "Except when it comes to marriage. There he limits himself even more."

"... and Titan will do the same."

Adrianna continued to stare at the wall of laws. "Yes. He will."

"So ... what now?"

"I don't know. I'm out of ideas." Her eyes finally felt tired. "Get married, I guess."

"Well it's a bit fast, but I suppose I accept."

Adrianna rolled her eyes. "You're a good friend, Reon. As much as it pains me to say it, I really mean that. But you and I both know we would hate each other."

Reon laughed. "That we would." He turned to the scrolls. "Maybe I'll look over these as well. Try to figure out who I'm supposed to spend my life with."

Adrianna shook her head. "I've been through each of them multiple times. They don't shed much light on the subject."

*****

Devvon filled his lungs with the crisp mountain air. It felt particularly real this afternoon. A perfect day for his ascension to immortality.

A mounted soldier galloped back to him and reined in his horse. "My lord."

"News?"

"Lexik, Alder, and Tressle have already arrived. No sign of Yuoran."

Devvon raised an eyebrow. "Lexik and Alder are already here?"

"Yes, my lord."

Good for you, Lexik. Devvon had feared an attack on the road might have turned them back. Apparently Lexik's devotion to this ridiculous charade of friendship was stronger than his logic. Devvon had made a bet. He needed Lexik present. And, as was happening more and more frequently, the odds appeared to be in Devvon's favor.

He blinked at the sudden rush of sunlight. They had cleared the tree line and were beginning the final ascent. Above loomed the enormous stone spike, their destination, the Tower. Built on the precipice of a thousand foot drop, the structure was hundreds of years old. Legend held it was where the Dragon had been killed and where the kingdoms had begun. Devvon had it on good authority that was idiocy.

There were three distinct camps surrounding the base, each flying their kingdom's colors. Two of the armies had distinctly fewer tents than the third. Devvon couldn't help but grin. He kicked his horse forward, leaving his own force to catch up.

"My fellow kings!" he yelled as he neared. He pulled his horse up short as he was confronted with dozens of spearheads and sword tips.

"Devvon." He turned to find the source of the growl.

"Lexik! Dear me, it can't be! The last year as king has been good to you, my friend."

"No closer, Devvon," a more familiar voice said. Lexik strode between two tents, cape flapping.

Devvon looked back at the youth before him. "Can this be Titan? My you've grown, boy." He dismounted and thrust the reins into the hands of a western soldier. "What in the Ragdons are you feeding him?"

"Devvon, enough." Lexik stopped ten feet away. Behind him, Devvon watched Alder approach in a similar huff. "Why did you attack us?"

Devvon clicked his tongue. "I hardly think a friendly question can be called an attack."

Lexik drew his sword. "You are a filthy rat."

Devvon gently shook his head. "Not a very good example, insulting a friend in front of your heir."

"What's your game? You weaken us, and then wait until another kingdom joins us before bringing your whole force to conquer?"

"My whole force?" Devvon chuckled. "I hardly think twenty men can be considered my whole force."

Lexik hesitated, glancing over Devvon's shoulder. He looked to his son.

"Nothing," reported Titan. "No movement whatsoever for miles about the entire day."

"You were spying?" Devvon widened his eyes and brought a hand to his mouth. "We're trying to hold a peace conference, but you fellows seem like you are looking for war."

Lexik took a step forward. "Give me one reason why I shouldn't kill you now."

Devvon met his eyes. "Because it's the law."

"A law you broke not three nights ago."

"Even if that were true, how does my breaking the law give you the right to?"

Lexik held his gaze. Devvon could feel the hatred pouring off of him. Finally, Lexik turned.

"Father!" Titan started towards Lexik.

Lexik held up a hand. "No, Titan. We honor the law. Even if the scum we have to deal with doesn't." He looked back at Devvon, the fire in his eyes turning to ice. "We're better than they are."

"That's the spirit," Devvon said.

Lexik slowly exhaled and turned. One by one, the soldiers surrounding Devvon lowered their weapons, though most stayed between him and their camps. The soldier holding on to his horse threw the rope at him. Devvon nodded with a smile, then turned to see his own force setting up camp. He led his horse on foot, cheerily greeting passing soldiers.

"That went fairly well," he said to the captain as he handed over the rein. He strode to a shaded chair, sat, and accepted a glass of wine. "Now we just wait for the last to show. Leave it to Yuoran to be last, even with us taking our time. The fool always did like making an entrance."

Yuoran's force of a hundred men arrived hours later. The king rode at the front of his soldiers as the picture of regality. A brilliant white cape billowed behind him, his breastplate gleamed in the failing light, and his jet black hair looked as though it were plastered in place with butter.

"It probably is," noted Devvon to no one in particular as he watched the procession.

The men behind him were in similar décor. A large part of Yuoran's power was derived from his image. People saw him as a kingly person, and so he was respected. Never mind that he was better at ballads than he was at swordplay.

Devvon raised his glass to the king as he passed. Yuoran beamed and returned a friendly salute.

"Captain," Devvon said. The soldier's heels clicked behind him.

"Yes, my lord?"

"Take King Yuoran a bottle of wine. As a gift."

"Yes, my lord." The man ran to fetch the bottle. He dashed past Devvon towards the newly arrived king.

They didn't even attempt to stop him, Devvon mused as the gift was delivered. He could hear Yuoran's characteristically hearty laughter as he accepted and popped the cork. He took a long drink, then turned and raised the bottle to Devvon.

Devvon nodded graciously. *And he drank wine given to him from an enemy king.* The stupidity of the man was like a foul stench one could smell from three hundred paces. Devvon beckoned to his soldier as he jogged back.

"Have you collected reports?"

"Yes, my lord."

"And?"

"The attack *was* successful."

"Wonderful." Devvon sighed, leaned back in his chair, and tucked his hands behind his head. "I imagine the other kings will allow Yuoran to settle in before attempting to begin." He looked at the sunset on the western horizon with its vibrant hues of red and orange. "All the better. The darkness should make for a better show."

How many years had he been planning for this night? Too long. A thousand years ago, Devvon's deification should have been sealed. Well, the time had come. Time to correct all the wrongs, all the injustice. Time to put fate and destiny back where they belonged: in his own hands. After all, was that not the purpose of a god?

CHAPTER 8

Titan double checked his leather armor. Secure. For this occasion, a steel breastplate on an aide would be seen as ... distrusting.

So why not wear it?

He brushed the flap of cloth aside and strode from his tent. The Tower loomed before him, its formidable height accentuated by the waning light. The first time he had seen it as a boy, Titan had been mesmerized by both the size and the significance. And, as a man, its allure hadn't diminished. He shivered.

At the base of the structure he could pick out a small group of soldiers. Aside from the kings, those men were the only ones let inside during the conferences, one man for each kingdom. They were tasked with keeping an eye on the offerings while the monarchs resolved inter-kingdom problems behind closed doors. Titan nodded as he passed a group of his own soldiers and crossed the short distance to join the other four.

"Evening, gentlemen," he greeted them. Three grunts and a glare were his only replies. Titan looked at each of the men, studying them in turn.

"I'm sorry about Toque," he said to the man in green.

The man just shrugged.

The man in white raised an eyebrow. "Who's Toque?"

Green didn't look up. "The captain. He was supposed to be here in my place." He grit his teeth. "Died in the fight coming here."

All eyes turned towards the soldier in red.

"I don't even know who the man is," Devvon's aide said.

"Doesn't matter," said the third in brown and yellow. "You're Devvon's. It might as well have been you who knifed him."

They're tense. Titan watched the men bicker. Everyone was thrown off and confused by the attack. All the more reason to keep a careful eye on them. Titan scanned the campground, noticing the distinct size difference between Devvon's army and the other four. Why bring so few men? Even with the damages Alder's force had taken, it still dwarfed the Eastern camp.

"You, you're Lexik's son, ain't you?" asked White.

"Yes. Titan is my name."

"Huh. Always wondered why Lexik doesn't even look at his soldiers in action before choosing. He always just brings you. The rest of us had to earn this honor."

Titan was taken aback. Yuoran and his kingdom weren't always friendly, but they were hardly ever hostile. He cleared his throat. "I've requested that he choose based on skill, but he refuses."

Red laughed a sharp bark. "He must be even stupider than Yuoran."

White growled. "Shut up, dog."

Red got up. "You gonna make me?"

"Take it easy," Titan said, stepping between them. Both men turned and glared at him.

"Pip squeak. Want a sword through your belly?"

Titan tried to look relaxed. "We both know you won't do it."

Red cocked his head to the side, his smile cold. "I guess we'll see about that."

Several minutes passed before the camps grew quiet, the soldiers within forming ranks. Lexik walked to the edge of the camp, some 100 feet from the base of the Tower, and waited.

A moment later Alder and Tressle each emerged from among their camps' tents and stopped at the edge of their men. Yuoran managed to knock over a rack of spears as he hurried to catch up, earning snickers from several of the aides beside Titan.

Devvon remained seated, sipping his wine and watching the other kings move to their traditional positions. After all were in place, he rose slowly and considered them. He turned and gave the glass to the man standing at attention, stretched his neck from side to side, and approached at a leisurely pace. He reached the edge of his own camp, his cape elegantly trailing behind him. He was joined by the other four kings as they approached the Tower.

They arrived as one. The aids stepped aside in silence and the kings entered the building. Titan allowed the other four guards to enter first and stepped through. He closed and locked the door behind him. Within was a large room, encased on all sides by stone with a curving rock stairway on the far side. Titan passed through the empty space to follow the last of the aids up the steps.

The first of the windows didn't appear until they had climbed for a time. Firelight glimpsed through from the camps, and Titan noted how with each circuit the lights grew further and further below. At last the stairway ended, opening into a sizeable antechamber with a stone table in the exact center. Several tapestries hung on the walls in various states of disrepair. The procession crossed the room to the door on the opposite side. Alder reached it first and swung it wide, its hinges quiet despite its obvious age. Beyond was a small hallway running both left and right, circling the perimeter of the Tower with stain glass windows at intervals. Straight across from the group was another door. The kings remained at the doorway, and Titan and the other four aides circled the perimeter, ending where they began.

Lastly, they entered the center room. Five chairs stood in a circle, the only furniture present. A staircase to one side led to a walkway that circled the room twenty feet above the floor.

Books lined the walls, intended as a diversion for the kings when a brief respite was needed. The room possessed an air of both simplicity and regality.

All kings gave a nod of agreement that the Tower was empty of anyone besides themselves. The group returned to the antechamber and the kings circled the table, each with his guard behind him.

"Devvon," Lexik said, jaw set.

"But it's not my turn."

"We've all decided it needs to be."

Devvon sighed forlornly. "Such mistrust." He obligingly stepped forward and raised his right hand. He slowly unlaced the ties that bound a well fit leather glove. He pulled it free, waved it at Lexik, and dropped it in the center of the table.

Titan felt the tension seep out of the others in the room. But why? He felt no such release from his own inhibitions about the situation. Devvon sacrificed nothing with his offering. Nor would any of the other kings. What was the point of an empty demonstration of goodwill when the man was still armed?

Devvon smiled, stepped back, and nodded to Alder at his left. Alder carefully placed one of his bracers next to the glove and motioned to Tressle. Tressle detached the nose guard on his helmet and set it beside the other two items. Titan closed his eyes and shook his head as Yuoran neatly set his necklace down in a coil.

Lexik step forward. He reached up and gripped the hilt of his sword hanging from his shoulder.

"Father," whispered Titan. "Please."

Lexik pulled the sword free. He considered the dark-tinted blade, let out a breath, and carefully set it next to the other offerings. Titan sighed. He glanced at the other four kings, noting their blades still firmly tucked in their sheaths. At least Alder would still have his weapon.

Lexik stepped back, and all five kings started towards the door leading to the center room. Lexik turned to Titan. He nodded and clapped him on the shoulder. "Take care of her for me." He turned and followed the others without another glance back.

The door to the antechamber closed, and after several seconds, Titan heard the door to the central room close as well. *So begin the peace conferences.* Peaceful was the last word Titan would have used to describe the situation. He watched carefully as the other four guards one by one found positions along the outer wall and sat. After being left alone, he too backed away and found a seat on the stone step leading towards the central room. He settled in and prepared to wait. The conferences would continue until all disputes of the year had been resolved. Conflicts among peasants ... bandit threats ... treaties and alliances (or lack thereof) with those kingdoms across the sea ... blatant attacks by the traitorous Eastern armies.

Titan sighed. This year's conference might take a while.

He watched as the other four men slouched lazily, some exchanging meaningless conversation. They seemed much less prone to arguing now that the conferences had begun. They even occasionally laughed at another's jokes. Part of Titan wanted to join them, but his sense of duty and his apprehension for the return journey kept him quietly contemplative. And so he listened and waited.

"My sister married some nobody from a farm. I told her not too, but she never listens to me."

He listened to the drab complaints of the man for a time. Stifling a yawn, he shifted his attention to the other two.

"... six years ago, almost to the day. The scar runs the full length of my thigh."

"Let's see then."

"Can't very well take off my clothes at the peace conferences."

"That's convenient, ain't it? You're bluffing."

Titan let his eyes close, trying to squeeze the sleep from them as he continued listening to the conversations as they shifted from topic to topic.

"And then I says to him, 'shut up or I'll break your face.'"

"Let me guess. He broke yours instead?"

"Very funny. No, the bloke goes on talking about how he could rip me limb from limb. I had to teach him a lesson. I like that tavern too much to let him feel comfortable there."

"Which was it?"

"The one a couple blocks south of the castle. Boar's Ale is the name."

"Yeah, I know the one. Peg-leg runs it, right?"

"That's right."

Titan's eyes snapped open. He looked to the pair of men who were conversing on the far wall.

"The ale's good there, but the meat's even better."

"Too true."

Slowly Titan stood. One by one, the other aids turned their attention to him.

"Stretching your legs?"

Titan shook his head and continued to stare at the two men. One in red, one in white.

"What's the matter with you?"

"You," he said, pointing at White. "How do you know what the meat taste like in a tavern just south of Devvon's castle?"

The silence hung heavily in the air. White rose to his feet. "I've traveled."

"Ragdons. No one travels to the east."

"You calling me a liar?" White took a step forward.

"I'm asking you a question."

Red stood up behind White. "Easy, son."

Titan pulled his sword from its sheath on his back. "Answer the question."

Yellow and Green both stood as well, looking back and forth between Titan and White.

White looked around at each aid before focusing his attention back on Titan. "Alright. Because before my last assignment, I went there every Thursday. A day off isn't any fun sober."

Titan stared at the man. "You defected from Devvon's army."

White laughed heartily. "Not a chance. I'm no traitor." He grinned at Titan as he pulled his own sword from its sheath. "Long live King Devvon."

"Long live King Devvon," said Red, arming himself.

"Long live King Devvon," Yellow and Green repeated in unison. Each reached for his own weapon.

Titan glanced rapidly between the other four men as each stepped towards him. "What are you doing?" he demanded, heart pounding.

"Carrying out orders," Green said softly as he circled the side of the table.

Titan watched the progression toward him, backing towards the alcove surrounding the door beyond. As he watched, the four men placed themselves between Titan and the table before continuing towards him.

Titan dreaded the answer before he even asked. "What orders?"

Red grinned. "To put a sword through your belly. Pip squeak."

The explosion from behind the door shook the stone floor. Titan's four opponents glanced to each other. Titan saw his opportunity, whirled, and threw open the door. The soldiers charged. Titan shoved the door closed and slammed the steel bar into place behind it. Another explosion sounded behind him. He spun again, reached for the handle, and grabbed nothing but air as the door was yanked inward.

Lexik barreled through, grabbed Titan by both shoulders and dove with him to the side. The hallway behind them burst into flames.

Titan froze, staring at the inferno. His eyes watered from the heat as the fire consumed the door he had just barricaded. The wood melted away like butter under a hot knife.

Titan was shaken out of his stupor by heavy hands. "Run!" Lexik yelled. Titan whirled, taking once last glance at the flames before following his father around the outside corridor. Lexik dashed half the length of the circumference and skid to a stop exactly opposite from the fire. A voice echoed off the stones behind them.

"There's nowhere to run, Lexik. You can either come back and die like a man or run and die like a whimpering dog."

Lexik's spun to face Titan. "Your sword." He didn't wait for Titan to offer it, instead pulling it from his hand. He lifted it over Titan's shoulder and slammed it back into its sheath.

"What are you doing?! What happened?!"

Lexik grabbed Titan by the shoulders and held his own face inches from his son's. "Do you remember your uncle Richards, the hermit?"

"What?"

"Richards, do you remember him?!"

"Yes! Why?!"

"Go to him. Tell him Devvon has killed the other kings. Tell him to tell you everything!"

"Father –"

"Shut up, boy!" Lexik squeezed his eyes closed. He took a deep breath, and when he looked at Titan again, a tear slid down his cheek. "Please. Promise me."

"I ...", Titan stared at his father, "I promise."

Lexik nodded, then pulled his son to his chest. Titan let his own arms wrap around his father. He abruptly felt very small and very unsure of himself. Lexik lowered his head to Titan's ear. "Now pray for Enlightenment."

Titan pulled back. "What?"

"There you are, old friend," Devvon said coolly from behind.

"Pray!" Lexik grabbed Titan by either shoulder and threw him, head first, at the stained glass beside them.

The window exploded with the impact. Titan flailed his arms wildly amid the broken glass but found nothing but empty air. Through the sparkling glass, he could see the base of the cliff the Tower sat on over a thousand feet below. He rotated as he continued to reach for something, anything to keep him from falling. He felt the intense heat of another explosion as fire spewed from the shattered window above him. His rotation continued, and Titan found himself staring at his own death, a thousand feet below, as it accelerated towards him.

INTERLUDE

Luff's sword connected, and the man fell with a gasp. He didn't get up. Luff nodded to his companions, and the other four moved towards the cowering woman and her children. She tried to press herself further into the corner, but was easily pried away. Luff sighed as the woman began her begging.

"Please, my children!"

Luff didn't look back as he ducked through the door. "You want us to take them as well?"

"I'm all they have! You … you can't –"

"Ah, but that's where you're wrong. I can, and I will. It's nothing personal. We didn't pick you out of hate." He turned a gave a shrug. "Next time don't live so far from the city."

The woman was near hysteria. "They'll die!"

Tuff turned to see the two children wailing in the doorway. The boy was probably ten, the girl a year or two younger. Pitiful little things. Underfed and overworked, no doubt, with the life of a farmer. Tuff turned back to the woman. "What's the boy's name?"

The woman shook her head, either unable or unwilling to answer. Tuff rolled his eyes and waved to the man holding her. The man took the base of his sword and knocked her unconscious. She fell silent, and two of the men hoisted her onto the horse and began securing her ropes. Tuff turned back to the pair of children. "You there, boy! Come here."

The boy obeyed. He wiped his eyes as he approached. Tuff nodded his approval as the tears stopped.

"What's your name?"

"Bental." His voice was little more than a squeak.

"How old are you, Bental?"

"Eleven, sir." *Sir* was a good sign. Let the boy show respect to his betters.

"Can you make a fire, Bental? Can you cook, wash dishes, chop wood?"

The boy hesitated, then nodded.

Tuff pointed at the woman. "Your mother wants me to take care of you now. Will you come with me and my men?"

Bental's eyes widened in fear. He glanced down at the sword that was still in Tuff's hand. Tuff looked down as well, then smiled. He sheathed the sword, then lowered himself to a knee. He pulled up a pant leg to reveal a long knife strapped to his calf. He quickly unbuckled it, then stood again.

"Coming would mean learning how to be a man." He held out the knife to the boy. "How to be a warrior. Would you like that, Bental?"

The boy slowly took the knife and stared at it in his hands. He drew it from the leather, the blade gleaming in the sunlight. He paused a moment, then stabbed the point at Tuff. The man fluidly stepped to the side and caught the boy's arm. He twisted sharply, though not to the point of serious injury. Bental yelped in pain and the blade fell.

Tuff released his hold. Bental began backing up, wide-eyed, as Tuff crouched and picked up the blade. He studied the boy, then offered the handle of the knife. "No blood, no retribution. Just don't try it often." Bental stared at the weapon. He reached up and grasped the handle, his arm immediately dropping to his side. Tuff placed a hand on his shoulder. "Come and learn. Be more than a farmer."

The boy raised his gaze and met Tuff's eyes. He wiped his eyes, then nodded. Tuff smiled. It was amazing what a gift, some forgiveness, and a little opportunity could do, even right after Tuff had torn the boy's family apart. Bental would try to kill Tuff again, and perhaps a third time. He would hate Tuff for killing his father, for kidnapping his mother. But that didn't matter, not really. As long as Tuff slept with an eye open for a month or so, the boy would succumb to the same call that Tuff himself had felt over twenty years prior. Life with power, and power without rules.

The boy sniffed. "What about my sister?"

Tuff glanced at the little thing still standing in the doorway, knowing she wasn't worth the effort. He looked back to Bental. "Where's your nearest neighbor?"

Bental pointed to the north. "About a day's walk."

Tuff nodded. "Then you'd better get her going."

"Can't we take her there?"

"I'm afraid not. We're headed south." Tuff walked to his horse and climbed into the saddle. "Besides, a group of bandits is no place for a little girl." He winked at Bental. "Maybe when she's older you can come back and get her."

CHAPTER 9

What is Devvon's game?!

Felk strode the length of the room for the thousandth time that night. Twelve hours had passed since he executed an innocent man, but he could still feel the weight of his axe in his hands. The man's voice echoed through Felk's head over and over again, the words twisting to condemn him dozens of times over. Felk hadn't saved him. It was his authority by which the execution had occurred. It was under his watch. And still he was powerless.

Ragdons. I didn't even bother asking his name.

Logic argued with the guilt churning in his mind. His hands had been tied. There was nothing he could have done. If Felk had let the man go, Devvon would have killed him and Felk's men would have been at the mercy of a merciless king. He yelled it at himself again and again, yet somehow the prisoner's quiet whisper was all he could hear.

But why had Devvon ordered Felk to carry it out? Why was he pushing Felk towards the edge? Hatred was an obvious reason, but though Devvon was one to loathe, he was no fool. Felk had survived six battles in the last year where he shouldn't have. He knew how to keep men alive, how to win battles against the odds. Even with the jealousy Devvon had towards Felk's favor with the people, he needed Felk.

No. Hatred and jealousy didn't explain Devvon's actions. At least not all of them. But what did? Fear of betrayal was absurd. Felk had loyally carried out every command since Devvon had taken the throne. Both men hated the bandit hordes and had dedicated large amounts of resources to wiping them out. What more did Devvon want?

Insanity. It was the only explanation Felk could imagine as he sat down in front of the small fire. He considered the idea, then shook his head in dismissal. There was an undeniable clarity in the king's eyes. He had his purposes, and they weren't those of a mad man.

But what are they?

*****

Adrianna strolled along the stone pathway that wove through the gardens west of the castle. Her late night the previous day had prompted a short rest during the afternoon that had gone unchecked. She found herself wide awake yet again, watching the shadows cast by the moon shift as the wind ruffled through the trees. The sky was devoid of clouds, instead showing off its vast collection of glimmering stars.

Adrianna sighed. She had studied both laws. Not just read, *studied*. She had considered the wordings, the circumstances that had prompted the creation of each law, the intentions, everything. The law wouldn't permit the marriage, and Titan wouldn't change the law. Her own sheet of notes was as clear as the night's sky.

Far less satisfying, though.

She stopped in front of a decorative bench and sat heavily. The clear night was accompanied by a chilled breeze, and she pulled her cloak close to keep the cold out. She closed her eyes. She was in love with a man who was in love with her, but refused to be with her for honor's sake. Adrianna loved and hated Titan for it.

The wind whistled softly as it played through the trees behind her. She could smell the flowers in full bloom.

Adrianna loved walking gardens at night. The plants were beautiful during the day, but at night one could focus on their irresistible scent. She breathed in deeply, trying to push the work of the day out of her mind.

"Princess?"

Adrianna jumped, quickly scanning the darkness. There. A dark figure stood a dozen paces off, his features hidden in the shadows. "Show yourself!" Her adrenaline gave the question an accusatory edge.

The figure stepped forward. "My apologies, my lady. I didn't mean to startle you." Jaron's blonde hair shimmered in the moonlight. "I didn't expect anyone here this late."

Adrianna let go of the breath she had been holding and leaned back. "Nor did I. That's why I chose the spot."

"I am sorry I disturbed you." Jaron turned to leave.

"It's alright," Adrianna said. "Some company might actually be good for me."

"A difficult day then? I didn't see you around the castle."

"You could say that. A painful day, at least."

"I'm sorry to hear it." Jaron approached. "May I sit?"

Adrianna nodded. "Of course."

"What happened?"

"Nothing," Adrianna said, a wry smile crossing her face without invitation. She took a deep breath. "I guess I'm something of a masochist. I spend my spare time causing myself pain."

Jaron paused. "You hurt yourself?"

"Only my heart."

"Ah," Jaron replied as he turned towards the garden. "Titan."

Adrianna looked at him. "You already knew?"

"Just a guess," Jaron said. "Reon gave me a stern warning this afternoon to keep my distance from you or Titan would have my head." He chuckled. "It was interesting receiving a reprimand again. I almost enjoyed it."

"Have you been general that long?"

"No, only a year or so. But it has been several since my last disciplining."

"And your refresher was from Reon," Adrianna said with a smile.

"Yes. Not even a military man."

"Might as well be, for as good as he is with the sword."

"Very true. And for as faithful as he is to his friends as well."

Adrianna paused. "Was he being faithful?"

"Of course. He was looking out for Titan's interests while he's away." Jaron continued to watch the darkened garden.

"But to what end?" Adrianna said. She sighed. Again. "I'm not Titan's, and I never will be."

The two sat in silence for a time, staring at the cloaked scene.

"So ... you are altogether unspoken for?"

Adrianna looked at him. "I suppose I am."

"And... are you ... looking to be spoken for?" He shifted on the bench. "What I mean to say is, though you can't marry Titan ... are you leaving your heart with him?"

Adrianna's gaze drifted back to the shadows. *Am I?* They would never be married. That was the single conclusion the day's studies had offered. Her chest ached. How long would it take before the pain stopped?

"I... don't think so. But I love him."

"And," Jaron cleared his throat, "can a woman love more than one man?"

Adrianna stared at her hands in her lap. "... I don't know."

"Would you allow me to try and find out?"

Adrianna looked up. Jaron's jaw was set as his eyes held her gaze. She had known him barely a week. He was an excellent companion, joining she and Reon daily for whatever their whims dictated. He treated her with chivalry, respect. And he was genuinely kind to Reon, something not even she or Titan could say about themselves. But ... she didn't love Jaron. Could she let him hope for an impossibility?

Or was it impossible? He continued to watch her as the conflict twisted within her. His grey eyes were a striking, particularly as the gleamed in the moonlight. As far as she could tell he was every bit as honorable and loyal to his kingdom as Titan. His status as the lead general of Lexik's army showed he was both intelligent and wise.

And he is an eligible suitor.

She broke his gaze and once again inspected her hands, clasped tightly in her lap. "Yes."

Jaron let out a slow breath. "Thank you, princess." Adrianna heard him stand, but couldn't look up. "Until tomorrow then, my lady."

"Yes," she whispered as he walked away. "Until tomorrow."

CHAPTER 10

The vibrant flames of several minutes melted down, then vanished as marvelously as they had appeared. The smell of smoke and burnt flesh filled the air, but Devvon refused to leave. He walked calmly forward and bent over the body. No movement. No breathing. No life. He straightened and smiled. Tressle, Yuoran, Alder, and Lexik were dead. Devvon closed his eyes, the fire within him continuing to burn. He breathed in deeply. The smell wasn't so bad.

He turned and briskly returned to the antechamber door. Or what was left of it. He threw the retaining bar aside and kick the remnants of the wood from its hinges. On the other side stood four soldiers, weapons drawn. As he stepped through the opening, his men lowered their weapons and snapped to attention. Devvon waved them to a side wall and walked to the middle of the room.

The table stood perfectly with the five offerings carefully placed on its surface. He picked up the glove he had left as his own offering and held it side by side with the one of the pair he now wore. Extraordinary leatherwork, indeed. He tossed the glove to the nearest soldier. The man caught it, studied it for a moment, and then raised an eyebrow at his companions. The man in white shrugged.

Devvon smiled again and moved on to the other four. Just like his glove, each was half of a pair. Their companion pieces were still strapped to their previous owners, cooling from the evening's recreation. Best not to handle them just yet. Burning flesh is a painful experience.

He lifted Yuoran's necklace, the metal glittering in the torchlight. A chain, uniform but for the black gem that hung from it. A circle, with the center cut out to allow it to sit around the stone embedded in the middle of Yuoran's breastplate. He carefully placed the item around his neck, the metal cool against his skin.

Tressle's nose guard was a shard of metal. The black stone that it bore was jagged along the top. The matching stone would be attached to Tressle's helmet, still capping the dead king's head.

Devvon gripped the handle of Lexik's sword and let the blade scratch against the table as he drew it off. Of the four, this item brought him the most joy. Not because of what it was, but because of where it came from. The great king of the west was gone. Devvon turned it in his hand, noting the half circle of black on the hilt. The sheath held the other half. Reverently, he set the sword down.

And finally, Alder's bracer. Once again, one of a pair. He crossed to a torch as he rolled up his sleeve, then used the closer light as he pulled the leather over his forearm and began tightening the laces. The triangular stone flickered in the light. Devvon flexed his arm and felt the strain against the leather

Godhood. The five were his. And the sixth would –

"My lord?"

Devvon turned. "Men, today is the dawning of a new era. You have witnessed this night ..." he trailed off as the soldier in green held something up to him. A paper, folded. It was smudged in several places, and one of the corners was folded up.

"What is it?"

"Don't know, my lord. It was on the table. Under the bracer."

Devvon crossed to him and accepted the paper. He turned it over. Alder's seal. *What in Ragdons?* He broke the wax, unfolded the page, and began to read.

Devvon,

As you are reading this, I assume that either I have been killed or I am running for my life. Lexik and I knew this day was inevitable, and we have been looking for deception in any shape or form. I wish to congratulate you. Your deceit has been perfect; I don't know in the least how you have stolen my bracers from me.

I hope they treat you as well as they have treated me. They have kept my forearms warm in the winter months and have saved my arms from countless bowstrings. However, you should know that is all they have done for me.

A number of years ago, I had this set made to be identical to the pair handed down to me by my father. Where the originals are at the moment, I can't very well say as I am likely dead. But what I can definitively say is that they are not on your arms.

May you die a thousand deaths and experience a hundredfold all the pain you have caused. And may the Ragdons keep you in their inferno for eternity.

Alder

P.S. I feel I can safely assume that if you have my bracers, you have some other items of importance as well. I would be careful trying out that sword. Lexik has let me in on one or two little secrets of his own.

The paper shook as Devvon read the last lines. He looked at the bracer on his arm. The sword on the table. The glove, now held by the man in yellow.

Devvon stumbled to the broken window. Fakes. They had made ... fakes.

He clenched the ledge, filled his lungs, and roared.

*****

Titan fell.

The dark ground hurtled toward him. Eight hundred feet below. His scream was forced back down his throat as the wind battered his face. Seven hundred feet. The shapes began to define themselves in the darkness, the ambiguity of the night giving way to the certainty of his death. Five hundred. The base of the tower raced past, and the smooth, stone wall gave way to the chaotic cliff face.

Moments of the past several days flashed through his mind at break-neck speed. Fighting Reon. Riding from the castle. Devvon's attack. His father's gift. Adrianna's farewell. His father's final words.

Pray.

Titan flew through the motions. Hands to the chest. Four hundred. Straight out, fingers together. Three hundred. Spread arms, heart exposed to Enlightenment. One hundred. He squeezed his eyes shut and braced for the impact.

Nothing. The wind still whipped over his skin, but it felt different somehow. Slower. He cracked an eye to find the ground racing fifty feet beneath him. Looking forward, he saw the line of trees standing guard ahead like an army of dark warriors. He was ... falling sideways. *What in the Ragdons?* He craned his neck towards the top of the tower.

A winged demon flew just over him. He screamed and threw his arms over his head. The thing held tight to his back. Titan rolled and squirmed to get free. Rather than freedom, Titan was yanked from side to side, and continued to hurtle into the darkness. He dared another glance upwards and immediately regretted it. Enormous, leathery wings stretched dozens of feet in either direction.

He screamed again and thrashed his limbs towards his attacker. The creature continued to weave back and forth, but refused to let go. Titan kicked even harder. The two flipped in the air and began to streak downward. Just before impact, Titan noticed that the ground shone in the moonlight. He jerked his legs to his torso and sucked in a lungful of air.

The impact and frigid water smashed the breath from his chest. He allowed himself to sink, then kicked hard away from the site of the crash. The thing had apparently been just as shocked as he, as he could no longer feel its grasp on his back. He swam hard, stroke after stroke, staying well below the surface. Unable to stand the burning in his lungs a moment more, he finally turned upwards and broke the surface. He sputtered and chocked on the first several servings of air.

He swam for shore, not daring to look back. As far as he knew, bats didn't swim. Hopefully the same also held true for their relative monsters. The water dragged against him more than he ever remembered. Fully clothed and armed, he fought for each inch. Just as his strength began to fade, his foot hit gravel.

He dragged himself to dry ground and collapse, his breaths and mind haggard. He closed his eyes and focused on breathing. In ... out ... in ... out ... in ...

Titan's muscles shuddered to stave off the cold. He needed a fire.

Fire. Father.

Groaning, he tried to roll to his back and hit something half way. He turned his head to look.

Wings.

Adrenaline poured into his body, warming and re-energizing. He was instantly on his feet, hand on the hilt of his sword across his back. He whirled to face his attacker, but found nothing but air. Knowing before he looked, he slowly lowered his arm and turned his head. It was clinging to his back once again. Had it let go at all?

Yet ... there was no pain. The thing didn't even weigh him down. Titan closed his eyes, took a deep breath, and cautiously craned his neck to see it in full. The wings hung to either side, dripping water. The body ... was missing. As far as he could tell, the wings butted right up to his back. It was as if there wasn't a demon, but the wings were ...

He reached a hand behind him and felt the leather of the wing connect directly to the sheath of his sword. He felt blindly along the sheath. His leather armor had been torn, as had his shirt beneath. The sheath sat against the naked skin of his back. No, not against. Attached. The sheath was fused to his spine.

His eyes grew wide as he reconsidered the wing to his right. In the dark it was little more than a silhouette of shadow obscuring a patch of starry sky. It hung still, limp, as did its companion to Titan's left.

How?!

His hand was still behind him, and he let it drift back to the wing. It looked to be a pelt, as if taken from a massive black beast. The thickness would withstand significant punishment, likely stopping an arrow before its head could break all the way through. The frame of the wing arched forward higher than his head, came to a point, than swept wickedly back. Narrower spindles grew from the upper ridge at intervals, stretching from the wings upper frame to its bottom edge.

Titan stared. The wings were attached to him. He wasn't being attacked by a monster. He *was* a monster. He closed his eyes and rubbed a palm against them. He looked again. They hung at his sides, resolute. But if they were attached to him, then that would mean –

Titan yelped as the wing twitched. He stared at it, breath coming faster again.

Ragdons help me.

They were ... his wings.

He bit his lips, and tentatively focused. Ever so slowly, the wing twitched again, then began to move. It stretched to the side away from him, reaching into the night. Fully extended, the tip hung over twenty feet from him. He looked to the other side, concentrated, and forced the other out as well. A fifty-foot wingspan.

My wingspan. They are my wings.

Titan felt terror returning.

What has happened to me?!

He stumbled backwards, the wings effortlessly following. Shaking his head, he let the wings drift back towards him until they hung behind him. He looked back upriver. The Tower atop the cliff loomed nearly a mile away. He had been carried along the course of the river that emptied into the far side of the lake.

Not carried. I flew here.

Titan sank to his knees. Twenty minutes prior he had been sitting calmly in the antechamber with the other aides. Twenty minutes.

The ... peace conferences.

He put a hand to the ground as the earth lurched beneath him. Devvon had betrayed them. He had betrayed everyone. The kings were dead. His father was...

His body began to shake again. He lowered himself to the ground as the first tear fell to the rocks beneath him. He was falling from the Tower again, spinning in the darkness, watching the ground approach. Only this time, he didn't sprout wings. He felt it slam against him, throwing him into a mercifully oblivious sleep.

CHAPTER 11

The chill breeze pricked at Felk's face as he walked down the street. His pacing within his home had driven him towards madness until he succumbed to the need for escape. He looked up and down the dark streets as he passed, though he knew he wouldn't find what he sought. One does not happen upon justification or answers in dark alleys.

I had a choice. I could have refused.

His feet followed the familiar path, winding from street to street until the city walls came into view. He glanced up. The walkway around the perimeter of the kingdom's capital would bring peace. It always did.

Devvon. Why kill me? What do you gain?

He climbed towards the top of the embankment, eyes focusing only on the next step. He reached the last and nodded to a soldier's salute. He didn't know the man, but didn't need to. Each soldier in the army was his man. Each put their lives on the line every time they were at their post. These men were to be respected by both the citizenry and their superiors. Why didn't Devvon understand that? These weren't just numbers bolstering the kingdom's forces. These were men. Lives.

Perhaps that was why Devvon hated Felk. Perhaps Devvon didn't see them as individuals, but a part of a whole. Perhaps Felk, by individualizing them, put the kingdom at risk. Was he willing to make sacrifices, let men die, for the good of the rest? The question had been presented hundreds of times during his military training, yet it now seemed more troubling. Could he let a man die?

"You can save lives if you alive. My friends' lives."

The prisoner's voice, accusing only minutes before, gave the answer. Felk *had* let a man die. And that man, with his final seconds, had sworn Felk to protect the rest. The sacrifice of one good, innocent man had likely provided the means for thousands to live.

So why am I questioning myself?

Among the cacophony created by the wind's low howl, the red flags as they jerked against their poles, and the indistinguishable voice of the night, Felk heard the faint whistle of an arrow and a thump as it found its mark. He whirled, axe in hand, and crouched.

Silence.

He turned to the soldier he had just passed. The man was gone. *Ragdons!* He looked further down the wall until his eyes came to rest on a pair of guards, chatting quietly. Anger rising, he strode quickly towards them.

"Soldier!"

The two men spun and saluted. "General," they said in unison.

"You are on duty. Do *not* leave your post. An arrow was just shot over the wall!"

The accused cleared his throat. "My apologies, General. I suppose you had left when we began receiving reports this way." He held up an arrow. Felk picked out the parchment rolled tightly around it. "This is the latest report from our lookouts. We're to open them in twos."

Felk looked from the arrow, to the man, to the large wooden post behind him. Dozens of notches were burrowed into it.

"They shoot them up here, and we pass them on. Makes it faster for them, and less likely they'll be seen by the gates."

Felk nodded. "Excuse me for my mistake. I was unaware of the practice. Carry on."

The men visibly relaxed. They carefully untied, then unrolled the report and scanned it. Felk, intrigued by the new process, stood quietly and watched. After several seconds, both men glanced at each other, then at Felk, as if awaiting further instructions. Felk raised an eyebrow.

"What is it, soldier?"

"Several large groups of bandits have moved closer to the city," came the reply. Felk took the paper as it was offered to him.

NE – 0
NW – 0
W – 0
S – 0
BDTS NNE – 1000 – CMP 4 mi
   E – 1700 – CMP 3 mi
   SE – 1800 – CMP 4 mi
   W – 500 – CMP 5 mi

Felk looked back up at the men. "What are still you doing here?! Double the wall guard and inform the general on duty!"

The men raced away. Felk scanned the paper again, then looked back out at the night. Five thousand bandits were within two hours' march of the city. No movement, but at that range there would be little warning of an attack. Five thousand would be far from able from taking the city, but there were more than five thousand. If there was anything Felk knew, it was that bandits were like cockroaches. Pests that had a talent for hiding.

And Devvon was gone. With no king within the walls, the bandit's attack would leave the four generals in complete command. Each deserved his station, but none of them saw eye to eye. An organized assault could lead to a power struggle and divided tactics without a unified leader. Devvon had his faults, but his presence demanded unity.

Felk turned and crossed back towards the stairs. *Ragdons help us*, he silently pleaded.

*****

Ragdons, Titan! Adrianna stomped through the trees, her long hair flowing behind her, trying to keep up. She didn't know where she was going, and with no destination in mind her path bent itself to her anger. The frustration of her studies, Jaron's visit and request, her response ... She had cried from laughter, anger, and despair all within moments without a sound explanation as to why.

Why do you have to be so ... honorable?! She silently yelled. No answer came, and she grew more exasperated. She loved him. Ragdons curse it all, she did. So was she angry at Jaron for asking to court her? Why should she be? Jaron saw her pain, obviously had feelings for her, and provided a solution to both of their complications. Yet how could she have agreed? She didn't love him! How could she let go of the hope that Titan would change the law when he became king?

And how long until that happens? Lexik was in good health and barely into his forties. Decades. Adrianna would likely be passed child-bearing years, further binding Titan to marry another in order to produce an heir. So did she gamble on Titan's heart being stronger than his will and wait? It was stupid and irrational. Jaron had earned royalty, he would be an ideal husband, and he would love and care for her until the day he died. He was the logical choice.

But will my heart listen to logic?

*****

Devvon brought both hands together, palms forward, his arms extended outward directly in front of him.

Time for a demonstration.

His gloves warmed to match the rage within him. He had killed Alder and Lexik. Too quickly. Not enough pain. Devvon had tried the sword and bracers. Alder hadn't been lying.

He screamed and let fly the flame. A ball of fire shot from his hands across the room and smashed into the door. Wood exploded from the force of the blow, the smoldering remnants scattering in all directions. Devvon watched as the fire consumed the remains.

Muffled yells carried through the crackling. The camps outside would no doubt be forming up ranks, scared and bewildered at both the explosions above and now in the Tower's entryway. Devvon's anger was soothed for a moment. At last the leash of countless generations was broken. He could finally use the power he had always been endowed with, but never permitted to wield.

The breastplate and helmet felt natural on him. They should. After all, they were meant to be used together. The pendant and nose guard had been reaffixed to the armor. He was missing the others, but he had enough to move forward. He took a deep breath, triggered the breastplate, and left mortality in his past.

The metal began to shift. New plates grew along his shoulders, then down his arms. Scales of impenetrable silver covered his vulnerability down to his wrists, under his gloves, completely encasing each finger. From the bottom edge of the breastplate more metal grew, extending to cover his thighs, calves, and feet completely. The neckline of the breastplate began to shift and grow. It encircled his neck, up around the back and sides of his head beneath his helmet, and across his face. Devvon shivered as it he felt the tiny interlocking plates wrap around his lips, along the inside of his mouth, over his teeth and tongue. And with a final grate of metal against metal, plates slid over his eyes, transparent from within.

He was invincible. He reached to the side and retrieved his cape, clasping it onto his shoulders. Time to convince the rest of the world.

He strode forward into the inferno. Flames enveloped him, a thousand wicked tongues lashing at his legs and arms. He felt ... nothing. The cool metal covering his body rebuffed the heat. Devvon smiled at the irony of Alder's letter. The inferno *would* keep him. And with that inferno he would rule the world.

Brilliant fire gave way to the dark night beyond. As his eyes adjusted, the nearby yells took on a new tone. Fear. Apparently seeing a metallic god walk through a raging fire was enough to make even grown men nervous. The camps came into focus, as did the hundreds of men in various stages of shock and panic.

He took a step towards the camp just in front of him. Tressle's yellow and brown flags swayed gently in the breeze, a distinct contrast to the chaos surging around them. Several dozen soldiers were still coherent enough to follow orders and were forming up ranks, spears leveled. Doubtful they knew who Devvon was, but it wasn't surprising that his entrance of steel and fire made a convincing argument for caution. He raised both hands towards the meager line.

Plunk.

Devvon turned. Another arrow struck his chest, snapping and falling to the ground. Lexik's army apparently wasn't waiting for an invitation. *Even better*, Devvon thought with a smile. Palms forward, he aimed at the center of the line.

Men were swept from the fire's path, and the blue tent beyond them exploded. Devvon turned to the next group and shot again. Men screamed in pain and fear. He shot again. Lexik's line broke and ran for cover. Embers rained down on the camp, peacefully igniting that which remained.

The few extra seconds were all that Tressle's army needed. Devvon turned to them even as their commander screamed his command. The hundred men charged toward him, the light glinting off of their spears and eyes.

Devvon raised his hands again. One, two, three, he swept from left to right. Four seconds passed in massacre, men flying through the air and fire consuming all. The handful that survived ran like children before a wolf. Their comrades were left to a fiery burial.

The blood lust consumed Devvon. Balls of death, bright against the night sky, raced unbiasedly towards those who ran toward and away from him. He would need survivors to tell stories. But he didn't need a lot of them.

A final eruption, sent as encouragement, boomed as the last of the soldiers disappeared into the trees. Devvon listened as their screams of panic slowly faded, replaced by the soothing crackling of his work. Scattered at his feet lay a surprising number of arrows. He hadn't noticed that so many had struck him during the encounter. He smiled and turned back to where his own army stood huddled like sheep.

He walked towards them. They remained, as they had been commanded, but did so with swords drawn. He stopped a dozen yards before them.

Devvon smiled, voice even. "You would attack your king? Your god?"

Hesitation. One by one, the tips lowered.

"Better. Captain, a drink and a chair. I need to think."

Devvon turned back to the Tower, letting the men resolve their anxiety on their own. The flames at the base were dying down, the heat intense enough that only a few minutes were required to eat away the wood.

"My lord ..."

Devvon glanced back at the captain. "There are three men in there. Assuming they didn't suffocate in the smoke, we'll collect them and leave at first light."

"... yes, sir. My lord, how did you –"

He turned to fully face the man. "It's none of your concern, Captain."

The captain flinched. "Yes, my lord. Your orders? Shall we hunt the survivors down?"

Devvon shook his head. "I need them alive. I need the fear that they now possess to spread like a plague through the kingdoms. I need them to describe the fate of their companions to every man, woman, and child they come in contact with." He felt the armor, still cool, against his arms and legs. "But we do need to hunt, Captain."

The soldier hesitated. "If they are to be left alive, who are we hunting?"

Devvon gritted his teeth. "A thief. We hunt whoever it may be that has stolen my inheritance."

CHAPTER 12

"It's … a man."

A long pause. "Never seen a man like that before."

Titan groaned. He heard a yelp, followed by the pounding of feet against gravel. He slit his eyes open and discovered the retreating backs of two small figures. Children. He closed his eyes again, took a deep breath, and pushed himself to his elbows. His head throbbed.

He struggled to get his legs under him. The night sleeping on the rocks hadn't been kind to him. He forced his eyes open and lifted himself upright, swaying slightly in the morning light. He took a deep breath of the crisp morning air and shivered. The night was over. And the nightmare?

He looked over his shoulder. Wings.

"Over there, papa!"

He glanced up the shore. Several hundred yards away he spotted a small group approaching. Six men, led by two children. Behind them stood a cottage, to their right was a dock with three boats tied up. In each man's hand was a hooked fishing spear.

"What is it, Lents?"

"Don't know. And I ain't going to ask it either. Something that big with wings that ugly don't come from the Ragdons."

Titan took a step backwards as the men came to within fifty yards, spears leveled. He cleared his throat. "Excuse – "

He jerked as an arrow whipped past the side of his head. "Wait, I'm – "

The man in front dashed towards him. "Don't let it speak! It'll curse us!"

Titan spun and ran from the small mob. He focused on pumping his legs. The group was getting closer. Titan felt the resistance of the air hitting his wings, making each step harder.

He stumbled. *The wings...*

Still running, he looked to the side. The right wing hung limp from its skeleton-like frame. *Stretch!* Hesitantly, lethargically, the leather began to obey. Titan strained his will, forcing his new appendage to obey. He looked left and began working on that side as well. The volume of the yelling behind him rose. Another arrow missed his cheek by inches.

His wings stretched to their full span. Placed, as it seemed, by the Ragdons themselves, a small hill appeared directly in front of Titan. He ran for it, the air resisting him all the more. He started up the incline as another arrow missed its mark by not enough. He reached the peak and barreled toward the opposite slope.

Ragdons, please let this work.

Titan dove, paralleling his wings to the ground. He drifted lazily down the hillside, falling forwards like the night before. Reaching the base, he reached for the ground with his feet and hit running. The group behind him reached the top of the hill.

Titan racked his brain, searching for the correct muscle. He glanced at the wings and took a deep breath. *Alright, here goes nothing.* He mentally pushed the wings down as hard as he could. For an instant, he felt slightly lighter on his feet. The leather slapped against the ground and began to drag, and gravity returned in full. Raising both wings once again, Titan forced them back down.

His feet left the ground. He stumbled as it came abruptly back up at him.

Faster. Up again. Back down. Up. Down. Up. Down.

His feet didn't touch the ground after his fifth pump. Up, down, up, down. He began to rise, still racing forward at a running pace. Up, down, up, down. The ground was three feet below. Then five. Ten. Twenty.

Titan beamed as he rose. Up, down, up, down. He concentrated on keeping his wings pumping and watched, eyes wide, as the ground continued to fall away. The yells grew more distant, and Titan looked back to find the group had stopped their pursuit. When Titan reached roughly fifty feet in altitude, he slowed his beating, trying to maintain rather than rise. He breathed a sigh of relief and returned his attention to the course in front of him.

A wall of pine trees. He pumped furiously and rose with the speed and grace of a three-legged cow. He wheeled his arms as the unforgiving boughs reached for him.

He lurched to the side. His wing brushed the needles, and he continued his flight alongside them. Titan glanced at the limbs as they continued to grasp at his leather wing. How did birds do it? Tilting their wings? He set his jaw and lifted his right wing.

The direction of lift shifted from straight up to viciously left. Titan felt his stomach lurch. *Too much!* He yanked his left wing up to match and was thrown in the opposite direction. He tumbled forward and down, back towards the surface of the lake. Swallowing hard, he forced his wings level.

The air caught him as his feet splashed into the cold water. He pumped his wings again and quickly rose. He soared over the lake, the cool morning air coursing through his hair. Titan took a deep breath and looked around him. The group of would-be-demon-killers stood watching him from the shore, waiting. Waiting for ... what?

I have no idea. He struggled to think of something, anything. What was he to do? After several more attempts at banking, he determined that he could gently glide with an only moderate chance of killing himself. But that still left him without a destination. And the opposite shore was fast approaching.

He gingerly tipped his wings again. The turn was by no means graceful, but nor was it out of control. He began towards the row of pines once again. He couldn't land or he would be skewered by the fisherman. Returning home in his current state would probably throw his own people into a similar frenzy. And ... there was nothing left for him at the Tower.

Anyone who sees me will assume I'm from the Ragdons' Inferno. He banked again, careful of his distance from the man with the bow.

Richards. His father's voice echoed in his mind.

"Go to him. Tell him Devvon has killed the other kings. Tell him to tell you everything!"

For the first time in his life, Titan had seen fear in his father's eyes.

"Promise me!"

Richards hated crowds. He lived by himself in a small valley to the southwest, miles from any would-be-neighbors. *Why go there?* Lexik had named the man Titan's uncle, but that was obviously untrue. The recluse was only a handful of years older than Titan, and there was absolutely no family resemblance. But Lexik had been adamant. Titan shook his head and flew higher. Getting his bearings from the mountain ranges to the south, he banked and started his journey towards the hermit.

He cleared the first wave of trees and continued to rise. The lake and demon-hunters disappeared behind him, covered by the flowing blanket of green. Titan looked up, picked out the mountain from its neighbors, and pumped harder. The vegetation below began to rush swiftly by, broken only by rivers and the occasional road. Lexik had said Richards had answers. The king's final command had been to find the man. Titan fought, stroke after stroke, to push both the air and the images behind him, his eyes undeviating on the valley in the distance.

*****

Felk gripped the rough stone, gazing out over the wall. The attack should have come either in the dark or at first light. It was passed midday, and still there was no sign of them. The entire army was on alert and had been for nearly twelve hours, waiting for the five thousand identified bandits and Ragdons knew how many invisible ones. No attack had come.

What in the inferno are they waiting for?!

The general shifted his attention to the steady stream of peasants flowing beneath him through the city's main gate. After it became apparent that the city proper wasn't in imminent danger, they had sent word to all surrounding villages with orders to seek the protection of the city's walls. Understandably, the civilians had all but run to safety. The increased number would put a strain on supplies, but without Devvon around to directly command that food be conserved for the army, refugees and citizens alike could live off less for a time.

The fix was temporary. Devvon would return in a week and throw the people back out to the wolves. The army was strong, and that strength required food. Farms didn't tend themselves, and an occasional missing daughter or slaughtered family was apparently worth the benefit.

So many people. Felk watched the thick crowd surge forward, unyielding. It was difficult to remember that the bulk of the kingdom's population lived without the walls. But as the throng continued, hour after hour, Felk realized the true gravity of the charge given to him by the prisoner. They continued, undaunted by the reddening sky. So many …

He let go of the stone and strode along the wall. A soldier, standing beside the post riddled with indents, snapped to attention. Felk knew him.

"Timot."

"Afternoon, General. All's quiet."

92

Felk looked back out at the forest. "I wish I felt like that was good news. When do reports come?"

"Around midnight, unless there is urgent information. It's the spy's choice, really. He decides when it's least risky."

Felk nodded. "Smart. Well, when it arrives tonight, I want to be informed immediately. The other generals and I will be sleeping in the barracks tonight."

"Yes, sir."

Felk crossed to the stone steps. With the surrounding villages empty and the army on alert, the bandits could do little harm. All Felk could do at this point was wait for them to show their treacherous faces.

CHAPTER 13

"So we're going to take it easy this time, right?"

"Of course," Adrianna said, batting her eyes.

"I know that look, princess," Reon replied with a wag of the finger. "Legally I can't let you out of my site outside the city. No funny business. You slow up."

"You had a difficult time keeping up last time, did you?"

Reon scoffed. "Yes, I did. It could have had something to do with the fact that you jumped over a mountain."

"It was a fallen tree."

"That was bigger than small mountains! Honestly, it took me ten minutes to find another way through that thicket." Reon patted his horse's neck. "These animals can't jump that high."

"Mine did."

"I don't think yours qualifies as a horse after the things I've seen it do."

Adrianna pushed her mount into a slow trot, chuckling. "You worry too much. What do you think is going to happen to me out there?"

"Nothing," came a voice from the side. Adrianna looked over to find Jaron pulling up beside them from a side street. "I swear it."

"What are you up to, old chum?" Reon asked, chin raised. "Aren't you supposed to be marching or something?"

"I marched quickly this morning and came straight here."
Adrianna assumed he was telling the truth, as he still wore
his armor.

"And what makes you think you're coming with us?"

Jaron nodded at Adrianna. "I received an invitation."

Reon whirled on Adrianna, annoyance spread thick on his
face.

"You complained so much about my leaving you behind
last time. I thought you would welcome the help."

Reon huffed as he kicked his horse forward. "I would
rather you just stayed close."

"What's the point of having the strongest animal in the
kingdoms and not riding him to his fullest?"

The three galloped across a city square and through the
eastern gate. The buildings disappeared to either side, and
were replaced by a think forest, lush with undergrowth. The
trees covered the sky nearly as completely as the greenery
covered the ground to either side of the road. The late
morning sun filtered through the canopy, lighting specks of
dust in the air, enchanting the path before them. Shards of
the sun itself hung and shifted at random. Several hundred
yards outside the gate, Adrianna veered off the road and into
the forest. She heard her two companions follow and smirked.
She leaned forward, her horse obediently quickening.

"Um, Princess?"

"Don't bother." Reon didn't sound pessimistic. More ...
resigned.

"But the trees..."

"We're only up to about half speed of what she likes to do."

True. She leaned harder, and the horse complied. Trees
grew dense to either side, choking off the path even as she
galloped through it. Her horse wasn't the largest in her
father's army, but it may have been the most agile. She had
created a unique relationship with it, an understanding. She
never used a whip or her heels. Her ride in turn responded
promptly to her gentle instruction. The pair leapt over a fallen

tree into a small stream. Water sprayed as they charged across and plunged headfirst into the underbrush.

"Princess," came Jaron's voice again. Further away, and more uneasy. "I really must insist."

Adrianna leaned lower. The wind and leaves pulled at her hair, the twigs at her dress. She had been riding the horse beneath her for years, and the two knew each other well. She rarely used the reins, instead guiding their course with shifts of weight. He invariably understood, and would frequently anticipate the changes of direction before she even moved.

"Let her go," she heard Reon's voice filter through the trees. "Not going to catch her now."

Adrianna pulled up and looked back. The other two had stopped and were completely hidden through the foliage.

"But we have to."

"Yes, we do. But try as you might, you aren't going to catch her. Don't worry about it, General. She always finds her way back."

"And if she runs into trouble? Or her horse stumbles?"

Adrianna could almost feel Reon shrugging. "Hasn't happened yet."

"So what do we do then? Just wait?"

"Well, General, I usually grab a bite to eat at the tavern just inside the city gates. Come on, I'll let you buy my meal with that general's salary of yours."

Adrianna shifted and the steed took off once again. Normally she would spend an hour or two riding, enjoying the increasingly rare moments of solitude. But today ... perhaps a bit more fun. She swung back at an angle, guessing at the direction of the gate. She knew the tavern Reon mentioned, as she'd found him there the year before, sulking.

The trees blurred to either side, and eventually began to thin as they drew closer to the city. The horse, surer now in its footing, charged ahead without further instruction. Adrianna lay flat against his back as they ducked beneath a low hanging branch. The road ahead materialized through the trees.

A sliver of metal flew by, an armored rider. *How?* She had both the shorter path and the element of surprise. She broke through the trees and leaned left onto the road. Ahead, sun glinted off the back of the man's breastplate as he hurtled towards the gates.

Jaron. Adrianna smiled, despite herself. She'd underestimated how well the general already knew her. He knew she'd enjoy beating them to their goal. She pushed on, determined to at least limit his win to a few hundred paces.

Jaron disappeared within the city, and Adrianna followed moments later, nodding to the sentries on either side and slowing her mount to a walk. She looked around the square. No sign of him. No sign of Reon behind on the road, either. She turned down a side street and trotted the half block to the tavern. Smoothly dismounting, she tossed the reins over a wooden post and pushed through the door, aware of but undeterred by her lack of an escort. A handful of occupants looked up. One apparently recognized her and nodded in deference, but none of the faces were familiar. She frowned and withdrew.

Jaron and Reon were just rounding the corner at the far end of the street. She folded her arms as they approached.

"How did you know we were coming here?" Reon asked as he dismounted.

"Where else would two men go to nurse their egos back to health?"

Reon opened his mouth. After a moment, he shut it again. "Right. Last year."

Adrianna looked to Jaron. "But I thought for sure you'd beaten me here."

"Why is that, my lady?" Jaron carefully tethered the horse.

"You raced ahead of me."

"Raced? A steady trot can hardly be called racing. We thought you'd be gone for some time."

"Oh." Adrianna frowned once again. "Must have been another soldier then. I assumed at his speed it was Jaron trying to get the better of me."

"Another soldier? Racing?"

Adrianna nodded. "Wearing armor like yours."

Jaron tapped his finger against his animal's neck. "Why would a soldier in full armor be riding that hard?"

Reon shrugged. "Eager to get home, I suppose."

Jaron hesitated. "Probably." He tossed the leather from the post and turned to mount his horse again. "But I'll feel better if I check in. Princess?"

Adrianna smiled. "Adrianna. Please."

Jaron's cheeks pinked. "Will you meet me this evening? In the gardens?"

"No," Reon replied.

"Yes," Adrianna said.

"Thank you," Jaron said. "Until then." He kicked his horse back the way they had come.

"'Yes'?" Reon asked, glaring at the princess.

Adrianna stuck her chin out. "Yes."

*****

Devvon, the half-god, rode east. Behind him trailed a group of less than twenty-five men, chatting amiably. A pitiful guard, but then, Devvon no longer needed numbers. Metal coated his arms, legs, even his face. What could an enemy do? He was invulnerable.

But not immortal.

He growled. The sword and bracers were gone, and the helmet atop his head was useless. He looked around him and imagine what it would be like, to see everything, hear everything, smell everything. He needed those pieces. The novelty of his breastplate had quickly worn off as he realized that being a half-god was laughable in comparison.

His soldiers joked with each other. The initial shock of his appearance had dissipated, and while he still likely looked like a fiend in the sunlight, the effect appeared to be far lessened. The men mingled, with the three "aides" frequently being barraged by questions from the others. They had been posing for years, working their way into the trust of their superiors. Years of work to create the perfect moment to ...

Devvon halted and stared at the forest ahead. The group pulled up behind him and quieted. Devvon slowly turned his horse. "You, you, and you."

The three glanced at each other, then nudged their horses forward. "Yes, my lord?"

Devvon gritted his teeth. "What exactly happened in the antechamber?"

"My lord?"

"WHAT IN THE RAGDONS HAPPENED?!"

The first paled, sputtering. The second cleared his throat. "Exactly what you planned, my lord. We waited until we heard an explosion, then rushed the boy. He was quick, so he made it through the door before we could reach him, but you killed him."

Devvon raised an eyebrow. "*I* killed him?"

The man hesitated. "Didn't you, my lord?"

Devvon pinched his metal brow. "How sure are you of that?"

The soldier glanced around for support and found none. "He locked the door behind him! We couldn't follow! And we heard the explosion, just outside, right where he was standing!"

Devvon raised a hand, stopping the man's panicked explanation. "What was your task?"

"To ... kill the son of Lexik and guard the offerings."

Devvon nodded. "I have a hypothetical question for you. Suppose you had in your possession one of the greatest treasures known to man. And supposed you were forced to leave it behind. But it's something you really don't want to part with for extended periods of time, so you want it close, just in case you need it. With whom do you suppose you would entrust it? Hmm?"

The soldier shrugged. "I'm not sure, my lord. Someone I could trust?"

Devvon nodded. "An astute observation. And, following your own logic, who do you suppose Lexik trusted most last night?"

"His … son?"

Devvon drew his sword and with a clean swipe took the man's head off. "His son." He kicked his horse into a run through the midst of the men. "Back to the Tower!"

Ragdons! How could he have been so blind? Titan had escaped his own execution. Lexik had run. He had thrown something threw a window, over the edge of a thousand foot cliff. And strapped to that something's back were two very large, black wings.

CHAPTER 14

The scene below was little more than a patchwork of greens, browns, and blues. The original plan was to fly a safe distance away from the fishermen and walk. Then Titan realized the necessity of landing in such a venture, and decided the safest option was to stay in the air a bit longer. It was an inevitably approaching experience, but procrastination seemed like a good idea at the time. He also soon realized that he was making exceptionally good time. The mountains loomed closer, and his journey would likely end sometime late that evening.

Titan was pleased, for the moment. His progress was steady, he'd only been shot at twice since his initial liftoff, and he was getting more used to his new limbs. He swayed from side to side, dipped and rose. It was ... exhilarating.

He expected to tire quickly, but found that such wasn't the case. His energy drained as if he had been riding a horse for several hours, but the wings themselves had little effect on him. He controlled the wings, but they flapped under their own power. As if they weren't really a part of him, just on loan.

He passed over another grouping of cottages and was rewarded with several more yells. He looked for the sources, but the trees soon obscured them. He would probably become a ghost story told to frighten young children. He only hoped that it wouldn't be a reality. He was still vividly aware that he was a freak, some sort of devil. The screams wouldn't end. Assuming he could convince them not to burn him for witchcraft, even his own people would be terrified of him. The thrill of soaring wasn't worth the cost.

I hope Richards has some answers.

*****

A knock. Felk rose from the table. He opened the door and was greeted by a salute. "General. You wished to see the scout report?"

"Yes, you have it?"

"I'm afraid not, General. General Dants is officially in command today. The report is with him. I wanted to make you aware of its arrival."

"Thank you." Felk stepped out into the waning light with the soldier and swung the door closed. Dismissing the man, he started towards the barracks to his right. Mist was beginning to appear, and the building was blurred by the haze. The day had come and gone, the city had finally received the last of the villagers, and the gates had creaked shut. Felk had stayed on the wall, watching and waiting. The sun was now setting, letting the night creep like death itself over the city. And still, the bandits held.

Felk passed tent after tent. The city streets were lined with them, and houses were being shared by as many as four families. Every space was filled, every room occupied. Felk shook his head at the sight. Devvon's breeding laws had had drastic effects over the last two decades. The population had swollen, and the first of the sons were just reaching recruitment age. The army would swell in like manner over the next handful of years.

Felk reached the door and pounded twice. A moment later it opened for him. The two torches blazing within illuminated the bunks that stretched away from those sitting around the table by the entrance. General Dants stopped his discussion, smiled, and reached a hand out to Felk.

"A busy day, old friend."

Felk extended his own hand and smile. "Indeed."

"I expect you will sleep well tonight."

"I'll sleep when I'm dead," Felk remarked. "You have the report?"

Dants nodded, sliding a paper across the table. He settled back, crossing thick arms. "You'll die sooner if you *don't* sleep. And you may want to sit down before reading."

Felk's heart skipped. *How many more?* He carefully picked up the paper looked over the scribbles.

NE – 0
NW – 0
W – 0
S – 0
BDTS – 0

Felk looked up at Dants. "This has to be a mistake."

Dants shook his head. "This is actually the second such report. I didn't believe the first and requested confirmation from another man."

"But, where?"

Dants took a sip from a cup. "Ragdons if I know."

"And the men who originally spotted them?"

Dants leaned back. "All of them gave the same answer. They came back to the city last night to give their report, and when they return just a few hours later, the bandits had vanished."

Felk looked back at the paper. "They knew they'd been seen and ran."

Dants paused. "All four camps? Miles apart? Within the same hour?"

Felk looked back up. "You're saying … they planned it? To be spotted and then flee? Why would they do that?"

Dants shrugged. "You know the bandits better than anyone. What do they gain?"

"Nothing. They prefer to ambush. Letting us know they're near isn't like them."

"Alright. So where did they go?"

Felk read the paper again. "I have no idea."

Dants grunted. "I'm keeping the army on full alert. We'll scout more extensively tomorrow."

Felk nodded. "Good. Keep the refugees here, too. They're too vulnerable outside the city. The last time ..." Felk trailed off. He quickly looked away.

"I know," Dants whispered. "My daughter was there."

"I ... apologize, Dants. It was not my intention."

Dants closed his eyes and took a deep breath. "Don't apologize, Felk."

"I ... I don't know what to say."

"No one knows what to say. That doesn't stop them from talking, though." Dants held up a hand as Felk opened his mouth to speak. "You and I both know you are a good man. Let's just keep the rest of the kingdom's daughters safe. It's worth whatever the cost."

"Yes. It is."

Felk stayed for another pair of minutes, then bid goodnight. Outside, the city was still. Devvon's breeding laws were about to achieve their purpose in growing the army. But over the last years, they'd first fulfilled the goals of the enemy. Foreigners across the sea had apparently taken a liking to the women of the five kingdoms and were willing to pay a premium for such a wife. The bandits in turn had established a thriving slave-trading market, capitalizing particularly on the increased number of eastern women working the fields. Most men within the army now had missing wives, sisters, or daughters.

Devvon, Felk thought as he strode into the evening, *whatever your game is with me, may the Ragdons destroy you if you don't protect your people.*

*****

The sun threw splashes of pink and red across the sky. Adrianna surveyed the gardens, noting the vast array of color choices. Ironically, they hadn't been commissioned by anyone of the royal family. Lexik didn't believe the reigning class should burden the common people with such frivolities, and so he kept much of his surroundings clean, but simple. The garden had been planted as a birthday gift for him by his subjects, despite his efforts to stop them.

Jaron was late, and Adrianna wasn't certain she knew how she felt about it. She stood amazed that he would abstain from coming to meet her, nervous about what he would say when he arrived, and worried at the implications of both emotions. She loved Titan, but Jaron was more respectful and less ... obstinate. She imagined the evening would bring with it a pleasant walk, friendly conversation, and utter propriety. A perfect gentleman.

Footsteps on the gravel alerted her to his approach. She looked and spotted him weaving between the hydrangeas and peonies. Adrianna breathed in deeply, straighten a fold in her dress, and beamed. *How I wish you were Titan.* She felt the thought taint her smile.

Jaron stopped a dozen feet away. "My lady," he greeted her softly.

"General," Adrianna replied. She patted the bench beside her.

"I ... think I shall stand."

"Oh. Very well." She pushed off the bench. "A walk then?"

Jaron shook his head. "And I think sitting would be better for you." She hesitated. He took a step forward. "Please, princess."

Confused, she obeyed. "Jaron, what's going on?" He was nervous. More so than the first day they'd met. Surely he wouldn't ...

He took in a slow breath, then let it out again. "My lady," he repeated. Adrianna felt her stomach tighten.

"What is it? What's so difficult to say?"

"I ... have some news. And I don't know if I have the heart to tell you."

Adrianna's throat went dry. "What news do you bring?"

"That rider that you saw. He ... was part of Lexik's guard."

Adrianna froze.

"He reported an occurrence at the Tower." Jaron swallowed. "With the kings inside, something ... happened. He said some sort of man-creature attacked them, covered in metal and breathing fire. It was over in minutes, the army destroyed. He thinks he ... might be the only survivor."

Adrianna stared. "And the kings?"

Jaron looked to the ground. "The soldier said the creature came from within the Tower." He shook his head. His lip trembled.

"My father ..." A ball of pain formed in her stomach.

"... yes."

Adrianna longed not to ask. Her voice cracked as she spoke. "And ... what of Titan?"

A tear slipped down Jaron's cheek. "Lexik always took his son with him inside."

Adrianna felt her heart collapse. Tears streamed freely as she leaned forward, the pit in her stomach burning. She felt Jaron sit beside her. "I am so sorry, princess." She fell into him as her chest convulsed with the sobs. He caught her and held her to him, his own body shaking as well. "I am so sorry," he whispered through his own tears.

Titan! She screamed in silence. A void was spreading from within, dragging her into it. She felt the world sway, moved by the pull of the wound, and she wept. Beyond pain and coherent thought, she heard a moan escape her lips. She closed her eyes to the sunlight and colors, searching the darkness for a comfort she knew wasn't there. And so, unable to do anything else, Adrianna lay in Jaron's arms, mourning for a lost love she had never really had.

CHAPTER 15

People of the East,

It is with great pride that I announce the birth of a new era. Long has our kingdom been subject to the wills of our four neighbors, with expectations placed upon us that have inhibited our ability to succeed, to thrive. This is no longer. As of this declaration, we are free. More than free. We stand not only apart, but above.

Within days, we will launch the greatest crusade ever known to man. We will reunite the five kingdoms under a single rule and working together, we will establish peace throughout this continent. We will at long last have the power to seek out and destroy the bandits that have long plagued our people. We are on the verge of a new destiny.

As with all worthy objectives, this reunification will also have its price. But, Ragdons willing, the cost will be brief and temporary. From this time forward, the recruitment standard for the army's ranks will be lowered to fifteen years of age. This may seem young to many, and I agree. For this reason, you have my word that those between the ages of fifteen and eighteen will never see battle. They will be used as scouts and messengers, allowing those currently used in those capacities to step forward and fight for their kingdom's honor.

While the enlistment of our sons is mandatory, I also ask that every able man enlist of his own volition, even if he has already served his required term. We will need all available men to make this dream a reality.

Do not fear the future. The peace conferences went exceptionally well, and most of the other kings have already been persuaded to cooperate in this vision. I am undergoing negotiations even at this time. We will win their allegiance. You have my word, not as your king but as your emperor.

Be strong, and train hard. I shall return shortly, and together we will march for victory.

  Emperor Devvon

Devvon signed the letter. He rolled and sealed it, then pulled out a second sheet. Re-dipping in ink, he addressed a second message.

Generals,

Within days you will have tens of thousands of new recruits. Train them fast and hard. At the end of a week, you are each to take a fifth of the men, leaving the final fifth within the city, and march on the other kingdoms. They will anticipate your coming. Conquer them at all cost.

  Emperor Devvon

He waved the nearby soldier forward as he sealed the second note. He handed over both and watched as the messenger mounted and disappeared into the waning light, headed east.

*****

The sun set as Titan entered the valley. Scanning the forest before him, he picked out a trail of smoke rising through the trees. As he neared, the cottage came into view with its surrounding clearing. Titan watched the ground continue to flash past below him. Letting out a resigned sigh, he banked toward the open patch below. After clearing the last of the trees, he banked sharply down. His speed shot up, as did the ground, and he hit running.

His clip was too much. In a flash he was tumbling forward, the wings making it impossible to guess where to reach for the ground as he rolled over and over. At last he stopped. As he lay for a moment catching his breath, he was happily surprised to find nothing more than scraps and minor bruises from the encounter. He rolled to his knees, pushed himself to his feet, and consciously tucked the wings back behind him.

He watched the small house for a time. Firelight flickered through the window, and a shadow occasionally crossed. As he listened, he could pick out a song being hummed, but didn't know the tune. Grateful for the darkness the night was now providing in full, he stepped towards the door. The wings would be harder to spot. Of course, his whole purpose in coming here was to tell the hermit about them, so what did it really matter?

Titan took a deep breath, raised his hand, and after a minor waver of fortitude, knocked. The humming stopped, and footsteps approached. The door was flung open, revealing a short, bushy beard and accusing eyes. The latter scoured the darkness, finally resting on Titan.

"Who are you? What do you want?"

Titan swallowed. "It's me. Titan. Son of Lexik."

Richards studied Titan's face, frowning. "May the Dragon take me. So it is!" He broke into a wide grin. "What in the devil are you doing all the way up here? Come in, come in. The night's going cold."

"I … I'm afraid I can't."

"Why not? Not in too big a rush to talk for a few minutes with your old uncle, I hope." Richards chuckled. The man didn't look a day older than twenty-five.

Titan shook his head. "No. It's just that I don't think it's a good idea for me to come inside."

Richards cocked his head. "Are you diseased?"

"No!" Titan closed his eyes. "Well, actually, in a way, yes." He took a deep breath and turned, exposing his profile.

Richards' eyes widened. He whistled softly. "Dragon."

Titan spun back. "It's still me, Titan, but these things are ... I need your help."

Richards nodded. "Alright, my boy, I'll do what I can. Give me just a moment and I'll build us a fire out in the back." He waved Titan around the side of the house, withdrew, and closed the door. Titan heard the lock click.

Great. Titan trudged around the side of the house, and plopped down on the log beside the fire pit. The man was likely finding a pitchfork or spear so he could –

The door flew open. Richards backed out, carrying an armful of wood. "I see you already found a seat. Good boy. Give me just a minute to get this thing going." He dumped his load to the side and set to work building a miniature cabin from the sticks. Titan waited in silence. After several minutes the fire was self-sustaining, and Richards sat back, throwing one of the larger logs on.

"Now," he said as he leaned forward onto his knees. "You can imagine it's not every day that an old friend shows up with wings strapped to his back. Care to elaborate as to what exactly is going on?"

Titan shook his head. "I have no idea. I was hoping you would have some answers.

Richards frowned. "What makes you think I've got them?"

"My father told me to come to you."

"Oh?"

"Yes. Just before –" Titan clenched his jaw. "Just before he was killed."

Richards bit his lip. "I am truly sorry. I didn't know." He looked into the fire. "Can you tell me about it?"

Titan rubbed his forehead. "We were at the peace conferences. I was my father's aide, and while I was in the antechamber I noticed something odd about the other four. They knew things about each other, like they were already friends. I asked them about it, and they attacked me."

Richards raised an eyebrow. "They attacked you? All of them?"

110

Titan nodded. "They said they were following orders. That their allegiance was to Devvon."

"I thought you people didn't allow more than one aid for each king at this thing."

"I don't know how he did it, but Devvon had all four of them, dressed as if they were from the armies of the other kingdoms."

Richards scratched at his beard. "To be chosen as an aide, don't you have to be fairly well trusted? Have a good track record? I imagine there was a lot of planning and waiting on Devvon's part, getting all of them in place."

Titan nodded. "They rushed me, so I ran for my father. That's when I heard the first of the explosions. My father came charging out, with fire chasing after him."

Richards dropped his head. "Fire chasing him."

"He hauled me down the hallway. That's when he told me to come find you."

Richards looked back up. "And then he was killed."

Titan looked at his hands.

"So ... how did you survive?"

"He threw me through the window."

Richards raised an eyebrow. "From the top of the Tower?"

Titan nodded. "Another explosion happened just behind me. Right where Father was standing."

"Titan. I'm sorry." After a moment of silence, Richards stood and added another log to the fire. "Now, that still leaves you falling out of the sky. That must be over a thousand feet."

Titan smiled weakly. "I grew wings."

Richards chuckled. "Just like that, eh?"

Titan shrugged. "Before he threw me, Father told me to pray. I did, and I guess the Ragdons sent them to save me." He shook his head. "Ironically, the next morning I was nearly killed for being a demon."

"You do look more or less like something I used to have nightmares about."

"I know. And as hard as I've tried I can't get the things off."

"What all have you tried?"

"... Pulling?"

Richards smirked. "No success there, eh? Exactly which Ragdon did you pray to while you were falling?"

Titan thought for a moment. "Enlightenment."

"And have you thanked Enlightenment for saving you?"

Titan cocked his head. "What?"

"Have you thanked him? Or is it a her? I never know with the Ragdons."

"Neither," Titan said. "They transcend gender."

"Ah," Richards said. "Well, have you thanked *it* then?"

"I guess I haven't."

"You may as well. It's the least you can do, seeing as how it saved your life and all."

Titan stared. "Now?"

Richards smiled, eyebrows raised. Titan hesitantly lifted his hands to either side. He swung them together, arms straight and palms together. Lastly, he pulled both hands back to his chest, completing the reverse motions of the prayer he had performed while falling.

"Satisfied?"

"Since when was this about my satisfaction? The question is, are *you* satisfied?"

"What do you mean?"

Richards motioned behind Titan. "The Ragdons give. The Ragdons take."

Titan looked over his shoulder and saw nothing. "I don't –" He stopped. He saw nothing. The wings were gone. As he whirled, he found that his shirt was still torn, exposing his back, but the sword swung free. He whipped back around and found the hermit beaming. He gave a theatrical, albeit awkward, bow from his seat.

"Poof!"

CHAPTER 16

NE – 0
NW – 0
W – 0
S – 0
BDTS – 0

Felk ground his teeth. Reports were coming more frequently, per Dants' command, and there was still no sign of them. They were out there, Felk was sure of it. But where? Waiting for what?

The obvious answer was reinforcements. But if they were aiming to attack the city, why had they let themselves be spotted? Perhaps their plan was to lay siege and wait for supplies to run out. Or perhaps they knew Devvon was away and would wait to ambush him as he returned, hoping to claim a ransom.

Felk returned the report to the soldier with instructions to inform the other generals. The horizon was growing grey. It should have brought hope that the night had ended without incident. But Felk would have appreciated the light that an incident would have shed far more than the light being given by the dawning sun.

Ragdons, he cursed.

The day was approaching when Adrianna opened her eyes again. She didn't remember falling asleep. Shivering, she sat upright. She looked up at Jaron, his arm still around her. His eyes were exhausted.

"Can you ever forgive me?" he whispered.

Adrianna closed her eyes again. "There isn't a need." She took a deep breath. "You have done nothing but held me. That's all anyone could have asked for."

Jaron studied her. "And now? What would you have me do?"

Adrianna shook her head. "I don't know."

Jaron nodded slowly. "And what will you do?"

Adrianna dropped her face into both hands. "I don't know that either." She attempted a laugh, but barely kept back a sob. She took a deep breath. "Any ideas?"

He laid his hand gently on her shoulder. "I wouldn't dare suggest." He paused. "But I imagine you will rule your people magnificently."

"Rule?" she asked, sitting up and facing him.

"Yes," Jaron replied, his smile sad. "Princess."

Princess? Her father had died. Her mother hadn't survived Adrianna's birth. That meant the right to rule fell ... to her. Law demanded that she be crowned within the week.

"Oh." She found herself at a loss. She had always known this day might come, but hadn't really believed it ever would. She turned back to Jaron. "And the west? With Lexik and –" She broke off and bit her lip. "Without a male heir ... the crown passes to ..."

Jaron was studying the rose bush in front of them. "The generals."

"And," Adrianna continued, studying his face, "you outrank the other two."

Jaron didn't look at her.

Adrianna joined him in watching the light creep across the grounds. "You will make an extraordinary king."

"I doubt I will ever measure up to Lexik," he replied. He hesitated. "Or Titan."

Adrianna shook her head. "You're as honorable as either. And that's what made them truly great."

Jaron didn't say anything for a long time. Adrianna wasn't sure whether conversation would be welcome, so she contented herself with the silence. Finally, Jaron cleared his throat.

"Princess?"

"Yes, Jaron?"

"Are you familiar with the laws governing western marriage?"

"Unfortunately, yes," she said. "That's what had me in such a foul mood the other night."

Jaron nodded. "So you understand the restrictions placed on the king."

Adrianna nodded "I do. The king must marry – oh. Yes. Yes, I see." Her heart began to ache again. "No royalty."

Jaron turned to her. "Marry me."

Adrianna stared at him. "What?"

"I know you have only known me a short time," he said, speaking quickly. "And I know the occasion isn't what I had hoped for in asking this from you."

"And it's against your laws," she said in confusion.

"No," Jaron said slowly. "It isn't."

Adrianna watched him. "I read the law not two days ago."

"Do you remember the words?"

"More or less. A king cannot marry a royal from any kingdom."

Jaron shook his head. "A king cannot *propose* marriage or accept a proposal of marriage to a royal." He paused. "But if he were already engaged to be married to such a person when he assumed the throne ..." He watched Adrianna intently as he trailed off.

"But you are king now."

"My coronation is scheduled for two days from now."

"So if I agreed to marry you before that time ..."

"Then no law would be broken."

"But," Adrianna said, turning the law over in her mind, "the king's successor is bound as well."

"Only his immediate heir." Jaron took her hand. "Adrianna ..."

Her spine tingled. Jaron had never used her name before, and the sound of it from his lips shook her. What was she to say? She didn't even know what to think. Only hours before her world had been torn apart. She had lost the two most important people in the world to her. Now she had two days to make a choice she had expected was still years away. She opened her mouth. No words came.

"I love you," Jaron said. "I have from the first moment I saw you, three years ago. It took me three years to gain the courage to even speak to you. My honor demands that I give you the same, but ..." His eyes glistened. "It's unfair and I know it, giving you two days to decide whether to marry a man you've known for less than a dozen. But if I don't ask now, I'll lose you before I even had the chance to have you."

Adrianna was exhausted. Her body and emotions felt battered, drained to the point of collapsing. "I ..." her heart pounded as she steeled herself. "Do you know what you're asking of me? By marrying you I give up my throne, my kingdom. I become a westerner."

Jaron's gaze was unwavering. "I know. But I offer you my throne ... and my life." He looked down at his hands. "You don't have to answer right now. I'm afraid to hear, anyways." He smiled weakly. "After all, we have two days."

Two days. Two days to decide the course of my life. There is nothing to be done with two days.

"I don't need two days," Adrianna said. Jaron looked back up at her. "I ... accept." She paused. "I will love you, Jaron."

A tear slid down his cheek. "I believe you, Adrianna." He pressed her hand to his lips. "And I will make you happy."

Adrianna forced herself to smile. "I know you will."

*****

"Nothing, my king."

Devvon gritted his teeth. "Emperor." He waved the man's stuttering away and returned his attention to the cliff. A thousand feet, with nothing but jagged rocks to cushion him. Devvon shook his head. Finding the body would have been both highly convenient and highly improbable. The boy hadn't fallen from the Tower. He had flown from it.

Devvon scanned the horizon. Where would Titan go? His home kingdom? If that was the case, Devvon would have to wait for his army. Unfortunately, that was the most likely answer. Still, Devvon wasn't about to sit and stew for days on end, and so set aside that possibility for the moment. He gazed down at the stream far below. He let his eyes wander along its course, through the trees. In the near distance it emptied into a small lake.

If he were running, Devvon would stay out of sight. Staying entirely below the tree line was the safest option. That left two choices: directly over the stream, either upstream or down. Upstream would lead the youth east, away from his home and towards Devvon. Not likely.

Downstream it was then. Devvon motioned to his captain and strode to his mount. He swung into the saddle and pulled the horse around. The boy was downstream. Devvon could feel it. He rammed his heels into the horse's belly and started down the incline.

CHAPTER 17

Titan awoke. He wasn't at home and he wasn't in camp. He was …

The world and his memory came back into focus. His dreams had been dark and disorienting, though he couldn't remember their content. Richards hut around him didn't help. Clothes were scattered, books stacked, and all was tainted by dirt. Richards himself only added to the disarray as he entered through the back door. He waggled several eggs at Titan as he yanked a pan from a hook in the wall.

"Hungry?"

Titan nodded, counting back. "I haven't eaten in nearly two days."

Richards crouched in front of the fire place and prodded the embers. "See, if I was a good host, I would have asked you last night if I could get you something to eat. But don't look for an apology, you aren't going to get one. There's a reason why I don't have any neighbors."

Richards added some sticks and the flame reignited. Titan flinched. He closed his eyes and shook his head.

"Now will you answer my questions?" he said.

"Don't get in a huff. You and I were both worn out last night. I wasn't coherent enough to give good answers, and you weren't coherent enough to receive them. But yes, now I will answer your questions." He cracked an egg into the pan and set it over the fire.

"How did you know how to get rid of the wings?"

"Thought you were the first person to show up at my door with wings, did you?"

"Actually ... yes. I did."

"It just so happens that a number of years ago I showed your father how to get rid of them as well." Richards chortled. "Course, that was after I showed him how to get them in the first place."

Titan stared. Richards sighed.

"Alright. How much do you know about the Dragon?"

"About as much as anyone, I guess," Titan said. "It was some kind of beast that terrorized the world a thousand years ago. The five kings from that time killed it."

Richards smirked. "Fairly accurate. Though the whole world is a bit of a stretch and I would have said 'ruled' rather than 'terrorized.' Sounds more human to me."

"More ... human?"

"Yes, human. A man, to be specific. Flesh, blood, two arms, two legs. The Dragon was a simple man with very un-simple gifts that made him more of a conquering tyrant than a proper king."

"I've never heard that before. Where did you hear it?"

"I didn't *hear* it. I was there."

Titan paused. "A thousand years ago."

"Mm-hmm," Richards said as he slid an egg from pan to plate. "And in case you're thinking it, know that you won't be the first to tell me that the years have been kind."

"And ... how?"

Richards stood and stretch his back. "I think the story from the beginning might shed a bit more light." He handed the plate to Titan. "If you'll allow it."

"Please," Titan said as he accepted the food.

"The Dragon was actually a man by the name of Yorth. Before he conquered the world, he was a treasure hunter of sorts. Looked for gold and trinkets and all that so he could sell them to those interested in antiques. He traveled extensively, being gone for weeks, sometimes months at a time. He would come back with the oddest things, smooth talk his way into the pockets of fools, and leave again. Always sold all of his wares, and he made a good living out of it.

"During one of his searches, he found something different, something special. Black stones, smooth and bright. He brought them back and decided that it was high time he kept something for himself. So, rather than sell them at the market, he brought them to me."

"So you actually knew him," Titan said.

"Yes," Richards said. "He was my brother." He held a finger to his lips, and Titan stifled his question. "Yes, I know, a thousand years ago. Impossible. Well, give me another few minutes and I'll see what I can do about that doubt of yours.

"Yorth came to me not because I was his brother, but because I was an apprentice of a talented alchemist. The man I worked under was obsessed with turning everything to gold, and as you might imagine, he failed miserably. But," Richards said, removing the pan again, "he did make another discovery. He figured out how to bond materials, no matter how different they were. He fused fabric to metal, wood to rock. Anything.

"As his apprentice, I paid close attention and had learned. Yorth asked a favor. He showed me the stones, and asked me to fuse them to a suit of armor. And so I did. In fact, I bonded one of the stones to that very sword you have there."

Titan looked at the sword, leaning against the wall. The black gem shone even in the dim light.

"I originally wanted to take several of the stones and break them into smaller pieces, but each stone only broke once. The stone in your sword split as you can see, creating semicircles. Beyond that, I couldn't so much as chip them. So, rather than creating many tiny stones, I took the halves and created matching pairs in Yorth's armor. The sword and its sheath. A pair of gloves. A helmet with a removable nose guard. Each stone pair would fit snuggly together when the armor was worn.

"Yorth was more than pleased when I was finished. After all, they were rather remarkable, if I may boast just a little. He first took the sword and, after donning it, turned and spread his arms for my approval. And, as he did so, wings spread from his back, black, leathery wings. The same wings you've now had a run in with. I must say, it scared the devil out of both of us.

"We calmed ourselves, and set to studying. The wings sprouted from the sheath, which had shorn straight through his leather vest and shirt and was sealed to his spine. Several more minutes of investigation brought the realization that he could control them. It was incredible to see, to feel the wind the first time he flapped them. Unfortunately for us, we didn't have a dear Uncle Richards to show us how to remove them, though in all actuality it was my idea that eventual got them off. Yorth hid for days until we tried reversing the movements that caused them. He immediately experimented with the other armor, and each brought new powers to him. His first movements after putting them on caused a reaction, and the reversal undid the binding."

Richards walked to a book shelf and selected a text. He flipped through the pages as he returned and gave it to Titan. Drawings, both of the armor and the movements. As Titan considered them, he recognized the prayers he had performed from childhood. Richards continued.

"The sword gave him wings, the breastplate covered him with armor, the helmet increased his senses a hundred-fold, the bracers gave him super-human strength, and the gloves allowed him to shoot fire from his hands. That last one was a fairly exhilarating discovery, as we were inside his house at the time."

Titan frowned, lowering the book. "The offerings."

"Yes," Richards said. "Each piece of armor required the two stones of its pair to be joined before functioning. Each king at your peace conferences was required to give up half of their power to ensure nothing happened while they gathered." He paused. "And, it would seem, Devvon found a way to sneak in both of his gloves."

Realization hit Titan. "The explosions," he whispered.

Richards nodded. "Devvon used the gloves to attack your father and the other kings. The other aides attacked you in order to secure the other halves of the pieces."

Titan stood. "We have to get them back."

"By this point, he has armor plating, can destroy at a distance, has the strength of a hundred men, and will hear you coming literally a mile away." Richards folded his arms. "Getting them back may pose something of a problem."

"So how do we stop him?" Titan asked.

"I'm still working on that part. Let me finish my story. So Yorth saw these new powers as a means to an end. Money, specifically. He began performing feats for audiences. He acquired quite a following, with fans coming from miles around to see him throw boulders and such. And it paid off. He made a mountain of wealth almost overnight.

"Unfortunately, Yorth told several close friends about the source of his powers, and rumors started to spread. Thieves started making grabs for the pieces, with some nearly succeeding. My brother became paranoid. He began wearing the armor day and night, keeping it bound to him. He became obsessed with the power he had gained. He stopped giving shows, pulled away from the world. When he got hungry, he would steal what he needed. And, as you may well guess, what he needed quickly became much more than food and water.

"Eventually he decided that the power he possessed gave him the right to rule." Richards finished his egg and returned the pan to its hook. "So began the reign of the Dragon. It was his stage name, and people remembered him well when he returned. He flew from village to village and demanded their allegiance. Some opposed him near the beginning. After making an example of those towns, there weren't many others who dared resist.

122

"But rather than build a castle, Yorth maintained his reclusive home in the mountains. He'd dug away a cave half way up a cliff wall. Impossible to climb up or down to it. He ruled as a demon from that perch for four years."

Titan stared. "You were really there."

"Yes. I was. In hiding, for the most part. Yorth knew I had made the armor for him, and feared I could unmake it or fuse more. He came back to silence me. My master was killed, as were his other two apprentices. I had run months before Yorth attacked. I knew him. When he reappeared, I knew it was only a matter of time."

"So ... how did the kings kill him?"

"Well, he was invincible in battle, but that didn't mean he wasn't without weakness."

"What weakness?"

"The same weakness that all men share." Richards pulled at his beard. "A woman."

*****

Felk felt like a fish swimming upriver. The throngs of people were oppressive, surging like some unstoppable force down the path. Deciding to take a break from the crowds to catch his breath, he ducked into the store to his left.

"Day to you, General."

"Morning, Tup." He took a seat at a small table and the old storekeeper shuffled over with a bottle. The man specialized in trinkets and oddities, but had a knack for finding good vintages as well. He set a small glass down in front of Felk and began to fill it.

"How's business?"

"Can't complain. Can't really boast, either, but it keeps me out of the streets at least."

Felk nodded, watching the said streets. "So many people," he said. "Amazing, isn't it?"

Tup snorted. "It's oppressive, you mean."

"More people means more business, doesn't it?"

"Not these type. These are refuges. They aren't interested in knickknacks. I've barely sold a dozen since they arrived."

"I'm sorry to hear it." Felk gulped down his drink. It burned pleasantly. "I'll buy the bottle."

"No you won't," the man said, re-filling the glass. "This one's on the house."

Felk raised an eyebrow. The old man was a friend, but a businessman first. He was firm when it came to his wares, particularly alcohol. "I don't mean to offend, but you've never offered me a free glass before."

Tup grunted and sat in an empty chair. "The way I see it, you deserve more than a drink." He glanced at Felk, then back out the window. "You forget, General. Everyone was required to be at the square."

Take care of them.

"Do you always let executioners drink for free?"

Tup snickered. "No offense to you either, but you'd make a lousy executioner. No flourish, no riling the crowd. Nah, the executioner that day was Devvon. You were just the axe."

Felk lowered his eyes to brown liquid. He picked up the glass and gently set it in front of Tup. "You see a lot for a simple storekeep."

Tup eyed the drink. "Not bad for being nearly blind." He lifted the glass and emptied it. "And I see more than that," he said, wiping his mouth with his sleeve.

"Oh?"

"Take a look at those young blokes out there. They have no respect, no honor. Too many of them, and the kingdom will collapse from within."

Felk looked out. "What makes you think they lack respect?"

"Just look at them. Extremes in every style, beards shaved in strips, designs carved into their arms." Tup huffed. "They don't respect themselves. After you lose self-respect, you start losing respect for everyone else. Only a matter of time."

The man was right. A group of youth were pushing past the window, their appearance anything but conventional. Felk didn't remember seeing such styles before his last battle. "I don't know if it's all that bad. Just a trend that will run itself dry before long."

"Mark my words, General. This kingdom will destroy itself from the inside out if we don't teach them respect." Tup saw Felk's smile and growled. "Maybe it's not just the younger generation that needs manners."

"Can I ask you another question?"

"Course, General."

"You called me ... the axe, rather than the executioner. Are you alone in that view?"

The old man scratched the stubble on his cheek. "I wouldn't think so. Most everybody knows you as a good man. Devvon's name was on the command that everyone be present. Two and two, General."

Felk nodded. "Thanks for the drink." He stood and stretched.

"Leaving so soon?"

"I'm afraid so. You take care of yourself, old man."

"Don't mind if I do."

Felk pushed the door open and joined the sea of bodies once again, headed toward the barracks. Dozens of patrols had been outside the city, combing the forest, and reports were due soon. As Felk walked, he noticed several more groups of men pushing the limits of what was socially acceptable. Devvon ruled with an iron fist, and was resented by many for it. Perhaps this new style was an unspoken push against his rule. But if that were the case, how long until these "rebels" took more extreme action?

Fantastic, Felk thought dryly. Between Devvon's lust for Felk's death, the vanishing bandits, and the potential rebellion brewing ...

He rounded the last corner to see a rider gallop through the gates. Dants and the other generals were already there waiting. Felk arrived as the soldier dismounted and handed over a rolled parchment.

Felk's stomach tightened.

NE – 0
NW – 0
W – 0
S – 0
BDTS – 0

CHAPTER 18

Adrianna's lonely procession dragged towards the front of the Temple of the West. Rows of onlookers to either side gawked, likely more at her dress than at her, while the high priest from the South stood behind the large, metal altar at the front of the church. The long train behind her had white stone woven into its green fabric, creating both beauty and significant weight. Each step was a struggle, making it all the more difficult to walk with poise.

Her advisors had recommended against holding the coronation in the west, but it seemed logical to Adrianna. While they hadn't made the announcement public, Jaron and her marriage would strip her of her citizenship. Why pretend that this coronation was anything but a formality? As soon as their engagement was widely known, the process of selecting a replacement for her in the South would begin. No, holding the coronation in the West was the best option.

The Southern priest stood in silence and waited for the gentle murmurs to stop. With his nose tilted into the air and hands folded neatly in front of him, he nodded condescendingly at Adrianna. *How does he manage to keep his nose up while nodding?* Adrianna looked down in hopes that he wouldn't see her irritation. She firmly believed that the Ragdons were ready and eager to help those who asked. That being said, she also believed that more times than not, ranking spiritual leaders more got in the way than helped the process.

Quiet ensued, and after an exaggerated pause, the old man squared his shoulders. He looked around the room, slowly. *Is he studying each face?* Adrianna thought. *Get on with it!* She wouldn't be queen for long, and she wasn't particularly eager for the responsibility, but the man's self-important air was insufferable and the dress she was wearing was designed for display, not breathing.

"My people," the priest said.

Your people? Adrianna asked silently.

"We are gathered to both despair and rejoice together. We despair at the loss of our great king. May the Ragdons keep him within their holy paradise for eternity as a just reward for his exemplary service to us." He paused, then looked down and smiled benevolently at Adrianna. "And we rejoice at the opportunity to see little Adrianna step forward to take on his responsibilities. May she grow quickly to fill the crown."

Adrianna's contempt boiled over into mental composition. *By royal decree, all present clergy are forthwith condemned, for excessive pomp, to be –*

"Princess Adrianna. Do you humbly swear to use your power to protect and provide for your people?"

Adrianna bowed her head. During the ceremony, only the priest was allowed to speak.

"And do you, Princess Adrianna, understand and accept the laws of the kingdom as they stand? Will you abide by them, allowing their power to supersede your own?"

Another bow.

"And do you swear before the Ragdons that you will subject yourself to their will, whatever the cost?"

I do.

The priest narrowed his eyes. He took a deep breath and raised himself to his full stature. He took another moment for quiet reflection.

Is he really considering whether my head bobs were sincere enough?

"Then ... may They keep you." A lesser priest approached, carrying the customary green pillow. The high priest lifted the diadem. He raised it above his head for all to see, and began to carefully, reverently, and particularly slowly, lower it. Adrianna watched the floor at her feet and counted off a full ten seconds before feeling both the metal of the crown and the weight of the kingdom rest on her.

"All hail Queen Adrianna!"

Cheers filled the hall, echoing off the painted ceiling far above. Adrianna turned and faced the crowd, most of which were not her subjects. Still they yelled their encouragement, seeing the South as a brother kingdom, just as Lexik and Alder had viewed each other.

She beamed and nodded her appreciation. Some in the audience bowed in return, but most were enjoying their rare opportunity to yell inside a church. She lugged her dress to the throne that awaited her opposite the priests, and with the assistance of several aids, negotiate the process of sitting down. The seat beside her was still awaiting its occupant, and the crowd hushed in anticipation as the high-nosed priest withdrew from the altar.

The doors at the rear of the chapel were carefully opened once again, and all eyes turned. Jaron stood beyond, stone faced, breastplate gleaming. The midnight blue cape hung resolutely from his shoulders, and the crowd whispered in excitement as he took his first steps into the room. He walked swiftly down the aisle, eyes firm on the altar before him, left hand on the hilt of his sword. Each footfall, with its accompanying clink, seemed to ripple wonder through the onlookers. Reaching his destination, Jaron dropped to a knee and bowed his head.

He looks ... regal, Adrianna realized. She had seen him in armor before, had seen him serious, determined. Yet something had changed. The crowd noticed it as well, the whisperings growing to murmurs. Awe shone in their faces as they regarded the man who would be their king. He held their devotion, even before being crowned. Adrianna smiled. Jaron would make an excellent king.

The second high priest in attendance rose from his chair and shuffled to the altar. Priest Wesling's eyes glistened, and his smile reminded Adrianna of a grandfather.

Adrianna's proximity just permitted her to make out his whisper. "A day neither of us thought would happen."

Jaron kept his eyes downcast. "I am truly sorry that it has."

"As am I." A tear escaped down the old man's cheek. He raised his head and addressed the congregation. "My people. A tragedy beyond words has struck down our king, and" his voice cracked, "his heir. And so it is with both grief and joy that I present General Jaron. I could give personal testament as to his worth and devotion, but to what end? You know this man. He has been our general, and is now our king. Will you have him?"

The crowd bowed.

Wesling looked back at Jaron. "As will I," he said quietly. "May you reign long and well." He stood up straighter than Adrianna would have thought possible. Raising his hands, he pushed them outward in a prayer for Power, swept them to either side for Enlightenment, clapped his forearms together for Strength, touched his forehead for Vision, and finally rested them over his heart for Protection. Despite his age, the motions were smooth and beautiful. The efforts of an old man to keep polished that which he held most dear, his connection to his gods.

"Your king!" he yelled.

The crowd roared once again, leaping to their feet. Many shed tears, the memory of losing their beloved king and prince creating a tempest of emotion with the joy at having another, equally honorable man take the throne.

Wesling placed a single ring of gold atop Jaron's head, and the crowned king of the West turned to the congregation and beamed. Jaron allowed them to cheer for several moments before he turned to take his own throne beside that of Adrianna. "Your majesty," he greeted her.

She shook her head. "We are of equal rank, now. And if we are to live happily beneath the same roof, I would prefer you didn't address me by my title."

He chuckled. "Very well, my love."

She tensed. *What else would you have him call you?* "That's better."

As soon as Jaron had sat, the small army of priests could bear no more and pounced like robbed lions, pleading with the cheerers to be quiet. The crowd was soon formally dismissed and began to disperse, being shushed the whole way out. The pair of high priests approached again.

"Congratulations, my children," the southern priest said, head held higher than ever. "An excellent ceremony, in my opinion. One the people won't soon forget. I think doing it here in the west was perhaps a good idea."

"Indeed," said Wesling. He reached and took Jaron's extended hand as the southern priest excused himself.

"My king."

Jaron shook his head. "Your friend, first."

The priest nodded. "You have more devotion within you than a dozen followers combined." He paused. "Don't let the throne change you."

Jaron smiled. "You think that it will?"

"I have seen more than one king loose his faith after rising to the position."

"Not Lexik, though," Jaron said. Wesling hesitated. Jaron raised an eyebrow. "He spoke always of the Ragdons, of the importance of prayer."

"True," Wesling said. "It just seemed more ... strategic, rather than believing." He still held Jaron's hand. "Do this one thing for me. Never lose faith."

The king nodded. "You have my word."

"I believe you." He smiled fondly. "So, when are you two announcing your engagement?"

Jaron and Adrianna glanced at one another. "We hadn't really discussed it."

"Might I give a suggestion?" the priest asked.

"Of course."

"Send out a proclamation today."

Adrianna started. "Today? Right after the coronation?"

"Wait too long," Wesling said with a shrug, "and people won't believe you when you say it happened before. And most people in the city are feeling exceptionally loyal at the moment. I think they would accept the idea willingly."

Adrianna opened her mouth, but no answer came. Wesling clicked his tongue. "No other arguments, then?"

Adrianna looked to Jaron. He shook his head slowly, finally shrugging. "I suppose not."

"Good," the old man said, turning. "Allow me to announce it. The church's approval can only help." He didn't wait for a response, exiting through a hallway to the side.

Adrianna stared at the closing door. It was happening. There was no going back after the kingdom knew, and word would travel quickly back to her own people in the south. She turned to find a smirk on Jaron's face. "What?"

"You can't fault that man for his earnestness."

Adrianna shook her head, smiling. "No, I suppose one can't. But today? Isn't that a bit soon?"

"Wesling's logic is solid. The sooner the better."

Adrianna let out a slow breath. "Well, alright then. Here we go."

*****

"To the inferno with you, demon!"

Devvon growled, then raised his left hand. The large oak just beside the cottage exploded in flames. Devvon moved his aim slightly, sighting the building between his fingers. "Speak!"

The leathery fisherman watched with wide eyes as the trees around his home crackled in the fire. To his credit, he didn't run. Love for his family, forced into the boat and onto the lake by Devvon's men, was apparently stronger than his fear.

"It wasn't us what brought it here. It appeared, crawled out of the water onto the shore. We are god-fearing folk, pray to the Ragdons night and day, we do!"

Devvon rolled his metallic eyes. "And I'm sure they listen ever so carefully. What did this water creature look like?"

"Some sort of bat. Huge, it was. It started speaking gibberish, cursing us, but we chased it off."

So the boy *had* fled downstream. Devvon's intelligence amazed even himself at times. "Which way did he go?"

The fisherman glanced back and forth between his home and his family. A limb fell and landed only a handful of feet from the house. Devvon's men kept their bows trained on the boat, floating several dozen feet off-shore. "Took to the air. Flew in circles, laying an invisible spell. Brought you down on us, it did."

Devvon raised an eyebrow. Circles? "Which way did he go?" he repeated.

The fisherman raised a shaking finger. "There," he said, pointing southwest. "Went straight that way. We watched him, made sure he was gone for good."

Devvon turned and looked. The sky was empty. In the distance he could pick out the mountain range that ran directly between Lexik's and Alder's kingdoms. If the fisherman was to be trusted, the boy would be off-course. He would end up miles away from his kingdom. There was nothing out there but –

Of course. Devvon smirked. "Good."

"Please. That's all I know. Now leave us be, fiend."

"As you wish, master fisherman." Devvon crossed to his horse, metal crunching on gravel with each step. He swung into his saddle and signaled for his men to follow. "'Fiend', however, is not quite accurate. You may call me 'God'."

Devvon raised his hand again. The cottage was torn apart by the impact, throwing stone and wood backward into the forest beyond. The man screamed in horror, and was matched by the wails of those in the boat. Devvon nudged his horse forward into a gallop, his men trailing behind him. The captain pulled up beside him.

"Where to, my lord?"

Devvon smiled. "We're going to pay an old friend a visit. A very old friend."

CHAPTER 19

"A woman," Titan repeated.

"Yes. Don't you find yourself at your weakest when the woman you love is near?"

Adrianna's face flashed into his mind. The glint of her eyes, the shape of her mouth, the curve of her jaw, as vivid as if she were in the room. He pushed her from thought. "I'm not in love."

"Then why the pause?" Richards said with a wink. "I may not know who she is, but a thousand years has taught me to recognize the signs."

"How was a woman Yorth's weakness?"

"You're changing the subject."

"I'm getting us back on topic."

"Ah," Richards said, grinning. "Well, one of the towns he came to conquer was home to a happily married couple, Jag and Rochelle. They were young and very much in love. Rochelle was strikingly beautiful, Jag was as honorable a man as they come. Everyone agreed they deserved each other. Yorth arrived, saw Rochelle, and as far as I can tell was immediately smitten. He had already taken the town's allegiance, but returned the next day and demanded her as well. He gave the village one month to deliver her or face destruction.

"Jag was infuriated. He refused to let her go, and attempted to convince her that they should run and hide. Rochelle hated the idea as well, but as with all women, she kept her head about her. She saw the danger for her friends and family. She also saw an opportunity, and tried to convince Jag. He wasn't ready to accept any idea that involved losing her, and so Rochelle ran. She went to Yorth herself, hoping that Jag would follow the plan she had laid out for him."

"What was the plan?" Titan asked.

"First rule of story-telling: never give away the ending," Richards replied. "When Jag found she had gone, he had no other option but to follow. He rode from village to village, recruiting men. Many had already lost much to Yorth. Jag instructed each man that, when a certain day came, they were to march, traveling completely alone where possible. No gathering, no training. Nothing for Yorth to suspect.

"It was several months before the date Rochelle had set arrived. When it did, men from miles around marched. In the dead of night they came to the base of the cliff, with Yorth and Rochelle sleeping above. Miraculously, Rochelle had used those months to gain Yorth's trust and convince him to remove articles to be human with her. That night, she took the helmet and the breastplate and moved to the edge of the cave. We'll never know exactly what happened, but I would guess Yorth awoke and found her about to betray him. Watching from below, Jag saw the flames smash against her and throw her into the night. Her body fell the hundreds of feet into the army's midst.

"Despite Rochelle's sacrifice, Yorth was still unreachable. Even without his helmet, he could easily see the army below. From the safety of his perch, he unleashed his anger on the forest below, shot after shot, until everything burned. The army was destroyed, men burning and choking to death in a matter of minutes. Less than two dozen men survived the night, with Jag among them.

"When dawn came, the fire had burned itself out. Yorth descended and began searching for his missing armor. As he sifted through the ash, Jag and the others rushed to kill him. Yorth quickly fired off a rapid succession of shots, killing most of the remaining men, then lifted into the air to seek the safety of his cave once again. Jag and the others fired arrow after arrow into the sky, some of which found their mark. Half-way up the cliff, my brother succumbed to his wounds and fell back to the ground." Richards let out a long, slow breath. "Over a thousand answered Jag's call and surrounded the mountain that night. Six survived."

"Six?" Titan asked. "I thought the Dragon was killed by the five kings."

"He was," Richard replied. "Five of the six men became kings. The sixth became a hermit."

Titan's eyes widened. "You ..."

"Yes. I helped kill my brother. Or rather, the man who had once been my brother. The six of us took the armor, but we feared keeping it together. We split the pieces between ourselves and vowed never to let any of them be used ever again.

"The land was divided into five kingdoms. The eastern kingdom was given to Jag, along with the gloves that had killed his wife. He hated them for it and never put them on. The northeast kingdom was given the breastplate, the northwest was given the helmet, the western the sword which you now possess, and the south was given the bracers."

"Why weren't you given a piece?" Titan asked. "You were there as well."

Richards smiled. "I *was* given a piece." He held up his right hand. On the middle finger sat two gold bands, each with a small black gemstone. The rings sat side by side, the gems fitting snugly together. "These rings were the last piece. It grants the wearer invulnerability to time and disease. I don't age, and I don't get sick while I wear them. And to answer your next question, it would be a bit suspicious if a king outlived his subjects' great-great-grandchildren, so no, I wasn't given a kingdom beyond these four walls. At the time I was known as Leth, but when I left mortality behind I left my old name behind as well. As the man responsible for creating the armor in the first place, I took it upon myself to warn those who would come after, the descendants of the first kings who hadn't seen and hence couldn't appreciate the danger their power could present."

Titan stared at Richards. "Aren't you lonely?"

"I was," Richards said with a shrug. "But loneliness wore off after the first few hundred years. During that time I married several times, more for some company than anything else, but outliving my wives only made the situation worse."

"I'm sorry."

"Me too," Richards replied. "But it's been over seven hundred years since the last passed away. While I still miss each of them, I've had plenty of time to resolve my emotions." He stood. "Well, that's the basics of the legend of the Dragon. And unfortunately, even with the arrival of a friend, the responsibilities of a man living off of the land must be taken care of. I'm going for some firewood." He grabbed an ax that was leaning against the wall.

"I thought you said you could live forever. Why get firewood if you can't die?"

"Didn't say I couldn't die. I said I didn't get old or sick. Freezing or starving to death is still perfectly possible. Even if it weren't, I would still want to be fed and comfortable. Care to join me?"

"Of course." Titan set his side bag against the wall and stood.

"Now what I don't understand," said Richards as he opened the door and stepped aside to let Titan through, "is how you can think of anything more important to carry around than food."

"What do you mean?" Titan asked as he crossed the room.

"Your bag there. You said you hadn't eaten for two days. So either you forgot about your food or you didn't pack any. Either way, you're dim witted. Apologies for speaking my mind."

138

Titan looked back at the bag. "Oh, that's not mine. I was carrying it for King Alder."

"What's in it?"

"No idea. He said it was something valuable to him. He didn't want to take it into ..." Titan trailed off.

"Is that so?" Richards asked, rubbing his chin. He crossed to where the bag lay and picked it up. "Something tells me this isn't a brick of gold." He held the bag out to Titan, who returned and accepted it. "Seeing as how Alder's dead, I don't think there's anything wrong with taking a gander."

Titan stared at the satchel in his hand. He undid the clasp, then lifter the leather flap and let it fall open. After a glance at a bemused Richards, he carefully turned the bag upside down, spilling the contents onto the bed beside him.

Richards chuckled. "Those, my boy, I have seen before."

Titan slowly picked one up. *Bracers.* He turned the worn leather over in his hand. The black stone gleamed dully from the light filtering through the dirty window. Its match was visible on the other bracer. "Ragdons. Why would Alder give these to me?"

"Alder and your father were both intelligent men. They talked to me several times about their concerns with Devvon. Looks like they were taking precautionary measures."

"But I saw Alder leave a bracer on the table as an offering." Titan was at a loss.

"Just like you saw your father leave a sword? Just like Devvon left a glove?"

Titan shook his head. "Fakes," he said flatly.

"It would appear so. All three of them. Devvon wanted to sneak his armor in. Alder and your father wanted to leave them out."

"But I still don't understand why? If they thought Devvon was going to try something, they should have kept their greatest weapons with them."

"Two problems," Richards said as he held up his fingers. "First and foremost, Lexik and Alder were honest men. They said they were going to leave their armor out, and so they did.

Second, the object wasn't to fight. It was to make sure that Devvon didn't get too much power when he played his hand. They knew they might be sacrificing their own lives, but Devvon's chances of success were greatly diminished if the sword and bracers weren't within arm's reach. Even if you died in the process, what would be the odds that Devvon would try *your* sword and satchel? My guess is that they would have laid with your body for quite some time."

Titan picked up the other bracer and examined it. *Three out of five kings lied. Are all kings liars, then?* He turned in response to a laugh from Richards. "What?"

"Oh, a little something that I just realized. Devvon is likely even angrier than you might suspect at present."

"Why is that?"

Richards stifled his laughter. "There's something about the armor that I didn't mention. It's used circularly."

Titan stared at him. "That makes no sense."

"Here," Richards said as he picked up the book he had given Titan several minutes prior. He started flipping through the pages. "As we tried the armor, we did so one at a time, just like I told you. But when we tried to use them together, we noticed an unusual pattern. Certain items couldn't be used together unless others were also being used."

"I still don't understand."

"Look." Richards stopped flipping and handed the book back to Titan. "Imagine all the pieces on a circle. Pieces can only be used if they are next to each other. If there's a piece between that isn't being used, then the two pieces won't work simultaneously." The word "Sword" was written at the top, then "Breastplate" below and to the right, "Gloves" just below, "Ring" centered at the bottom of the paper, "Bracers" above and to the left, and "Helmet" just above that.

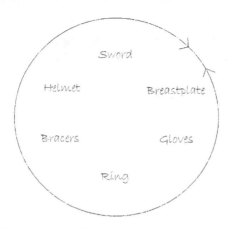

Richards watched Titan's face as he studied the page. Titan shook his head. Richards sighed. "I won't call you dense, but only out of respect for your father. Here. Suppose that a person was using the sword, flying about, and wanted to use the gloves to rain destruction on their enemies from above."

"Like Yorth from his lair."

"Ah, but there he wasn't flying. When he was using his wings, trying to fly back up there, he didn't shoot fire. That's because he was no longer using the breastplate. While using the wings, he couldn't shoot with the gloves without first activating the breastplate. If he was using the bracers, he'd have to use the helmet before he could use the sword. While using the items together, no gaps allowed. Circular."

Titan slowly nodded his head. "Right. So Devvon is particularly angry ... because he doesn't have the missing items to complete the circle."

Richard beamed. "Even more than that, he can't use the helmet at all without leaving himself vulnerable. He'd have to deactivate both the breastplate and the gloves."

Titan scratched his forehead. "But that's increased senses, right? Perception? I don't see how that helps all that much, he's still impossible to kill and shoots balls of flame."

Richards shrugged. "At least he won't hear your screams quite so well."

"That's comforting."

"You know, if you spent half as much time trying to think of a solution as you do making witty comments, we'd already have this problem licked. Now, what would you do if you were in Devvon's position?"

Titan looked back at the paper. "Well, I'd probably use the breastplate all the time and forego the helmet's power."

"As would I. He'll likely still wear it to keep it close, but won't use it. What would your next move be?"

Titan thought for a moment, realization quickly hitting him. "I would find the other pieces."

"Right you are, my boy."

"I guess it's a good thing he doesn't know where I am."

"Agreed," Richards said, "but unfortunately he does know where I am."

Titan started. "How?"

"What do you mean, how? I brought him here to show him how to use his gloves. He drops by on occasion to visit or ask questions. At least he used to. He's lost a lot of his gratitude over recent years."

"You trained him? But he's ..." Titan couldn't come up with a good word.

"The bad guy?" Richards supplied. "He wasn't always like he is now. And even if he was, it's my duty to keep the kings aware of the past. All of the kings, even if I don't agree with how they rule their people."

"Then he wouldn't dare kill you. You have to stay alive."

"Why?"

"To tell the kings ..." Titan trailed off.

Richards nodded. "To tell the kings exactly what will happen if all of the pieces are possessed by a single man. Turns out not all of them see that as a bad thing."

Titan stuffed the bracers back in the bag. "We've got to get you out of here."

Richards set the ax over his shoulder and made his way to the door again. "There's no hurry, He won't arrive for a least three or four days yet."

"But why wait? We need to put as much distance between us and him as possible. That means we leave now."

"Not necessarily. We have an advantage."

"And what advantage is that?"

Richards smirked, then winked. "Your wings, of course."

CHAPTER 20

Felk strode across the field, approaching the other three generals. They stood in a circle, conversing, and opened a space as Felk arrived. Each nodded a welcome. Felk returned the gesture, noticing the letter being read to his right. "Good morning, gentlemen. What's going on?"

"It would appear that our focus is going to shift."

"What do you mean?"

Felk received the paper in place of a response. "This just arrived from the Emperor."

"Emperor?" Felk said as he accepted the page. He read through the short letter and looked up. "Is he serious?"

"Very," said the general across from him. "I spoke with him about certain plans he had before he left. He means to conquer."

"But we're needed here!" Felk said. "The bandits could attack any day!"

"They haven't been sighted since that first night. And Devvon has stated our numbers will increase dramatically."

Felk's stomach twisted. "How?"

"With this," Dants said to Felk's left. He held out a second piece of paper. "Devvon's dropping the recruitment age and asking for volunteers from the older generation."

Felk accepted the page and scanned it. "Fifteen!" he exclaimed. "They'll be barely able to lift a sword, let alone swing one."

The general to his right grunted. "Agreed. But we've vowed to uphold him and his decisions." He beckoned for an aid. "Soldier, have this letter copied and posted by morning. With all of the refuges still in the city, it'll take a lot less time to get word out. Add a deadline to the bottom that all recruits are to report by sundown tomorrow."

"Yes, sir."

The gathering broke, and the three other generals dispersed, calling out orders. Felk stayed, looking back and forth between the two papers clutched in his hands. *Conquer at all costs.* Felk had been in command long enough to know that Devvon's promise to hold back the youth from the front lines was a blatant lie. He would force them to fight with only a few days' training, and would use their blood to claim his victory.

And even with increased numbers, a fifth of the army couldn't withstand a determined attack from the bandits. Felk didn't know how many young men were available for recruitment, but he guessed the number wasn't in the tens of thousands. Those asked to volunteer had already honored the law with their own military service and wouldn't readily join again.

Devvon was insane. And the sons of his people would die for it.

*****

A knock sounded at the door. Three times, slow, and hard. Adrianna knew before she moved that the inevitable was happening. She rose and crossed the room. Since her engagement, she had been visited and congratulated by countless people of nearly as many ranks. It appeared everyone in the kingdom had come to wish her luck. Everyone but her next visitor.

She pressed her dress, put on a smile, and swung the door open. "Hello, Reon."

"Wench," he replied curtly, pushing passed her.

"Reon, I know –"

"How much I must hate you?" he ventured as he sat himself in the chair she had just left. He put his feet up on her desk. "Then inform me. How much do I hate you?"

Adrianna hesitated. Reon brushed everything off, from insults to injuries. This was a side of him she didn't remember ever seeing before. "... a lot?"

"A lousy description, but I'll take it for the time being. And why, dear queen, would I have reason to hate you 'a lot'?" He tapped a finger on the wood, eyes boring into her.

Adrianna sighed, leaning against the desk. She looked down at her hands. "Because I'm getting married?"

Reon shook his head. "We all knew it was an inevitable fate." He glared at her. "What about *Titan*?"

Adrianna met his gaze. "What about him?" She struggled to keep her voice even.

Reon didn't waver. "Two days. You waited two days before you were engaged to the next guy in line."

"Reon, it was the only way."

"Ragdons."

Adrianna flushed. She shoved his feet off the desk. "What should it matter, anyways? We were never going to be together! Who cares if it's two days or two years?"

Reon leaned forward. "I care," he said quietly. He looked down at his feet. "Titan deserved twenty years. Even if it was impossible."

Adrianna felt shame pour through her. "I ... Reon, I didn't mean to –"

"Yes you did, Adrianna."

She stood and turned to face him square on, fists clenched. "You have no idea what the last few days have been like for me!"

"No," Reon said, rising. "I only know what they've been like for *me*. And I'd rather go through the inferno." He pointed a finger in her face. "You professed to love him, but you seem fine. Your majesty, I *did* love him! Like a brother I loved him! I would have given my life for him! And Ragdons help me if I don't speak my mind to the woman who dares to dishonor him!"

"Dishonor!? What dishonor!? It wasn't *legal!*"

"And if it was, would you have done differently?"

Adrianna hesitated. "I don't know," she conceded.

"Wench," he spat again.

"So what am I supposed to do? Die alone because the man I loved but could never have died?" She wiped a tear from her cheek. "Die an old maid because I lost a friend that I've had since before I can remember?"

Reon shook his head. "No. As far as I care, you can die a *young* maid." He pushed passed her and stormed across the room to the door. He turned back. "And you haven't lost one friend of countless years, your majesty. You've lost two." The door slammed behind him.

Shaking, she lowered herself into the chair. Sobs of anger and frustration poured out, and through their persistence the fury melted back into despair. She was back in the garden, having her chest ripped open once again. Reon was wrong. She *had* loved Titan. More than her own family, more than her own life. How dare he suggest otherwise? *I hate you, Reon.*

She repeated the phrase over and over in her mind, willing it to be the truth. Reon was wrong, he was bitter and misjudged her. She pushed herself to her feet and stumbled to the bed. The blankets caught her as she fell, and she gladly pulled them around her. Better to sleep. Better to allow her own mind to trick her, numb her to the pain. Better to dream that the reality she faced was a forgotten nightmare.

Yet sleep evaded her for just long enough to allow her a final realization. She didn't hate Reon. She was angry, but not because of his words. She yearned for him to return, to tell her she was right, her decisions were good. No, the anger she felt was at herself. Reon's accusations were nothing compared to her own self-condemnations. She was angry because, unlike herself, Reon had proved his loyalty to Titan.

*****

The horse whinnied in pain as Devvon drove his heels deeper into its sides. Another town was just ahead; the company could trade out mounts again there. The peasants in the last village had needed encouragement, and Devvon hoped the same wouldn't be true in the next. Killing a man wasn't a problem, it was the time it took to bridle his horse after he was dead. Giving a direct command and being obeyed was much more efficient. And time was the issue at hand.

Every village reported the demon flying overhead, though descriptions were subject to the given breed of insanity of each group. The boy was flying straight, unwavering. He might as well have left painted arrows in the dirt. *As much an imbecile as his father.*

Yet … Lexik had outsmarted Devvon. He'd switched out his offering first. He'd made a fool out of a god. Devvon gritted his teeth and kicked the horse again. Five days' worth of travel had taken just three. Given their pace, the mountains loomed closer by the minute. By sunset tomorrow they would arrive on the hermit's front step. The "old" man would get what had been coming to him for a millennium. Titan would pay for his impudence. And Devvon's birth rite would finally be restored.

CHAPTER 21

"Again." Richards wiped juice from his chin as he munched. "Wait just a bit longer this time."

Titan nodded, took a deep breath, and leapt from the top of the tree. He hurtled towards the ground. Pushing off the moment for as long as his nerves would let him, he gave a fierce pulse with his wings just before hitting, and landed heavily. He stumbled several steps before regaining his balance.

"Landing is probably one of the techniques you'll most want to master," Richards said as he stood from his seat and crossed toward Titan. "A nasty landing kind of impairs your ability to take off again."

"It's harder than it looks," Titan said with a smile. "I've watched birds land for years and never thought twice about it."

"Birds have the advantages of weighing almost nothing and living their entire lives in the air," Richards replied. "Let's do it again."

Titan shook his head. "I need to breath. I must have climbed that tree more than twenty times already."

"You're free to fly back to the top."

"We tried that once, remember?"

Richards laughed. "That I do. Alright, time to try out the bracers."

Titan started. "You want me to actually use them?"

"Why wouldn't I? You don't think you'll be able to defeat an invincible man with a pair of wings alone, do you?"

"Well, no, but I thought the plan was … " Titan scratched his cheek. "Do we have a plan?"

"Not yet, but whatever it is it won't hurt to add a little strength to the mix." Richards held out the bracers. "Put them on."

Sighing in resignation, Titan accepted the pair and began tugging at the lacing.

"I don't think I've ever known an adolescent boy that regretted being strong."

"I just thought the whole point of your being alive was to not let any one person have more than one of these."

"See that's your problem," Richards said as he folded his arms. "You're so good you don't know when to be bad in order to achieve the greater good."

"Bad to bring about the greater good? When has that ever worked?"

"Rochelle lied to Yorth."

Titan slid his arm into the leather and began to tighten. "Her story didn't exactly end well."

"But you can't argue it didn't benefit humanity." Richards watched like a brooding mother as Titan pulled the laces on his second arm. Once finished, the prince flexed his arms, feeling the animal hide pull against his skin. He looked up and nodded at his mentor.

"Ready?"

"Ready."

"Good. Pray for Strength."

Titan raised his hands. "I hate this, you know."

"Don't, we've been through this. The keys to unlocking the power had to be remembered somehow. We couldn't very well write an instruction book and leave it lying around for someone to find." After a moment, Richards chuckled, but waved Titan's interest away before he could ask.

"But inventing a higher power? Hundreds of thousands of people look to the Ragdons for help. They would die defending their religion, their gods. It's the one thing that pretty much everyone in the five kingdoms agrees on. Meanwhile, we've been lying to them all this time, telling them there's something more when there's nothing.

"The Ragdons were created to perpetuate what have come to be known as the 'prayers,' yes. But that doesn't mean there's nothing there."

"Oh? What then?"

Richards shrugged. "Somebody had to originally create the six stones. Somebody with more power than you or I. Is that not the definition of deity? A higher power?"

Titan sighed. "I really believed, you know. I always thought the Ragdons and their power created our societies."

"Interestingly enough," Richards replied with a wry smile, "the opposite is truer. Our society, ruled by men possessing the armor, created the Ragdons." Richards clapped his hands. "Now, let's see what you can do. Pray for Strength."

Titan nodded and raised both arms. He placed his forearms together, careful to let the triangular stone on the left fit between the two triangles on the right. He closed his eyes, pulled them out and to the side, and waited for the surge or strength.

None came. He cracked an eye, glancing at his arms. He lowered this arms and looked to Richards. "Did I do something wrong?"

"I don't think so. Looked good to me."

"But I don't feel any stronger."

"When you wear the wings, do you feel their weight?"

Titan remembered the night at the tower, swimming across the lake, dragging himself onto the beach. "No, I guess I don't."

"Then not feeling stronger fits the pattern. Let's see if we can't *prove* your strength." Richards walked to the fallen tree he had been giving flight instructions from and patted the bark. "My view from here isn't nearly the angle I need for proper tutoring. Please move this tree for me."

Titan didn't move. The trunk was some forty feet long and over two feet think in diameter. "I'm that strong?"

"Don't get cocky thinking this is you. But yes, the bracers are that strong. Remember, Yorth used to lift and throw boulders for money."

Titan shrugged and crossed to the tree. He squatted and slide his arms as far under as they would go, then shifted his feet back and forth to firm up his stance.

"Easy does it," Richards murmured. He took a step back.

The bark was rough against Titan's hand. Taking three quick breathes, he forced his legs straight, the tree pulling from the ground like an enormous sliver being torn from the world. The wood left his hands as he came fully upright and continued upward, peaking some thirty feet above the ground. Titan yelp and dove backwards as the timber came crashing back to the ground. The earth shook as it hit, limbs flying in various directions.

Titan stared, breathing heavily. "Ragdons."

"Yes," Richards chuckled as he reached a hand down to Titan. He immediately jerked back. "On second thought, why don't you help yourself up. You'd likely rip my arm from its socket."

Titan nodded and gently pushed himself to his knees, then feet. He was uninjured, but felt as though he should be. When he looked up, Richards smiled, then nodded back to the tree. "Again. This time, try to bring on the strength a little slower. Just lift the tree, don't throw it."

Titan turned. He gingerly stepped up. "Now that I know I can do it, I'm a little less sure about this idea."

"I would say that a healthy fear of power is a good thing."

Titan stooped and carefully wrapped his arms around the trunk, his hands not touching on the opposite side. He planted his feet beneath him again. He began to stand as slowly as he could and was rewarded with the snapping of twigs and branches. He continued until he was fully upright, paused, then lifted the tree over his head. "I can barely feel it," he breathed.

"That's because it's not your strength. You don't get tired from the wings because they aren't a part of you, just as this strength isn't a part of you either. You are directing power. It is not a part of you, but an asset."

"So I can lift as much as I want without tiring?"

"Yes and no," Richards replied. "The bracers have their limits as to weight, but when you cross that line you simply won't be able to lift. Repeated use isn't a problem, the bracers aren't human like us so they don't get tired. They have their maximum weight, but other than that, they're limitless."

Titan looked up at the tree above his head. "I could get used to this kind of strength."

"Yes, you could. In fact, the hope is that you will. The bracers are tricky, in that you will have to learn to use a different amount of strength than you would expect in order to do things. It's like learning to use a different set of limbs. It will take some time."

"Time we don't have."

"Right."

Titan scanned the clearing. "So where do you want this?"

"Over there's fine. I'll have the next man who receives the bracers bring it back over here in fifty or sixty years if I don't like it."

Titan laughed. He drew his arms back, then threw the tree in the indicated direction. The massive projectile shot past its goal and crashed into the forest beyond, shattering and knocking over several more. "Uh ... whoops?"

Richards waved as he tromped across the meadow. "How do you think this clearing came to be in the first place?" He came to one of the newly fallen trees, brushed aside some dirt, and sat down. "Now thank Strength."

Titan took a breath, then reversed the prayer he had performed minutes prior. "Good," Richards said. "Now trigger them without the prayer."

Titan obeyed. The morning after Titan's arrival, Richards had explained that the prayers were the initial binders. After a piece of armor had been bound the first time to a person, that person could trigger its use simply by willing it to be so. Titan walked to a boulder at the edge of the clearing, placed a palm against the cool stone, and gave it a gently shove. The boulder crashed to its side.

"And off again," Richards commanded. Titan obliged, then pushed hard against the boulder with both hands to prove as much to himself as to Richards that the bracers weren't active.

"Very good," Richards said with a smile. "Now that we've established that you're extremely strong, we've removed all your lazy excuses. Let's get you up that tree again."

*****

Felk watched the mass of men slowly calm and form lines before him. He stood patiently, aware that while a soldier would never be excused for how long the process took, these were not soldiers. Not yet.

They needed training. Much more training than they would receive with Devvon's looming command to march almost immediately. As Felk scanned the crowed, waiting for the gentle rumble to die down, he noted the disparities. There were boys, some with grins, others without. There was the occasional man who was quick to attention, clean shaven, scars visible on the faces of the nearest handful. And then there were the rest, those who took the longest to quiet. Men who had either been out of the army for too long or who hadn't been disciplined while enlisted. These were the majority of the volunteers.

It would fall to the sergeants and the captains to do the actual training, but Felk had another purpose. Outside of battle, a general's charge was to inspire. To lead. Before him stood one of four groups that were gather today, each headed by its own general. Felk's trained eye did a quick estimate. His group had nearly somewhere near sixty thousand.

How could Devvon have known so many would volunteer? Felk wondered in amazement. Within minutes of the announcement being posted, men and poured in through the streets. Lines formed and men stood for hours to renew their enlistments. The idea of conquering the other four kingdoms had appeared impossible when the letter had arrived, ridiculous even. But with the number that had stepped forward for the cause, it now felt all but inevitable.

Perhaps I was wrong, Felk thought. *Perhaps Devvon is more aware of his people than I thought. Perhaps ... he really can pull this off.* Felk felt no desire to shed blood, but he wouldn't pass an opportunity to place the kingdoms under a single banner. Hidden or not, the bandits would be driven before a unified army and people. But even if Felk couldn't see a better world on the other side of this crusade, he understood himself well enough to know he would obey regardless. He was sworn to Devvon, and his honor wouldn't allow him to waiver.

Felk waited atop the wooden platform, hands clasped behind him, until the last of the conversations were put to silence by the glares of their neighbors. He let the quiet sit for a moment. The calm before the storm.

"Soldiers," he yelled.

"General," came the unified reply from too few. Others realized their missed opportunity and tried shouting it out late. Felk waited until the crowd quieted again.

"My brothers! Welcome to the greatest army ever to exist! With the addition of you to our ranks, we now stand supreme." Scattered cheers broke out, but Felk raised a hand. "We are in a position of power. We have within our reach the most momentous event to happen in a millennium. The reunification of the world!"

Felk didn't attempt to silence the men as they cried out in unison. He looked out at them. He studied individual faces. If these men were going to fight for him, he wanted to be sure that he knew who they were. As he looked from man to man, he noticed that the old shopkeeper's observances were true. The majority of the men before him had some extreme style of one sort or another. *But he's wrong,* Felk thought as the noise died down, *because they are here. We are united.*

"My men! You are here to wage war, and so we shall. But let us not forget the purpose of this war. We are uniting, not destroying. Men will die. But let us remember that whether one of ours falls or one of theirs falls, at the end of the conflict it is the same. The united world will stand one good man less. Let us remember that. Let us kill only with purpose, never with rage.

"We have one week before we march to the west. One week for you to learn a lifetime of combat training. Train hard, men! Obey your commanders! And in seven days, march with me!"

The men broke into cheers again as Felk stepped back. *Seven days,* he thought as he stepped off the platform and looked back into the faces of those yelling. His admiration for them grew as he pondered the true potential of this army. *Seven days until we can stop the skirmishes with the other kingdoms and focus on ridding the world of the true enemy.*

*****

"I'm going to miss this," Jaron said softly as they walked passed a line of soldiers.

"Commanding?" Adrianna asked.

"In part, yes. But more just being with the men."

"You can still be with them," Adrianna said with a smile. "Your king, after all. You can do whatever you want."

Jaron smiled at her. "I can, but I shouldn't. So I won't. I'm needed for other things now."

Adrianna nodded. "An occasional break to come down and visit won't ruin the kingdom, though."

"True," he conceded.

A passing group of soldiers saluted in respect to their new king. Adrianna could see loyalty in every look, every gesture. These men had seen Jaron at their head and had grown to trust him and his orders implicitly. Men that would follow him to the death.

Why is it the leaders of the West gain such devotion from their first day in command? She wondered silently.

"I would give my life for any one of these men," Jaron said, as if answering her unspoken question. "These are good men."

"You *are* giving your life for them," Adrianna countered. "You're just doing it by living instead of dying for them."

"My liege," a soldier saluted as Jaron approached.

"General," Jaron replied, saluting in return.

"Several of the men have seen you here and were wondering..." the general tried to hide a smile, "if becoming a ruler has gotten to you at all."

"Gotten to me?"

"They say that perhaps ... it has made you soft."

Jaron smirked. "Which men?"

The general shrugged, chuckling. "It has just been on their minds."

"Well, we can't have the men doubting me, now can we?"

"That would be detrimental, sire."

Jaron turned to Adrianna. "Will you excuse me for a few minutes?"

Adrianna nodded her assent and Jaron strode with the general to a nearby tent. Several minutes later he reemerged wearing a thoroughly dented breastplate and a faded helmet. He picked up a sword from the nearby rack and gave it a swing, instantly proving his adeptness with the weapon. "Who dares challenge me?" he bellowed.

It seemed that every soldier in the kingdom heard Jaron and yelled in return. Adrianna yelped as they dashed passed her, several pausing long enough to apologize for their haste. The crowd encircled the king, converting the bard patch of ground into an impromptu arena. Jaron lifted his sword and swept it in a slow arc, pointing it at the men as they continued to cheer.

"Well?" he yelled.

"I challenge," came a loud voice from the side. The group of men parted and a large man with thick arms stepped forward in matching armor.

156

"Telchin? Already in armor, ready to ambush? Surely someone with a stronger backhand is available."

The man smiled, swishing his sword through the air. "Apologies, but my wife is still at the market, sire."

Jaron barked a laugh. "Then I'll suppose I'll settle for the next best. Come on, then!"

Both men raised their swords and ran at each other. Jaron neatly parried the first blow, spinning to land his sword against the giant's back. Telchin growled and spun back towards the king. His swings came faster, from the right, below, left. Each swing gave a sharp clang as it was met by Jaron's weapon. Jaron ducked, then landed another blow across the man's chest.

"Two," he said with a smile and a wink.

Telchin shook his head. "Just want you to feel comfortable, your majesty." He swung again. Jaron stepped to the side, the sword completely missing, and tapped his own on Telchin's shoulder.

"And three."

Telchin burst into laughter. "Ragdons. If you weren't royalty I'd suggest we see who fairs better without steel."

"I think I'll pass," Jaron said with a smile. The large man clapped the king on the shoulder as he passed him on his way back to the crowd. Jaron raised an eyebrow at the still cheering men. "Next?"

Another man stepped forward. "Ulrich," Jaron greeted him.

"Your majesty," the man replied with a smirk. Jaron beckoned and the man rushed him. Within a minute the man was on his way back to the edge, laughing.

No wonder he was general, Adrianna thought with a smile. He was obviously exceptional.

"I'll challenge," came a voice from behind her. The men began to part and Adrianna turned to see Reon step forward, breastplate and helmet in place.

"Reon," greeted Jaron, lowering his sword.

"You're not a soldier yet, young lad," said the general.

"Let him," Jaron said, waving Reon forward. "He's the best there is and I need the practice."

Reon stepped into the circle. "You calling me practice, King Jaron?"

Jaron frowned. "I didn't mean it as an insult."

157

Reon smirked. "I know, sire. Just pulling your leg." He lifted his sword.

Jaron mirrored him. "Are you ready, then?"

Reon nodded, sword steady. "Are you?"

"As I'll ever be." He stepped forward, closing the distance. Reon didn't move, keeping his sword trained on the king. Jaron began circling Reon, waiting for the inevitable attack. Reon was unwavering as he kept Jaron directly in front of him. After a moment, Jaron swung and the two engaged. Steel met steel as they exchanged blows, neither finding their target. Reon took a step back, and Jaron pushed forward. Another step back. A third.

Reon's blade hit the armor beneath Jaron's arm as the king swung above his head. "One," Reon said. "Three steps back will bring out the opponent's pride, making him sloppy."

The general started forward, but Jaron waved him away. He faced Reon. "That's good advice," he said, smiling. Reon raised his sword again and waited as the king regrouped. Jaron stretched his neck from side to side and advanced.

Again the two clashed. Reon's blows came swifter now, forcing Jaron to defend. Blow after blow, each leaving no time for Jaron to assemble his own assault. Jaron bumped into the rack he had pulled his sword from. Reon took a half step back, giving the king room. Jaron lunged forward, sword coming down hard from overhead.

Reon raised his sword, but let go as soon as the two swords met. He stepped deftly to the side, snatched another sword from the rack just behind Jaron, and laid it across the king's back with a sharp clang. "Use all of your available assets. Ignoring them is idiocy."

Several of the soldiers started yelling accusations of cheating at Reon, but both he and Jaron ignored them. Jaron nodded. "A mistake I won't make again."

Reon waited until Jaron lifted his sword, then attacked with fury. The speed of his attacks made it appear as if he had been merely playing with the king before. Adrianna realized she was squeezing the life out of her other hand. She forced herself to relax. Reon was anything but disloyal. He wouldn't hurt Jaron. Jaron was his ruler.

Reon hates him. Her hands clenched once again as she watched him land hit after hit against Jaron's sword. The king was stumbling backwards, staving off the attacks, but at the cost of all opportunities to attack or gain ground. Reon pressed harder. Jaron stepped back again, planting hard in a small patch of mud. His foot slipped out from under him, his knee hit the ground, and Jaron reached down to catch himself.

With Jaron's head down, his helmet was tilted forward and the back of his neck was fully exposed. Reon stepped forward and swung down hard with his sword. The blade hissed through the air, aimed expertly at the strip of naked skin. Adrianna knew that while the blunt sword wouldn't go all the way through, it would go far enough.

A loud smack sounded from the impact, silencing the men. "And no matter who you are or think you are," Reon said as he lifted the sword once again, "the better swordsmen can and *will* kill you."

Jaron reached his hand up to the back of his neck. The flat of Reon's blade had left a dark red welt. Jaron knelt before Reon, head down for several seconds as he rubbed his neck. Reon stood solidly over him, as if the two's social stations were suddenly reversed. Jaron rose slowly and met Reon's eyes. "I'm sorry, Reon," he said quietly.

Reon was stoned face. "So am I." He dropped the sword and strode calmly from the circle. The men parted in silence for him as the general rushed to Jaron's side.

"Are you alright, my liege?"

Jaron continued to rub his neck as he watched Reon across the yard. "Yes, captain," he said softly. He gestured toward the retreating figure. "How long until he's eighteen?"

"Two months, sir."

Jaron nodded. "Have him leading as soon as possible. We need more men like him in command."

CHAPTER 22

Devvon raised his hand, the moonlight glinting off his metallic fist. His men halted and all noise ceased but murmurings of crickets and the occasional owl. The small army had tied their horses several miles behind and had finished the last of their journey on foot to give themselves the element of surprise and to give the sun plenty of time to finish its daily ritual. Devvon peered through the trees. Across the small clearing before him stood a small cottage, with light flickering through its windows and smoke seeping from the chimney.

The building was only a hundred yards away, just within range of his gloves. For a normal mission, the firelight should have been enough evidence to proceed. But this was no normal mission. His men's mistakes at the Tower were fresh in his mind, and he wasn't about to take anything for granted. Staying to the shadows, he stalked forward.

He crept up behind the decrepit wagon that sat halfway between his men and the hovel. He crouched, holding his breath, and waited. He could just make out the smell of meat cooking, and heard the occasional crackle from the fire.

A voice came, soft as the wind. Devvon closed his eyes to concentrate.

"So we leave tomorrow?"

"Right. Devvon won't arrive until at least the next day. A day's head start should be enough with your wings."

Devvon smiled as he opened his eyes. *They're* my *wings, now.* He slowly raised his arms, pressed his hands together, and took careful aim.

*****

Richards set another log on the fire, then sat on a stool beside it. "So," he said, rubbing his shoulder. "You're getting better with those wings of yours."

"I kind of had a crash course," Titan said dryly.

Richards chuckled. "Just think of your fall from the Tower as a test."

"With no room for error."

"Pass or fail tests are usually the easiest kind," Richards said, smiling. "And the bracers are coming along as well." Titan raised an eyebrow, earning another laugh from Richards. "Relatively speaking.".

"So what now?" Titan said as he spooned stew into his mouth.

"We keep practicing. You keep getting better, and when the time is right you find Devvon in a dark alley and somehow either force him to surrender his armor or kill him."

Titan nodded. "Sounds simple enough."

"Impossible plans usually do," Richards replied as he stirred the fire.

Titan started. "Wait, I've got it!"

"You've got what?"

"How to kill him!" Titan waited for a response, but was only rewarded with a raised eyebrow, so he continued. "We drown him! I hold him underwater using the bracers' strength. Don't you see? He'll suffocate!"

Richards nodded. "That's a good idea." He spooned a bit of meat into his mouth.

Titan waited. Richards continued eating. Titan sighed, shoulders sagging. "Alright, tell me why it won't work."

"Same reason it didn't work four hundred years ago when Shio tried to kill Tomeril. Something about the armor acts like a filter. Shio reported that after fifteen minutes of holding him there, Tomeril was still breathing, bubbles still coming out of his mouth. The man was mad as anything when he got free. I didn't want to raise Tomeril's ire, so I waited until the next generation to start testing it out. Seems like the armor acts as some sort of filter, pulling air from the water."

"There's air in water?"

"Apparently."

Titan chewed. "How about starvation?"

Richards shook his head. "You'd have to hold out just as long as him. Without sleep."

"What if I tied him up?"

"While he's blasting fire at you? He's the impervious one, remember."

"While he's asleep."

"And when he wakes? He only needs one hand kind of pointed in the right direction. Even if that direction is down at the ground, he won't feel the heat and can keep fire coming until it eats up whatever you've tied him with."

"So we slip him a sleeping drug to keep him knocked out. Wait, what about poison?"

"Same as with drowning. Filters it out."

"You actually tried poisoning someone? Just to see if it would work?"

Richards pointed his fork at Titan. "Before you get to judging my methods, I'll have you know that Wels knew perfectly well what he was eating. Besides, he didn't even catch a cold." He stabbed another piece of meat.

"How does he eat?"

"Just like I'm eating. I don't know how it happens. It just does. The armor protects him from everything that intends him harm, but lets everything else pass."

Titan studied the contents of his own bowl. "So what then? What haven't you tried?"

"I tried everything I thought of. But for the time being, I think it would be advisable to continue praying to the Ragdons. On the off chance that whatever Supreme Being that does rule the universe honors supplications to them as well." He winked at Titan.

"Devvon is likely closing in on this place," Titan said, changing the subject. The Ragdons were no longer a source of comfort. Thinking of them brought conflict and confusion. "We should leave soon."

Richards nodded. "I think you are right, my boy. This cottage has served us well, but I believe it's about time that we made a change."

"So we leave tomorrow?"

"Right. Devvon won't arrive until at least the next day. A day's head start should be enough with your wings." Richards coughed through a patch of smoke. "That combined with the fact that—"

The cottage behind them exploded. The force of the blast knocked both Richards and Titan from their stools around the fire pit behind the home. Titan whirled and watched as the flames completely engulfed the building, the heat washing across him in like waves from the inferno.

"Actually, I think we should leave tonight," Richards said, grabbing Titan's shoulder and forcing him to his feet.

Titan shook his head clear, then reached to his side and swung both his sword and Alder's bag onto his back. Richards turned away from Titan and lifted his arms. Titan grabbed the man in a tight hug, spread his wings, and jumped into the air. They had attempted the process before, and while it had been possible, it wasn't easy. Titan couldn't tap the strength of the bracers while flying, so clinging to a passenger proved to be extremely tiring.

They rose slowly, angling away from the inferno. As they cleared the tops of the trees, Titan heard yells coming from behind him.

"Faster, my boy," Richards said.

Titan pumped harder, shooting them forwards and over the forest. The yells intensified. *Almost there.* Titan grit his teeth. *That was close.*

A ball of heat and fire shot passed their right side. Titan swerved away from it, just as another blast passed where they had just been.

"TITAN!" Devvon's scream echoed off the mountains surrounding them.

Titan swerved back to the right as a third blast seared by, nearly grazing them. He focused on speed. The trees behind him finally created a barrier for them as the skimmed the tips.

"YOU'RE A COWARD!" Several more explosions sounded, and Titan glanced back to see trees engulfed in flames. "JUST LIKE YOUR FATHER!"

Titan maintained their altitude and pushed harder. His arms ached with the weight of Richards in them. Just as

Devvon was limited by the circularity of the powers, Titan was similarly handicapped.

"Good flying," Richard said. His voice contained more sincerity than Titan had ever heard. "For only a few days' practice, you did admirably."

After another pair of minutes, Titan dipped between the trees and pumped hard to slow their speed. Giving a final burst, the pair dropped to the ground and stumbled away from each other.

"And your landings have much improved as well," Richards said, steadying himself against a tree.

Titan ripped open Alder's bag and pulled the bracers from them. "Good idea," Richards said, righting himself and helping slide them onto Titan's forearms. "These things will be safest on you."

Titan pulled at the laces. "I'm going back."

Richards grip tightened. "Now why in the world would you want to do something as foolish as that?" Titan pulled his arm free and continued lacing. Richards hesitated, then spoke again. "Both you and I know that Devvon's insults meant nothing. Lexik was the bravest of men."

"He's in the dark, and he's without his army," Titan said, moving to the second bracer. "Only a couple of minutes ago you told me I needed to use this kind of opportunity to kill him."

"*After* you've had time to practice!" Richards said. "I admitted you were getting better, a couple of days are not near enough to master the wings and bracers! Devvon has had years!"

"Only with one of the three. With the other two he is just as fresh as I am."

"The other two?! Titan, what kind of practice do you think someone needs being protected, or having superhuman senses? *He doesn't need practice with them!*" Richards grabbed Titan's arm again. "Titan, don't do this."

Titan shrugged him off and finished with the leather. "I'll be careful. I have the element of surprise now. He will expect us to run, not return and fight. And if it turns south, I'll just fly away."

"He shoots *fire!*" Richards was nearly yelling. "We were lucky to escape once!"

Titan saluted and spread his wings. With a pair of flaps, his feet left the ground. He ignored Richards protests as a gentle breeze bore him up and over the treetops, back in the direction they had fled from. Without the added wait of a passenger, the return trip was considerably shorter. He circled to the opposite side of the meadow from the cottage, staying out of sight, and gentle dropped to the ground. He waited for cries of surprise, and when none came, began picking his way between the trunks and bushes.

CHAPTER 23

Felk walked along the wall as the mist swirled around him. It was nearly sunrise, the edges of the sky just beginning to show glimpses of gray. He continued slowly, surveying the forest beyond the city wall. Dark and shrouded in mist, the sight was eerie. Felk stared out into the night, his mind going over not for the first time what the weeks before him might bring.

He heard the familiar sound of an arrow digging into wood and began making his way towards where he knew it had struck. After several moments of walking, the soldier came into view, reading the paper over.

"Soldier," Felk greeted him.

The soldier jumped, his hand grasping at his sword as he whirled. "Who's there?"

"Your general," Felk said, continuing forward. "You have the report?"

The man didn't relax as Felk neared, but held out the paper. "Yes, sir."

Felk reached and took the report, studying the man. "Are you a new recruit?"

The man nodded slowly. "How did you know?"

Felk shrugged, looking down at the parchment. "Standing orders are to open all reports in twos. You probably weren't made aware."

"No, I wasn't. Forgive my error."

"Of course," Felk said, reading the report. Nothing. Not a single bandit. At least none that were visible. He turned back and looked out once again at the army of shadows among the trees. "Ragdons."

"Sir?"

Felk glanced at the man. "Not a sign of the bandits." He cocked his brow as the man tucked a sheet of paper into his pocket.

"Sorry, general, a letter from my daughter. I probably shouldn't be reading that either while on duty." The man cleared his throat and ran a hand through his hair. "Isn't it a good thing that they're gone, sir?"

Felk shook his head. "They were there, then vanished. Knowing where an enemy is camped is much preferable to not knowing."

"Perhaps they went home?"

Felk nodded. "That seems to be the general consensus." He looked at the paper again. Perhaps the others were all right. Perhaps he was simply being over-paranoid, the bandits had realized their surprise attack was discovered, and they had retreated back to wherever they came from. He took a deep breath, the feeling of indecision and uncertainty finally breaking him. For whatever reason, the bandits were gone. Felk would concentrate on the impending crusade and leave the protection of the city to Devvon. Devvon had known men would step forward when asked. Perhaps he knew the city would be safe.

"As you were, soldier," Felk said, and the man returned to his vigil, glancing back only once as the general continued his walk along the stone wall. Felk sped his pace, pushing the bandits from mind.

*****

"He's a good man," Jaron said as they walked.

"Yes," Adrianna agreed. "Just be careful around him. Reon is full of hate right now. He might do something rash."

"You know him better than I do, so I'll be careful. But I don't think he's really a danger."

"And what of the fight?" Adrianna could see the welt clearly, even in the dark of the night. "I thought it was against the rules to hit skin."

"Slapping with the flat of the blade isn't considered a damaging strike. He was perfectly within the rules."

"Just be careful," Adrianna said again.

"I will." Jaron paused. He glanced at her. "You're beautiful in the moonlight."

Adrianna felt her cheeks grow warm. "But not in the sunlight?"

"What I meant was—"

"I'm sorry, I shouldn't play with you. I know what I meant. Thank you."

Jaron chuckled. "I'm sure going to miss you."

"And I you. But my advisors are right," Adrianna replied, sighing. "My people have heard that they have a new queen, but that she is abandoning them within a pair of months. Changes like that need the presence of the leader to stabilize things."

"I couldn't agree more. I just hate to see you go."

"I know." Adrianna smiled at him. "I'll miss you too."

"Perhaps I should go with you?"

"You know as well as I that you need to stay, for the same reasons that I need to go. Your people need you here as a reminder that they are taken care of."

"I know." Jaron kicked at the pebble. "But I can't help but wish it wasn't so."

"I'll be back soon. And after that, there will be no reason for us to ever be apart."

"I look forward to it," Jaron said with a smile. He reached out and grasped Adrianna's hand, pulling her to a stop. "I love you," he whispered.

"I..." Adrianna took a deep breath. "I love you, too."

Jaron smiled, reaching a hand up and brushing her cheek. "I believe you." He stepped closer.

Adrianna felt herself leaning towards him. His breath was hot against her cheek as he gingerly placed a kiss. "Be safe, and come back soon."

Adrianna could feel the side of her face tingle. "I promise."

Jaron pulled back and winked. "I know you will."

*****

"COWARD!" Devvon screamed at the darkness yet again. His only answer was the crackling of the flames as they consumed the forest. Titan had escaped. Again. And unlike his first flight, he now was armed with an ally who possessed incredible knowledge, one who would direct him to travel at night, avoid people at all costs, and leave no trace whatsoever. Titan had just disappeared.

Devvon cursed every deity man had ever invented. His own lust for power had betrayed him yet again, prompting an attack before ensuring that the voices he heard were actually coming from *inside* the cottage. His opportunity was gone, and with it his best chance at true invulnerability. Fate, once again, had pitted itself against him.

A soft cough sounded behind him. "Sir?"

Devvon whirled, cape flapping wildly behind him, and glowered. "What?" he hissed.

"Do we follow, sir? If so, we need to get going as fast as possible. The horses are still several miles –"

"To what end, Captain?"

"To ... I thought ..." The captain silenced himself and saluted. "Orders, your majesty?"

"Save me the trouble and slit your own throat." Devvon left the man to sort out the conflicting instincts of loyalty and self-preservation. Instead, the not-quite-omnipotent god returned his attention to the inferno and began to systematically shoot fireball after fireball to the edges, urging the flames to devour every last foot of the infernal place. Trees exploded, burned, collapsed. Perhaps if he caused enough damage, Lexik's spawn would return to stop him. Devvon didn't have a better plan yet, so he continued to burn this little corner of the world.

Smoke and ash filled the air as he continued his work. Each fallen tree seemed to feed Devvon's rage, spurring him towards the next. He let the anger consume him and began firing in faster succession. Fireball after fireball savagely attacked the forest. So much destruction with so little effort. Yet he had tried twice to steal a simple sword and had failed. He shot again.

A man yelled from behind Devvon. He turned and raised a hand towards the sound. *Let them be silent or let them be dead.* He waited as his eyes readjusted to the darkness of the woods, the blaze vivid in his sight even when looking away. As the glare cleared, he found the men fighting, swords drawn. Weary even of destruction, Devvon dropped his arm and let out a breath he hadn't realized he was holding. The men were afraid, so they fought. Perhaps fear was how he could draw the boy out.

Devvon strode towards the fight. Four of them were ganging up on a fifth, and from the looks of their swings they wouldn't be satisfied with anything short of blood. Devvon really didn't care whether or not a man died. He didn't need them. Chances were that he himself would kill one or two when he reached them. He did need obedience, however. He would teach them to fight when commanded, not when they felt like it.

Yet ... the fifth man was different. His stance, the way he held the sword. And he lacked the armor the rest bore. The man wasn't part of the company. He didn't even appear to be an easterner. Devvon scanned the nearby forest and realized that these four were all that were standing. The rest of his men lay, dead, scattered near and far from the fight. Whoever this newcomer ...

Titan. Devvon took a moment to let the realization sink in. The impetuous prince had returned. The skirmish continued, and the four eastern soldiers seems to have the situation under control. Titan was slowly retreating, being forced back by the barrage of attacks. The soldiers pushed forward, their success bolstering them. Noting the loss of his men as a necessity, Devvon raised both hands and prepared to end the conflict.

Titan swung, sweeping his sword at chest level. All four men made to parry the blow, their training and instinct overcoming the logic that only one of them would need to. Steel met steel. His own soldier's sword snapped in two, the top half wiping through the darkness as the man was tossed sideways. Titan's swing continued, shearing through the three other weapons as well, throwing their owners. Titan stepped back, watching as the four men half-ran, half-crawled away from him.

Devvon's steel jaw sat agape. That wasn't just a swing. That was power like he had never seen before. Power to cut through steel, to send four men flying. Power ... of a god.

The fool Alder had wagered. He had bet his most powerful asset on a mere boy. Devvon's smile grew wide as he felt the fire course from within his chest, down through his arms, and blast out through the palms of his hands.

CHAPTER 24

More men than I would have thought, Titan thought, silently counting the men staring at the fire as Devvon continued his ruinous work. Titan had been expecting to attack Devvon alone, taking him by surprise. He couldn't fight all of them, not at the same time. Titan glanced toward his father's murderer, the metal glinting in the firelight. Perhaps there was still a chance for vengeance, to stop the nightmare before it gained momentum. While they were all watching the display.

Titan crept forward, from shadow to shadow until he was within arm's reach of the first of his foes. Titan reached an arm towards him, but hesitated. *I'm no assassin. I don't know the first thing about silent killing, and there's not a chance I'll get to all of them without someone noticing.* The situation wasn't right. His father wouldn't have done it. And as soon as the thought occurred to him, Titan knew he wasn't going to either. He stepped back, felt the stick beneath his foot just as he committed his weight, and heard the crystal clear snap.

The burning forest provided no shortage of cracks and pops, but Titan knew this one would be heard, even amidst the fire's cacophony. The man whirled, and Titan reacted without thought. He lunged forward and punched the man with all his might directly in the nose.

Rather than knock the man unconscious, as was his plan, the skull collapsed and the man's body flew some forty feet backwards, smashing two other soldiers heavily into a large tree. The trio slumped to the ground, none of them rising.

Titan looked down at his arms. He had triggered the bracers while creeping and had forgotten he was using them. *Perhaps ...*

A yell from his other side made the decision for him. Titan whirled, drawing his sword from his back just in time to parry the blow. He returned with a swing low and wide. The man blocked in return, but was sent whirling back from the force of the impact.

Four, Titan counted silently. Reon had taught him to use numbers in a fight. Count the swings, the parries, the hits. Count to keep from thinking. Too much thinking would lead to hesitation, consideration, and such lapses in action could get a man killed. Instead, he focused on the numbers and let his muscles and instincts do as they had been trained.

Another man charged, and Titan similarly threw him backwards with a single swing. Despite creeping fears that the force would break it, his sword held firm. Richards had said the armor was indestructible, but it wasn't until Titan sheared straight through the next attacker's sword that he fully believed him.

Six. Seven. Nine, he counted as two more men crumpled. Half the group was already either unconscious or dead. Titan found himself in awe at the raw power at his command. He was unstoppable. No one could stand in his way. He was omnipotent, and so he deserved to win.

Titan hesitated. *No. Don't let yourself think that way*. The power felt consuming, but Titan knew it shouldn't. Devvon sought power. Titan was trying to bring him down for it. As he hit the next group of men, Titan realized how easy it would be to slip from "liberator" to "replacement." The force of his blows was incredible. He would have to be extremely careful. He took a deep breath and switched the bracers off. His fear spiked in response, but Titan felt his conscience calm.

Three men had grouped up, but waited outside of his sword's reach. They had seen what he could do, and were obviously not enthusiastic about their future. Titan waited for the attack in a crouch. A fourth man joined them, and Titan realized that he was facing the last of Devvon's entire force. He spared a quick glance around and found the ground littered with bodies in every direction. He felt a moment of dizziness.

The four men started forward. Titan held his ground reluctantly. He glanced down at his bracers again, knowing that by not using them he was ignoring one of his greatest assets.

I will not be Devvon, he thought. *Winning this battle isn't worth losing my will.*

Or ... was it? Wouldn't Devvon subjugate the world if Titan lost?

The first soldier swung. Titan parried the half-hearted attack and retreated a step. The men began to encircle him, each occasionally swiping, trying his defenses. As his own swings became more human in their eyes, Titan felt more and more strength come behind their attacks. He continued to retreat, ensuring that he kept the soldiers on either side from circling entirely behind him. The soldiers pressed on, finally pouring their full strength into their attempts. Titan was forced to dodge more than block as he continued to stumble backwards.

He tripped. A branch caught his foot, and he was forced to grabbed onto the tree beside him. The blow came swiftly and would have taken off his head if he hadn't jumped back. As it was, it left a superficial, but painful gash on his left shoulder. As the blood began to seep, Titan realized exactly how this fight would end – as did the four soldiers.

I'm going to die. The men rushed him as one, swinging harder than ever. Titan watched the blows come. He couldn't block all four, and no matter how he dodged one of them was bound to wound him again. *I can't stop Devvon if I'm dead. And that has to be more important than not losing myself to the power.* He triggered the bracers, dismissing his worries about internal corruption. He could reclaim his moral ground after surviving the night.

Titan ducked a blow as he whirled. He brought his sword around hard. He was too far away from any of the men to reach their bodies, but instinct told him he wouldn't have to. Each raised their sword in unison. Titan pushed his own sword harder. The four swords were ripped in half by the force of the impact, and their bearers were thrown. Titan brought the sword over his head, ready for the next attack.

The men didn't rise immediately, whether from a lack of ability or a lack of courage. Titan lowered his sword and surveyed the damage as two of them struggled to their feet and limped away. Devvon's small army lay scattered, the bright flames of the king's enraged attack shining brightly off of each man's armor. Satisfied that he had eliminated all sources of his enemy's support, Titan turned towards his real goal.

Devvon was staring at him, his silver eyes locked on Titan, with both hands raised and pointed directly at him. Fire erupted from his palms, forming a ball of flame that flew from his hands and streaked toward Titan. With nothing between the two of them but the night air, Titan realized he was completely exposed. Diving behind a tree would be of little use when the flames enveloped the area.

Titan jumped. A branch below him snap from the force his bracer-enhanced legs exerted. He whipped through the branches and leaves, which hurt, but no doubt were less painful than remaining on the ground. He cleared the tops of the trees as his speed slowed, the starry expanse now interrupted only by the silhouette of the mountains to either side, yet dimmed by Devvon's rage-induced fire.

The forest below him exploded. Titan slowed to a stop as the wave of heat reached him, burning his skin even from this distance. Gravity was relentless, dragging him down as if the Ragdons themselves were dragging to his destiny. And should gravity win, as was usually the case, Titan was unsure whether he would even be able to survive the heat rippling through the air towards him long enough to die from the impact.

Titan swung his sword, still in hand, up over his head and slammed it into its sheath. An instant later a pair of wings shot out to either side. The heat waves that continued to pulse upwards caught the prince, pushing him further up into the night sky. He flapped wildly, banking away from the clearing.

Another fireball hit Titan's left wing and set him to spinning. He plunged down, back towards the inferno. He scrambled, legs, arms, and wings flailing. Righting himself just as he sunk below the tree line, he cried in pain as the heat once again caught him and buoyed him up. His arms and face pulsed in agony, the heat strong enough to raise blisters even from the distance. Titan shoved thoughts of his wounds aside and pumped his wings harder still.

He jerked to the side instinctively, and another fireball soared by, the heat quickly bringing Titan's injuries back to his attention. He flew as low as the heat would permit him, flapping wildly. Another fireball passed, but was off its mark.

"Coward!" came the scream from behind. "I'll burn the world if I have to! I'll find you!!"

Once clear of the fire, Titan banked right. *This must end now.* He knew that Devvon was exaggerating, but he also knew that he wasn't overstating by much. Devvon didn't care about lives. He would kill thousands to get at Titan.

Titan banked towards a patch of darkened forest and dropped to the ground. He quickly surveyed his wounds. His right arm was black from the burn, but after muscling through the pain he found it was still completely functional. The wound to his left shoulder looked as though it had been partially cauterized by the flames and hurt no more than the rest of him. His face felt as though it were still in the midst of the fire. Knowing he needed a healer, Titan looked back towards the clearing. If Devvon hadn't expected him to return before, he certainly wouldn't expect him a second time.

Gritting his teeth, Titan stalked forward once again. The raging fire that was once Richards' home slowly became distinguishable from the back drop of the burning forest. Devvon stood before it all, hands clenched at his sides as he stared into the blaze. Titan continued forward. He doubted he would be able to sneak up on the man if he was using the helmet. Luckily, Titan could still see light glinting off the armored face.

Devvon raised his hands again and another section of the forest exploded. Then another. Titan crept onward. A smoldering tree had fallen between the two of them. Titan approached and wandered the length until he came near the roots. The wood had a section that appeared unscathed, and while the trunk was still warm, Titan could grip it.

He reached down and as gently as he could, lifted the tree. It cracked and groaned from the shift. Titan glanced up at Devvon, but realized that his fears were unfounded. The entire forest was moaning from the night's abuse. He raised the tree gently over his head and began forward once again. He judged the tree to be thirty feet tall. *Twenty more feet until I can reach him.* He crept towards his foe, awed once again by how easy it was to lift the impossible weight. *Five feet.* Three more steps forward.

Devvon turned. Titan swung with all of his strength as Devvon's surprise spread thick across his face. The tree connected with Devvon's shimmering chest. The impact sent Devvon flying backwards towards the middle of the clearing. Titan watched as he slammed back first into the cottage, breaking through the outside stonewall.

The punishment of the flames and the impact proved too much for Richards' house. It collapsed, the walls as one falling inward, the roof collapsing, and the dwelling being reduced to nothing but a blazing heap of rubble. *With Devvon inside it*, Titan thought with a sigh. The stones settled, and the pile grew still, save for the fire dancing across the bits of wood that hadn't yet been consumed. Titan stood and stared for a long time. Nothing. The forest continued to burn, the flames roaring in Titan's ears.

The rubble exploded again, this time blown outwards. Titan jumped back as several rocks landed near him and scattered. In the crater that had appeared in the middle of the pile, a figure stood up, shaking off the debris that clung to him.

Titan stumbled away. *Ragdons*. Devvon shook his head as he climbed from the pile. He looked dazed, but otherwise completely unharmed. *Time to go*, Titan knew. He spread his wings and leaped into the air.

Devvon was invincible. Titan couldn't think of a way to produce more damage than he had just done. And Devvon had walked away from it unscathed. Titan closed his eyes as he soared. Even with all of Richards explanations, logic, and warnings, a demonstration was much more potent in convincing Titan of the only possible conclusion.

I can't beat him. No one can.

INTERLUDE

"Father?"

"Please, Ason, come in. Have a seat."

"Thank you."

"Yes, there's fine. How are you? How are the studies coming along?"

"Well enough, I suppose. I've been particularly interested of late in the seventh century revitalization. It strikes me to hear of the passion the priests of those days exhibited. Such fervor."

"Indeed. They are to be admired and commended for their work. It is largely due to their efforts that the church is as strong as it is today."

"Yes! It fills me with hope."

"It does so for me as well."

"... is that all you wanted to see me for, Father?"

"I'm afraid not. Though I do enjoy hearing what inspires an individual. Salvation is a very personal thing, you know. But the purpose of my inquiry is more to do with your sermons. How are those?"

"As good as can be expected, I suppose. I feel the fire of the Ragdons within me as I speak, and I trust that those listening feel so as well."

"Are your sermons well attended?"

"I'm afraid only twenty or so on average are present. And only a handful come consistently. I imagine the rest in attendance are simply finding the time as they can and aren't looking for a specific priest. I lament not being a better instrument to bring more men and women to the Ragdons."

"I can honestly say, Ason, that I'm not the least bit concerned. For one so young in the church, those numbers are nothing to be ashamed of. My concern has more to do with the subject matter of your teachings."

"... I apologize. Have I offended you, Father?"

"Offended is a strong word. I am merely being cautious. I've listened in on one of your sermons last week, and you spoke of the war. I conferred with some of the others who have had more opportunity to observe you, and you seem to broach the subject consistently. "

"It is on the people's minds. Their sons have marched, and the king has sworn to conquer the other kingdoms. It feels appropriate."

"To be sure. But what of the outcome of this war? If the East wins and establishes dominance?"

"I should think that the people would be proud of their kingdom. That they would be proud of their kin who have fought."

"True, but there is a risk as well. The kingdoms will inevitably associate more than ever before. And with that conquered and conqueror relationship, a rift could be created. And a rift between the people could potential lead to a rift in the church itself. Even while the priests are holding true to each other, regardless of their allegiance, the people would have a devastating effect on the church itself."

"... I see."

"We live in a golden age, Ason. The Ragdons are universally accepted between the people of the five kingdoms. You would be hard-pressed to find a man, woman, or child that doesn't have at least some faith within them, either here in the East or anywhere else. Their religion binds them together. And we cannot allow political and military maneuverings to affect their spiritual destinies."

"Understood, Father. And again, I apologize."

"I'm not worried about you, Ason. You're a good man, with a better heart. But allow the voice of age to give you this bit of counsel. Remember that while kingdoms will come and go, the

Ragdons are eternal. The kings lead and direct, and we pledge fealty whenever our conscience allows us to do so. But the day very well may come that the Ragdons give us something better. And when that day comes, we need to be ready."

"I see wisdom in your counsel, Father. Thank you. I won't discuss the topic again."

"Thank you, Ason. I couldn't be more pleased with your progress. Even us old priests at times forget that no matter what happens, we serve the Ragdons first, the kingdom second."

CHAPTER 25

Felk walked among the groups of men as the practiced. Many were adept in combat, the sword acting as an extension of their arm rather than an addition, so their work took the form of a reminder rather than a true training session. The older men had grown unaccustomed to proper formations and how to best defend as a group, but even some of the younger men, those who had been out of the military a relatively short time, had trouble grasping some of the techniques they no doubt had mastered only a handful of years prior. Felk stopped and watched a man in his early thirties attempt a simplistic parry four times, his trainer correcting his form every time. The man huffed in frustration.

"Why can't I just parry my way? Why do I need to learn to do it 'correctly'?"

Felk interjected before the captain could. "Because, soldier, your commanding officer told you to." The group snapped to attention, apparently having been unaware of who was observing. The trainee began an apology, but Felk instead took the sword from him.

"Don't think of parrying," Felk instructed as he performed the exercise. "The hand motion is the exact same as when praying to Enlightenment. Pray with your right arm while your left defends."

The soldier looked confused. "Pray instead of fighting?"

Felk pinched the bridge of his nose. "You don't actually have to say a prayer, though if you're in combat it couldn't hurt. Just use the motion."

The man looked to his comrades, uncertain. Felk returned the weapon, placed his hands behind his back, and stood expectantly. Finally, the man performed the move again, showing no improvement whatsoever over his first attempts. He looked to Felk. "Like that?"

"More or less," Felk muttered to no one, then moved on. Fortunately, the man had some basis for his argument and most of these men appeared to be naturals with the sword. Their moves weren't standard any longer, but they were used to fighting.

Defending their farms against bandits, no doubt. He forced the bitterness that surfaced to the back of his mind as he approached another group.

"... to not break the line," the commander was saying. "We have the advantage of numbers from here on out. Let's not lose that strength by letting the enemy break our formation. Seek the good of the kingdom, not your own."

A man with his back to Felk just in front of him turned to his companion and whispered. "Forget the kingdom. Just show me the women." He ran his hand through his hair, the shaved stripes on his head shining slightly in the sunlight.

Felk shoved the man hard from behind. He stumbled into the middle of the circle, stopping himself just short of running into the commander. "I believe," Felk growled, "that this man had a comment."

The commander raised an eyebrow. "Oh? What do you have to add, Gyonit?"

The man straightened himself and flashed a glare at Felk. "Nothing, sir."

"So you lack all honor," Felk said flatly, stepping forward. "You insult your country, your wife, and now you lie to your commander's face."

"I ain't got no wife," the man snarled.

"Thank the Ragdons," Felk replied. "Because you just merited a death sentence. And I hate seeing a woman widowed."

"You going to kill me, General?" The man's hand went to his sword at his side.

Felk pulled his ax free from its scabbard. "No."

The man laughed, turning to his friend. Felk raised the ax over his head and swung it hard. The man struggled to free his sword from its sheath, pulling it out and raising it just in time. Felk's ax wasn't aimed for flesh, but instead caught the sword near the hilt and ripped it from the man's clumsy grip. The man stumbled back as Felk strode confidently forward.

"You're going to get *yourself* killed," Felk said calmly. He turned to the rest of the group. "Why do you think your commander is instructing you to stay in formation during combat?"

The men shuffled, eyes dropping to the ground.

"Because," Felk continued, "he is smarter than you. You are all good men, but you've rarely been in a real battle, or haven't been in years. Your commander has been at my side in nearly a dozen battles and has consistently kept more men alive than any of my other reports." He sheathed his ax. "It really doesn't matter what he tells you to do. Do it and you will live. Don't," Felk turned back to Gyonit, "and you will be your own executioner."

"Yes, sir," Gyonit replied, humbled for the moment at least.

Felk nodded for the commander to take over again and strode away. Gyonit's impudence bothered Felk. The number of men who had stepped forward to join the army had been astounding. It had led him to believe the kingdom was unified. But the man's lack of respect had been right in line with what the old shopkeeper had said. His radical hairstyle seemed to be an outward expression of a one-man-rebellion against convention. And there were possibly tens of thousands of those one-man-rebellions within the army now.

The commander had been spot on. Every unit in the army needed to stand their ground, to keep their formation intact. But what Felk understood was that this applied to more than just where their feet were placed. A formation included the unity of purpose, the bond between the men as they fought for the same goal. An army that had split motives was as weak as one whose line broke during combat.

Felk continued to walk, mentally preparing the address he would give to his men just before they began to march west. What good would motivational speeches really have for the fragmented group?

*****

Adrianna mounted her horse, focusing on her grace and then waiting for the compliment. And because her observer was Jaron, it came.

"You know, I think that's better than most of my men can mount."

"Of course it is," Adrianna replied. "I'm a woman."

Jaron cocked his head. When Adrianna offered no explanation, he chuckled. "I get the impression that life will never be dull with you at my side."

"I should hope not," Adrianna said with a smile. "Marriage, even among royals, should never be dull." She waved a guard forward. "Are we ready?"

"Yes, your majesty," the man replied with a nod of respect. "At your command."

Adrianna looked back to Jaron. "This is it then."

"No," he said, stepping forward and taking her hand, "this is just the beginning." He pressed the back of her hand to his lips and held it there for a moment. "Please be careful," he said as he stepped back.

"You know me," she replied with a wink.

Jaron smiled and nodded. "I'm starting to." He offered a small bow. "Until next we meet, my lady."

"May the Ragdons hasten time until then." She leaned forward on her horse, and the animal began its forward movement. She turned and returned the king's wave, finding herself sad to be leaving. Jaron was the upmost of gentlemen. She would miss him during the weeks of separation.

The procession of soldiers surrounded her as she passed through the castle's courtyard and continued out into the city. The hundred men were all on horseback, and a carriage was being drawn for her. She had elected to ride for at least the first part of the journey. She felt better on the back of a horse than on pillows.

They rounded a bend and the city gate came into view. Adrianna took a deep breath. While she had been crowned for several days now, she felt as though she wasn't really bearing the responsibility. And even though she wouldn't have to for long in her home in the south, it still felt like a daunting task. She urged her horse into a faster walk.

"Why so eager, your majesty?"

"Because I'm afraid that if I don't get there as soon as possible I'll turn back."

"Oh? You're stronger than that, my lady."

Adrianna shook her head. "It would appear not, Captain. Each step seems even harder than the last."

"You act as though you were the one doing the walking. It's your poor horse that has to haul that oversized dress."

Adrianna furrowed her brow as she turned to the side. Reon rode beside her, smiling devilishly. "And technically I'm not a captain."

Adrianna turned to find the captain of the small army riding on the other side of Reon. He gave a sheepish shrug. "Heaven help us if you ever become one," Adrianna replied, turning back to Reon. "I wonder, do any rules apply to you?"

"None that I've found so far. But I'll let you know."

"So are you coming with us?"

"Nah. Just wanted to wish you well."

Adrianna studied him. "Even though you're angry with me."

"Wouldn't you be? One of your best friends is getting married and you don't even get an invitation." He turned and winked.

Adrianna sighed. "That part actually was on purpose."

"I resent that. But, lucky for you the groom has asked me to be his best man."

"What?!"

"Don't act so surprised. It's not like the bloke has that many friends."

"But ... you're ... "

"Irresistibly attractive? I warned our good king of just that problem. With me up there, who's going to notice you two?"

Adrianna shook her head. "Jaron invited you to be his best man." She chuckled. "I don't know why I'm surprised."

"I don't either," Reon said with a sniff.

Adrianna let out a sigh. "So ... we're okay?"

Reon looked over at her and smirked. "I'm magnificent. But the two of us averaged I guess comes out to right around 'okay'. Seriously, that dress looks as though it's going to smother your poor horse."

Adrianna glared.

"Fine," Reon huffed. "I'll join you at 'okay'."

Adrianna took a deep breath. "I'm glad."

"So am I, princess — I mean, queen. Speaking of, don't expect me to call you by your new fancy title."

"I wouldn't dare," Adrianna said, shaking her head. "That would be a rule."

"Exactly! Finally, somebody gets it!" He winked at her mischievously. "Well, you best be getting on." He reached a hand over and gave the rump of Adrianna's horse a solid smack. The horse continued its deliberate, steady pace. Reon looked back up at Adrianna. "Well, that was anticlimactic." Adrianna patted her horse's neck. "The very best." She turned and slapped Reon's mount. The horse bucked and charged forward, Reon holding on for dear life.

"Until your return, old friend!" he yelled back to her.

Adrianna laughed out loud as he rounded a corner ahead, not of his own volition. She leaned further forward on her horse, the beast responding by breaking into a trot. Immediately she heard the hundred horses surrounding her follow her lead. With Reon once again as an ally, Adrianna found herself even more eager to return.

*****

Seven days of hunting, and not a single trace of them. Devvon took a deep breath and closed his eyes. With Titan's wings and Richards' experience, it would be impossible to predict where they had landed. No tracks to follow, and no one for ten miles had seen them. Chances were they flew by night, staying on the move to keep Devvon from getting anywhere near them. It was what he would do in their place.

It was also infuriating. Devvon had destroyed countless homes during his week's search, trying to quell his anger. But each time he used his gloves he was made that much more aware of his missing pieces. Titan was alive and directly interfering with Devvon's invulnerability. And he was uncatchable.

Devvon reined his horse in and looked up to the mountains once again, reaching a decision he had been turning over in his mind. *If I can't find the bat, I'll make the bat come to me.* He turned his mount northeast. By now the generals should be marching. Whichever general was marching to the west had the longest stretch before them and wouldn't arrive for another week. Devvon would find them. And with an army at his back, he would march on Titan's home and burn it to the ground.

Let's see how long he can watch before trying to stop me.

*****

Titan jumped. Up he soared, easily clearing the tops of the trees and continuing upwards into the sky above. At the pinnacle of his jump, Titan estimated himself at two hundred feet. He spread his wings and glided in tight circles back to the ground. Pumping once, he landed lithely on his feet.

"Best yet," Richards said from the side.

"Your best student or the best I've done?" Titan asked with a smirk.

Richards smiled amiably. "I've been doing this for a thousand years. Let's not get delusional." He looked back up to the sky. "That is a pretty good distance you get, though. Not much fear in you, is there?"

"Not from heights," Titan replied.

"What does scare you then, my boy?"

Titan thought about this. "At the moment, fire." The pain had subsided, but his face and arms now had layers of skin peeling away. Not exactly a good appearance for someone who already had a set of demon wings.

Richards nodded. "I would say that given our current predicament, that's a healthy fear."

"I can't beat him."

Richards continued his nod. "And that's a logical conclusion."

"If it's logical, why do you expect me to?"

"What I expect is irrelevant. What's important is that you try. Your father died when he had one of the six greatest weapons ever created at his disposal. Why?"

Titan closed his eyes. "Because it was for the greater good."

"And what is our greater good now?"

"The downfall of Devvon."

"So we do it," Richards said with a sad smile. "I don't know how, but we do it."

"He'll head for my home, you know."

"I do," Richards replied. "If the decrease in forest fires over the past three or four days is any indication, I'd say there's a good chance he has already started that way."

"We need to be there when he arrives," Titan replied.

"*You* need to be there."

"You're not coming with me?"

"I'm afraid not, my boy. Too dangerous."

"What? And it's not for me? Didn't you just say we needed to sacrifice for the greater good?"

"If he kills me," Richards replied calmly, "then the world loses its one link to the horrors of the past. This situation would have happened centuries ago if I hadn't been a voice of warning. And it will happen again if I don't survive. My purpose supersedes even Devvon's downfall."

"How can you say that? Thousands of lives will be lost!"

"And if Devvon has the ring? If he goes on living forever, impervious to age or sickness? Is it worth the gamble? If you don't beat him, the only thing that will is time. I'll wait him out."

Titan clenched his teeth, angry but knowing that Richards was right. "Shouldn't I leave the sword and bracers behind as well? By taking them I risk giving him even more power."

"Agreed," Richards replied. "But I don't think you or anyone else stands a chance at defeating him if you don't use them."

Titan sat heavily on a log. "Even with them I don't think we do."

Richards sat beside him. "You'll find a way."

"Oh? What makes you so sure?"

Richards lifted his gaze. "Because, my boy," he said as he stared out at the setting sun. "You are your father's son." He put a hand on Titan's shoulder. "And no man with that kind of blood fails easily."

CHAPTER 26

Felk sat and watched his men, huddled around innumerable fires in the waning light. The food was good tonight, and the day's training had given the army a healthy appetite. It seemed that each individual was part of a continuous cycle, first drinking, then laughing, then ripping chunks of meat straight off the bone, then drinking again. Felk smiled at the familiar pattern, inspired by hard work and good friends. After swallowing the last of his own meal, he stood.

"Soldiers!"

It took time, but a quiet slowly spread through the army. Even with the noise at the level of a whisper, a dull roar persisted. Such was inevitably with only a handful of days' training. Still, it wouldn't matter. Felk would speak to those who could hear. Honor was like a disease. Instill it in a small part of the whole, and given the right conditions, of its own accord it would spread to consume the group.

"For the East!" The men echoed the cheer in unison, but with less force than Felk would have liked. Still, all the men raised their mugs and drank. *For love of country or love of ale?* Felk wondered. The men closest to him took a swig and lowered their drinks, returning their attention to him. Those who had elected to sit further away continued to drink, seeking the bottoms of their cups. When they finished, a good number turned back to their meals. Felk shook his head in disbelief, but continued. He couldn't help but notice the distinct hairstyles.

"We are but a two days march from our goal," he continued. "Two days until battle. Are you ready?"

The men cheered once again, this time with fervor. *At least they all want to fight*, Felk thought. "Indeed you are. Our time together has been short, but I would trust any one of you with my life." Those on the outskirts turned back to their food again. "You are *my* men! Follow me!"

The close groups yelled energetically. Those further didn't bother. Felk sat, more disturbed than ever. The differences of the men were stark. The new recruits were being ostracized, sitting together away from the army central. It wasn't healthy, either for the trip or the battle. Felk looked to the closest circle of men and waved a soldier over.

"Yes, General?"

"Wents, isn't it?"

"Yes, General." Wents puffed up his chest. Felk had learned long ago that learning a name bought loyalty much faster than a higher wage.

"Tell me. Why aren't the new recruits accepted by your companions?"

The man suddenly looked uncomfortable. "We haven't tried to push them away. It's just ..."

Felk raised an eyebrow. "Just what, soldier?"

"They don't like us. They prefer to be together." Wents shrugged. "Maybe they're intimidated."

Felk smiled. "A distinct possibility, trying to live up to this army's standards."

Wents smiled broadly. "Thank you, sir."

"Thank you, Wents." Felk dismissed him and returned to watching the army. Two thirds of his men being intimidated by those with more experience wasn't the worst scenario Felk could think of, but he didn't like it either. He had two days to unify the army. Felk had elected to lead an army to the West, and none of the other generals had argued. It would undoubtedly be the most difficult kingdom to subdue. But with the divisions in his men, he began doubting their ability to take it at all. *Two days*, he thought with a tired sigh.

*****

"There it is, my lady."

Adrianna leaned to her side to peer out the window of the carriage. She had ridden on horseback most of the trip, but the captain had insisted that the new sovereign of the kingdom needed to arrive in proper fashion. Hence, Adrianna was confined to the carriage, once again wearing her coronation dress. She was sweating profusely. While she was grateful for the protection from chaffing that they offered, the fitted pants and shirt beneath the dress only added to the heat.

The city wall had just come into view. She breathed a sigh of relief at the bright green flags billowing in the wind on either side of the main gate. Though she sometimes felt more at ease in the west, her home kingdom represented her childhood. She dearly loved the people, and was rewarded with their loyalty for it.

As they approached, the gate slowly opened, revealing a gathered crowd on the other side. Adrianna stood and leaned out her window. The basic purpose of her return was to be seen. No sense in losing time sitting in a carriage. Adrianna's wave was answered by a cheer from the crowd. She waved again from the other side of the carriage and was met with a similar response.

Such trust. She had been crowned less than two weeks prior, news of her engagement and consequential abandonment had no doubt reached the city, yet they still cheered her. She lifted her chin. Short though her reign would be, she would ensure their faith wasn't misplaced.

"Strange," the captain mumbled as he rode beside her.

"What's strange, Captain?"

"Oh, it's nothing. My wife usually stands on our balcony to welcome me home." He pointed. Adrianna followed his signal to spot an empty balcony above.

"She's probably waiting in the castle courtyard so she can kiss you as soon as possible."

The man grinned. "Undoubtedly, my lady."

Adrianna returned her attention to the crowd and continued to wave. One of her habits as a child that she had never lost was studying faces. She loved to imagine what a person was thinking. She glanced from face to face, trying to discern their unspoken secrets. The man with the black beard looked anxious. Perhaps he had a son returning? The man in the yellow tunic kept making remarks to his companion. Surely the two had served in the army together and were swapping stories about the old times. The man near the back didn't move or speak at all. Most likely he didn't approve of the peace conferences.

As her focus shifted from person to person, Adrianna slowly grew uneasy. A man with a staff. A man smiling through the window. A man bowing nearly to the ground. She lowered her voice. "Captain?"

"Yes, my lady?"

"Do you notice anything ... strange about the crowd?"

The soldier scanned the faces. "Such as, my lady?"

Adrianna continued to watch the passing faces. "Where are all of the women and children?"

The captain watched the crowd pass for several moments. "That's ... odd."

Every face belonged to a man. *There must be a logical explanation*, Adrianna thought, mind beginning to race. Perhaps, as with the Captain's missing wife, they were waiting in the castle courtyard. Such a welcome would be moving. *And unlikely.*

"On your guard, Captain," Adrianna commanded quietly.

"You're worried, my lady? These are your own people."

"Just a precaution."

The captain nodded. "Yes, my lady." He steered his horse towards several nearby soldiers and relayed the command. Adrianna watched as the message went from soldier to soldier until it had reached all one hundred men. Adrianna reached behind her and quietly loosened the back straps of her dress.

They approached the castle, the hordes of men on either side becoming more and more frightening with every step. What was going on? Adrianna's carriage was pulled slowly into the castle courtyard, and Adrianna looked around yet again. All men.

The crowd quieted as a soldier opened the carriage door. "Welcome home, dear queen," came a loud voice from the side. Adrianna looked to her left and spotted Nitin, her father's closest advisor approaching, trailed by a group of aids. He appeared ... what, sad? Possibly worried?

Adrianna tipped her head in greeting, keeping her eyes on him. "It's good to be home," she replied with a smile.

"As it should be," Nitin answered. He stopped a dozen feet from her, his smile paper thin.

"How ... are things in the kingdom?"

Nitin hesitated. The aide to his right stepped forward with a ready smile. "Never better, my lady."

"That is good to hear," Adrianna said slowly, watching Nitin's face. "Anything to report?"

Nitin shook his head. "Nothing, my lady."

Adrianna cleared her throat. "And ... what of the peasants' petition for extending the city wall? Has there been any resolution?"

Nitin paused, confusion obvious on his face. The aide to his side spoke again. "I'm afraid not yet, my lady."

Adrianna smiled. "I see."

She turned to face the crowd. "My people! It is with both excitement and regret that I make my first announcement to you as queen." The men on the outskirts of the courtyard began to come closer, striving to pick out her words.

She turned. "Captain, will you help me?" He neared and offered her a hand to step up onto the driver's bench of her carriage. As she placed a hand on his shoulder, she dropped her voice to a whisper. "Have my horse brought up to the other side of the carriage and get ready to run for the back gate of the keep." He nodded almost imperceptibly as she righted herself.

"I have been fortunate enough to receive the affections of His Majesty Jaron of the western kingdom! And in less than two months' time, we shall be wed!"

The people looked at each other. *They aren't sure how to react*, Adrianna thought. *They don't know the implications.*

"As you know, at that time the law requires that I step down from my throne and become a westerner. I beg of you both your forgiveness for leaving you so soon, but also your blessing." She waited patiently. Several of the closer men nodded their assent. She saw out of the corner of her eye a horse being led to stand beside the right side of the carriage. The captain approached astride his own horse on the other side. He gave another nod as she glanced down at him.

"And so," she continued slowly. "It is with both hope for the future and regret for what I am leaving behind that I tell you that I am leaving this fair kingdom."

"But why leave," came a voice from the side, "when we want you to stay so much?"

Adrianna turned to face the speaker. Nitin's aide had stepped forward once again. He slowly removed the robe he had been wearing to reveal a full set of armor beneath. "Don't you see, Your Majesty?" he continued. "We will do anything to keep you here."

"And who are you?" Adrianna asked casually.

"General Dants, my lady," came the relaxed reply, "of the East."

Adrianna nodded. "I see. And these are all your men, General?" She waved to the crowd.

"Every last one of them, excepting your Nitin here."

The captain at her side drew his sword. Adrianna kept her eyes on Dants. "And what are you doing in my city?"

"I'm afraid this city isn't yours anymore. Not since it was claimed by the armies of Emperor Devvon three days ago."

"Emperor?"

"I believe that's the proper title to give someone of his ruling power."

"And what exactly am I supposed to do? Simply step down?"

Dants smiled kindly. "That is the hope, your highness."

"And if I don't?"

The general shrugged. "You have barely a handful of men left to you and you're surrounded by thousands of soldiers. Your cooperation is appreciated, but far from required."

"Not one to pull punches, are you General?"

"You would prefer lies?"

"At least then I'd know for sure you were here at Devvon's bidding."

The smile on Dants' face faded. "My lady, I have orders to capture you and your men. But know that alongside those orders I also have permission to dispose of you. Don't test my hospitality."

Adrianna let her shoulders fall. She fidgeted from foot to foot, praying to the Ragdons that her motion looked more like a nervous tick than it felt. "Please accept my apologies, Dants. I spoke brashly."

"Indeed. Now yield."

Adrianna glanced at her men. She looked down at her dress. She reached behind her and pulled the last of the straps on her back free. "This dress was to symbolize my assent to the throne. Finding my throne occupied by another, I think it's a bit out of place." The dress fell free, leaving Adrianna in her fitted shirt and trousers. She stepped out.

"The Emperor appreciates your cooperation." Dants motioned towards the hundred men surrounding her. "Please command your men to similarly disarm themselves."

Adrianna eyed Dants. "Are you going to kill them?"

"We are conquerors, my lady. Not murderers. You have my word that assuming they are cooperative, not one will be harmed."

"And what of the rest of my people? Where are they?"

Dants motioned. "They are under guard in the northern sections of the city. We didn't want them giving away our little surprise." He nodded his ascent to her unspoken question. "They won't be harmed either."

Adrianna nodded slowly. "Captain. Order your men to remove their armor."

The captain glared at Dants. Slowly he reached up and pulled the strap at his shoulder. One by one, the soldiers began to obey. Within a pair of minutes, all hundred men sat astride their mounts wearing no more than cloth pants and shirts.

"And their swords, my lady?" Dants smiled. Each soldier's sword was still in its sheath, strapped to the horse.

"Is that really necessary? You of all people know how attached a soldier can grow to his sword. It would be like removing a limb." She reached up and removed her crown. "Wouldn't you settle for a tiara? As a gift of peace to your emperor?" She weighed it in her hand.

"I won't settle, but I'm sure he will be most grateful for the thought." He held his hand outstretched towards her.

Adrianna nodded and tossed the crown high in the air towards Dants. As the general watched the crown rise, Adrianna leaped from the carriage. In one fluid motion she landed in her horse's saddle, deftly tucked her feet into the stirrups, and kicked it forward. "Now!" she yelled.

One hundred horses bolted forward. Each man drew his sword as the stampede hit the first line of men. The group of easterners dove out of the way to avoid the hooves and blades, and after a brief moment, the stampede was through the courtyard and once again in the city. With Adrianna riding directly in the middle, the small army began their flight towards the outer wall.

"After them!"

Adrianna leaned low over her horse. "Captain, split your men up!"

The captain complied without question. Four groups of men split off down side streets as Adrianna, the captain, and nineteen others charged ahead. They had seen thousands of men on their way in, and Dants had said the women and children were being watched in the northern section. Adrianna had hoped this would leave most of the rest of the city empty and was rewarded with vacant streets.

She glanced back to see enemy horsemen pouring out of the castle courtyard. The men paused at the intersection where the other groups had broken off. Adrianna lowered herself to the horse even more. Without her dress and with her soldiers without armor, the only thing that would distinguish her from them would be her longer hair and figure. There were more than enough eastern horseman to catch all five groups, but a moment's hesitation might make all the difference.

She glanced back again to find pursuers barreling towards them once again. She turned her attention forward. "Captain?"

He looked back, then reached to his side. "Arrows, men!" He drew a bow from beside his sword and deftly aimed it behind him. His first arrow glanced off of a breastplate, but the volley from the rest of the soldiers managed to drop several enemy soldiers. As Adrianna looked again, she saw the fallen quickly replaced by those who had been riding behind.

Another volley of arrows struck the enemy, but with less effect. The men were prepared and were hunkered low over their mounts. As Adrianna watched, several of the lead soldiers pulled bows of their own from their side. She realized quickly that without armor, the men around her would fall within moments.

"Left!" she yelled as the first enemy arrows zip towards them. They veered down a side street as several of the men cried out in pain. Three men fell, including the soldier to her right whose beast continued on beside her without its rider. Adrianna glanced at the empty saddle, deftly reached over, and drew the bow from its leather straps. She swung it over her head and shoulder, fetched the arrow pouch, and veered to the right with the rest of the group as another spread of arrows whipped past them.

"My lady!" The captain called. He motioned ahead to the gate. She glanced up to find it solidly closed.

"Order it open, Captain!"

"My lady, they control the city!"

Obviously, she berated herself. Two men stood on the wall above, one steadying a bright red flag. Beside them she saw the lever that operated the gate. Smoothly she pulled the bow from her back, grabbed an arrow and notched it. She lifted the bow and took careful aim. At these speeds on horseback, she knew it was an impossible shot. Even if she hit the lever, chances were slim it would do anything more than bite into the wood.

She let the arrow fly and immediately saw it was off course. Rather than hitting the lever, it struck the man just beside it. He grabbed his side, staggered.

Ragdons, Adrianna thought as she grabbed another arrow. They were running out of room. She looked upward once again, raising the bow just in time to see the wounded man fall to the side directly onto the lever. It slammed down under his weight, and the gate creaked as it began to open. *Well*, Adrianna thought, *that's fortunate*. She let her notched arrow fly, catching the second eastern soldier in the leg.

"Go, my lady!" the captain yelled. "Men, keep the gate!" He reined his horse in, along with the eight other men who were still with them. "You there, to the top! Close the gate!"

Adrianna slowed, realizing that all but five of her companions had been lost. The captain whirled on her. "No, my lady! You must go!"

Adrianna saw the enemy soldiers round the last corner into view. Her throat constricted as she realized the captain was right. She was their goal. She had to escape. "May the Ragdons keep you!" she yelled, her voice cracking as she spurred her horse on. Five unarmored men wouldn't last long. A tear slipped from the corner of her eye and was whipped back into her long, billowing hair. She had to be sure their deaths weren't in vain.

She barreled down the road, dust leaping into the air at her passing. She looked back in time to see the gate creak all the way closed, her men on the inside. The eastern soldiers would soon open the gate and have her easily in view. Adrianna looked at the straight road ahead. Nowhere to hide. She turned her attention to the dense forest on her left and waited for an opportunity. After an excruciating moment, she saw her opening and leaned hard. The horse turned sharply, jumped a fallen tree, and charged full speed into the undergrowth.

CHAPTER 27

The horse whinnied as Devvon drove his heels into his mount's flanks. He had taken the horse, just as he had taken those before it, claiming ultimate ownership as the emperor over all the kingdoms. He had reached the Tower the day before and had found evidence that a large encampment had spent a night there. After that, it had been easy to follow their course. If his estimates were right, this army would be nearly sixty thousand strong. Hiding such a force was impossible.

Except Devvon knew that it wasn't. One just had to know where to put them. He simultaneously cursed and praised his actions once again as he kicked his horse onward.

*****

"So, any last advice?"

"Yes, actually." Richards smiled. "Make sure this advice isn't your last advice."

Titan lifted the sword over his head and shoulder. "That's good advice."

"The only kind I give," Richards said with a smile. He held the bracers out for Titan. "Good luck, my boy."

Titan took the bracers, slipped them on and began tightening the bindings. "I still have no idea how to beat him."

"Nor do I." Richards paused. "He's missing pieces, so he's not at full strength. Just as the Dragon was beatable once several pieces were removed, Devvon is too. The armor is meant to be a single unit."

"But the Dragon was missing the breastplate."

Richards nodded. "That he was." He clapped Titan on the shoulder. "You'll figure it out."

Titan flexed his arms against the leather bracers. "I hope you're right." And with a mock salute, he jumped. At the peak he once again spread his wings and began pumping. In the twilight he would be barely visible, but he kept low to the treetops to be safe. No fires meant Devvon was likely not around anymore, but it wasn't worth the risk. Better to travel at night and arrive home in secret.

The waning light gave way to utter darkness. Titan had to slow to make sure he was going the right direction, as the mountains weren't visible to gauge his course. The slower pace meant that it would take him several days to arrive home. Hopefully it would be fast enough. Chances were good that if Devvon got there first, he would take out his anger on the city.

*****

Felk sat outside the command tent, watching the resting army. He had trouble sleeping when his men were uneasy. So he sat in the night, thinking of the battle to come. For once, the odds were on his side. More than sixty thousand men against an estimated twenty thousand men inside the West's city. Other soldiers would be about on assignment, but not enough to make a significant impact. Assuming Felk's line didn't break at the first march, the city was as good as theirs.

That knowledge didn't soothe Felk. Winning had never been Felk's main objective. Keeping men alive was a much nobler goal.

Felk turned his attention as a soldier came running up. "General!"

"What is it?"

"Sentries have reported the sound of horse hooves approaching."

Felk stood. "How many?"

"Just one, sir. At a run."

Who would be traveling this late at night? Felk motioned for the man to lead and followed him towards the rear edge of the camp. Several guards saluted as Felk approached. "Report?"

"General, I heard horse hooves several minutes ago on the wind." He set his jaw. "I apologize for not informing you then. I assumed it was my ears playing tricks on me. But then I heard them again several minutes ago and sent for you. They have been persistent since then."

Felk listened carefully and could pick them out. "Just one horse."

"Yes sir."

Felk nodded. "Raise a squad and bring them here. Keep listening for the direction of approach so we're ready when whoever it is arrives."

The man saluted and strode off. Felk waited patiently for his return. The soldier soon reappeared with twenty sleepy looking men behind him. The sound of hooves was distinctly clearer.

Felk watched the dark road behind them. He was grateful for the night's full moon, allowing him to see a considerable distance down the road. At last, he caught a glimpse of light flash as the mystery rider rounded a corner a half mile away.

"The man's wearing armor," he said quietly. He heard the men behind him shuffle.

As the rider drew nearer, he picked out the billowing cape. When the man came within three hundred feet, Felk order the men to draw their swords. He then strode out to the middle of the road and yelled. "Who goes there?"

Rather than reply, the rider barreled onward. Fifty feet from Felk the horse was reined in, and the rider smoothly dismounted. He strode towards Felk, helmet reflecting moonlight in the darkness. The stride looked familiar.

"Identify yourself," Felk commanded again.

The man continued forward. "I'm your emperor, fool."

The voice fit, but the face did not. The figure now two dozen feet before him was covered from head to toe in metal. Felk shivered as he caught sight of the cold, metal eyes.

"Stand down," the figure said, still not slowing its pace, "or I'll have the lot of you beheaded."

Still wary, Felk waved a hand behind him, and the men unwillingly lowered their weapons. Felk heard more than one muttering fearfully as Devvon passed and Felk fell into step beside him.

"We weren't expecting you."

"So I gathered," Devvon said dryly as they passed a man slowly sheathing his sword.

Felk felt his anger rising, but forced it down. "Where have you been, my lord?"

"It's none of your concern."

Felk stole a glance at the steel plates covering Devvon. "What has been done to you?"

The metal face whirled on him. "Felk, you are despicable. I would like nothing more than to take your head off this instant. But if I did that, I'd lose half my men, so I can't." He calmed his outburst, then continued. "Not yet."

Felk took a deep breath. "Duly noted, my king."

"Emperor," Devvon hissed as he continued walking. He strode to the command tent and threw open the flap. "I'll take this for my quarters." He snapped and a soldier dashed forward. "Fetch me some —" Devvon stopped short when he saw the man's face.

"Something wrong?" Felk asked.

Devvon pointed a silvery finger at the man. "How long have you been in the army?"

"Nearly three weeks, sire."

Devvon growled. "Get out of my sight." The man glared at the king, then turned and left. Devvon turned to Felk once again. "Never do that again."

Felk furrowed his brow. "Do what?"

"My safety depends on the soldiers who surround me. From this point on, no new recruits are allowed within fifty paces." He glared at Felk. "Or it's your head."

Felk nodded slowly. "As you command." He waved another soldier forward. "Jert has been in the army for six years."

Devvon ordered the soldier to bring food and turned back to Felk. "Report, General."

"Everything is according to your plan and on schedule. We received your letters and the new recruits poured in." Felk hesitated. "I was surprised at the number of men, but you seemed to expect it. How did you know?"

Devvon crossed his arms. "Is it so astonishing that I know my people better than you, General?"

Yes, Felk thought angrily. "No, my liege. I'm just trying to learn that I might better estimate the next time."

"There will be no next time," Devvon said as he accepted a cup from a nearby soldier. "This will be the last war."

201

Felk nodded. "True, my lord."

A soldier nervously approached and began to unbuckle Devvon's cape. The king whirled and shoved the man to the ground. He drew his sword and strode forward. "What in the inferno are you doing?"

Felk stepped up beside the cowering man. "This is Teh. He was removing your cape. It's in tatters." As Felk looked closer, he saw scorch marks scouring the cloth.

"No one touches me," Devvon growled.

Felk watched Devvon carefully. "Yes, my lord." Felk extended a hand to the fallen soldier, pulled him up, and ordered him away. Felk looked back to Devvon. "We'll reach the west tomorrow. Any specific orders?"

Devvon turned and strode into his tent. "Burn it."

CHAPTER 28

The moonlight filtered through the trees above, creating an eerie path of shifting shadows before Adrianna. After several hours of hard riding through the thick forest, she had slowed her horse to a walk. With the darkness, she wasn't even sure which direction she was going. She needed to find the road to make good time, but the road meant soldiers.

The horse stumbled over a fallen branch. "I know," Adrianna said softly. "You need a rest too." She looked around and soon located a small clearing. It wasn't large, but it would be big enough for a small campfire and room for both of them to lie down. She didn't bother tying up the horse, instead setting herself to gathering nearby wood. A fire would be more visible, but not having a fire meant spending the night in only her thin pants and shirt.

Soon the fire was small, but sturdy, and Adrianna set herself to making a bed for the two of them. After the stones and sticks had been removed, she sat and found the ground extremely comfortable, all things considered.

Stress and long rides will make anything comfortable, she thought. She coaxed the horse to the ground and lay down leaning against it. The fire was like a beacon in the darkness, ever drawing her gaze to it. She watched as the flames leapt from side to side, a beautiful dance of light. The fire would create one image, then in an instant tear it apart to create another. Scene after scene flashed before Adrianna as she watched, ever mesmerized.

Just like life, she thought sadly. She had loved Titan, but he had been torn from her. Reon had left, only to return to her side just as she was leaving. Jaron's affections were immediately followed by her departure from him. Her journey home, only to find it occupied. Her flight saved her life, but probably lost the lives of all hundred men that escorted her.

Adrianna continued to watch the dance. Back and forth, side to side, rhythm covertly emerging from chaos. Yellows, reds, and whites, twisting like scarves being whipped through the air together. Always changing, never the same. Always changing ...

Adrianna awoke with a start. She rubbed her eyes against the brilliance of the fire. Something had snapped in the darkness. She tried to peer into the surrounding trees, but found nothing.

She jerked her head at another snap. Close. She squinted against the fire's light. Finally she was able to pick out a silhouette of a man, sitting directly across the fire from her. He picked up another stick, snapped it in two, and threw the pieces into the fire.

"You're fire was getting low," he said smoothly.

Adrianna stayed quiet as the figure came more into view. A husky looking man with a full beard. His clothes showed obvious signs of wear. "Who are you?" she ventured.

The man chuckled. "Nobody of real consequence. The question of the hour, fair maiden, is who are you?"

Adrianna didn't answer. The man clucked his tongue.

"Not very nice of you to deny me the privilege of listening to your voice."

She shrugged. "I'm no one of consequence either."

The man smiled widely. "Very well. My name is Hulkins."

Adrianna hesitated. "Kalyn."

"Pleasure to meet you, Kalyn. And what might a pretty little thing like you be doing out this fine hour? It's late, and this forest is a dangerous one." His smile persisted. "Very dangerous indeed for such a pretty thing."

Adrianna took a slow breath. "Just passing through."

"Oh? That's too bad." He stared at her. "And all alone, too."

Adrianna swallowed. "My brother is following. Should arrive any minute."

Hulkins clucked his tongue. "Not very becoming of a lady to lie. There's nobody for miles." He shook his head like a disappointed father. "I'm prone to believe your name isn't even Kalyn." His smile faded. "You shouldn't lie. Such wrongs must have consequences."

Adrianna jumped for her bow and yanked it free. Without looking she reached for an arrow, but grasped only air. The man across from her snickered.

"I'm afraid arrows can be dangerous. Much too dangerous for a young lady like yourself."

She stood and held the bow like a sword.

Hulkins snapped his finger. Adrianna gasped as a second man materialized five feet to her right. She swung back and saw a third to her left. As she spun, she counted six more emerge from the darkness.

"Never travel alone at night," Hulkins chided her. "My mum taught me that when I was a boy, so I never do. Much too dangerous." He stood, his massive form matching that of his eight companions. "Now, why don't you come with us, sweetheart? Such a pity to be all alone in such a dark place."

Adrianna jumped onto the back of her horse. The horse immediately stood upright and jerked towards the forest. A thick rope snapped taut, and the horse's head was jerked to a stop. Adrianna was thrown off balance by the sudden stop. She grasped at the reins, dropping the bow in the process. She finally righted herself, looking down to see the horse firmly tied to a tree.

"Ah, yes," Hulkins said. "You shouldn't leave your horse untied, neither. Why, he might've wandered off if it weren't for us." He walked slowly forward, the other eight men circling the horse. "And riding in the dark? My, my, my. You do have a lot to learn about safety." He reached a hand out to her. "I imagine you've already learned a thing or two."

Adrianna spat at Hulkins and jumped from the other side of the horse. She was seized by strong hands before her feet even hit the ground. "Let go of me!" she screamed as she tried to tear her arms free.

Hulkins wiped his face with his sleeve. "Not very nice manners. I fed your fire." He sounded resentful. Adrianna drew still as he approached, pushing backwards into the men who held her. Hulkins reached out a hand, and Adrianna flinched as it brushed her cheek.

"More learning to do," he whispered as he brought his face close, his rancid breath hot. "But don't you worry. We'll make a proper wife out of you yet."

*****

"So what is your main goal?"

Devvon glared at Felk. "I don't need to explain myself to you."

Felk held his gaze. "No. You don't. As my ruler, I am bound by my own honor to do my best to obey your every command." He folded his arms. "But how am I to do my best if I don't know what in the Ragdons we are doing?!"

"We will take the city," Devvon said calmly.

"I gathered that. But all of your orders thus far have been to destroy as much as possible." Felk shook his head. "There's no sense in killing the entire population. Your expanded empire as it stands will need all of the laborers it can get. You know this. I heard you explaining that very fact as one of the reasons behind your population laws. More sons meant more total births, more births were required to produce more peasants to work the fields, and more peasants were required to expand the empire."

"We will have the peasants from the other three kingdoms."

"But why not this one?!" Devvon could hear the anger rising in Felk's voice. "Why wipe this one off of the map?" Felk stood up straight. "I respect your authority and your decisions, but I feel compelled to voice my concerns. This move isn't a wise one."

Devvon watched Felk. The general was nervous, stealing glances at the metal covering Devvon's body. Devvon smiled to himself. *Perhaps I can have him killed during this crusade,* he thought. *A war casualty. No foul play suspected.*

"Why?" Felk demanded again.

Devvon let out a deep breath. "Because I need Titan."

Felk's brow furrowed. "Lexik's son? Why in the Ragdons do you need him, and how will burning the get him?"

"Because," Devvon said evenly, "he is the new ruler of the kingdom. Lexik died several weeks back, along with the rest of the kings. Each of the kingdoms is on the verge of uproar. All they need to be pushed over the brink, and thereby be entirely unprepared for our attacks is to have each new leader assassinated as well. While I have had no reports, I assume that such has been the case in the other three kingdoms, and I will not settle for less here."

Felk continued to stare at Devvon. "You killed the kings."

"Yes," Devvon replied curtly. "An unfortunate, but necessary decision."

Felk nodded slowly. "Unfortunate, yes. Whether it was necessary or not, I don't know. What I do know is that your orders still don't make sense. We're not going to surprise the kingdom by killing Titan *after* we've already razed the city to the ground."

Devvon closed his eyes. "You will obey, Felk. I need Titan, and this will bring him to me."

Felk rubbed his chin. "That is true." He paused. "But it still leaves you with the problem of losing potential field workers."

"And what other way do you propose, my all-knowing general?"

Felk visibly chaffed. "I propose, my liege, that we don't throw away tens, if not hundreds of thousands of lives. Take the boy by deception."

"And what deception did you have in mind?"

"Hold a knife to the city's neck," Felk said, "and let his own honor capture him."

CHAPTER 29

Titan landed just below the crest of the massive hill. The city was still several miles off, but he wanted no risk of being seen in the air. He walked to the summit and looked down on the familiar valley beyond. Nestled between the mountains stood the seat of his kingdom, his father's castle. Well ... Titan's castle, he supposed. The thought brought on a surge of emotions. He pushed them aside and for the moment allowed himself to simply be glad to be home.

Titan froze. To the east of the city was encamped a massive army. Even from the distance, he could easily pick out the red flags flying among the tents. Titan did a quick count. *With a camp that size, the army must be sixty thousand strong*, Titan thought in wonder. *Sixty thousand men. Devvon must have brought his entire army*. Even then, it didn't seem possible that he had amassed that many soldiers.

Titan stared down the hill at the city. It appeared that the entire force was gathered on the one side. Likely there would be spies posted around the entire perimeter, but by keeping his force entirely together, surprise attacks from the West would be all but ineffective. Titan aimed to arrive on the back side of the city. Sneaking past the spies would be easy. They would be watching for people coming out of the city, not going in.

How did Devvon get his entire army here? Titan had feared that he might have to face Devvon upon his arrival home, but had never dreamed that the entire kingdom would be under attack. He must have left orders with his generals. He couldn't possibly have known that Titan would escape with the sword and bracers. Regardless of how Devvon had managed it, Titan was glad to see that all of the gates were firmly shut and that the walls still flew the blue flags of the West. *No smoke*, he added mentally. Perhaps Devvon wasn't here yet.

Within the hour Titan arrived at the city wall. He approached a familiar tree that stood at the edge of a large forest several hundred feet from the stonework. After carefully scanning the surrounding forest to be sure that it contained no spying eyes, he deftly slid into the hole hidden at the base of the tree by a small bush.

The stone tunnel smelled dank and moldy. It extended for a quarter mile, passing directly beneath the city wall. His father had shown it to him on multiple occasions, explaining it as an escape route for the king in a time of invasion. Titan had accused his father of cowardice. Lexik had calmly explained that the king represented the kingdom. Capture the king, and you crush the people. If the king was free, their desire for freedom would burn on.

Titan reached the end of the tunnel and felt in the darkness for the handle in the roof. *Here's hoping the horses are grazing*, he thought as his hand found the metal ring. He gave a gentle push upwards. Dust and light filtered through the crack, and Titan pushed harder.

The straw fell away from the door, and he found himself in an empty horse stall. The stall hadn't been cleaned all that recently, but the stench was bearable considering how easy he had made it through. He closed the trap door behind him and scattered straw over it until he was satisfied that it was properly hidden once again.. Making his way to the stable doors, he peeked through to find several stable hands tending to the royal horses a short distance away. Titan glanced around, waited until all eyes were elsewhere, and darted around the corner.

He paused in a dark corner as a messenger boy passed. Titan wasn't sure why he wanted to stay hidden, but he felt that it was important for the time being. He spotted a discarded cloak nearby, probably belonging to one of the servants tending to the horses, and he threw it over himself. With the hood up, the sword was thoroughly hidden, as was his face. He took a deep breath and strode out into the street, being careful not to draw attention.

He was not surprised when he encountered only a handful of people on his way to his first stop. *They're scared*, he thought to himself. *Besieged by an enemy army without a king.* He approached his destination and knocked three times.

"Coming," came the call from within. The door was flung open to reveal a robust woman with a wooden spoon in her hand. "Can I ..." she trailed off as her expression filled with recognition. Titan darted inside and closed the door behind him.

"Good to see you again, Gentra," he greeted her.

"My ... prince," she replied, obviously still in shock. "I ... we ... thought you were dead."

"Dead?" Titan paused and realized the conclusion was a logical one. No doubt word of the attack at the Tower had reached the city, and with Lexik dead and Titan missing, it was a reasonable guess. He smiled. "Well, I'm glad to say that I'm not."

"I'm glad to hear it," she replied, mouth slightly agape. She turned as the door opposite the one she just opened was pushed wide.

"Mum, have you seen my ..." Reon trailed off as Titan came into view.

"Afternoon, Reon," Titan said with a smile.

Reon walked slowly over to him. "Titan," he said matter-of-factly. "I should have known better than to assume you dead without actually poking a body. Typical prince drama, upsetting the whole kingdom when you're still alive. Not very decent of you."

"You know me," Titan replied, smile widening.

"That I do," Reon answered, grabbing Titan in a firm hug. "Ragdons curse me for it." He turned to his mother. "I assume Titan can join us for dinner?"

"I'm afraid I just stopped in to let you know I was okay," Titan interjected. "I don't have much time."

Reon chuckled. "Right. Gotta go save the kingdom and all." He turned and grabbed a sheathed sword that was leaning against the wall. "So where are we off to?"

Titan hesitated. "I'm ... not sure."

Reon watched him carefully. "Well," he finally said, "let's get going anyway." He led Titan to the door and waved to his mother. Still in shock, she didn't seem to even register that they were leaving.

Reon pulled Titan across the street and into the tavern on the other side. After finding a booth, he sat and folded his arms. "Now. Where are we off to?"

"I told you."

"Titan, I'm not buying it. That cursed brain of yours can't help but think five steps ahead."

Titan took a deep breath. "I can't get you involved. It's too dangerous."

Reon laughed. "You forget, I'm the better swordsman. If either of us is to go on some dangerous mission, it should be me." He paused. "And I'm better looking."

"It's not —"

"Now." Reon glowered at him.

Titan took a deep breath. "You asked for it," he muttered.

For the next hour, Reon's expression didn't change. Titan kept expecting outburst, questions, disbelief, something. But Reon just watched, speaking only when the barkeep came around. Titan continued on, detailing all the events that had happened over the past several weeks. "So," he finished, "I really don't know where I'm going."

Reon chewed on his lip. "A magic sword?"

Titan nodded.

"And magic bracers?"

Titan lifted his arms to show them.

"And Devvon is invincible."

Titan nodded again.

"Okay," Reon said slowly. He thought for a moment, opened his mouth to speak, and closed it again. He rubbed his forehead. "We could ..." He shook his head and closed his eyes. He reopened them excitedly. "Or, once he ..." he trailed off again and slumped back. Finally he raised his eyes back to Titan. "You got me."

Titan nodded. "It's impossible."

"Yep."

"So you still want to come?"

"Yep."

Titan smiled. "Figured as much."

"It's the least I could do for my ex-prince."

"Ex?" Titan raised an eyebrow.

Reon nodded. "Sorry, Titan old friend. You have officially been skipped when it comes to the line for kingship. Jaron was crowned just days after news of your death arrived."

"Really? General Jaron?"

"Yep."

Titan chewed on this. He wasn't bothered by the fact that Jaron was the crowned king. He simply found it odd that the throne had been filled at all. He hadn't even realized the city would think him dead until an hour ago. "Where's Adrianna?"

Reon nodded. "Wondered how long it would take you to get around to asking about her. She left for home more than a week back." He paused. "She's the queen now, you know."

Titan nodded. "That part I did guess."

"And ... there's something else," Reon said quietly.

"What is it?"

"Adrianna ... when you faked your own death –"

"I didn't fake anything. I've been trying *not* to die."

"Nuances. Anyway, after that happened, Adrianna ... made some decisions."

Titan waited. "What decisions?"

"Well ... she kind of got engaged." Reon said.

Titan stared at Reon. "To be married."

Reon answered with a slow nod. "In two months' time."

Titan took a deep breath. "I didn't realize she even had any prospects."

"Well," Reon said as he rubbed his forehead, "when you left, she didn't."

Titan let out a hefty sigh. "I guess that's her decision. She is her own woman."

"Titan!" Reon sounded suddenly angry. "What ever happened to fighting to win your love?"

"Reon, we've discussed this before. Whether I love her or not is irrelevant. It's against the law."

"So Jaron can do it, but not you?"

Titan hesitated. "She's engaged to Jaron?"

"Yep. Engaged to the crowned king of the West."

"But ... that's against the law."

Reon shook his head. "It's against the law to accept or offer marriage while king or next in line to do so. Jaron was third in line and did it before he was crowned."

Titan thought for a moment, finally lowering his gaze to the table. "Then it's legal."

"That's what everyone keeps saying." Reon watched Titan from across the table. When Titan didn't move, Reon cleared his throat. "I'm sorry, Titan."

Titan closed his eyes. "Don't be. She was never mine."

"Ragdons, man! I'm supposed to console, and you're supposed to get mad! Not the other way around!"

"Reon, the law –"

"To the inferno with the law! Jaron found the loophole, so he got the girl! Why won't you bend your unbreakable loyalty to the West for your own happiness just for once?!" Reon stood. "For being a prince, you sure are stupid." He turned to leave.

"Reon, wait," Titan grabbed his sleeve. Reon looked back, obviously still angry. "Get out of the city."

"Why?"

"Because Devvon only cares about getting to me. It's only a matter of time before he attacks."

"Shouldn't I stay and fight?"

Titan shook his head. "Take your family and leave. Devvon is invincible. There's no sense throwing your lives away." He paused. "I'm going to talk to Jaron, try to figure out a way to get the rest of the people out of here. You remember that mountain lake where we used to fish?"

"Yeah."

"If you're still interested in helping, I'll be there tomorrow at noon."

Reon sniffed. "I'll be there."

Titan smiled as he watched his friend walk away. He stood himself and followed, but turned down the street, rather than following Reon back to his home. A short distance away stood the castle walls. He strode forward, focusing on his people's escape rather than the impossible task that was to follow.

*****

He won't attack, Felk reassured himself once again. The Western army wasn't a threat; there was nothing to be gained from slaughtering them. And after discussing Felk's plan, Devvon had admitted it was the better idea. Lay siege to the city. Titan was bound to return. And when he did, make sure that the officials in charge were seeing the situation clearly. The West was honorable, something Felk yearned for in his own kingdom. The kingdom's leaders would see the logical choice.

Devvon won't attack, Felk told himself again.

*****

The horse below her turned once again. Adrianna had tried to keep track of where they were going, but she hadn't known where they had started from. Her hands were bound behind her, her eyes were blindfolded, and her mouth was gagged. Her kidnappers had said little to her after tying her up, only telling her to duck when low branches were in the way. "Can't be damaging the wares," they snickered several times.

It hadn't taken long to deduce that they were bandits. And it had taken even less time to guess what they intended for her. Adrianna had heard of the slave-trading market that thrived among them. Women were kidnapped and sold at auction as brides for foreigners. If rumor was correct, it was exceptionally lucrative. The bandits had undoubtedly spotted her fire the previous night and seen her as an opportunity. She cursed herself yet again. Without her bow she was defenseless. And with her eyes covered and her hands bound behind her, escape didn't seem plausible.

Wait for an opening, she silently coached herself. She wasn't sure what it would look like or when it would come, but there was nothing to be done until it appeared. If she tried to escape and got caught, they'd keep her on an even tighter rope. But thoughts of her fate urged her to action. She undoubtedly had a long boat ride before her. If they didn't unbind her before then, she knew there would be little hope of escape. She would be half a world away before another opportunity arose.

*****

Devvon flexed his hands, searching for the familiar feeling of leather stretch against his skin. There was none. The protective plates had glided beneath the gloves, leaving only the cool metal to be felt. He hadn't removed any of the armor since the Tower, and he doubted he ever would. The leather was impervious to water, use, or damage, as were the breastplate and helmet. Taking them off was Yorth's downfall. Devvon would not repeat his mistake.

"Here we go," Felk muttered beside him. Devvon followed his gaze to spot a blue flag on the castle's wall waving slowly back and forth.

"I'll take care of this," Devvon growled, starting forward.

"No, Devvon," Felk commanded. Devvon snarled. "Wait for the right moment. It's only going to get easier the longer we wait."

"Oh? And if you're wrong about this new king?"

Felk shook his head. "I'm not."

Devvon stepped back, his back to the stone wall. "You had better not be. I'm betting quite a bit on your instincts." *More than you know.*

CHAPTER 30

Titan was greeted at the castle's gate by two stunned faces.

"Prince Titan," the soldier to the left managed to get out.

"Yes," Titan replied smoothly. "I need to speak with King Jaron."

"Of course, my lord," the man quickly said, waving to the soldier on top of the wall. The gate slowly began to open. "It's just ... we thought you were dead, sire."

Titan shook his head. "Not yet." He strode through the gate and across the courtyard. It was empty. No doubt the soldiers were at battle stations, watching for an attack. He entered through the familiar door to the left of the main entrance to find an empty corridor before him. A servant saluted from the side.

"Where is King Jaron?"

"In the map room. Do you require directions?"

Titan realized the man didn't recognize him. "No, thank you." He continued down the hallway to the stone stairs at the end. He climbed to the next floor, walked quickly down the next corridor, and began up another flight of stairs. The castle around him was completely silent. Apparently the siege had everyone taking cover.

He reached the top of the stairs and found the thick wooden doors already open. He walked quietly through them to find Jaron seated beside a large table, already staring at him. *The same table father and Alder had been discussing giving me the bracers.* Jaron stood, the crown on his head

216

catching the light from a nearby window, and beckoned Titan forward.

"Welcome home, my prince."

"Not your prince anymore, majesty," Titan said, accepting the proffered hand. "You don't seem surprised to see me. I thought I was assumed dead."

"You were," Jaron said with a small smile. "But I try to make a point of not underestimating those of your bloodline."

"We can be a bit unpredictable," Titan said with a smile.

Jaron motioned him to a chair at the table. "But always for the good of your people."

"I hope my return is for their good. It looks like we're in a problematic situation."

Jaron shook his head, smiling. "That's putting it mildly."

"Has Devvon made any demands? Though it seems like he could take the city without negotiating."

Jaron nodded slowly. "A couple of messengers have been sent."

"And?"

Jaron shrugged. "Their requests are fairly simple. Simple enough that I suspect Devvon has other motives."

Titan paused. "What are they asking for?"

Jaron watched Titan. "You. They seemed sure that you would return, hence I wasn't startled at your arrival. They have promised that upon delivering you to Devvon, the city will be left in peace."

Titan nodded. "I expected that."

"Oh?"

"Yes. Devvon has been chasing me for the last several weeks."

Jaron furrowed his brow. "Why?"

"It's somewhat complicated."

"I see myself as an intelligent man. Try me."

"Not that kind of complicated. Just ... " Titan took a deep breath. "Just trust me that it's better that you don't know."

Jaron nodded slowly. "I've trusted you and your father for much of my life. I suppose I can manage this time as well."

"Thank you, Jaron." He paused. "What did you tell the messengers?"

"That you weren't here."

"And when I returned?"

"That I would speak to you."

Titan nodded. "That will buy us time. They didn't see me coming into the city, so they won't expect an answer yet. We need to get the people out of the city. The army is grouped on the east, but if we escape through the opposite gates, we might be able to make it to the mountains with them."

"That many people will be nearly impossible to move without detection. And an army can move faster than a population."

"Well, we have to find a way. They can't be here when Devvon attacks."

"What if he doesn't?"

"You just said that unless they get me, they'll attack."

Jaron didn't say anything. Titan studied him carefully. "You think I should give myself up to them."

The continued silence was enough of a reply. Titan shook his head. "I can't do that, Jaron."

"You have to," the new king said as he leaned forward. "Your people are in danger, and we have the solution."

"I can't."

"Titan, see reason! We can save tens of thousands of lives!" Jaron took a deep breath. "I have served you as best I could for years, and I would die defending you. But is your survival more important than your people's?"

Titan remembered his father's lesson from the escape tunnel. "I'm a symbol of hope for the people."

Jaron shook his head. "The people think you are dead. Giving yourself up at this point is just giving yourself up as a man, not as a prince. Please, Titan."

Titan closed his eyes. "I can't, Jaron."

Jaron furrowed his brow. "Why not? You've never been one to cave to fear."

"It's complicated."

Jaron shook his head. "When it comes to the lives of the people, nothing is too complicated to skip. Why can't you give yourself up to Devvon? It's what your father would have done."

Titan snapped his eyes back open. "How dare you speak of what my father would have done."

Jaron set his jaw. "How dare you not do it."

The two sat glaring at each other for a long minute before Jaron broke the silence. "This is because the suggestion is coming from me, isn't it?"

"Why would that matter?"

"Because Adrianna has agreed to marry me."

Titan felt his teeth involuntarily clench. "That has nothing to do with this."

"What then?!" Jaron yelled, standing.

Titan watched him carefully. He had first met Jaron when he was appointed general just over a year before. The man was exemplary when it came to honor and trust. And he was the crowned sovereign of the west. Titan sighed.

"Because my capture will mean his victory."

"Why?"

Titan closed his eyes. "He wants my sword and bracers. They're—"

"None of his concern," came a voice from behind. Titan whirled, the chair behind him falling to the ground. The two wooden doors swung closed, revealing behind them two men in full armor. The one sported a thick beard and a large battle ax. The other bore a chilling, silvery face.

"Devvon," he hissed.

Devvon gave a mock bow. "So good to see you, my young friend. And how is your father?"

Titan felt anger spread through his body as if his veins carried molten lava rather than blood. "I'll kill you."

"Not likely," Devvon said, raising his hands to reveal the gloves in place. "At least you haven't had much success with that endeavor thus far."

Titan glanced around the room. Devvon was right. He wasn't prepared. He needed to find a way out. There were several windows in the walls, but none close enough that he could reach them. He glanced back at Jaron, who hadn't moved. "Betrayer."

"I didn't lie," Jaron replied. "These two were the messengers I told you of, and they have promised as I said." He paused. "But I am sorry. I admired you and looked forward to your reign."

Titan watched as Devvon and the other man slowly approached. "So you'll leave this city alone then, Devvon?"

Devvon sneered. "Of course not. An emperor can't have a rebellious city within striking distance."

Jaron growled. "Devvon, we had a deal."

"Yes. If you convinced Titan to give himself up, I would spare the city." He smiled. "But you didn't convince him.

You've left that to me. That's twice that you have made empty promises." He took another step towards Titan. "There's nowhere to run, boy."

Titan looked around himself and knew it was true. While he could break through the stone and woodwork of the walls with a jump using the bracers, his body likely wouldn't survive the impact. The closest window was directly behind him. Even if the table and Jaron weren't in the way, it was still too far a distance to cover before Devvon killed him.

"Jaron," Titan said quietly. "You need to leave."

Jaron drew his sword. "I'm not leaving you outnumbered."

"It's not worth the risk of the people losing another king."

"Then let's make sure we kill them before they kill us."

The silent man next to Devvon hefted his ax. Devvon smiled. "If numbers are all you're concerned about, that's easily remedied. General, leave us." He nodded towards Jaron. "That gives you freedom to leave as well."

"My liege," the man beside Devvon argued.

"Leave, Felk."

The general didn't move. "Devvon, don't be a fool."

"NOW!"

The general gritted his teeth and turned. He strode to the door, swung it open, and stormed out. Devvon returned his attention to Jaron. "Your turn, lad."

Jaron hesitated. "Go," Titan said calmly.

"Yes, lad. Prince Titan and I need to discuss his surrender. You and I can re-open negotiations once we're done."

Titan heard Jaron take a deep breath and slowly exhale. He crossed to the door, cracked it open and walked through.

Devvon kept his eyes on Titan as he backed up to the door. He reached a hand out and swung the steel crossbar into place. "Now," he said, walking forward again. "I will kill you." He raised his hands and pointed them at Titan. "Last words, young prince?"

Titan glared at him. "I hope you got as good a laugh out of those fakes as I did."

Devvon growled and let loose a fireball. Titan dove to the side as the shot struck the table behind him and threw it against the wall behind. The flames began to consume the wood as the heat immediately filled the room. Titan rolled to his feet, then darted again as another shot rushed at him.

"No sense in moving, boy," Devvon snarled. "You're only delaying the inevitable." He aimed again.

Titan triggered his bracers. As the next shot came, he jumped out of the way with as little strength as possible. His shoulder hit hard against the bookcase ten feet to his left. He gasped from the pain, but righted himself and leapt again in time to avoid the next fireball. He looked back towards where the first shot had struck, the wood of the table and window being devoured by the flames. As he glanced around, he realized that all three of the walls surrounding him were engulfed.

"Nowhere to go," Devvon smiled. "No more room for those fancy dives you're so fond of." He raised his hands again.

"Leave my people alone," Titan gasped through the smoke.

Devvon lowered his hands slightly. "I'm afraid I can't do that."

"You've got what you came for." He raised his arms, showing the bracers. *Keep him talking.*

"Boy, if I don't conquer them now I'll just have to conquer them later." He paused. "Where is Richards?"

Titan shook his head. "Don't know."

"Liar. Tell me."

"Or what? You'll kill me? You'll attack my people? What more could you possibly threaten?"

Devvon smiled wickedly. "Do you happen to know where Queen Adrianna is? I assume that's the same Adrianna you and young Jaron were speaking of. Unless he is marrying two girls named Adrianna."

Titan felt his blood pouring through his veins again. "Leave her alone."

"Where is Richards?"

Titan glanced around himself, silently counting.

"There's nowhere to run, boy. The room is being consumed. It's only a matter of time before the flames do my work for me."

Titan shook his head. "The flames were your mistake."

"Oh? And how is that?"

"Because it let me do this." Titan jumped straight backwards as hard as he could. He soared across the room and smashed back first into the fire directly behind him as Devvon raised his hands once again. The wood, already weakened from the intense heat of the fire, gave way easily.

He burst through the window and found himself hurtling at a break-neck speed toward the city beyond. He quickly released the bracers and triggered the wings, spreading them to slow his fall.

He heard the scream of rage from behind, followed by a quick succession of explosions. Titan banked hard to the left, out of the line of sight of the window he had just burst through. It would be only a matter of seconds before Devvon left the map room and found another window to shoot from. Titan turned his attention towards the mountains beyond the city wall.

He yelled in pain as his back began to burn. He glanced back and found his shirt on fire. *Ragdons*, he thought, trying to swat at the flames. He hastily looked for a nearby source of water. There were several lakes within view, but nothing close enough. He made a snap decision and brought his wings in close to his body.

He immediately began plummeting, head first towards the ground. His speed increased steadily, the wind whipping through his hair while the ground grew ever closer. With enough air flow, the fire would be snuffed out. But with limited room, Titan felt himself begin to panic. He watched the buildings rush up at him as he counted in his head.

One. Two. Three! He spread his wings and swooped just over one of the city's marketplaces. He pulled up hard, barely clearing the roof of the house directly in front of him and began to pump his wings. He glanced back and sighed when he found the fire extinguished.

At the sound of a scream his attention was jerked back to the ground below. A woman was pointing up at him, her other hand over her mouth. Another scream from behind. Titan realized he was still smoldering, and that combined with his bat-like wings was likely a terrifying sight. *Oh well*, he thought. Not much he could do about that. He returned his attention instead to the mountains before him.

*****

Felk watch the new king carefully as he closed the door behind him. The king turned, sword held firmly in his hand.

"And you, general?" Jaron held his sword at the ready.

Felk shook his head. "I have no interest in fighting you." He slid his ax into its leather case at his side.

Jaron stood where he was, though his sword lowered several inches. "Do you hate me, Felk?"

"No, Jaron. I don't hate you."

"But you think I'm a traitor to my country."

Felk furrowed his brow. "From my point of view, you had to choose either your conscience or your duty. And you chose."

"You think I chose wrong."

"I'll let Devvon be your judge."

Jaron's sword lowered further. "He's going to kill me, isn't he? Promises mean nothing to him, only power." Jaron hesitated. "You seem a reasonable man. Help us stop this massacre."

"I'm not like you, Jaron. I won't turn on my own king, even if I don't agree with him."

Jaron hesitated. "So you deny that the man is insane?"'"

Felk folded his arms. "I didn't deny anything."

"You dishonor him."

"It is unfortunate, but at times he dishonors himself, against my counsel."

"Oh? And when Devvon said this idea was yours, to trap Titan here?"

Felk shook his head again. "You really don't see it, do you? Devvon will destroy this city. By leading him here, I had hoped to spare lives."

An explosion sounded on the other side of the door. Felk's ax was back in his hand in an instant, while Jaron's sword whipped back up to the ready. They eyed each other as Jaron stepped to the door. He leaned against it, but the sturdy wood held firm. He turned his full attention back to Felk and advanced. "What's going on in there?"

Felk raised his ax slightly. "Careful, boy. You're making assumptions again." Jaron stopped just out of the reach of Felk's axe. Another explosion sounded from within the room. Jaron clenched his jaw.

"Open the door."

Felk held his ground. "Can't, lad. It would appear Devvon has locked it from the inside."

Jaron leapt forward and swung his sword. Felk swung his ax to the side, blocking the blow. "You lie," Jaron growled as he began to circle Felk.

"Stop it, Jaron." Felk eyed him warily. "As I said before, I have no interest in fighting you." Another explosion. "Devvon is his own man. I, nor anyone else, can control him."

Jaron stopped. He eyed Felk for a moment. "You really don't approve of this, do you?"

Felk held his gaze. "No." Another explosion.

Jaron glanced back to the door. "Then what is happening in there?"

"Ragdons if I know." Felk strode over to the door, careful not to let Jaron out of his sight. He pushed hard against the door. The door felt ... warm. "Whatever it is, Devvon didn't tell me about it. Is there another way in there?"

Jaron shook his head. "That room is a fortress unto itself. One way in and out, with doors that would take some time to break down."

They heard an angry scream, followed by three explosions in quick succession. Felk heard the crossbar moving on the other side and stepped back just in time to avoid the doors being slammed open. A wave of intense heat washed over them, and both stumbled back. Bright fires were intensely ablaze on all sides of the room. The metallic Devvon stood in the doorway. He looked around, seeming to be gathering his bearings, and ran between the two down the hallway.

"Devvon!" Felk yelled after him.

"Shut up, fool! And dispatch of the traitor!" Devvon turned a corner and disappeared.

Felk stared after him for a moment, then turned back to Jaron. The young king was already at the ready with his sword. He was glancing quickly back and forth from Felk to the burning room. "What have you done with Titan?"

"I told you, I don't know." He took a step towards Jaron. "I don't agree with Devvon, but he is my king."

"And you obey your delirious, demonic king's requests? Wouldn't you rather follow your conscience?"

Felk hefted his large ax and took a deep breath. "I am bound by my honor." He took another step forward.

Jaron backed away slowly. "You call following that man honor? He's not even human anymore!"

Felk continued forward. "No. But I do call keeping my word honor. And I am sworn to obey him."

"Even to killing the innocent? You will attack the city, then, when he commands it? You will slaughter thousands of women and children?" Jaron's back bumped into the stone wall behind him.

Felk stopped in front of him. "I am bound."

CHAPTER 31

Two days of riding blindfolded and bound had made Adrianna both sore and sick. They had let her sleep on the ground at night, but had neither untied her nor removed her gage. Instead, they had insisted on binding her legs together as well and tying them to a tree. Her wrists were worn raw, as was the skin on either side of her mouth. It seemed as though the horse would simply plod on forever at her expense.

On the morning of the third day, the procession came to a stop. Without the men's feet and the horse's hooves beating against the ground, she could pick out the sound of waves crashing a distance away. Adrianna heard a single set of footsteps move off a short distance.

"Wait just a minute, chaps." Adrianna recognized Hulkins' voice.

"There's no more room. We'll be back next month for another shipment." The second voice had an accent Adrianna hadn't heard before.

"No more room you say? You haven't even seen her."

"I can see her fine from here. And it doesn't matter; beauty has little to do with how many we can fit."

A chuckle. "I think you'd better take a look. I've half a mind to hang on to this one for myself."

The second voice sounded annoyed. "We're casting off in ten minutes. If it will appease you, I will look at her and make an offer. But as I said, there's no more room."

She heard the men draw near and held her breath. Rough hands began working at the knots at the back of her head.

The blindfold fell away first, and Adrianna was immediately blinded by the brilliant sunlight.

"You see, my man? A real beauty."

The gag was removed next. Her jaw ached as she stretched it. The world finally came into focus. The white, sandy beach her horse was standing on was starkly contrasted by the blue water that filled the rest of her view. She had been to the ocean before, but every time she was amazed by its immensity. A rowboat was tied to a tree a short distance away. She looked out to the ocean and picked out a large ship anchored several hundred yards out.

Her eyes finally came to rest on her kidnappers. She was still surrounded, but Hulkins now stood with an extremely distinct looking man at his side. The strangers face was flat, his jet black hair and eyes a huge disparity to his pale skin. A thin, manicured mustache occupied his upper lip, and the man's diminutive frame was covered in black from head to toe. His intense gaze made her uncomfortable. She squirmed at the ropes tying her hands behind her back, but the bandit left them in place.

"Now, how much would you say something like this is worth?"

The foreigner looked her up and down. "Twenty."

"Twenty? I can probably sell just her hair for as much."

"Thirty then."

"Friend, you're teasing me. Notice the length of the hair, the developed figure, her piercing eyes. I guarantee this one will fetch a very good price. All I'm asking is that you share the profit with me."

"I'll pay you," Adrianna interjected.

Both men gave her a glance, then returned to their conversation. "Fifty."

"Closer, but we're still not there yet. Let's make it an even hundred."

The foreigner scoffed. "I won't deny she's a fine prize. But is she really worth four others combined?"

Adrianna coughed. "I'll pay you a thousand."

"Look at her, man! There's not a woman we've given you that has been this well taken care of."

"I will pay you!" Adrianna's voice rose.

One of the bandits standing beside her chuckled. "You keep on trying, little miss. Just don't be disappointed when no one hears you. You're not the first to try it." He smirked. "Hulkins listened once. He strangled the girl when she couldn't make good on her promise. It's probably best you just keep quiet."

Adrianna scowled. "But I *can* pay."

"Eighty then. Surely we can agree on eighty."

"I'll give you no more than seventy."

"I'd settle for seventy, but we're going to have to feed her till you return. Food is expensive these days. Eighty is really the best I can do."

The foreigner looked at her again. "Seventy. And I'll find room for her on this boat."

A wide grin spread over Hulkins face. "Thought you'd change your mind. Seventy it is." He held out a hand, and the man shook it. The foreigner pulled a small pouch from the inside of his coat and delivered it to Hulkins.

"Half now, half if she survives the voyage. As always."

"Of course," Hulkins pocketed the bag and waved the bandit guiding the horse forward. "She's all yours."

Adrianna watched as the reins were held out. In the moment where one hand opened before the other one closed, Adrianna leaned hard to the right and forward. The horse jumped into motion, barreling between the foreigner and one of the other bandits, knocking both to the ground. She leaned harder, and the horse darted into the long grass surrounding the beach.

"Idiots, after her!"

Adrianna spared a glance behind her to see the bandits run towards a group of horses tied up a short distance away. *Ragdons*, she cursed. They hadn't been in view during the negotiations, and she had been banking on the fact that her kidnappers would be on foot. She hadn't eaten or slept well in two days, and the horse had been walking for miles already without a rest.

She bent further forward, careful to stay balanced on top of the horse. With her hands tied she doubted whether she could stay in the saddle through any sharp turns. *Can't out maneuver, can't outrun.* She heard the sound of horse hooves start up behind her.

She burst into the trees. Her horse leapt over a fallen log, then swerved to avoid a tree as Adrianna leaned away from it. The forest wasn't thick enough to lose her pursuers. She doubted she even could with her hands bound. *I have to try.* Around a bush, between two large trees, across a creek. She gasped as sticks and leaves slapped at her face. She no longer had to strain to hear the horses behind her. They were definitely getting closer.

The trees gave way to a dirt highway. Making a snap judgment, Adrianna swerved to her left and pushed the horse into a dead run. If she could create some distance through a burst of speed, then swerve back into the trees, she might be able to lose them.

A rider darted out of the trees in front of her. He pulled at the reins of the horse, bringing the animal to a stop. She looked back and saw three more horsemen emerge from where she had just come from. She searched the trees on her right for an opening, but found none. Finally, she turned back to her left to re-enter the woods she had just left.

Hulkins burst through the foliage, followed by three more of his companions. Adrianna pulled up hard, bringing her own horse to a stop. She whirled again, trying to find an escape. The horse beneath her was gasping for breath from the exertion. Both sides of the road were block, as were the forests on either side. There was no way out.

Adrianna sighed, resignedly. She waited patiently as the men neared on all sides, creating a circle around her. All of them had their swords drawn. Hulkins stopped directly in front of her.

"You think you're clever?"

Adrianna didn't say anything.

Hulkins growled. "Now you've got some real learning to do. Only one way to teach a woman the lessons you need to learn." He gave his sword a swing.

"Please," Adrianna said quietly, fear suddenly filling her. "I can pay you."

"I told you, wench. Women shouldn't lie. And even if you could, you couldn't pay what you've already cost me. The ship is gone, and on it the richest trader from the east. And he just broke an arm because of your little stunt. He likely won't buy from me ever again." Hulkins clenched his teeth. "And that makes me angry."

Adrianna backed her horse away, but was cornered by swords on the other side. "I can pay you thousands."

"Not enough," Hulkins said as he continued forward, "to make it worth not killing you."

"How about your own life?" came a voice from the side. Adrianna looked to find a familiar figure walk into the circle between two of the bandits. Reon smiled broadly. "That's a fairly good trade, your life for hers."

Hulkins stared at Reon. "And who are you?"

"Reon."

"And you threaten me?"

"Anything for a friend." He shrugged.

"This girl is your friend?" Hulkins smiled. "All the better. I'll make her watch while I kill you, *and then* I'll kill her." He dismounted from his horse and walked towards Reon.

Reon held his ground. "Do I get a sword?"

Hulkins continued forward. "Should have brought your own."

"Well that's not very fair. Especially seeing as how I'm offering you your life for such a low price." He winced. "Sorry, Adrianna. Didn't think about that one before I said it."

"I guess the odds really aren't in your favor, boy." Hulkins lifted his sword.

"Then how about I even them?"

Hulkins paused. "How?"

Reon just pointed behind Hulkins. Hulkins slowly turned, keeping an eye on Reon. "What is it? I don't see –" He cut off as an enormous, dark shape swooped down from the trees and smashed him to the ground. Adrianna screamed in surprise. Reon smiled.

"Told you, mate."

The shape solidified into a man. He spun and threw Hulkins' unconscious body into two other bandits, smashing them off of their mounts. Adrianna leaned forward, aiming straight for where Reon was standing. "Reon, get on!"

Reon nodded, grabbed the saddle, and climbed on behind her. "Yes. It's probably best that we remove ourselves from the situation. Let these gentlemen sort things out."

Adrianna leaned forward and the horse took off once again. Reon yelped and reached around Adrianna, grasping at the reins.

"Ragdons, woman! You don't even have your hands free!"

Adrianna glanced back in time to see three more men be thrown from their mounts. She leaned harder. *Out of the frying pan and into the fire.*

"I think we're far enough away, don't you?"

"We need to put space between us and them!"

"Why? I guarantee the bandits are going to lose."

"Because when whatever that was finishes, it's likely to come for us." She pulled the horse to a stop. "I need my hands. Untie me."

Reon chuckled as he started working at the ropes.

"Reon, this isn't funny!"

"I actually think it is," Reon said, finishing with the knots and dismounting. "After all, that bloke thought quite a bit of himself. All of them getting whipped by a single man? That's exceptionally funny."

Adrianna looked back towards the fight, rubbing her wrists. She saw several horses trotting both towards her and away, all of them without riders. She could see her kidnappers lying in heaps. "Reon what was that thing?"

His response was a wide grin. "I bet he'll be around shortly to introduce himself."

"Why are you smiling? Whatever it was, if it can clear through that many men that fast, we need to get out of here."

"Nah. This one is all muscles, no brains. I'm sure we can trick him into not attacking us. Just bat your eyes at him."

Adrianna spun as she heard footsteps approaching from the forest. A shadowy form hesitated behind the bush beside the road.

"Who are you?" she demanded.

No reply.

"Adrianna," Reon said slowly. "Try to stay calm. This might be somewhat jarring for you."

Adrianna continued to stare at the shadow. She realized her hands were shaking. "Show yourself!"

After another moment's hesitation, the shadow walked forward. It pushed aside the leaves and stepped into the full light. An all-too familiar smile spread across the man's face. Her vision blurred, the world around her swaying.

"Hello, Adrianna."

"Titan," she gasped, even as she felt herself falling from the horse's back.

CHAPTER 32

"The city's quiet," the captain said at Devvon's side. "We haven't seen any movement since you came back, my lord."

Good, Devvon thought. *Less men required to hold it.* "Any spy reports?"

"Nothing, sire."

"Excellent. Send for General Felk."

The captain saluted and strode quickly off. Devvon had intended this army to overwhelm the city. But with the city hiding in their basements, it wouldn't take the full sixty thousand to keep the peace afterwards. He would leave those necessary, and take the remainder with him on his hunt. Perhaps sheer numbers would prove the deciding factor. Devvon reached his tent, crossed to his chair, and sat. An aide brought him a glass of wine without further prompting.

Felk entered the tent. "You asked for me, my lord?"

"Yes. I wanted to congratulate you."

"Congratulate, sire?"

"Yes. Whatever you did to this young king has had drastic effects on the kingdom. It would appear that the entire city is in a panic, even so far as to stay out of the streets. There is no movement." Devvon raised his cup. "I said dispatch of him, not paint the city with his blood, or whatever it is you did. I commend you for it."

"Thank you, sire."

Devvon nodded. "With the city in this state, it should take considerably less men to hold it once we have attacked. Once the city is ours, we will take forty thousand men with us to track Titan down and leave twenty thousand in the city."

"Forty thousand to hunt down one man?"

"I want no mistakes this time. And if we can't find him, I want a large enough force with me to affect my original plan." His smile had faded, his jaw clenching. "Burn him out."

Felk nodded. "How did he escape?"

Devvon stood, strode over to the general, and backhanded him across the face. Felk stood firm, despite the metal slap. "That's none of your concern, general."

Felk glared. "When do we attack?"

"As soon as you can arrange it. After that, we will take these legions with us and depart by sundown." Devvon proffered a list to Felk.

Felk scanned the paper. "These are all the new recruits."

"Yes."

"I was under the impression that you preferred to deal with veterans."

"The last unit listed. I want my personal guard to be comprised of veterans. As for the new recruits, I don't dare leave them here. We must take all of them with us, as they're not properly trained yet to hold a city."

Felk nodded. "I believe they would do fine, but as you wish."

Devvon waved a hand of dismissal and Felk left through the tent door. Two hours later, Devvon still sat in his chair, now outside the tent, and watched as the last of the blue flags in the city was replaced by a red flag. He smiled, then waited patiently as a soldier emerged from the city's gate on a horse. *That went even faster than I had hoped*, he noted as the soldier approached.

"You have a report?"

"Yes, my lord." He handed a paper to Devvon.

Devvon unfolded it and read for a moment. He looked up. "No casualties whatsoever?"

The soldier hesitated. "No, sire."

"How is that possible?"

"The ... the city was empty, sire."

Devvon stood. "Empty? How?"

"We're not sure, sire. General Felk has asked if you still intend to leave with this news."

Devvon nodded slowly. "Yes. Wherever the people are, we'll find them. But we have a more important task at hand.

Tell the general to leave the securing of the city to the captains and to bring those leaving with us immediately."

"Yes, sire." The man returned to his horse and rode swiftly back towards the city.

Empty? Devvon stared at the red flags, now less momentous then they had seemed a moment before. He shook the thoughts from his head. He would deal with that mystery in due time. At the present, his goals were much simpler: find Titan, take back the sword and bracers, and make sure to get Felk killed in the process. And more than anything he knew his timing would have to be perfect.

*****

"Adrianna." Titan gently shook her shoulders. Reon was leaning against the wall of the cave, beaming.

"You know, she's likely to faint again if she wakes up while you're that close. Your breath is awful."

Titan ignored him. He shook her again. "Adrianna, wake up." When she didn't respond, Titan held his hand out to Reon. "Here."

"I want to do it."

"Reon," Titan said sternly. Sullenly, Reon handed over his water pouch. Titan emptied a small pool into his palm, then sprinkled it onto Adrianna's face. She immediately squinted her eyes and began sputtering. Titan watched her intently as she wiped the water from her face. After a moment, she cracked her eyelids open and her eyes slowly focused on Titan.

He smiled. "Hello, Adrianna."

Her hand hit him hard across the cheek. Reon burst into laughter as Titan stumbled backwards. "Easy, it's me! It's Titan!"

Adrianna sat slowly, watching him. She didn't say anything.

Reon stifled his laughter. Titan took a step back towards her. "Are you okay?"

She continued to watch his face. "I just wanted to be sure," she whispered. A tear slid down her cheek. "You're alive."

"I am," Titan replied. "I'm … sorry. I didn't know everyone would assume I was dead. I would have come back sooner."

Adrianna gave a quiet laugh, the color slowly returning to her cheeks.

"You're ... not angry?" Titan asked carefully.

Adrianna shook her head. "How could I be angry for getting exactly what I asked the Ragdons for?"

Titan felt a pang of guilt. Not only had he left her thinking he was dead, but her only recourse had been imagined deities. "I still think anger would be understandable."

Adrianna slid herself over to the side of the cave and leaned against the rock wall. "If you were alive, why didn't you come back after the attack at the Tower?"

Reon smiled. "That story is actually quite interesting."

Titan took a deep breath. "I've been running from Devvon."

"What better place to run than your city with its soldiers and walls?" She looked down to her hands. "To your friends?"

Titan sat with his back to the opposite wall and began to rehearse his experiences from the previous weeks to her. She listened carefully, asked questions occasionally, and voiced her doubts as to his sanity.

"You're crazy."

"That idea has crossed my mind."

"A magic sword?"

Titan swung the sword off his back and handed it across the short distance to her. "Notice the black stone on the hilt."

She looked at it briefly, then leaned the sword against the wall beside her. "Titan, this is ludicrous. What you speak of can't happen."

Titan stood and crossed to a nearby boulder. He reached down and gripped it firmly with his hands, triggering the bracers on his forearms. He lifted the enormous rock easily above his head and heaved. It crashed into another boulder twenty feet away, both of them cracking from the impact. He turned again to find Adrianna's face pale once more.

Reon was already moving to her. "Might have been a bit fast for showing off, all things considered."

Titan reached her other side and lowered her gently to the ground. Reon grabbed her legs and lifted them into the air, forcing the blood back to her head.

"Water," she whispered.

Reon handed over his pouch once again and Titan put it to her lips. She closed her eyes and took long, slow swallows. When the pouch was empty, she opened her eyes again. "I need to eat." Titan helped her to sit as Reon fetched several bags, pulling from them bread and cheese. Adrianna accepted them with thanks and ate.

Titan and Reon stayed close, watching for signs of another bout of fainting. Every bite she took seemed to cause visible improvement in her steadiness. After several minutes she put the food down. "That's all I should eat for now."

"All you should eat?" Reon examined the remainder as it was handed back to him. "That was enough for Titan and I combined."

"I haven't eaten in a few days."

Titan clenched his fists. Adrianna looked at them, then up at Titan's face, smiling. "I'm better now."

Titan closed his eyes. "I didn't even know you were in danger. I should have been here."

"You're here now." She reached over and took his hand. He looked down at it, then up at her.

"Adrianna ..."

She held his gaze, leaning towards him slowly. "I love you, Titan," she whispered.

"I ..." Titan felt his pulse quickening as words escaped him.

Reon coughed. "I think I'm going to go for a walk." When his statement wasn't acknowledged by either Adrianna or Titan, he chuckled, stood, and brushed off his pants. He started whistling as he rounded the corner out of the cave.

Adrianna continued to lean closer, watching Titan's mouth. Titan felt drawn to her by an unavoidable, undeniable power. It reminded him of the feeling of being dragged back to the world below when jumping with the bracers.

She is my world, he realized. *I would do anything for her.* He had been denying the emotion for so long, it was a relief to finally admit defeat. He loved her. He ached for her.

Adrianna closed her eyes as her warm breath tickled at his cheek.

"Adrianna ..."

She pulled back several inches and met his gaze. She reached a hand to his face, stroked his cheek. "Don't say anything," she whispered, leaning in again.

Titan gently gripped her hand. "It's the law," he whispered in return, hating the words even as they left his mouth.

"Laws are meant to be broken." Her lips brushed playfully against his.

He took a deep breath, her scent filling him with desire. "And ... you're engaged."

She froze, unmoving, the space between them immeasurably small. She pulled back slowly, eyes still closed. Her back came to rest against the stone wall as she let out a long, slow breath. "I didn't know you knew." She nodded slowly, eyes still closed. "But you are right. I am engaged." A tear streaked down her cheek.

Titan yearned for her to return, for her to make the decision and press through his defenses. The brush of her lips still had him reeling, inwardly gasping for breath. He watched her as she brought her knees up and rested her arms and head on them. She was so beautiful, even after days of forest living. She had professed her love for him without reserve, and he had thrown it in her face. Titan closed his eyes and thumped the back of his head against the stone wall.

Neither spoke for a while. They sat, starring at the wall across from them, the inches between them gradually becoming miles. Titan swallowed.

"I'm sorry."

Adrianna wiped the tears from her cheeks. "You've only ever done the right thing, Titan. Don't apologize for being the better person." She let out a long sigh. "So what do we do now?"

"I don't know. I haven't known what to do for weeks."

"Titan!"

Both Titan and Adrianna leapt to their feet at the sound of Reon's yell. They darted outside and searched the forest around them, but saw no one.

"Titan!" came the yell again. Titan looked up to see a figure with a pair of large, black wings plummeting towards them. Reon was falling, the wings flailing uselessly to either side. He dropped the last thirty feet and slammed into the ground. He gave a sharp cry of pain.

Titan and Adrianna ran towards him. "Reon!" Titan said as he dropped to his knees by him. "Are you okay?"

Reon whimpered. "My arm," he gasped. He rolled over slowly to reveal a small, flat rock beneath him. His left arm was bleeding. He yelled in pain as Titan gingerly moved it to rest on Reon's stomach.

"It looks broken," Adrianna said quietly.

Reon's laugh was cut off by another gasp. "It *feels* broken," he managed to get out.

Titan closed his eyes and shook his head. "What in the blazes were you thinking, taking the sword?"

"What? Let you –" he bit his lower lip "—let you have all the fun?"

Titan let out a sigh and set his jaw. "I'll go get something to wrap it in."

Reon grabbed his sleeve as he made to stand and pulled him back down. "We have to leave now," he wheezed.

"Why?"

"I may have been ... seen."

Titan's heart sank. "Devvon will hear about it."

Reon nodded, wincing again. "I imagine so, seeing as how it was his men who saw me."

"What?!"

Reon nodded towards the northwest. "The East's army is headed this way. I didn't see them till I heard them yelling."

Titan sighed in exasperation. "Let's get your arm wrapped. You won't be able to ride without it secure."

"Why don't you carry him with the wings?" Adrianna asked.

"Yeah?" Reon grimaced.

"Because I'm carrying you," Titan said.

"Don't be stupid, Titan. He needs you more than I do."

"I let you fall into harm's way once. I'm not doing that again."

Adrianna stood, hands on hips. "His arm is broken, Titan. He can't ride."

Titan looked to Reon. "Then he'll have to wait here until I can come back for him."

"And face Devvon? They know we're here. Reon, how long do we have?"

Reon shook his head. "Not sure. An hour, maybe?"

Adrianna turned back to Titan. "You can't make two trips to far enough away in an hour."

"I won't –"

"And I'm the better rider," Adrianna interrupted. "You are going to fly him out of here, and I'll meet up with you ..." she paused. "Where?"

Titan sat back in defeat. "The Tower. It's far enough, and it's the place I most want to stay away from. Devvon will rightly assume it carries with it bad memories." He took a deep breath. "Just ... be careful, okay?"

Adrianna nodded. "I will. Let's get moving." She moved to pull the sword from Reon's back.

"You can't remove it," Titan said.

"Why not? You took it off."

"It's bound to his back." He pulled at Reon's shirt, showing that the sheath was literally attached to his spine through it. Just as had happened with his own shirt, Reon's had been torn down the center of his back. "He'll have to reverse the prayer.

"But his arm ..." Adrianna trailed off.

"Yes," Titan said quietly. He turned to Reon. Reon's eyes were wide, but he gave a nod. "I'll need some help."

Titan fetched a stick for Reon to bite down on. Reon took it between his teeth, took several deep breaths, and closed his eyes. Titan and Adrianna carefully guided his broken arm in the reversal prayer to unbind the wings. Reon collapsed in tears once the sword was off, and Adrianna set to wrapping his arm to his chest. Titan swung the sword onto his back, feeling comforted by its familiar weight. He reached down and with Adrianna helped Reon to his feet.

After making sure Reon was steady, he turned to find Adrianna already mounting her horse a short distance away. She turned back. "May the Ragdons –" Titan shook his head, cutting her off.

"May *God* keep you."

Adrianna nodded her understanding, smiling sadly. "And you." Titan watched as her horse bolted forward. Within moments she was out of sight. He listened longingly to the fading beat of the horse's hooves.

I love you.

CHAPTER 33

Felk rode to Devvon's right at the head of the vast army. Even having left twenty thousand men in the city, the number of men was still daunting. *Forty thousand*, Felk pondered again, *for one man*. Devvon was correct that killing a king would unhinge a kingdom, and that by killing his successor the kingdom would fall into chaos. But they had taken the capital of the west. What more was to be gained?

Devvon said nothing as they rode, preferring instead to glare at the road ahead. Felk watched the forest round about, but saw nothing. Trees, bushes, and the occasional bird. Even those were sparse as the forest creatures ran from the throng of men. Felk looked off to his left and could pick out the tower in the distance. Several low mountains were scattered throughout the forest surrounding it, but nothing large enough to hinder his view of the looming structure.

Devvon's not telling me something. That much had been obvious since the night the king arrived enveloped in steel. But Felk sensed there was more to this quest for Titan than Devvon was letting on.

"Sire!"

Felk turned to find a young boy running towards them from the trees to the right. The boy was obviously underage. Felk growled under his breath at Devvon's stupidity.

Devvon pulled his horse to a stop and Felk followed. "What is it?"

The boy skidded to a stop. "There's something in the forest, sire. Something big."

Devvon clenched his jaw. "What was it?"

"Some kind of demon. It looked like a man –"

"How far?"

"Two miles east."

Devvon turned to Felk. "Bring those on horseback, order those on foot to come as quickly as possible."

Felk nodded. "And our search for Titan?"

"Just do it, fool." Devvon kicked his horse into a gallop in the direction indicated.

Felk gave the orders and pushed his own horse into a run. *A demon?* Since when did Devvon even believe in such nonsense, let alone chase after it? The thousand horses thundered down the road, the noise drowning out all else. Whatever Devvon was really after, it was apparent that he was intent on making no mistakes this time.

Due east was through the forest, but the road nearly paralleled that course, angling slightly to the north. Two miles would pass in only a handful of minutes without the hindrance of trees. Devvon rode at the front, his skin gleaming and his cape flapping wildly. As Felk rode behind him, he could still pick out the burnt edges of the red cloth.

Devvon raised a hand and the procession came to an immediate halt.

"Horse hooves," Devvon said, sounding surprised. Felk cleared his throat, but Devvon silenced him with a sharp gesture. "Why would he be on a horse?" he mused quietly.

Felk paused, picking out the echoing clapping. "Shall we follow?"

Devvon nodded and pointed towards the forest. "He's coming from that way." He closed his eyes and waited for a moment. "Headed almost due north. He will have to cross the road ahead. Let's make sure we're waiting for him when he does."

Without further explanation Devvon spurred his horse on, and once again the beating of the hooves grew to a roar. Devvon hunched low in his saddle, pushing his horse faster and faster.

The small army rounded a bend in the trees and began down the straight road beyond. Felk raised his head in time to see a flash of color dart across the road several hundred yards in front of them. As quickly as it was there, it was gone again in the forest to their left.

"After him!" Devvon roared and banked his horse in pursuit of the rider.

Felk and the thousand followed. Felk gave the command to his captains to branch off and flank the rider from either side. Whoever it was, they stood little chance riding through the thick forest outnumbered a thousand to one. Felk pushed his horse faster, struggling to keep Devvon in sight. Devvon plowed on, undeterred by the whipping branches.

Felk looked to either side to see the line of horses tearing through the forest. Even if they lost the rider, the line was long enough that their query had no choice but to barrel forward at full speed. Any angle to the left or right would mean capture within moments.

"Titan!" Devvon yelled as he continued to ride. No answer was heard, but Devvon didn't appear to be expecting one. Instead he lifted his body off the back of his horse, transferred the reins from his hands to his teeth, and pointed both palms directly ahead of him.

Felk cocked his head at the sloppy prayer. *I didn't realize he –*

A blast of fire shot from Devvon's hands and streaked through the forest. It slammed into a grouping of trees, blowing them apart and igniting their wood. Felk yanked at the reins of his horse and stared. Devvon rode on, his hands still raised. Another ball of flames shot forward, hitting another patch of forest. As it struck, Felk could pick out a single rider darting away from the fire.

The rider charged to the side, but was blocked by yet another blast. The horse reared up on two legs, then darted off again. *What in the Ragdons?!* Devvon still had his hands raised, but had coaxed his horse to a stop. Another ball of flame. He watched patiently, then another. *How?* Felk wondered in fear and awe.

He looked to his sides and saw the line of horsemen had pulled to a stop on either side of him. Each pair of eyes was riveted on the spectacle. Felk watched the terror grow.

Devvon continued his work. Within moments, a circle had been made, one side enclosed by men, the other by flames. Devvon lowered his hands and watched the rider a hundred feet before him search desperately for a hole. Felk glanced around and quickly deduced that there was none. The rider soon came to the same conclusion and stopped the horse's turning. He faced Devvon square on.

"Well this is interesting," Devvon said loudly. "I hunt for one royalty, but I catch another." He beckoned the rider forward.

Felk studied the unknown figure as the horse slowly moved towards Devvon. The man was wearing a simple shirt and trousers. His face was covered in dirt and ash, as were his clothes. His blonde hair – Felk squinted through the smoke. The rider wasn't a man. As she approached Devvon, Felk finally placed her.

"Queen Adrianna," Devvon said flatly.

"Devvon," came the angry reply. She stopped her horse ten feet from his. "What do you want with me?" Felk furrowed his brow. Unlike every soldier in his army, she didn't seem surprised by Devvon's appearance and had no question as to his identity. Had she seen him already as he was now?

Devvon cocked his head. "Shouldn't you be in the South with your people?"

"I'm afraid my kingdom is occupied by the enemy at present." She glared.

Devvon chuckled. "I'm not your enemy. We're more like … partners." He paused. "Where is Titan?"

Adrianna shrugged. "Isn't he in the West?"

"No." Devvon studied the girl. "Where is he?"

She held his gaze in silence.

Devvon shrugged. "I guess the answer to that is of relatively little value now."

"Oh? And why is that?"

Devvon smiled. "Because it is more beneficial to know where he is going to be."

"So you can see the future now?"

"It doesn't take seeing the future," he said calmly, "to know that a man in love will come after the object of his desires. Especially, my dear, when she is in danger."

Adrianna raised her chin. "Titan is nowhere near here. He doesn't know I'm in danger."

"I very much doubt that."

Several men to Felk's right began to yell. Felk looked up to see a large black shape falling from the sky. Two enormous bat-like wings extended from either side of the shape. The yelling increased as the creature continued its course. Right towards Devvon and Adrianna.

Devvon raised his hands. More flames erupted into the air, forcing the demon to bank hard. Another shot forced it up and over the tree line again. It disappeared for a moment, then reappeared on the opposite side of the circle of flames. Devvon already had his hands raised and fired again. The demon darted away again, trying to get to the ground. Devvon continued firing, cutting off all routes to himself and Adrianna.

"Felk!" Devvon yelled. "Tie her!"

Felk waved to four other horsemen and kicked his horse forward. She backed slowly away as they approached, but the roaring fire behind her quickly stopped her retreat. Felk dismounted and crossed to her. He held out a hand. "Your highness."

She hesitated. Another shot of flames from Devvon pushed the demon away once again.

"I have orders, your highness. And I will see them done." Felk glanced up as the creature's shadow shot over them.

Adrianna held his gaze. "To the inferno with you."

Felk nodded and drew his ax. "Very well." He darted to her and swiped at the underbelly of the horse. His swing missed the creature's flesh, but sliced through most of the leather belt holding the saddle in place. The beast reared in fright. With the horse vertical, Adrianna's weight was too much for the damage strap. The loud snap was followed by her falling in a heap to the ground.

Two of Felk's men leapt from their horses and helped her to her feet, keeping their hands locked around her arms. Another took the reins of her horse and pulled it away. The fourth dismounted, crossed to her and bound her arms behind her back.

Felk nodded. "Hide her among the men."

The soldiers nodded and hauled her back to the rest of the soldiers. Felk looked over to see Devvon duck as the demon swooped at him, then fire another fireball.

Felk ran to him. "Done, my lord."

Devvon kept his eyes on the forest. "Now bring down that bat."

Felk nodded and ran to his men. He swung up into his saddle. "Bows, men!"

Within a moment a thousand bows were trained on the sky. The forest grew silent, save for the crackling wood of the fires surrounding them. The men watched the sky warily, some visibly shaking. Felk looked to Devvon again. The emperor was turning in a slow circle.

"To your left!" Felk bellowed, just as the demon swooped over the trees again. It dodged Devvon's flames, and most of the men hadn't even turned in time to lose their arrows by the time it was gone again. Several pierced the enormous wings of the creature, but didn't cause enough damage to bring it down.

"After it!" Devvon yelled, kicking his horse forward. Felk ordered the men to follow, noting Adrianna tied on horseback nearby, wearing an eastern helmet and cape. From the air she would be indistinguishable.

The army leapt forward as one and barreled after Devvon through the forest. Felk looked up to see a small plateau before them. The sides were completely vertical, and the top harbored only a few dozen yards of flat ground and a handful of trees. As he watched, he saw the demon swoop down and disappear on top of it.

"Surround it!" Devvon yelled. "Keep your bows at the ready!"

The men quickly circled the area. Felk watched as the demon attempted to take off again from the far side. It appeared to be carrying a man. Devvon shot another fireball alongside the dozens of arrows fired from the soldiers. The demon darted back to the top of the plateau. Within a minute, the men had created a circle five men deep around the entire base.

The horses stilled as the bows were trained once again at the top of the plateau, waiting for any sign of movement. Felk watched intently, but saw nothing. There was just enough room on top for the creature to remain out of view from all sides, and apparently it had chosen to do so. Felk studied the surrounding cliffs, but found no way to scale them. The thing was out of reach, but trapped.

Devvon nudged his horse forward. "Titan!" he yelled.

His voice echoed softly in the silence. There was no answer.

"I have Adrianna, and I *will* kill her! Show yourself!"

More silence from the top.

Devvon took a deep breath. "You're trapped, boy! You have nowhere to run, and I have enough men to keep you up there for a very long time! Tell me, would you rather die quickly by the sword or slowly by starvation?!"

Devvon waited for a moment. After no reply, Devvon nodded. "Very well, fool! You have until dawn to show yourself! If you do so, I'll let Adrianna go free! If you keep me waiting, the only thing for you to gain will be a slow death rather than a swift one!"

He turned to Felk. "Tie the girl to a tree. I don't want him swooping in and carrying her off."

Felk waved a hand to her guards nearby. "Devvon, what was that?"

Devvon dismounted and looked back up towards the top. "It's Titan."

Felk glanced back at the small mountain. Jaron's words echoed in his mind. *And you obey your delirious, demonic king's requests?*

Perhaps Devvon was delirious. Felk hadn't believed it, despite the ludicrous commands he had given. But what if it was true?

"Devvon," he said quiet enough that only the emperor could hear him. "What did you do back there?"

Devvon didn't look at him. "It's none of your concern, Felk."

"I think it is, my liege. You show up like some metallic monster, you shoot fire from your hands, and now you claim Titan is a winged fiend. The men are all terrified of you."

"As well they should be," Devvon countered. "I have more power than they or you can imagine." He pulled his gaze from the mountain. "I want a full thousand with bows trained on that mountain at all times, day and night. There will be no mistakes this time." He strode off towards where Adrianna was now firmly bound to a thick tree.

Felk dismounted. *Your delirious king.*

INTERLUDE

Uyt's axe sank satisfyingly into the wood. He pulled it free, then swung again. Another good bite. Over and over, chipping away at the massive tree. Each swing was small in comparison to the task at hand, but needed to complete the job. One doesn't fell a six foot diameter tree simply by looking at it.

The tree really was a marvel. The only of this size for at least twenty miles. It stretched up into the sky, rising far above any of its neighbors. Uyt had never before cut down a tree so large.

He swung again and again, smiling as the single chip turned into dozens that combined to make a four foot crack, two inches wide. Another man to his left was swinging as well, as was a man to his right. Weaken the base enough, and the whole thing would come down. And the price this much wood would fetch would be well worth the effort of the trio.

Uyt enjoyed the work. Some men didn't like getting blisters or sore backs, but Uyt found it satisfying. A man was built to work. Those who didn't work got soft and bored. Besides, the muscle of his right arm earned him several coins every weak in the tavern's matches. Nothing to complain about.

Uyt's axe bounced off the wood. *What in the –*

He stopped himself. It wasn't right to use a deity's name as a curse, even in his head. Most people believed firmly in the Ragdons and their power, but one did not honor them simply by believing.

Uyt examined the trunk. Lost in thought, he had swung several inches lower. As he looked, he couldn't see even a blemish. The bark below his own gash was as perfect as ever.

"Uyt, if you don't put in your share of the work, don't expect an equal share of the profit."

Uyt stood and smiled. "It isn't work if you love it."

Rews rolled his eyes, not looking at Uyt. "Please don't start again ..."

"The word work, you see, has a bad feeling behind it."

"Just swing your axe, man."

Uyt hefted the tool, still smiling. "And I don't have a bad feeling when I work."

Rews swung again, harder than before. Uyt chuckled. He enjoyed work, but he also sometime enjoyed annoyance. Surely the Ragdons wouldn't condemn him for that.

"So let us not use the word 'work' to describe what we all can agree –"

The wood groaned. Uyt decided to save his counsel for the journey home and the three men stepped back.

"Leaning to the left there."

"Hmm. Bring the horses, we'll hitch them and see if we can topple this thing between those two trees."

"Yes, sir."

Uyt went for the beasts while Rews and Bynil threw their ropes up into the branches in order to give the horses better leverage. Uyt returned with the four animals and they were soon hitched and pulling.

"Careful there, boys. Easy does it."

The tree shifted.

"Here she comes. Watch it. Watch it!"

Time slowed as the wood gave way and the giant began to lean. Limbs of nearby trees were snapped like twigs as the thing gained momentum. The slow beginnings gave way to steady acceleration, and the last dozen feet flew by in a blur. The crash rang through the small valley, and the three men hollered their approval. They unhitched the horses, tied them carefully up again, and set to removing branches. Uyt walked to the base of the tree, whistling.

He rounded the base and stopped short. There was something ... wrong about the stump. He stepped towards it, head cocked. The sides showed the abuse of the axes, and most of the remaining was jagged from the break. But there in the center ...

"Bynil? Sir?"

Bynil's head appeared between several branches atop the tree. "Yeah?"

"It's the trunk, sir."

Bynil wiped sweat from his brow. "What about it?"

"It has ... rings."

Rews whooped in laughter from the far said of the tree. Bynil just stared. "It's a tree, Uyt."

"No, not like normal rings. These rings look carved."

"Don't worry about it, Uyt. Keep chopping."

"Just come look, sir!"

Bynil stretched his back. He climbed down and strode closer. "Fine, Uyt. I'll humor you. I think you're an idiot, but I'd also like to think ..." he trailed off as he stepped up alongside Uyt.

"See, sir? Rings."

"Huh ... ain't that strange."

Rews joined the other two. "What's Uyt found this time?"

Uyt pointed and Rews stepped closer, squinting. His eyesight wasn't that good. He reached a hand over the jagged edge left by the tree and felt. "Smooth. And this one here stops."

Uyt looked closer. "Looks like maybe it goes underneath the broken part." He looked at Bynil.

Bynil folded his arms, and the other two waited. "Alright. Get the tools."

Uyt returned with a hammer and chisel for each of them. They worked carefully at first, not wanting to damage the unnatural circles, but soon found that while they were smooth to the touch, the wood was harder than steel. They chipped pieces of wood away, slowly revealing the oddity. Brushing away the last bits, they stepped back and stared.

There were five nested rings, growing in size from the middle to the outside. The largest circled the entire tree an inch from the where the bark began. Along each carved line was a series of notches at varying intervals. The very middle of the trunk was notched as well, in the exact center of the smallest ring. While most of the notches were no more than round divots in the wood, one of the notches on the third ring was different. It looked a bit larger, and the notch came to a point on one end. Almost like ... what, a drip of water?

Uyt whistled. "Never seen anything like that before."

Rews shook his head. Bynil just frowned.

"So ... what do we do about it?"

Bynil turned. "Nothing. It's just some weird freakish thing that has nothing to do with us."

Rews shrugged at Uyt and turned to follow.

"But we can't just ignore it, sir! This is a sign from the Ragdons!"

Bynil turned back. "Agreed. But them and me have an understanding. I stay out of their way, and they don't kill me. If that's from them, I don't want to mess up their plans for it."

Uyt's jaw dropped open as he turned back to the trunk. "But sir –"

"Come on, Uyt. Your share of the money means your share of the work. Let's keep moving."

CHAPTER 34

Adrianna didn't pull against the ropes. Her wrists were still raw from her previous capture. *Wasn't once enough?* she thought, forcing herself to smile. The last time the sentence was life as a slave-wife. This time it was death. Her smile faded as Devvon approached. While Titan had prepared her, the metal face was still unnerving. She steeled herself, desperate not to show weakness.

"My lady," he said with a sneer.

Adrianna tried to spit at him, but found her mouth was too dry from the days of dehydration.

Devvon smiled. "It seems as though you have had several rough days in quick succession. I would think you would be grateful for the hospitality of a friend."

Behind Devvon another man approached. Adrianna glanced at his beard and ax, then turned her attention back to Devvon. "What do you want, Devvon?"

Devvon stared at her for a long moment. "I think you know exactly what I want." He glanced back up at Titan's hiding place. "In fact, if you can convince Titan to give them to me, I might be inclined to just let you go."

"Liar," Adrianna hissed.

Devvon chuckled. "I prefer to think of it as teasing. That's what lying is among friends."

"And I suppose you were teasing when you said you would let me go if he comes down?"

Devvon spread his arms. "You see? Only allies know each other that well."

Adrianna nodded. "You will kill both of us no matter what we do."

Devvon dropped his arms. "Yes, my dear. I will."

"You're a mindless murderer."

"Strategic assassin turned god."

"Oh? There's a method to your madness?"

"Madness?" Devvon shook a finger at her. "I have thought about my actions in some depth. I want you dead to further unhinge your people's sanity. And I want Titan dead ... well, I suppose I do just want to kill him. We're both right, to an extent." He smiled again. "You see? A partnership."

Adrianna hesitated. *What if* ... She struggled to softened her face. "And what if I agree to a ... partnership?" She held his gaze, putting forth all of her effort to remove any trace of hate. She let her fear briefly show through. "A god needs a goddess."

Devvon's steel face showed nothing, but he hesitated. "You offer yourself to me?"

Adrianna slowly nodded. "In exchange for our lives."

Devvon smiled. "That is an appealing offer, my dear. But it sounds just a mite too familiar." He stroked his chin. "Now let me see ... Oh that's right!" His smile vanished. "That's how the last god was killed. A mistake I won't be making." He bent until they were at eye level. "And pretty though you may be, you're no goddess."

Adrianna growled. "He'll never come down, you know."

Devvon nodded as he stood again. "I have thought that might be so. But as I see it, that's an even better solution for me. If he stays up there, he gets to die slowly, with the last thing going through his mind being how he was responsible for the death of the woman he loves." He smiled in satisfaction. "I can't think of a better fate for the boy."

Adrianna shook her head. "He'll escape."

Devvon set his jaw. "I doubt that." He snapped a finger, and the man to his side stepped forward. "Have her gagged as well. We don't want her spoiling the surprise for Titan."

As the cloth was pulled tight around Adrianna's mouth, she watched in anger as Devvon strode away from her, red cape billowing behind him.

*****

Devvon watched as the men on foot began setting up tents against the backdrop of the sun slowly sinking in the sky. "Captain, have your men start fires. I want large blazes every thirty feet. If something moves up there during the night, I want to make sure our men see it."

As the captain moved off to obey, Devvon returned his attention to the plateau. Titan was trapped, Adrianna was caught, and the kingdoms were already conquered. With Titan's death, the last piece of Devvon's plan was falling into place. After that, it was only a matter of time before he found Richards. And with complete invincibility, he would re-establish the reign that was his right.

Within three or four days Titan would starve, and justice would finally be restored.

*****

"How many?" Reon lay against one of the seven trees on the top.

Titan was on his belly. He shifted forward and did a quick count. He yanked back just in time for three arrows to zip harmlessly by him. He crept back to where Reon was and leaned against another of the trees. "With the new comers? Forty thousand."

Reon whistled. "Forty thousand. All to kill you." He chuckled. "You should feel flattered."

Titan took a deep breath and let it out slowly. "Maybe if we weren't going to die."

Reon nodded. "That does seem to sober one's mood."

Titan had been hoping to leave and rescue Adrianna by cover of nightfall. But Devvon had read his move like a book and had started bonfires around the entire perimeter an hour earlier. He had positioned his men on the inside of the fires, meaning they reaped all the benefits of the light without utterly destroying their night vision. And with only a forty foot drop from the top of the plateau to the ground below, Titan very much doubted he would be able to sneak off.

"So," Reon said quietly, "we die then?"

Titan watched as the last of the sun disappeared below the horizon. He nodded slowly. "I don't have a better plan."

"Maybe if you throw the sword and bracers down to him?"

Titan laughed bitterly. "That would only give him the method to get up here."

"But he hasn't practiced with them." Reon chuckled meekly. "He might break a bone or something."

Titan laughed quietly in response. He closed his eyes and rested his head back against the tree. "Turns out this wasn't a very good spot to hide you."

"Nah. It was fine till you showed up. You do have a tendency to bring trouble with you wherever you go."

"Sorry about that."

"Apology accepted," Reon said with a smile. "Just don't let it happen again."

Darkness crept along the expanse of land before them. Without the defense of a moon, everything gave way to it. It consumed the forests, the mountains, and even the men below. All that was left was fire.

Fire stands supreme, Titan thought bitterly.

An arrow zipped through the night and struck a tree near the edge of the plateau.

"They're getting bored," Reon said flatly.

Titan saw a trail from the arrow in the darkness. "Reon," he said slowly. "There's a rope tied to that arrow."

Reon sat up straight. "Cut it before they start climbing."

Lying flat, Titan drew his sword and moved towards the arrow. He hesitated. "Why would they ..." he trailed off as he pulled it from the tree. He looked at it carefully.

"What is it?" Reon asked. "What's wrong?"

Titan looked over at him. "There's ... a paper rolled around it."

*****

Felk walked boldly through the darkness. He was, after all, a general. He had no reason to hide among his own men.

Treason, an ownerless voice whispered to him in the darkness.

Felk walked passed Devvon's tent. He could hear the king inside, quietly sipping at a drink. Felk shook his head. The king was delirious. Possibly possessed. Something had to be done.

Felk approached the large tent a few dozen yards away. He nodded to the guard on either side of the tent. They were the same two veterans Felk had spoken to several hours earlier. They nodded in return, then returned their vigil to the night. Felk calmly opened the flap of the tent and slipped noiselessly inside.

Adrianna stared angrily at him from her spot at the base of the tree. Devvon, in his madness had ordered a tent be constructed around the tree. As Felk approached, she began to struggle against her ropes. He stooped and put a finger to his lips.

"Your highness, stop struggling," he whispered. He grabbed both sides of her head and forced her to look into his eyes. "I'm here to help you."

She stilled, but her eyes were filled with mistrust.

"If I remove the gagged, will you stay silent?"

She didn't move.

"Adrianna, Devvon is currently sitting not fifty feet from here. We can't let him hear you."

She kept his gaze. After a long moment, she slowly nodded. Felk grunted in approval and reached his rough hands behind her head. As the gag fell away, he put a finger to his lips. "Quiet," he whispered.

She watched him, warily. "Who are you?"

"My name is Felk. I'm a general in Devvon's army."

"And what do you want with me?"

Felk took a deep breath. "I'm going to free you."

Adrianna stared accusingly at him. "Why?"

"Because," he said slowly, "Devvon is insane."

Adrianna laughed bitterly. "You're just now coming to that conclusion?"

Felk shook his head. "I mean literally insane. The man is raving about the impossible." He paused. "I fear he is involved in some sort of devilry. And I won't have a man without his faculties ordering others killed."

Adrianna nodded slowly. "So what are you going to do? I doubt your sentiment is shared by the entire army."

Felk shook his head. "No. But I do hold loyalty with a number of the men." He took a deep breath. "Especially those guarding Devvon. Those immediately around this tent."

He rounded the tree and began working at the ropes around her hands. "I've arranged for your horse to be waiting for you at the edge of the camp. I will escort you there personally. After that you're on your own. Run to the mountains and hide there." The ropes fell to the ground.

Adrianna rubbed her wrists. They were raw from the ropes. Felk cocked his head. Too raw.

"Are you alright?"

Adrianna nodded. "It's not the first time I've been tied to a tree in the last few days."

"You were mistreated when Dants captured your kingdom?" Felk was surprised. Dants wasn't above killing a man if it furthered his cause, but he never mistreated women. The loss of his daughter had cemented that trait in his manner.

"No. I escaped, but was captured by bandits that night." She met his gaze. "Escape from you to be captured by bandits. Escape from bandits to be captured by you." She smiled. "I can't win."

Felk felt fury welling up within him. He held out a hand to her. "Let's get you going."

She stood. "Get me to the edge of your camp, and I'll take it from there alone."

Felk shook his head. "Not alone. I've made some arrangements for an escort." He held up a hand to her protest. "It's better this way. Trust me."

He crossed to the tent flap and cracked it open. The guards to either side nodded to him again as two more soldiers approached from the right. They entered quietly and deposited Eastern armor on the floor.

"Put it on," Felk commanded, and Adrianna obeyed. The four exited between the two guards and began striding towards the outer edge of the camp. Felk was saluted by all soldiers they passed. *Too much attention,* he thought. His rank worked for him in getting to her, but worked against him in getting her out.

Felk held his breath as they passed in front of Devvon's tent. He could hear the king inside cursing at an attending soldier. He heard the swing of a sword and the man's cry of fear abruptly cut off. Felk walked faster and rounded the next tent.

"Captain!" came the call from behind. "Get someone to clean this mess up."

Felk waited for another fifty feet before he released his breath.

"He kills his own men," Adrianna whispered, her face white with shock.

"Regularly," Felk answered without looking at her.

"And ... you follow him?"

"I am bound by my honor."

"But you're letting me go."

Felk nodded. "He hasn't directly commanded me not to." He nodded to another group of saluting soldiers. "And you have an important task." The edge of the camp approached.

"And what is that?"

Felk nodded towards three horses ahead. One she recognized as her own. The other two already carried riders. "To take these two and get as far as the Ragdons will allow from here."

Adrianna nodded. "And who ..." she trailed off as they approached the two horsemen.

"Hello, Adrianna," Titan whispered.

She looked in astonishment between Felk, Titan, and Reon. "What –"

"This here general," Reon cut in, "appears to be a right good gentleman."

"He called off some of the men, creating a gap," Titan said, pulling Adrianna's horse forward so she could mount. "He even sent us the rope to climb down with."

Adrianna tuned back towards Felk. "Why are you doing this?"

"Devvon has some sort of power that I don't understand." He pointed at Titan. "As do you. I don't know what's going on. I don't know how he managed to shoot fire or how you sprouted wings. But I do know that if Devvon gets his hands on that power, the world will burn before his mad thirst is quenched."

Adrianna nodded slowly. "And what of you? He'll know I was freed."

Felk nodded. "I will face whatever the consequences. The last time I freed an innocent man, I wasn't strong enough to keep him from being killed. I won't make the mistake again."

"You'll let him kill you?"

Felk nodded. "If it's necessary."

Titan extended a hand down to him. "Let's hope it's not."

Felk accepted the handshake. "Now go. The change of guard is only thirty minutes away. Walk your horses for that time to avoid being heard, then run for your lives. I'll point the army in the wrong direction."

Felk watched as the three horses disappeared slowly into the pitch black forest. It had been relatively easy to arrange. Without a moon, the cliffs' surfaces had been difficult to watch. He had simply assigned several loyal soldiers to the area right around where he had told them to lower the rope, then let them slip by on the ground. Everyone's attention was in the air, so neighboring guards hadn't even noticed.

Felk turned and strode back towards the camp, dismissing both of his escorts to their tents. He could pick out the two large tents ahead, the first holding Devvon, the second now empty of its previous occupant. Thirty minutes should be enough.

Devvon burst from his tent, causing Felk to freeze. The king stretched, looking up at the night sky, the firelight gleaming off his cheek. He looked left, then right. He calmly crossed the short distance to the prison tent, swept between the two guards, and entered without a word.

Devvon's screamed was enough to confirm to Felk. Thirty minutes had just become thirty seconds.

CHAPTER 35

"That doesn't sound good," Reon said, turning in his saddle to glance back at the still clearly visible camp.

"Agreed," Titan said. "Time to move."

The three horses shot forward at the command of their riders. It seemed, for whatever reason, that Felk's promise of thirty minutes wasn't going to be upheld. Adrianna pushed her own horse harder, eager to create as much distance between herself and Devvon as possible. She glanced to the side to see Titan barreling along beside her. He spared a glance in her direction with worry in his eyes.

Adrianna looked to her other side. Reon was keeping up, but barely. He had his arm wrapped tightly to his chest, but the jolting of the horse was obviously causing him significant pain. He saw her looking at him and stopped grimacing long enough to wink.

Adrianna turned back to Titan. "Titan," she began.

"No," Titan responded without looking towards them. "We aren't separating again. Last time that almost got us all killed."

"And if Devvon catches us?"

Titan didn't answer, and Adrianna didn't have the energy to argue any further. As she rode, she felt the drain become all consuming. Being captured twice in a handful of days, bound, and starved. All she wanted to do was lay down and rest.

She blinked hard, attempting to rid the fatigue from her eyes, and spurred the horse on. Lying down meant Devvon finding them. The last time Devvon had given them the night to decide. She doubted he would make the mistake of ever letting any of them live again. Devvon would kill her. And though he fought his own emotions, Titan would kill himself trying to avenge her.

*****

Devvon emerged from his tent, stiff from his journeying of the past several weeks. He stretched, looking up towards the stars. The night was clear without a moon. The crisp breeze gently drifted across his cheeks. It felt good. Adrianna was captured, and even if Titan didn't come down in time, Devvon would have the pleasure of killing her with Titan watching.

Devvon glanced to the left, then to his right. The men surrounding the area were saluting in respect. According to his orders, those immediately camped around him were only comprised of veterans, those who had been in the army prior to his mandate. Devvon would have preferred to have only the new recruits with them, but he didn't have all the armor yet. Such a decision could have had significant risk.

He glanced over at the prison tent. Adrianna was bound within, likely in tears at the situation. Devvon smiled as he turned and strode over. The only thing better than beating an enemy was being able to gloat about it before killing them.

The soldiers posted at either side of the prison tent saluted, staring straight forward. Devvon strode between them, pushing the tent flap aside and stepping into the darkened tent.

"And how are we ..." He trailed off as his eyes focused on the tree. The girl wasn't there. He glanced around the tent quickly, searching. He quickly circled the tree, staring in disbelief as his eyes came to rest on the ropes lying on the ground.

"Impossible," he said slowly as the anger began to build. He sucked in a deep breath and let his fury take audible form. The girl had been rescued.

The soldiers from outside burst into the tent. "My lord, is everything—"

"Awake the camp!" he screamed at them. They saluted and darted back out into the night. Devvon blinked hard, continuing to stare at the ropes, willing them to rebind their escaped prisoner. The girl was gone. And if the girl was gone, he knew full well that Titan would be gone as well.

He raised his hands and let loose a fireball. He watched as it smashed against the tree, the wood exploding in splinters and flames. The tree creaked and began its descent. Devvon drew his sword and sliced through the tent wall as the tree crashed behind him.

A hundred yards ahead he saw a group of new recruits sitting around a campfire, one with a spoon halfway to his mouth. Devvon raised his hands and let lose another fireball. The men screamed as the flames smashed against them, throwing them backwards. With the heat and impact, they died before sliding to a stop.

"Devvon!" came a yell from the side. Devvon whirled and raised his hands again as Felk came running towards him. He shot another fireball, but Felk dove out of the way. "Devvon, what are you doing?!"

Devvon growled and turned, destroying another group of soldiers. He watched as men ran in all directions. He lowered his hands slowly and let out the breath he had been holding. *I need these men*, he thought, hating the idea even as it came to him.

"Devvon!" came the yell again. He turned to see Felk standing cautiously a dozen yards away.

"Get the men moving!" he commanded, turning back to see that the fallen tree had smashed several tents, likely with men in them.

Felk continued to approach cautiously. "Where are we going?"

Devvon hesitated. He ached to trigger the helmet, to pick out the slightest sound of movement over the panicked chaos all around him. But he would have to drop his defenses. He turned in a slow circle, searching for a clue. The night was black, moonless, and home to a cacophony of men and horses screaming. There was no way.

Devvon turned to Felk. "I need your tent."

"My lord?"

Devvon ignored him. He brushed past and walked the short distance to the general's quarters. He whirled as Felk followed. "Alone! Any man who enters will be executed on the spot." He left Felk staring as he pushed the flap aside and ducked in.

He stopped and took a deep breath. His hands trembled. He had vowed that he would never let his armor down. He was invulnerable to everything besides himself.

Titan was escaping.

Devvon released the breastplate. The metal scales melted away from his fingertips, up his arms, and across his shoulders. He looked down to see the armor climbing back up his legs until it disappeared into the bottom of the breastplate. And as he watched, he felt the steel slide off of his eyes, across his cheeks, and back down his neck. The cool night air and his sense of mortality sent a shiver through him.

No time. He immediately raised his hands and triggered the helmet. The tent around him broke into vivid colors, the waning light more than enough to show each and every detail. Devvon staggered as scents filled his nose, dirt, wood, sweat, and most of all smoke, each of them attacking him to the point of gagging. Worst of all was the sounds. What had been screams were now deafening screeches, the cracking of the nearby blaze turned into a raging inferno that seemed to burn in every direction.

Devvon took a deep breath and steadied himself. He closed his eyes and reached up to plug his nose. With sight and smell at least partially diminished, he focused on the sounds around him. He strived to listen past the yelling, the running, the noise. There was so much. Horses clomped from hundreds of directions. How could he possibly ...

There. Three horses, at a dead run, much further than any others, headed directly away from the camp. Devvon breathed a sigh of relief, and released the helmet. He triggered the breastplate once again, pushing the comfortable metal back into place in little more than an instant. He shivered again at his own vulnerability. The return to mortality, lasting less than a minute, was more horrible than he had even imagined.

Felk still waited for him outside the door. Devvon turned towards the escaping horses and peered into the darkness. A tall building was silhouetted against the stars.

Felk cleared his throat. "Did you kill the girl?"

"No," Devvon replied calmly. "She's escaped, and Titan with her. They're headed for the Tower."

"They ..." Felk trailed off, looking astonished. He glanced over his shoulder at the barely visible structure. "Why there? If I were them, I'd head south, away from any point of recognition."

"Shut up, Felk. Break camp now, get the men moving."

Felk saluted. "Yes, my lord."

Kill him and be done with it, Devvon ordered himself. But his hands didn't rise as Felk turned and walked away from him. He needed Felk. Without Felk, he wouldn't have the support of the veterans. And without either the veterans or the armor, he was at the mercy of an army he knew wouldn't follow him. An army that, unless he achieved complete invulnerability, would find a way and kill him.

*****

Titan pulled his horse to a stop and looked up at the enormous structure. It rose majestically into the air, the ancient stonework standing like a beacon, dwarfing the surrounding hills. Reon and Adrianna came to a stop as well as Titan dismounted. "Hide the horses inside," Titan commanded even as he pulled at his own horse's reins.

"Devvon might find us here," Reon said yet again as he dismounted carefully. He winced at his arm. "Should we keep moving?"

Titan pulled the horse through the broken door. Devvon's handiwork was easy to identify. "Felk promised to lead him away. He might find us wherever we go. And if he does find us, I have another idea I want to try that I need the Tower for."

"What idea?" Adrianna asked as she pulled her own horse through the entry.

Titan tied the horse's reins to a pillar, out of sight of the path to the stairs that wound up the belly of the structure. He looked to the side to find Adrianna doing the same. She turned and folded her arms. Titan accepted the reins from Reon and tied them up as well. "We'll make Devvon fall."

Reon chuckled. "Titan, I hate to point this out, but that's..." he trailed off as his smile turned to a frown. "You mean literally fall?"

Titan nodded, beckoning for them to follow him up the stairs. "The pieces are meant to be used together, right? And because Devvon doesn't have all of them, we can use his gaps against him. He doesn't have the wings, meaning that he is just as subject to falling as any of us. We simply throw him from the top and let the thousand feet do the rest. It would be like falling from the same height in a steel barrel. Even if the barrel survives, the passenger wouldn't."

Silence fell as they continued to climb. As they rounded the last curve in the stairway, Titan looked up to see the door to the antechamber ajar, the same room where the four imposters had attacked him. He approached and slowly eased the door open. Within appeared as though nothing strange had happened there, as if the betrayal of the kings had no bearing whatsoever on reality. As if it was all a bad dream.

Titan heard the other two enter the room behind him. A hand slipped into his. He turned to protest Adrianna's advance, but hesitated when he saw her pale face. She was staring ahead, towards the opposite side of the room. Titan followed her gaze to the door at the other end. The side that faced the inside of the Tower was charred black. Titan looked back to Adrianna, remembering the horrific scene that most likely awaited them.

"You don't have to go in," Titan said, squeezing her hand reassuringly.

Adrianna slowly shook her head, her eyes lightly glazed. "I didn't get a chance to say goodbye."

She and Titan crossed the room. He stepped through first, trailing her behind him, and crossed the hallway to the inner chamber beyond. The door was in ruins from the flames. He pushed it slowly open, catching his breath at the sight within.

Everything was in charcoal and ashes. The stairs and balcony surrounding the perimeter of the room were intact for the most part, but the wood had been gnawed away to near nothing by the fire. The stone walls were stained black in sweeping patterns, the rugs destroyed. And in the middle of them, Titan could distinguish three figures, burnt passed the point of being recognizable.

They stood and stared for several long minutes, neither daring to enter further. The bodies of the three kings were sprawled throughout the room. One was crumpled on the far side against a wall, another entangled with an upturned chair. The last was lying halfway between the circle of chairs and the exit.

"Father," Adrianna whispered.

Titan nodded solemnly. "I'm sorry, Adrianna."

"He was almost out," she said, motioning towards the closest.

"He must have been right behind my father," Titan replied.

Adrianna hesitated. "Not right behind. Right in front of."

Titan glanced at her, confused.

"Look at how he's lying. On his back. He was likely facing away from the door when Devvon killed him. He was between Lexik and Devvon."

"He sacrificed himself," Titan whispered, realization hitting him, "for my father." He turned and embraced Adrianna as she collapsed into tears. "I'm so sorry."

Adrianna buried her head in his chest. "Don't be. He loved Lexik. I can't imagine a better way for him to pass."

Titan held her for a moment, but she quickly composed herself. She pulled back, wiped the tears from her cheeks and met his eyes. "What now?"

Titan watched her. "If Devvon comes, you and Reon hide. I'll surprise him and throw him to his death."

"We can't say 'if' anymore," Reon said from the outside hall. "Devvon's army is only about a mile away and headed straight for us." He lifted a sword. "On a brighter note, look what I found."

Titan walked to him and took the weapon. "Father's sword," he said softly.

"The replica that fooled Devvon." Reon smiled. "Can I keep it? It gets me laughing every time I look at it."

"If we survive the day, you have my word."

"Not sure if I can trust that. You made us all believe you were dead just so we would like you when you came back."

Titan let Adrianna's hand drop and walked to a nearby window. Devvon's vast army consumed too much of his view already.

"You know," Reon said as he stepped up next to him. "This plan also depends on his army putting down their weapons after we kill him."

"I'll make them," Titan said as he set his jaw. "They've conquered my home, all of our homes for nothing more than a lust for power. I'll use the armor to ensure they back down."

"Sounds like an entertaining plan," Reon said with a smile.

"Well, let's work on the first part first." Titan turned back to Adrianna. "Once he is here, you two are to go around the outside corridor and lay down out of sight. I'll come get you when it's done."

Reon saluted. "Yes, my liege. We shall hide like cowards."

Adrianna's face showed no emotion. "You think it will work?"

Not really, he thought. "I do."

Adrianna nodded slowly. "And if it doesn't?"

"Then stay hidden until the army is gone and leave the kingdoms with whoever you can. If Devvon gets all the pieces, there's no telling when he'll stop."

"And why don't we just leave now?"

"Because," Titan said, taking a deep breath, "this is the right thing to do. If I have any chance whatsoever of beating him, I have to take it."

"Well," Reon said at the window, "you're about to get your chance. They're here."

CHAPTER 36

A full minute passed between when the order was given and when the entire army finally came to a halt. Felk looked over his shoulder. Forty thousand men, eager and ready for battle. Before them lay the Tower. To Felk's left, he could see Devvon staring up at the top, thoroughly convinced Titan was up there.

"Orders, my king?"

"YOUR EMPEROR!" Devvon roared, whirling on him. "I AM YOUR GOD!"

The man is insane, Felk remembered. "My emperor."

Devvon took a deep breath and turned back to the Tower. "My orders are to shoot anything and everything out of the sky. I will go after the boy myself."

"Yes, sire."

Devvon shook his head. "I hate you, Felk."

Felk clenched his teeth. "I know, Devvon."

Devvon nodded. "Then I assume you are already expecting your execution?"

"That's what you've tried to do over the last year, isn't it? Sending me into battle, outnumbered and in the worst possible positions? Killing thousands of your own men just to kill me?"

Devvon closed his eyes. "Yet you survived."

Felk felt a stab of pride at the annoyance in Devvon's voice. "And I will continue to survive while the men following me support me."

Devvon opened his eyes. "Then I'm afraid that ends today. When I come down from that Tower, I will be omnipotent. The army will then serve me."

"Power has never created loyalty. These men know and trust me, just as I know and trust them."

"Do you?" Devvon asked with a smirk as he urged his horse forward. "Tell me Felk, how well do you really know these men?" He continued, leaving Felk and the army behind.

Felk watched him disappear into the base of the Tower. *How well do I know them?* He turned and looked at the man to his right, then to the man to his left. He knew both by name, knew that the first had four children while the second's wife was expecting their first. As he looked around, he mentally stated each man's name and situation. He knew these men.

He hesitated when he reached a man he didn't know, a man he recognized as a new recruit. He hadn't had enough time to get to know many of them with the speed of the training and the march. As he looked over the ranks of men outside the perimeter of veterans that Devvon had demanded, he saw the rows and rows of new recruits.

Hardly any youngsters, he thought again. Most were middle aged, likely from the villages outside the east's capital city. Farmers, for the most part. Felk continued to scan the new recruits.

He froze. The beards. Many of the new recruits wore the odd patterned beards that his shopkeeper friend had warned about. As Felk looked back, he realized that not one of the veteran soldiers had the peculiar designs. The distinction made him uneasy. It was as if ... they were two different cultures. Felk felt his stomach tense.

"Captain," he said softly. "How many men are in your unit?"

"One hundred, general."

Devvon's personal guard were all veterans. One hundred veterans among ... forty thousand recruits.

The hordes of people flooding into the city after the bandits were sighted. The influx of soldiers, far beyond how many should have enlisted. The inability of the new recruits to master techniques that mirrored prayer movements. The segregation of the men, instituted by the new recruits, not the veterans.

"Move them into the Tower."

"Why, sir?"

"Just do it."

The man saluted, then turned and yelled for his men to move into the Tower. Felk watched as the men began towards it. The new recruits began to murmur among themselves. Finally, one man stepped forward.

"What's going on?"

Felk didn't answer, backing his horse towards the Tower.

"Why you leaving us out here? Why are you leaving your men, general?"

Felk glanced back to see the last of the men slipping inside. With the door destroyed, it wouldn't provide much protection. He looked back and met the man's eyes. "You are not my men."

"Not your men? We've marched behind you for weeks!"

Felk paused at the doorway. "No man that sells a woman as a slave wife will I ever call my own."

The man didn't waver. "Is that a fact, general?" He turned back to the rest of the men and yelled. "I think it's time that our kind general steps down!"

Felk ducked inside as the yelling began to pulse through the forty thousand like wild fire.

"General," the captain beside him said nervously. "What are you talking about?"

"The Tower is one of the most defensible locations in any of the five kingdoms. Approachable only on one side, with only one door in or out, stone walls thick enough to repel an enemy army for hours." The roar outside had become deafening. "We will hold them."

"But from whom are we defending, general?"

Felk felt the anger as though it would burst from his chest. Devvon had known. He had likely orchestrated the invasion. He had sold his country for power. "An army of bandits. An army of bandits that outnumbers us four hundred to one."

CHAPTER 37

"Hide," Titan commanded as he pulled the helmet down over his head.

Adrianna and Reon obeyed without arguing. They followed the hallway until the doors to the antechamber and to the center room were out of sight. Adrianna's heart was thumping loudly enough that she was sure hiding wouldn't matter. Devvon's helmet could surely pick it out. *He won't be using it,* she reminded herself. Reon eased himself to a window and looked down at the screaming army below. Adrianna felt her blood run cold.

"What are the odds we make it out alive?"

Reon looked at her. "Zero. But that's just a rough estimate."

"Not one to spread hope, are you Reon?"

Adrianna could easily see the fear in his eyes. "I don't have any to spread." He smirked. "You know, you still owe me a kiss."

Adrianna furrowed her eyebrows. "Why?"

"I read for you. That awful law stuff. I told you the price was a kiss."

Adrianna tried to make her laugh sounds genuine. "I'll kiss you after Devvon's dead."

Reon smiled. "Fair enough." He turned back to the window. "There are a lot of angry men out there."

Adrianna crossed and looked down with him. She studied the crowd, growing confused. "But … they aren't yelling up at us. They're yelling at the base of the Tower."

Reon shrugged his shoulders. "Never pegged Easterns as intelligent types." He continued to watch them, his brow furrowing. "They're fighting at the base of the Tower."

Adrianna peered out and could see that what he said was true. They were swarming the Tower, but she could see dead men being carried away. As she listened carefully, she heard metal hitting metal. It looked as though the army was fighting itself.

A crash behind them caused the two to dive to the ground. Adrianna looked to Reon, but he shook his head. "Didn't come from the room. Must be Devvon blasting through the antechamber. Trying to scare us."

"It's working." Adrianna forced a laugh.

Reon nodded, watching the hallway intently. "That it is."

"Titan!" Devvon's voice echoed through the corridor. The two fell silent.

"Show yourself, boy! There's nowhere to run this time!"

"I'm not running," Titan's voice answered.

"Ah! There you are. Thought you weren't going to show up."

"Didn't know we had an appointment."

Devvon laughed. "Oh, we've had this coming for a while now. You've known this would be your inevitable fate since you stole from me. You're no match."

"How about we trade a glove for a bracer and we'll see whether or not I'm a match then?"

Adrianna heard the explosion, then instantly felt the vibration of the stone below her. *This isn't going to work*, she thought. She began to inch her way towards the door.

"Where are you going?" Reon hissed.

Adrianna ignored him, continuing forward.

"Sure, Titan. You go first." Devvon's voice was full of triumph.

Another explosion. Adrianna jerked back as Devvon's cape came into view. He was standing in the doorway, the only way in or out of the room. Titan was trapped.

"As you wish." Titan's voice seemed casual. The room went quiet, and she could hear the crackling of the rekindled fires. Devvon's hands were still raised, but he wasn't firing.

"Catch, Devvon."

Adrianna watched as Devvon tilted back, lifting his hands upwards. Adrianna's breath caught. *Titan is giving up a bracer?! How can he believe Devvon will follow through?!*

Devvon crashed backwards as Titan plowed into him. They flew out of the center room, across the hallway, and through the opposite door into the ante chamber. Adrianna scrambled to the doorway, reaching it in time to see Titan stand, lift Devvon fully off the ground, and smash his fist square in the middle of Devvon's chest. Devvon soared across the rest of the room and exploded through the stonework, his legs and arms shimmering in metal. He fell out of sight amid the fragments of the Tower's outer wall.

"Titan!" Adrianna yelled as she leapt to her feet and ran for him. He turned and caught her as she threw her arms around his neck.

"Careful!" he warned. "Not too fast. I still had the bracers working."

Adrianna pulled back. "But you ..." she trailed off as she saw the bracer on his left arm, and only a shirt on his right. "You gave up one of them."

Titan smiled. He reached down and pulled the sleeve of his shirt back to show the other bracer beneath. "I only had a moment after you two hid. I found the discarded replica bracers your father had made and pulled one of them on."

"All royals are liars," Reon said as he entered the room behind Adrianna. "I'm convinced of it. Good or bad, you can't help yourselves."

Titan smiled, then turned to the hole in the wall behind him. The three walked solemnly over and peered down below. The army had converged on the Tower, but Adrianna couldn't hear anyone climbing the steps. She could see a hole in the army where the stones had fallen. Several men lay dead. A figure covered in metal from head to toe was sprawled in the middle of the mess, unmoving.

"Why are the men fighting?" Titan asked.

Reon shook his head. "Some sort of division in the army. Maybe it's that general fellow who let us off the mountain. Maybe the army found out about it and didn't think it was a good idea."

Adrianna continued to stare at Devvon. "He's dead," she whispered.

Reon nodded solemnly. Titan said nothing.

"I guess the armor doesn't—"

"There," Titan interjected. He pointed, his face hard.

Adrianna looked back down towards Devvon. He rolled onto his knees. As she watched, he lifted himself to his feet, then looked back up towards them.

"He's alive." Titan's voice was emotionless.

Adrianna felt a tear roll down her cheek as the figure started back towards the Tower again. "Fly, Titan."

Titan shook his head, pointing outward. "Half of those men still have their bows trained on the skies. It's the middle of the day. Even if all of them are poor archers, there will be twenty thousand arrows in the air in a matter of seconds."

"You have to try," Adrianna said quietly. She clutched his hand. "You might make it."

Titan shook his head. "We stick to my plan. You two hide. I'll draw him back into the center room. Once you have a chance, make a run for it."

Adrianna closed her eyes. "So you die at Devvon's hand, and we die at the army's."

Titan sighed. "You might make it," he said softly.

Reon cleared his throat. "Like I said. All royals are liars."

Titan didn't take his eyes off of Adrianna. "I love you," he whispered.

Tears continued to stream down Adrianna's face as the pain coursed through her. "Now you tell me?" Her smiled collapsed into weeping as Titan embraced her.

"You know that I've always loved you," he whispered.

Adrianna laughed. "Typical man. Can't talk about your feelings to save your life."

"We're not dead yet," Reon said softly from the side.

Adrianna felt Titan nod his head. "You two have to try. And there's still a chance I'll kill Devvon."

Adrianna pulled slowly back and studied Titan's face. She knew the look. He was resolved. She looked to Reon for help.

Reon shook his head, letting out a sigh. "Titan, I love you too. Not like her, mind you, but I do love you. And so, it is with great regret that I must inform you that your plan is downright appalling."

*****

Devvon lay, staring up at the sun directly overhead. He groaned and rolled to the side, several rocks sliding off of him in the process. He turned over to his hands and knees, then slowly pushed himself to his feet. He shook his head several times before he looked back up at the top of the Tower.

To the inferno with that boy! He turned to a nearby soldier. "You! Keep your bows trained on the sky!"

Devvon looked back towards the base of the Tower. The bandits were swarming the place, but with only one doorway to get in or out, their numbers weren't benefiting them. There was already a pile of dead men on the outside, and a number of bandits were pulling them out of the way to make room.

Devvon strode towards battle. He could see men on the inside of the Tower, fighting for their lives. Felk would be among them. He had chosen his position well, but it was only a matter of time. They couldn't hold out forever. At the very least the raw exertion of fighting would undo them.

But there's no reason why I can't speed the process.

Devvon raised his hands and aimed towards the doorway as he walked. The fire shot across the battle field and exploded right in the middle of the men. Bandits were thrown in all directions, including directly through the door, clearing the area for a moment. Devvon aimed again and fired. The ball of flame shot through the doorway and exploded inside. He nodded in satisfaction. There would be survivors, but a fair number would be dead.

He once again noticed the cool metal of the armor as he approached the flames. He calmly walked through them and into the Tower. The scene within would have made a weaker man tremble, but Devvon casually strode among the bodies and through the door beyond. He spared a glance for Felk, didn't see him. The general liked to fight alongside his men. The blast had probably killed him as well.

Devvon began the climb up the stairs once again. Undoubtedly Adrianna was up there with Titan. Devvon still needed her to ensure the south was thoroughly conquered. He would kill Titan first, then the girl. He was briefly tempted to capture her and kill her in front of her own people, but quickly dismissed the idea. No more mistakes.

He rounded the last corner and cautiously approached the antechamber. Empty. He crossed the room quickly, then peered either way down the hallway. Nothing. He looked up and saw the fires within the center room were already dying down. There was little wood left to burn.

He stepped slowly across the corridor and into the doorway. He glanced from left to right, but saw nothing. He took another step inside.

A sword smashed against the side of his helmet. He quickly ducked to the side, his attacker pursuing him into the room. Devvon hissed as he turned.

"I'll kill you, Titan."

Rather than answer, the boy swung the sword again, knocking Devvon's hands away as he tried to raise them. Titan was in full armor, likely taken from the dead kings, up to a breastplate, helmet, and shield held close to his body. He swung again, and Devvon reached up and blocked the blow with his forearm. He made to raise his hands again, but Titan swung again.

"Die, you rat!" the boy yelled.

Devvon slapped the blade aside, his anger building. He yanked his own sword from its sheath. He swung at Titan, but the blow was deftly parried. Another swipe landed on Devvon's shoulder, harmlessly bouncing off.

"You can't win, boy," Devvon growled as he swung again.

Titan attacked again, swinging fast and hard. Devvon stumbled backward as he parried most blows, allowing his armor to ward off the rest. Devvon would have been annoyed at being bested by a youth, but he actually found it amusing. Each time his opponent's sword got through, it had no effect. Let the boy wear himself out.

Devvon lowered his sword, and Titan swung three times in quick succession, each blow bouncing innocently away. The boy hesitated. Devvon watched through the eye slit in his opponent's helmet, spotting fear in his eyes.

"That's right," Devvon snarled. "You're going to die, and there's nothing you can do about it."

"That may be true," came the answer, "but I'm not the one who you should worry about."

"Oh? And why is that?" Devvon raised his sword again, glancing behind the boy towards the doorway. Empty.

"Because even commoners can be liars." Titan whirled, swinging his sword in a large arc and smashing it against the back of Devvon's helmet.

His head jerked forward, chin slamming against his chest. At the same time, a weight landed on his shoulders. Large black wings swept to either side. An instant later they were gone, and with them the weight. Devvon looked up to find a second figure flipping over the boy in armor. As the newcomer landed on the far side of the room, Devvon saw him throw something. Some sort of metal chain. As it soared, the black jewel hanging from it glinted in the sunlight.

Devvon reached up to his chest and felt the place where the stone was missing. He watched in horror as the girl, now standing in the doorway, snatched the piece out of the air and disappeared through the antechamber.

*****

"But it's the best plan we have."

"That's a bit boastful, don't you think?"

Titan glanced at Reon, noting the characteristic the twinkle in his eye. "What's your idea?"

"Each piece of the armor has two stones that have to be connected for them to work, right?"

Titan nodded slowly.

"Then let me fight him. I'm the better swordsman, I'll keep him busy. You climb up to that walkway in the center room and wait. I'll force him so he's facing the doorway with his back towards you. When I get him in position, I'll force his head down, and you swoop in. Snatch the necklace, jerk it free, and throw it to Adrianna who will be waiting. She runs and either hides or gets past the army, haven't really worked that part through yet. And poof, Devvon's without armor."

Titan stared at him. "Reon, that's brilliant."

"Thank you, sire."

"But he'll be wondering where I am."

"No he won't. He'll be thinking he's fighting you." Reon walked over to one of the king's corpses. "Help me get this helmet and breastplate on. The eye-slit is thin enough he won't be able to tell."

"And your arm?"

Reon bit his cheek. "Hmm. Maybe he won't notice?"

"The shields," Adrianna interjected. "There are several of them hanging in the antechamber. We strap one to him, covering the arm."

Titan looked back and forth between the two of them. "It's dangerous."

Reon laughed. "More dangerous than escaping through the middle of an army?"

Titan hesitated. "I guess that's true."

"Hurry then. He's probably already on his way back up."

Titan and Adrianna ran opposite directions. Titan eased the breastplate and helmet off the body and turned to Reon as Adrianna returned with a shield. They both helped Reon don the armor and tied the handgrips on the back of the shield to the straps of the breastplate. Reon winced as they worked around his broken arm, but urged them on whenever they paused.

Titan and Adrianna stepped back. Reon was indistinguishable.

"Told you," Reon said, the smile evident in his voice.

Titan held up the replica of his father's sword and Reon took it, giving it several ginger swings. "Alright, off with you two. It's time for a real man to teach Devvon a lesson."

Adrianna ran and rounded the corner down the corridor. Titan hesitated. "He might kill you."

Reon shrugged. "I honestly don't think any of us are going to live through the next few minutes. We keep confronting death. It's only a matter of time until our luck runs out. And I'd rather die fighting."

Titan nodded. "Let's hope this works."

"It won't if you're still in sight when he gets to the top of those stairs."

Titan nodded and ran for the stairs to the overhead walkway. He carefully tested his weight on the charred wood. He slowly climbed, testing each step before proceeding. He reached the top and hid behind a charred tapestry that was hanging in tatters on the wall. He whirled as he heard the first clash of steel.

Devvon stumbled into the room with Reon following quickly. Titan peered through a hole, watching as Reon attacked again and again. While it appeared that Reon was attacking in fury, Titan was able to pick out the carefully placed blows that force Devvon backwards and towards Titan.

Reon was magnificent. Devvon continued to stumble backwards, despite the fact that Reon was only fighting with one hand. Had Reon been part of the army, Titan wondered if he wouldn't be the best swordsman the kingdom had to offer.

Below, Devvon lowered his sword. Reon laid into him with all his might, delivering three mighty blows. Devvon waited, nonchalantly.

"That's right. You're going to die, and there's nothing you can do about it."

Reon stood firm. "That may be true, but I'm not the one who you should worry about."

"Oh? And why is that?" Devvon's sword came to the ready again.

"Because even commoners can be liars."

Titan swept out of his hiding place, spread his wings and jumped. Reon had spun to the side and was bringing his sword around. Titan swooped down, head first, directly towards Devvon. Reon's sword connect, forcing Devvon's head forward, and Titan landed. He stuck his left hand on Devvon's should for balance, his right hand slipping underneath the chain draped across the back of the neck. He pumped his wings, rotating himself and flipped clean over Reon as he ducked out of the way. He felt only a minor tug as the necklace came free. Titan's feet hit the ground as he let the rotation pour into his throw, praying to an unknown god that Adrianna would be in the doorway.

She appeared, snatched the stone and chain out of the air, and took off through the antechamber. In a flash, she was gone. A deep sense of triumph swelled within Titan as he whirled at the sound of Devvon's scream of rage.

The man was advancing on Reon. And he was covered in head to toe with metal. Titan's heart sank. They had failed again. Even with the necklace gone, Devvon's armor remained.

The king of the East lunged. Reon had turned to watch Titan throw the necklace, and was turning back too slowly. While the eye slit had hid his identity before, it now gave him limited vision.

Time seemed to slow. *He doesn't see Devvon,* Titan realized in a panic. Reon was turning back, but Devvon would be on him. Devvon's sword was extended, aimed for beneath Reon's good arm where the side of his chest was exposed. Titan sprang for Reon, urging his body to move faster.

Reon cried out as Devvon's sword sank deep into his side.

CHAPTER 38

Titan grabbed Reon, activated the bracers, and jumped backwards. Devvon's sword was ripped from both his hand and Reon's side. The two friends crashed into the bookshelf behind them, the weakened wood absorbing some of their impact. Titan felt dazed, but not broken. His focus landed once again on Devvon just as the Eastern king raised both hands towards them. Flames erupted from his palms.

Titan leaped to the side, the fire consuming the spot just behind them. Their landing was rough, and he stumbled to his knees, trying not to crush Reon with his increased strength. Devvon aimed again and released yet another inferno. No time to jump, no time to dodge.

Titan swept the wings around them, enveloping them in thick, black leather. The ball of fire crashed into them, smashing the duo back into the stone wall. Titan could feel the heat around them,, but the fire didn't penetrate their impromptu shelter. Titan stood, dragging Reon with him, and started circling the room towards the door on the far side. Another blast shoved them into the wall once again. Titan's head struck hard, his vision blurring for a moment.

The next attacked knocked him from his feet. Reon cried out as they hit the stone floor. The door was too far. There were no windows in the interior room of the Tower. Titan had the strength to break through the stone, but even if Devvon didn't incinerate them as soon as he lowered his wings, breaking down a wall would likely collapse the roof.

Another blast. Titan's head hit again. Reon whimpered. The room swam. Another blast. And another. And another.

Reon's helmet came free. His eyes were closed, his teeth gritted. "Titan," he gasped, "we're going to die." Another blast.

Titan looked at his friend. As he saw the face contorted in pain, he remembered his argument with his father before leaving for the peace conferences. *He is too young. We're both too young. How did we get here?*

Another blast. "YIELD!" Devvon yelled.

Titan closed his eyes. He took a deep breath. "Alright! Just stop!"

There was a pause. "Lower your wings, boy!"

Titan bit his lip. "You'll just kill us."

Another blast struck. "I'll kill you either way!" Devvon's voice had taken on an edge of hysteria. "YIELD!"

Reon opened his eyes and met Titan's eyes. He gave a slow nod. "I'm ready," he whispered.

Titan understood. They had escaped this fate too many times. Luck only held on for a time, and they had received more than their fair share. The time had come, and the two wouldn't die cowering. Titan nodded his own agreement to Reon. After a pause, Titan embraced him, and Reon wrapped his good arm around the prince.

Releasing Reon, Titan grit his teeth. He stood slowly, raising Reon to his feet beside him. Devvon had fallen silent. Slowly, Titan began to pull the wings apart. Through the crack, Titan glimpsed Devvon once again. Head to toe, covered in steel, arms poised. His usual smile was gone. He just stared, motionless as Titan pulled the wings further apart. He pulled them around behind him, and with what he knew was his final thought, released them. The sheath shifted on his back, no longer bound to his spine. Devvon remained still, no more than five yards from them.

Titan closed his eyes. "Please. Spare us."

The gloved hands lowered a fraction of an inch. "I can't do that. I won't do that."

"At least spare Reon."

"Look at him, Princeling. He's already as good as dead. As are you." Devvon raised his hands again. "Say hello to your father for me."

"Wait," Titan said, taking a deep breath. "Look, I'll give the sword to you." He reached carefully up and lifted the sheath's strap over his head. "Just – just don't ..."

Devvon cocked his head. "Don't what? You have no room for negotiation."

Titan took a deep breath. "Don't hurt Adrianna."

Silence filled the room. Titan stood holding the sheathed sword, waiting. There was nothing that could be done, they were completely in his power. But Devvon held. Finally, he gave a small nod. "Alright. Give me the items you have stolen from me, and I won't kill her." A pause. "But I'm still going to kill you."

Despite the gravity of the situation, Titan allowed himself to feel some relief. Devvon could very well be lying, but at least he had promised. That was more than Titan expected. Titan had been tasked with saving the world. He had failed at that. But he had managed to protect what he considered to be the most precious part of that world. The irony struck him as he realized he was finally doing what Reon and Adrianna had urged him to do for several years now. Abandon his duty and heed his heart.

Titan took a breath and tossed the sword through the air. Devvon kept his left hand trained on the pair, but reached out his right and caught the weapon. He hefted it, feeling the weight. He swung the belt over his head and shoulder, allowing the sword to rest against his back. He brought his hands together, pushed them straight out, and spread his arms. The prayer of Enlightenment, having been obviously practiced for years. The wings sprang from behind him, stretching across nearly the full length of the room. He returned his focus and his aim to the boys. "Now the bracers."

Titan nodded. He slowly lowered Reon to the ground. Then he stood and pulled at the laces. After freeing both, he tossed the pair. Devvon caught them. He slipped them on, foregoing the straps, and returned his attention to Titan. "Thank you for your cooperation, Titan. Now the last piece."

Titan hesitated. "What piece?"

Devvon smirked. "Why the necklace, of course. You stole that from me not five minutes ago." Titan remained silent, and Devvon chuckled. "If you don't, I'm afraid you're going back on your word. And unfortunately, that means I'm at liberty to do whatever I like with the young lady you tried so hard to protect." He took a deep breath, a peaceful smile spreading across his silvery lips. "I know it's cliché to ask, but any last words?"

Titan grit his teeth. "You'll never find her."

Devvon laughed. "I already have. She's hiding just down the stairwell, no doubt trying to peek and catch one final glimpse." He tap his helmet. "You forget, you haven't just given me wings and strength. You've given me omnipotence. Forget hearing the girl. I can *smell* her."

Titan felt his throat constrict. "Adrianna, RUN!" he yelled.

Devvon shook his head. "My dear boy, she's in love. She'll stay and watch until the bitter end. So, what image shall we give her as her last? Your body engulfed in flames? Or me tearing you limb from limb?" He knelt and smashed his fist into the floor, the stones crumbling before his strength. He stood again, facing them. "But no. I believe I have an even better idea."

His wings retracted until they disappeared behind him. He reached over his head, and slowly pulled the sword from its sheath. Titan's sword. No, *Lexik's* sword. The artifact that for over a millennium had been at the heart of Western kingdom, now gripped in the Eastern demon's hand. And with a swipe through the air, Devvon advanced. "Goodbye, Titan."

Devvon froze. His smile vanished as his eyes widened. There was a pause, and Devvon staggered forward. He continued staring at the pair, disbelief flooding his face. He flinched, lowering a hand to the ground to steady himself. Another flinch. The would-be god collapsed, face down.

Three arrows had spouted from his back. Titan stared at them. *How?* He finally raised his gaze to the doorway. Across the hall and on the other side of the antechamber, his eyes came to rest on a crouching figure. Adrianna held the bow firmly, another arrow already notched. She slowly stood, lowering the bow to her side.

"Figures she'd interrupt something as important as me dying," Reon whispered.

Adrianna dashed forward as Titan pulled Reon from the surrounding flames and carefully laid him on the ground. He turned to her as she skidded to her knees beside them.

"How?"

"His breastplate had a slit."

Titan looked back at Devvon. The three arrows on his back were in a neat vertical line, all along a three-inch wide stretch of bare skin. Titan glanced at his own back to find a similar cut in his own shirt.

"The sword. It bound itself to Devvon's spine ... right through the breastplate."

Adrianna was taking a closer look at Reon's wound. "Didn't that old hermit say the pieces were meant to work together?" She pushed against Reon's side, earning a gasp.

Titan nodded. "And Devvon separated them." He shook his head, staring at the fallen figure. "He was invincible. And he gave it up to be cruel."

"A true idiot," Reon said, grimacing.

Titan looked back down at Reon. "You're going to be alright."

"Liar."

Titan looked at Adrianna. She shook her head, tears slipping down her cheeks. "It's too deep. He's lost too much blood."

Titan looked to the armor. The wearer would be invincible ... unless they were already wounded.

Titan looked back at Reon. "You're going to be alright," he repeated.

"Saying it more than once isn't going to make it true." Reon took a sharp breath, his teeth clenched.

"But ..." Titan was at a loss for words.

Adrianna reached a hand to Reon's cheek. "What can we do?"

Reon looked over to her. "You owe me a kiss."

Adrianna sniffed. She wiped her eye, nodded, and leaned down.

"Wait," Reon stopped her. "Marry me."

Adrianna laughed through her tears. "To the end, you try to —"

"I'm serious, Adrianna. Marry me." He closed his eyes as his jaw went rigid.

Adrianna watched his face carefully. "Why? You're ..." Another tear rolled down her cheek.

Reon took several deep breaths, then opened his eyes again. "Because I'm a commoner from the West."

Titan furrowed his brow. "That doesn't matter, Reon. You're the best man I've ever met."

Adrianna was watching Reon intently. "My laws state that if I marry, I join my husband in rank and allegiance."

Reon nodded. "And our laws state that a widow can remarry." He gasped. "And Titan is bound by our laws to marry a Western commoner."

Titan looked up at Adrianna. She was staring at him. "If I marry Reon, after he dies I'll be a widowed commoner from the West." She burst into sobs.

"You better hurry," Reon wheezed.

"Reon," Titan said, turning back to him. "I'm not going to use you like that as you lay dying."

Reon met his eyes. "I've worked to get you two married since the first day you saw her. Think of this as favor to me. You're helping me complete years' worth of work." He turned to Adrianna. "Will you marry me?"

She took a deep breath, wiping tears from her cheeks. "I will," she whispered. She bent down and gingerly kissed his lips. "Thank you, Reon."

Reon closed his eyes. "You're welcome, your majesty." He smiled. "Now how about you fetch me a drink?"

Adrianna's laugh was sad, but genuine. "You always were lazy."

"To the death," he whispered, still smiling. He grabbed Titan's hand. "Take care of my wife."

Titan nodded, numbness filling his body. "Thank you, Reon."

Reon smiled. "My prince ... you are welcome."

Reon's hand went limp. Titan continued to grip it as he watched Reon's chest heave up, then down, and finally come to rest. Titan and Adrianna watched his face for several moments, neither speaking. His face was relaxed. Happy, even.

Titan looked and met Adrianna's gaze, a single tear rolling down his cheek. Adrianna reached a hand out and brushed it off. She smiled. "You have work to do."

Titan nodded as he looked back down at Reon. "Take care of him."

Adrianna's lip trembled. "I will," she promised.

Titan stood, and with a determination he had never felt before, strode to Devvon's corpse.

*****

"Do a count of those still alive."

The soldier leapt into action. He returned too quickly. "Twenty seven, general."

Ragdons, Felk cursed. Before Devvon's attack they had only lost a handful. His blast had killed over sixty in a moment. The bandits had likely lost no more than one hundred. The odds were even worse than when they started.

Felk spared a glance at the flames by the door, discouraged by how much they had already died down, and walked briskly through the small room. "Pull the wounded to the back of the room, by those horses. Then get back to the door. Those bandits aren't going to wait long."

As if to prove his point, one bandit came barreling through the flames. His shirt caught fire from the intense heat, and Felk cut him down with his axe. "Hurry, men!"

Those who were dragged out of harm's way were few. Most of the men scattered around weren't in danger any longer. Felk cursed Devvon once again, wishing more than anything that he could leave this fight to contend with Devvon. But his men were here. He was needed here.

Another bandit burst through, followed quickly by four of his companions. Felk and the men beside him engaged, picking through them quickly. The bandits had the definite advantage of numbers, but lacked the skill gleaned from years of coordinated training. Felk's men were the better warriors.

He knew it didn't matter. Even if the odds were still four hundred to one, it was impossible. A man didn't have the strength to cut down four hundred men, let alone contend with them. It was only a matter of time before they were simply too tired to continue. And with the blast and the heat, Felk was certain that time would be sooner rather than later.

A swarm of arrows shot through the door. Felk had purposefully positioned his men to the sides, knowing that every man on the other side had a bow, but despite his preparations several more men fell. Their numbers dropped to twenty two.

Felk roared as more bandits charged through the door. He ducked beneath a swing of the sword and sheared the man's leg off. He immediately dodged back and brought his axe down on another attacker. Most men preferred the sword, due to its agility in combat. While Felk's axe wasn't as fast as a sword, it had enough power to cut through thin armor. Each blow was usually lethal.

Another soldier to his left fell. *Twenty one*, Felk counted. The bandits continued to burst through the door. Their numbers were endless. Felk swung at the first. The bandit ducked to the side and swiped at Felk's exposed side. Felk let go of the axe with his right hand, swinging it to block the blow. The sword cut through the leather on Felk's forearm and sliced into his arm. Felk swung the awe with his left and cut the man down.

He glanced down at his arm. The wound stung, but wasn't deep enough to cause any real damage. He looked up and took down the next bandit. Another stepped up into his companion's place. There was always another enemy.

Felk took a step back as the man swung. He stumbled over a body, not having seen the man to his right be killed. *Twenty*, he thought even as he wheeled in the air, trying to keep his balance. His foot went out from under him and he fell back, his eyes riveted on the man coming at him. He landed flat on his back on top of several bodies. The man lunged. Felk brought his axe up, managing to get the handle in the way of the sword. The metal cut through the wood, but was deflected enough that it glanced off his breastplate rather than his head. The man raised the sword again.

One of Felk's soldiers tackled the man, driving him and a companion out of the way and to the ground. Felk seized the opportunity, grabbed a sword from the ground beside him, and jumped back to his feet. The soldier who had saved his life was cut down. *Nineteen*. Felk glanced around and realized he hadn't seen all that had fallen. They were closer to twelve.

Felk gritted his teeth, snatched a second sword from the ground and barreled forward. He swung again and again, cutting down four men in as many seconds. The bandits stumbled out of the way, and he pushed onward. He reached the door as two more burst through and quickly took them down, kicking them back through the opening as he pulled his swords free.

The bodies clogged the doorway once again, and the bandits on the other side abandoned their weapons for a moment to drag the corpses out of the way. Felk whirled to see the last of the bandits inside the Tower die at the hand of one of his men. Felk did a quick count, coming up with nine others. Ten men with less than a minute to live.

"Strength, men," he said calmly, standing up straight. "We will die today. But we will die killing the beasts who have stolen our wives and daughters. Fight for them!"

The small group inside in unison raised their weapons and roared. Felk turned back to the doorway, swords raised, and waited for his fate.

The screaming outside changed from a battle cry to panic. Felk watched as the bandits pulling at the bodies around the door looked upwards, terror on their faces. They dropped their swords, pulled their bows from their shoulders and began firing.

Felk jumped forward and sliced down two of the bandits that were within reach. Another bandit turned towards him and Felk ducked to the side as an arrow zipped through the opening. An explosion sounded outside. Felk peered around the side of the door and saw flames consuming the spot where the archer had been standing.

Felk looked upwards as a shadow passed over the sun. He heard his own men behind him approach. Something with giant wings swooped down over the bandits, fire erupting from its hands in quick, successive waves. The creature banked, making a low, tight arc around the Tower, firing again and again until the bandits were forced back.

"The Dragon," a man behind him whispered.

Felk watched as the bandits scattered as the winged figure dove for the ground. *Is it Titan or Devvon?* With the helmet in place and the armor covering his body, Felk couldn't be sure. The figure began to fire fireballs in quick succession at the bandit army.

"Whatever it is," he said, turning to the last handful of survivors, "we currently share an enemy, making it our ally. Move these bodies."

The soldiers hesitated, glancing to one another. One cleared his throat. "The Dragon was an ally to no one."

"That isn't the Dragon," Felk said, pointing his sword out at the figure. It had hidden its wings somehow and was taking mighty blows at the ranks of bandits. Multiple men were thrown dozens of feet with each swipe. "Look at its shape. It's a man."

The men shifted uncomfortably. "We trust you, General. But we don't agree. Look at how strong it is. How do you know it won't kill us?"

Felk looked back out at the figure as he threw four men into another oncoming group. Why would Devvon bring an army, then attack it? Felk gritted his teeth.

It has to be Titan.

Felk shoved a body out of the doorway, then plunged through the opening. There was a gap between where two fireballs had landed through which he could see the figure whirl. Felk ran through the gap, giving both of his swords a swipe in the air.

The figure whirled on Felk, hand at the ready as Felk slid to a stop. There was a moment of hesitation.

"Where are your men?" Titan's voice brought a wave of relief to Felk.

"In the base of the Tower."

Titan turned and smashed through another group of bandits. He raised his hands and fired on another a short distance away. "How many?"

"Ten, including myself."

Titan nodded. "Let's go." Titan fired another blast and whirled to follow Felk. Both sprinted back to the entrance.

Felk ran through the doorway first. "Swords down," he commanded.

Titan's entrance caused them to shy away. "You are to stay here." He waited until Felk nodded. "Do not leave, I will take care of this army myself." He glanced toward the stairs. "And do not climb."

Felk glanced at his men, then back at Titan. "You killed Devvon."

Titan stood firm. "Yes," he said calmly.

Felk nodded. "It had to be done." He paused. "Thank you for doing what my honor forbid me from doing."

Titan nodded. "You're welcome, General." He turned and slid through the door.

Felk made to follow to watch the fight continue, but pulled up short as he watched Titan lift a nearby boulder clean off the ground. He turned and gently placed it in front of the doorway, completely sealing them in.

CHAPTER 39

It had taken less than a quarter hour to break the army. Adrianna cradled Reon's head throughout, her tears accompanied by the yelling of men and the clashing of metal. Finally Titan had returned, visibly weary. He had carried Reon downstairs, then returned for the bodies of the kings. Adrianna began to argue when he emerged with Devvon, but Titan simply walked to the other five bodies and laid the would-be emperor beside them.

A sword-turned shovel made short work of the digging, and within an hour the two of them stood before six graves. Each was marked with a stone block from the Tower's center room, their names etched by Titan's armored finger. Adrianna gripped Titan's hand tightly. For the moment, it was once again flesh and blood.

"Great men, every one of them," Titan murmured.

"Except Devvon," Adrianna replied.

Titan shook his head. "Devvon was great. He just misused his greatness." He lowered his eyes to his hands, still wrapped in Devvon's leather gloves. The black stones on the thumbs sparkled in the sunlight. "The power corrupted him."

Adrianna nodded. "Luckily that power is in better hands now."

"Is it?"

Adrianna looked up at Titan's face. "Of course it is."

Titan shook his head. "I can't help but feel the pull for power. I've only had these pieces for a handful of weeks, and already I feel the craving." He sighed. "I think that in time, power will corrupt anyone."

Adrianna looked back at the graves. "Perhaps," she whispered.

The sound of footsteps alerted them to the approach of ten men. Adrianna recognized the first as Felk, the general from the eastern army. They had left to wait in the forest after Titan had asked them to let him bury the bodies alone.

"Prince Titan," Felk greeted as he approached.

"General Felk." Titan shook his hand.

"I wanted to thank you again. You saved the lives of my men."

"Just returning a favor," Titan said with a smile. "Where will you go from here?"

Felk smiled. "Home, of course. Where does any man yearn to go?"

"They'll be angry that you survived without Devvon."

"Unlikely. Devvon wasn't as popular with the people as most foreigners think. They will accept the change of leadership and continue their lives as normal."

Titan nodded. "May I ask a favor?"

"Of course."

"Pull your men out of my city. I don't want to kill any more than I have to."

Felk smiled. "Devvon left men we could trust, not the bandits there. I hold quite a bit of sway with them. That shouldn't be a problem."

Titan nodded. "I don't suppose you could do the same for the South?"

Felk hesitated. "My men there are outnumbered by bandits, though they may not know it yet. Once word of Devvon's death reaches them, the bandits will likely revolt and take control."

Titan nodded. "I understand." He paused. "How did Devvon coerce them into obedience in the first place?"

Felk shrugged. "I'm not sure. All I know is that any mercenary responds well to money. He likely promised them women."

Adrianna shuttered. "So many bandits," she whispered.

"We'll take care of them," Titan responded, sounding confident.

Adrianna looked up at him. "I believe you," she said with a smile.

"We should get moving," Felk said. "Those bandits will run for those armies. That only gives us a week's time at the most."

Titan nodded. "It should take us less than a day to make it there."

Adrianna shook her head. "But you're moving us one at a time."

Titan smiled, raising his arms to show the bracers. "Not anymore. I'll be back in a few minutes."

"Where are you going?"

He motioned toward a lake in the near distance. "I'm going to buy a boat to carry you all in."

CHAPTER 40

The general planted his feet. "I am bound."

Jaron lifted his sword. "Then let's get on with it."

Felk stayed where he was. "There's no need for a fight. Devvon's only command was to get rid of you. And that's exactly what I plan to do."

Jaron watched Felk's face carefully. What was this man playing at?

"You are to leave," Felk continued, his axe still at the ready. "Titan is right. The city needs to be evacuated. Take every man, woman and child and get out of the city."

Jaron lowered his sword several inches. "You want us to leave the safety of our walls?"

"Your walls aren't safe any longer. Our army will consume this city, and there's nothing you or I can do to stop Devvon from attacking. Get your people out of here. Hide them."

"Where do you propose we go?"

Felk shook his head. "I don't know, and I don't want to know. I am bound by my honor to obey Devvon's commands. If he asks me, I will tell him. Better that you come up with the plan." Felk sheathed his axe. "But make it happen tonight." He turned and walked away.

Jaron watched his back disappear around the corner. *Why would he do this? And how do we get the people out of the city?* Jaron sheathed his own weapon and turned to look back into the map room. The flames raged on.

We can't fight this, he thought. *We have to run.*

Jaron slowly followed the direction Felk had gone. If Felk was being honest, Devvon had to believe he was dead. If Felk was lying, there was likely some sort of ambush prepared for him. Either way, Jaron needed stealth.

Jaron looked both ways at the bottom of the staircase to find empty corridors. He took a careful step out, but jumped back in as a crash sounded down the hallway to his right.

"Curse that boy!" Devvon's voice was infuriated.

"Devvon," Felk's voice answered, "what happened back there?"

"Shut up, fool!"

The sound of both men's footsteps gradually grew distant. Jaron peered around the corner to see the last of Devvon's cape be yanked out of view at the far end. Jaron carefully crossed to a window and watched the courtyard below. A moment later, two horses charged from the keep's courtyard, carrying Devvon and Felk back towards the outer walls of the city.

Jaron waited until they were out of sight and dashed down the nearby stairway. He had ordered his guards to remain close, but out of sight for the negotiations. He burst into a large dining hall. The two hundred men gathered around the various tables leapt from their seats and saluted.

"Divide the city into sections, each man taking one. Spread the word that every person is to bring a week's worth of provisions and gather in the castle's courtyard as quickly as possible." He took a deep breath. "We're leaving the city."

The men saluted and charged away. Jaron watched them leave, nodding in encouragement as several of them looked to him in concern. Jaron maintained the skin-deep strength until the last had exited. He closed the door and sank into a chair. He had been king for only weeks and he was already giving up the kingdom.

No, he thought, pushing the oncoming despair aside. *The people are the kingdom. Keep them safe.*

*****

Sweat poured from Jaron's brow as he bent in the newly planted fields, clearing more land for additional seeds they had been able to gather from the surrounding forest. They had fled the city through the escape tunnel beneath the stables that only the royal family and several choice officers knew of. Three days of walking, three fire-less nights for fear

294

of being spotted, and several dozen miles had brought them to the valley where the newly crowned king now stood. He had immediately given orders to start planting with the hope that the race between the harvest and the first frost would end in their favor.

Even with the harvest, there won't be enough food. Not for this many.

"My liege!" came a call.

Jaron stood and waved to identify himself from the rest of the hunched group. The soldier quickly crossed to him and held out a paper. "Scout report from the city."

Having scouts watch the city after they had left had proved beneficial. They had observed as Devvon had quickly seized control, then marched with a large portion of his army elsewhere, leaving enough men to make retaking the city unlikely.

Jaron accepted the latest report. He unfolded the paper and read. After he finished, he looked up at the waiting soldier.

"When did this arrive?"

"Just, my lord."

Jaron scanned the paper again. "Send for the generals. Tell them to meet me at my tent immediately."

The man saluted and left. Jaron slapped a fellow laborer on the shoulder and began towards the large grouping of tents. Wood homes were already under construction, many of them finished due to the man power available, but Jaron had refused to accept better accommodations than those he worked beside during the day.

Upon reaching his tent, he washed in a basin. He was drying his face when the two generals entered.

"You called for us, my lord?"

"Welick, you know me better than practically anyone. There's no need for titles."

The man smiled. "Very well. What's going on?"

Jaron nodded to the report lying on his bed roll. Welick picked it up and both generals read through it.

"Are we sure?"

Jaron shrugged. "As sure as we were that the first portion left."

"But the entire army? Why would Devvon pull them out?"

"I have no idea. That's why I asked for you to come. What do we do with this? Ikes?"

The second general stroked his beard. "It feels like a trap."

"But to what end? Why would Devvon pull out of the city? Walls are worth thousands of men in a battle. Why give them back to us?"

Neither general spoke. Ikes scanned the paper once again, eyebrows furrowed.

"Seems risky. We have to remember our goal here. To keep the people safe."

"Agreed. But for whatever reason, Devvon doesn't seem interested in the West any longer. The safest place for these people come winter will be within those walls, with food and water to spare. The question is, is it worth the risk?"

Both men considered. After a moment, Welick nodded. "I think it may be."

Jaron turned to the other. "Ikes?"

Ikes smiled. "You're king. I don't like the risk, but I'll stand by your decision."

Jaron nodded. "I think we should head back. Welick, take half the men and make sure the city really is empty. Ikes and I will follow a day behind with the rest of the army and the people."

He took a deep breath. "Let's go home."

*****

The gates finally closed. Titan leaned back against the embankment and sighed. The city was secure, and the people were once again safely within. He chuckled.

"What's the laugh for?" Adrianna leaned against the wall beside him.

"I was just remembering the look on Welick's face when he saw the two of us just waiting for them to show up in the castle's courtyard. As if I don't know my own generals' habits."

Adrianna joined him in laughing. "Most of them thought you were dead."

They watched the city from their perch above the gate as night began to fall. One by one, lights came on in the thousands of windows before them. *Fire*, Titan thought. *Ironic that it now gives me hope. I guess that's the key. Fire unchecked brings destruction. But when harnessed, it can bring peace.*

"So what will you do now, Titan, son of Lexik?" Adrianna raised a meaningful eyebrow at him.

Titan smiled. "I think it's my turn to kiss you." He leaned in, closing his eyes.

Adrianna's hand caught his mouth. "I've only ever kissed one man before, and that was to seal our marriage."

Titan cracked an eye. "You expect me to match that kind of commitment?"

Adrianna pulled back and folded her arms. "Yes. I do." Titan hesitated. "Well get on with it."

Titan smiled widely. He knelt carefully before her and took her hand in his. "Adrianna. I love you. Ever since the first day I met you I've been arguing with myself over the matter. But it turns out, my heart is stronger than my head. And with your consent, I would like to make your happiness the pursuit of the rest of my life. Adrianna, will you marry me?"

"Yes." She smiled. "Did you practice that?" She burst into laughter as he felt his face grow warm.

"Did it come out alright?"

Adrianna nodded, beaming. "Perfectly." She reached a hand to his cheek. "Just how I imagined it would be."

Titan stepped closer. "And … that kiss?"

Adrianna closed her eyes. "You may get on with that part as well."

Titan lowered his face to hers. As their lips touched, Titan felt a shock ripple through his body. His fingertips tingled as he brought them around her, pulling her body close to his. The soft warmth of her embrace pushed all memories aside. He abruptly became only aware of the moment.

She slowly pulled away. Titan's eyes fluttered open. She was inches away, her vibrant eyes glossy with tears. "I love you," she whispered.

"I love you." He pulled her to his chest. She clung to him. "Not too hard," he joked.

"I don't want to ever let go."

Movement ahead caught Titan's eye. He glanced up to see a familiar figure disappear down the stairs, and instantly realized the entire exchange had been watched. "That's fine with me," he replied to Adrianna, still watching the space where Jaron had been standing.

CHAPTER 41

The city walls were bare of flags. Felk was unnerved by the sight.

His returning force was camped a dozen or so miles behind him. That was where the spies and met them. The same spies that reported groups of bandits surrounding the Eastern kingdom had once again reported bandits, this time camped inside the city walls. As Felk had feared, he had left his men in a trap. A week after he left to conquer the Western kingdom, the bandits had revealed themselves and overcome the loyal soldiers in the city.

Since that time, bandits had continued to come. Felk had no idea there had been so many, but it was now estimated that the city contained over 80,000 men. Felk was renowned for overcoming the odds, but a force one fourth as strong against an enemy guarded by walls was impossible. Even with equal numbers, Felk would have hesitated; Devvon's paranoia had made the walls tall and thick.

Felk turned and started back down the hill to the handful of men waiting for him. His second, Kalorn, followed. "Ideas, General?"

Felk shook his head. "None at the moment. We're outnumbered and they have the high-ground." He frowned. "If we attack, we lose."

"We can't just give up ... our families ..."

Guilt struck Felk. Kalorn was young. He was an experienced soldier and a good man, but his true dedication was to his wife. She was expecting their first-born. Felk shook his head again. "We're not giving up. We've got some time."

"All due respect, General, but these are bandits. They kidnap women and sell them on the slave market. I wouldn't list 'time' as one of our assets."

"We can't win with a frontal assault. We have to *make* time our asset." Felk and Kalorn rejoined the small group and mounted their horses. "We lay siege. We intercept everyone going in or out. We stop them from receiving more men and we stop them from selling our women. And then we wait them out."

Kalorn didn't look convinced. "Devvon had food stockpiled."

"We poison it."

"And starve our own people at the same time? Whatever food is left is going to be reserved entirely for that army. Nothing will go to the population."

Felk turned his horse to face Kalorn and the rest of his men. "I don't have all the answers. What you say is true and wise, but we will find the solution. I promise you this, men. I will do everything in my power to protect you and your families. I will give my life for them. We will re-take what is ours." He took a deep breath. "Do you trust your general?"

The men sat in silence for a moment. Kalorn cleared his throat. "We trust you. We always have and we always will." He turned to the others. "But I think I speak for all of us when I say we no longer trust our general; we trust our king." He drew his sword and stuck the point into the air. "I, Kalorn, pledge fealty to the uncrowned king of the East, King Felk."

Felk hesitated. "We are without a kingdom."

As the rest of the group raised their swords, Kalorn smiled. "But not without a king."

*****

"This is most unusual," the high priest said, wringing his hands.

"But merited," Jaron said, gaze steady. Titan stood quietly beside him.

"Well … perhaps." Priest Wesling looked back and forth between the two. "But you have already been crowned, Jaron. That is a binding agreement."

299

"But I was unlawfully crowned. I was third in line for the throne, and the direct heir was still alive. Surely you believe this is a qualifying exception."

"To be sure. But it has never been done before. Who am I to start?"

Jaron shook his head. "I will not have Prince Titan as a subject. The throne belongs to him."

Priest Wesling hesitated again. After a long pause, he lowered his head. "Yes. I do believe you are right." He beckoned Jaron forward. Jaron obeyed, kneeling before the withered man. "King Jaron, I hereby relieve you of your duties as king of the West." He gingerly lifted the crown from Jaron's head. Jaron stayed bowed.

"Thank you, Wesling," he whispered.

The old man's eyes twinkled with tears. "However short your reign, you were a magnificent king." He turned to Titan. "And I'm sure you will perform just as well. We'll hold the official inauguration in three days." The priest looked back at Jaron with a sad smile, then walked slowly from the room.

Jaron stood slowly, facing neither of the remaining two occupants of the room.

Titan cleared his throat. "I'm not sure that my presence here is needed. I'll be in the hallway."

Adrianna smiled at him as he left. She turned back. "Jaron," she said softly.

He closed his eyes. "It's alright, Adrianna. I never wanted to be king."

"But ..." she felt her hands trembling. "Titan and I ..."

He open his eyes as he faced her. A tear was rolling down his cheek. "I won't say I never wanted you."

Adrianna lowered her head as she felt the guilt poor through her. "I'm so sorry."

Jaron chuckled. "Why? I knew from the beginning that you loved him. All I asked was for an opportunity to taste that love." He stepped toward her and lifted her chin. "And you gave me that. Even knowing that this was going to happen, I still would have chosen as I did."

"You must hate me."

Jaron shook his head. "No, Adrianna. I love you."

"I know." Adrianna felt tears forming in her own eyes. "And I love you."

Jaron smiled. "So a woman can love more than one man?"

She smiled. "Yes."

Jaron nodded thoughtfully. "But she can't marry more than one." He raised a hand as she began to speak. "I release you from our engagement. I want you, Adrianna. But more than that, I want you to be happy. If your happiness depends on being with Titan, then that is where I want you to be."

Adrianna felt as though her heart was crushed and soared at the same time. She clenched her eyes shut. "Thank you, Jaron. You deserve a woman far better than I."

His hand cupped her cheek. "I deserve nothing." She let him pull her closer to him. His lips brushed against hers. A warmth spread through her as he gingerly placed a kiss on her lips. "Goodbye, Adrianna."

He pulled slowly away. She opened her eyes several seconds later to see him stride across the empty room and quietly exit through the opposite door.

CHAPTER 42

"I do," Adrianna said. Jaron's heart wrenched.

Priest Wesling cleared his throat. "Then I bind you. May the Ragdons keep you forever, together."

The crowd roared as Titan turned and swept Adrianna into his arms. After watching the kiss for several excruciating seconds, Jaron tore his eyes from them and surveyed the crowd. Everyone was cheering exuberantly. No one seemed to be bothered in the least that Jaron wasn't the groom at the wedding.

As it should be, Jaron told himself.

The inauguration had happened only a few minutes prior. With that kiss, Jaron's place in Adrianna's life was officially destroyed. He was no longer king and she was no longer his. He looked back at Titan. The newly crowned king was grinning uncontrollably as he escorted his bride down the aisle of the church.

As he should be, Jaron mentally repeated.

Jaron allowed himself to be pushed with the throng of people towards the exit after them. The courtyard beyond would be filled with the people of the city, awaiting their new king and queen. Jaron heard them screaming their approval before he could see them. He shielded his eyes against the sun to see the crowd, tens of thousands strong yelling in celebration.

As they should be.

Titan and Adrianna were standing in the middle, their arms raised towards the people. The cheering continued to fill Jaron's ears as he pushed towards the newly married couple.

One by one the generals and priests, leaders of the people's physical and spiritual defense, would be the first to congratulate them. He stepped up alongside the others and waited his turn as first Ikes, then Welick stepped forward and bowed. They both swore their allegiance emphatically to the crowned king.

Jaron took a deep breath and stepped forward. He accepted Titan's proffered hand. "I wish to congratulate you two. May the Ragdons keep you forever."

"And you, General Jaron," Titan responded genuinely. "I want to thank you for saving our people. You protected them when I couldn't."

"I tried to serve them as best I could," he said. "But I think that service is over now. My liege, if you will allow me, I wish to officially request stepping down from my position as general of the army."

Titan frowned. "On what grounds?"

Jaron glanced at Adrianna. "On grounds you are already aware of."

Titan nodded his understanding. "Jaron, I realize this situation isn't what either of us would have. But at the same time, how can I fault a man for falling in love with the woman I love?" He smiled. "If you must step down, then I will allow it. But I would ask you to stay. I know that despite the situation, you will serve the kingdom better than any other man I know."

Jaron closed his eyes. "If my king wishes it, I will see it done."

Titan gripped his shoulder. "Jaron, I won't force you into this. Why don't you leave your command for a time and consider? We need you, but not if the price is too high." He drew closer. "And in the end, regardless of your decision, I will respect and admire you for the rest of my life."

Jaron met his eyes. "Thank you, sire. I ... agree that some time would be beneficial."

Titan nodded. "I'm glad to hear it. But call me Titan."

Jaron bowed and stepped back to allow the next in line come forward. *Can I serve him?* He knew the answer was yes. But he also knew it would be one of the most difficult things he had done in his life. He didn't hate Titan. At least, he didn't think he did. His emotions seemed to be telling half-truths and weren't to be trusted. But Jaron knew that the sight of the king would cause him pain for a very long time.

"Richards?" Jaron turned back at the sound of surprise in Titan's voice.

"In the flesh, my boy," came the reply from a young man with a wide smile. "Couldn't miss a day such as this."

Titan grabbed the man in a bear hug. "I'm glad you didn't."

Richards laughed. "I can tell." He pulled back and surveyed the couple. "So, we won then?"

"We won. Devvon is dead."

"And ... the armor?"

"I wanted to speak with you about that."

Richards looked around. "Now is as good a time as any."

Titan hesitated. "Alright. I don't want it."

"Oh? Limitless power doesn't suit you?"

"It doesn't suit anyone. It's too much for a single man."

Richards shrugged. "So give the other pieces back to the other kingdoms."

Titan shook his head. "We've seen the damage that even one piece can do. I don't want anyone to have any of them."

"So what do you propose?"

Titan smiled. He slid a leather envelope from beneath his coat and held it out. "I'll be sending you a package."

Richards hesitated before he accepted the gift. "Aren't I a man?"

"A person that has lived forever no longer qualifies in my opinion."

"I feel insulted."

Jaron watched the exchange in confusion. What was the armor they were talking about? His attention was torn away by someone grabbing at his elbow. He turned to find Priest Wesling smiling beside him. Jaron returned the smile.

"And how are you holding up, General?"

Jaron nodded. "Well enough, in light of everything."

Wesling turned his gaze to the king. "This is a joyous day. But I imagine it is a hard day for some of us as well."

Jaron nodded. "I won't lie to a priest of the church."

The priest squeezed Jaron's shoulder. "Don't worry, my son. The pain will pass."

"I hope you are right."

"Have I ever been wrong?"

Jaron chuckled. "I suppose not. I take your words in the chapel on faith, why wouldn't I take them on faith outside?"

Priest Wesling's eyes glistened. "The strength of your beliefs is inspiring. What I wouldn't give to have a kingdom full of your devotion."

Jaron smiled. "Perhaps that is what is pulling me through. The Ragdons support us through trials. Leaning on them makes the process easier."

The priest nodded his approval. "That is right, my son." He bowed and withdrew.

Jaron turned back to find Titan and Adrianna conversing with the first of the commoners that had reached them. They were genuine in their speech, and the people readily accepted Adrianna as their new queen. No one questioned that the law had been upheld. With Titan involved, how could they?

Jaron turned and began to make his way through the throng. With each step he felt as though his chest would collapse. The hole within him was consuming.

The Ragdons taught that each individual had his burden to bear. A life without trials wasn't a life worth living. But how much was one man expected to survive? Jaron clenched his teeth. He didn't need time to decide. The agony he felt at losing both the throne and the love of his life wouldn't fade. Jaron had learned to walk away from his past, but that only meant he knew the path before him all the better. It is possible to leave people and places behind, but one can never leave memories.

His mind began to race. Run away again to be haunted forever by his own memories? Stay and serve, enduring the nightmare that was becoming his reality? And a third question, more frightening than the others.

Were accepting or running his only options?

EPILOGUE

Leth stood in the door of his newly re-built cottage. He had laid it himself, nearly stone for stone, exactly how his previous home had stood. The house would once again last Leth another 100 years or so. Assuming of course that another power-hungry despot bent on killing him didn't come to power in that time.

Leth watched the wagon pull slowly into the clearing. A single soldier climbed down from the seat and tied the horse to a nearby tree.

"I seek one known as Richards."

Leth nodded. "That's me. What can I do for you?"

"King Titan sends a gift. May I enlist your help in moving it?"

"Of course." Leth followed the young man to the back of the wagon. There sat a wooden chest, heavy by the looks of it, with a thick, metal lock firmly in place. Richards grabbed one side, with the soldier opposite. They slid the chest to the edge of the wagon, than hoisted it into the air. The box was meant to withstand considerable punishment, as evidence by the weight.

They stumbled to the door, and Leth nudge it open with a foot. It had taken months to fix his home. Fortunately, when the walls had fallen they had covered some of his more prized possessions, saving them from the flames. Leth could still smell the smoke.

The pair crossed the room and deposited the trunk against the far wall. After stepping back, Leth looked back to the soldier. "Key?"

The man saluted. "No, sir. But he also sent you this." He lifted a bag from his shoulder and held it out. Leth opened it and peered in, then laughed.

"My clothes from the wedding. He even folded them for me." Leth chuckled again. "Tell your king he is most gracious."

The soldier saluted and strode from the house.

Leth watched him go, then looked back at the bag. "Since when do you wash laundry, Titan?" He turned the bag upside down and dumped the shirts and pants on the ground. He did a quick count. Three shirts, two pairs of pants, a few odd socks, and ...

Leth smiled. He reached down and pulled the leather bracer from the pile. He admired it, then crossed to where the other was hidden beneath a floor board. He pulled them swiftly on, not bothering to tighten the laces. He triggered the bracers. Gingerly, he laid hold of the lock and gave it a sharp tug down. The metal ripped itself free from the wood, splinters flying in all directions. Leth disabled the bracers and slid them off. He gingerly lifted the lid of the chest and stepped up to look inside.

The breastplate gleamed brightly, even in the shadow of the roof. Above it lay the helmet, below were the gloves, and tucked neatly beside Leth could see the sheathed sword. He calmly dropped the bracers on top of the breastplate and stared, half in awe at the completed set. Titan had given away supremacy.

A man willing to give it up is one of the few that deserves this type of power, he thought. He slowly closed the lid as he pondered. What to do with the armor? It was indestructible. The only option would be to hide it.

Leth looked down at his ring. If he hid the rest of the armor well enough, his own purpose in living forever would be negated. He found himself smiling at the prospect of growing old and, in due time, passing on. He glanced up at the roof. He was intrigued at the idea of meeting whoever or whatever had originally created the stones.

A sharp pain shot through him like lightning. He gasped from the shock and looked down at his chest. A length of metal was protruding from it. His mind muddled as he tried to comprehend why it would be there.

A sword, he finally realized. Blood gushed from the wound, quickly soaking his shirt. He felt his legs beginning to buckle, and dropped to his hands and knees to steady himself. He gradually became aware of someone standing behind him.

The figure lowered itself until he could feel the hot breath on the back of his ear. Richards' vision narrowed, the edges growing black as a voice hissed quietly behind him.

"Long live the king."

Dan Hoffman received his MBA from Arizona State, is a private pilot, works as a senior analyst for a major airline, and aspires to be a heritage farmer. He currently lives in Dallas, Texas with his wife, his four children, and two herding dogs. *The Mortal Gods* is Dan's first novel.

CPSIA information can be obtained
at www.ICGtesting.com
Printed in the USA
LVHW022203150920
666084LV00004B/921